The critics on Robert Ludlum

'His best thriller yet' *Kirkus Reviews*

'Robert Ludlum is, of course, the bestselling thriller writer of all time, having sold more than two hundred million copies of his twenty-two novels, and he has become known for the sweep and intricacy of his plots ... Now he brings us *The Prometheus Deception* ... his most ingenious novel yet ... Ludlum transcends the genre' *The New Yorker*

'The pace is fast, the action plentiful ... a must read' *Booklist*

'Don't ever begin a Ludlum novel if you have to go to work the next day' *Chicago Sun-Times*

'Ludlum stuffs more surprises into his novels than any other six pack of thriller writers combined' *New York Times*

'Ludlum is light years beyond his literary competition in piling plot twist upon plot twist, until the mesmerized reader is held captive' *Chicago Tribune*

'Robert Ludlum is an acknowledged superstar of the political thriller' Amazon.co.uk

'A typically baroque concoction boasting more twists than a packet of pretzels ... a hugely enjoyable caper' *Sunday Times*

'Olympic style, all-out espionage ... Good news for Ludlum's countless fans' *Daily Express*

'Huge in scope ... Ludlum spins it all together with lots of suspense' *Sunday Telegraph*

Robert Ludlum is the author of 32 novels, published in 32 languages and 40 countries, and at one time was the world's bestselling author with his blend of sophisticated plotting and extreme pace. There are more than 210 million copies of his books in print. He is best known for *The Scarlatti Inheritance*, *The Chancellor Manuscript* and the Jason Bourne series – *The Bourne Identity*, *The Bourne Supremacy* and *The Bourne Ultimatum* – among others. Visit his website at www.CovertOne.com.

Patrick Larkin is a best-selling novelist specialising in historical and military fiction. His collaborations with Larry Bond have won critical acclaim for their suspense, realism, and unblinking appreciation of geopolitical and modern military realities.

By Robert Ludlum

The Bourne Legacy
(*with Eric Van Lustbader*)
The Tristan Betrayal
The Janson Directive
The Sigma Protocol
The Prometheus Deception
The Matarese Countdown
The Cry of the Halidon
The Apocalypse Watch
The Road to Omaha
The Scorpio Illusion
The Bourne Ultimatum
The Icarus Agenda
The Bourne Supremacy

The Aquitaine Progression
The Parsifal Mosaic
The Bourne Identity
The Matarese Circle
The Gemini Contenders
The Holcroft Covenant
The Chancellor Manuscript
The Road to Gandolfo
The Rhinemann Exchange
Trevayne
The Matlock Paper
The Osterman Weekend
The Scarlatti Inheritance

THE COVERT-ONE NOVELS

The Altman Code (*with Gayle Lynds*)
The Paris Option (*with Gayle Lynds*)
The Cassandra Compact (*with Philip Shelby*)
The Hades Factor (*with Gayle Lynds*)
The Lazarus Vendetta (*with Patrick Larkin*)
The Moscow Vector (*with Patrick Larkin*)

Also by Patrick Larkin

The Tribune

With Larry Bond

Red Phoenix
Vortex
Cauldron
The Enemy Within
Day of Wrath

THE
LAZARUS
VENDETTA

ROBERT LUDLUM

A Covert-One novel

Series created by Robert Ludlum

Written by Patrick Larkin

ORION

An Orion paperback

First published in Great Britain in 2004
by Orion
This paperback edition published in 2005
by Orion Books Ltd,
Orion House, 5 Upper St Martin's Lane,
London WC2H 9EA

A CIP catalogue record for this book is available
from the British Library.

Printed and bound in Great Britain by
Clays Ltd, St Ives plc

ROBERT LUDLUM'S

THE
LAZARUS
VENDETTA

PROLOGUE

Saturday, September 25
Near the Tuli River Valley, Zimbabwe

The last rays of the sun were gone, and thousands of stars shimmered weakly against a dark sky high above a rugged, arid land. This region of Zimbabwe was dirt-poor, even by that troubled nation's rock-bottom standards. There were almost no electric lights to illuminate the night, and there were few paved roads connecting southern Matabeleland's isolated villages to the larger world beyond.

Twin headlights suddenly appeared in the darkness, briefly illuminating thickets of gnarled scrub trees and scattered patches of thorn bushes and sparse grass. A battered Toyota pickup truck swayed along a worn dirt track, gears grinding as it bounced in and out of a series of deep ruts. Drawn by the flickering beams of light, swarms of insects flitted toward the pickup and spattered against its dust-streaked windshield.

'*Merde!*' Gilles Ferrand swore softly, wrestling with the steering wheel. Frowning, the tall, bearded Frenchman leaned forward, trying to see past the swirling cloud of dust and flying bugs. His thick glasses slipped down his nose. He took one hand off the wheel to push them back up and then swore again as the pickup nearly veered off the winding track.

'We should have left Bulawayo sooner,' he grumbled to the slender gray-haired woman beside him. 'This so-called road is bad enough in daylight. It is a nightmare now. I wish the plane had not been so late.'

Susan Kendall shrugged. 'If wishes were fishes, Gilles, we'd all be dead of mercury poisoning. Our project requires the new seeds and tools we were sent, and when you serve the Mother, you must accept inconveniences.'

Ferrand grimaced, wishing for the thousandth time that his prim American colleague would stop lecturing him. Both of them were veteran activists in the worldwide Lazarus Movement, working to save the Earth from the insane greed of unchecked global capitalism. There was no need for her to treat him like a schoolboy.

The truck's high beams silhouetted a familiar rock out-cropping next to the track. The Frenchman sighed in relief. They were close to their destination – a tiny settlement adopted three months ago by the Lazarus Movement. He didn't remember the village's original name. The first thing he and Kendall had done was re-name it Kusasa, 'Tomorrow' in the local Ndebele dialect. It was an apt name, or so they hoped. The people of Kusasa had agreed to the change and to accept the Move-ment's help in returning to a natural and eco-friendly method of farming. Both activists believed their work here would lead a rebirth of wholly organic African agriculture – a rebirth rooted in absolute opposition to the West's toxic pesticides, chemical fertilizers, and dangerous gene-tically modified crops. The American woman was certain that her impassioned speeches had won over the village elders. Ferrand, more cynical by nature, suspected that the generous cash grants the Movement offered had carried more weight. No matter, he thought, the ends in this case would amply justify the means.

He turned off the main track and drove slowly toward a little cluster of brightly painted huts, tin-roofed shacks, and ramshackle cattle pens. Surrounded by small fields, Kusasa lay in a shallow valley edged by boulder-strewn hills and tall brush. He brought the truck to a stop and lightly tapped the horn.

No one came out to meet them.

2

Ferrand killed the engine but left the headlights on. He sat still for a moment, listening. The village dogs were howling. He felt the hairs on the back of his neck rise.

Susan Kendall frowned. 'Where is everyone?'

'I do not know.' Ferrand slid cautiously out from behind the wheel. By now dozens of excited men, women, and children should have been thronging around them – grinning and murmuring in glee at the sight of the bulging seed bags and brand-new shovels, rakes, and hoes piled high in the Toyota's cargo bed. But nothing stirred among Kusasa's darkened huts.

'Hello?' the Frenchman called. He tried out his limited Ndebele. '*Litshone Njani?* Good evening?'

The dogs only howled louder, baying at the night sky.

Ferrand shivered. He leaned back inside the pickup. 'Something is very wrong here, Susan. You should make contact with our people. Now. As a precaution.'

The gray-haired American woman stared at him for a moment, her eyes suddenly wide. Then she nodded and climbed down out of the Toyota. Working swiftly, she set up the linked satellite phone/laptop computer they carried in the field. It allowed them to communicate with their home office in Paris, though it was mainly used to upload photos and progress reports to the main Lazarus Web site.

Ferrand watched her in silence. Most of the time he found Susan Kendall intensely annoying, but she had courage when it counted. Perhaps more courage than he himself possessed. He sighed and reached under the seat for the flashlight clipped there. After a moment's reflection, he slung their digital camera over his shoulder.

'What are you doing, Gilles?' she asked, already punching in the phone code for Paris.

'I am going to take a look around,' he said stiffly.

'All right. But you should wait until I have a connection,' Kendall told him. She held the satellite phone to her ear for a moment. Her thin-lipped mouth tightened. 'They've already left the office. There's no answer.'

Ferrand checked his watch. France was only an hour behind them, but it was the weekend. They were on their own. 'Try the Web site,' he suggested.

She nodded.

Ferrand forced himself to move. He squared his shoulders and walked slowly into the village. He swept his flashlight in a wide arc, probing the darkness ahead. A lizard scuttled away from the beam, startling him. He muttered a soft curse and kept going.

Sweating now despite the cool night breeze, he came to the open space at the center of Kusasa. There was the village well. It was a favorite gathering place for young and old alike at the end of the day. He swept the flashlight across the hard-packed earth . . . and froze.

The people of Kusasa would not rejoice over the seeds and farm equipment he had brought them. They would not lead the rebirth of African agriculture. They were dead. All of them were dead.

The Frenchman stood frozen, his mind reeling in horror. There were corpses everywhere he looked. Dead men, women, and children lay in heaps across the clearing. Most of the bodies were intact, though twisted and misshapen by some terrible agony. Others seemed eerily hollow, almost as though they had been partially eaten from the inside out. A few were reduced to nothing more than torn shreds of flesh and bone surrounded by congealed puddles of bloodred slime. Thousands of huge black flies swarmed over the mutilated corpses, lazily feasting on the remains. Near the well, a small dog nuzzled the contorted body of a young child, vainly trying to rouse its playmate.

Gilles Ferrand swallowed hard, fighting down a surge of bile and vomit. With trembling hands, he set down his flashlight, took the digital camera off his shoulder, and began taking pictures. Someone had to document this terrible slaughter. Someone had to warn the world of this massacre of the innocents – of people whose only crime had been to side with the Lazarus Movement.

Four men lay motionless on one of the hills overlooking the village. They wore desert camouflage fatigues and body armor. Night-vision goggles and binoculars gave them a clear view of every movement made below while audio pickups fed every sound into their headsets.

One of the observers studied a shielded monitor. He looked up. 'They have a link to the satellite. And we're tapped in with them.'

His leader, a giant auburn-haired man with bright green eyes, smiled thinly. 'Good.' He leaned closer to get a better view of the screen. It showed a series of gruesome images – the pictures taken only minutes before by Gilles Ferrand – slowly loading onto the Lazarus Web site.

The green-eyed man watched carefully. Then he nodded. 'That's enough. Cut their link.'

The observer complied, rapidly entering commands on a portable keypad. He tapped the enter key, sending a set of coded instructions to the communications satellite high overhead. One second later, the digital pictures streaming up from Kusasa froze, flickered, and then vanished.

The green-eyed man glanced at the two men lying flat next to him. Both were armed with Heckler & Koch PSG-1 sniper rifles designed for covert operations use. 'Now kill them.'

He focused his night-vision binoculars on the two Lazarus Movement activists. The bearded Frenchman and the slender American woman were staring down at their satellite hookup in disbelief.

'Target acquired,' one of the snipers murmured. He squeezed the trigger. The 7.62mm round hit Ferrand in the forehead. The Frenchman toppled backward and slid to the ground, smearing blood and brains down the side of the Toyota. 'Target down.'

The second sniper fired an instant later. His bullet

caught Susan Kendall high in the back. She fell in a heap next to her colleague.

The tall green-eyed leader rose to his feet. More of his men, these wearing hazardous materials suits, were already moving down the slope carrying an array of scientific equipment. He keyed his throat mike, reporting through an encrypted satellite link, 'This is Prime. Field One is complete. Evaluation, collection, and analysis proceeding as planned.' He eyed the two dead Lazarus activists. 'SPARK has also been initiated . . . as ordered.'

PART ONE

CHAPTER ONE

Tuesday, October 12
Teller Institute for Advanced Technology, Santa Fe,
New Mexico

Lieutenant Colonel Jonathan ('Jon') Smith, M.D., turned off Old Agua Fria Road and drove up to the Institute's main gate. He narrowed his eyes against the early-morning glare. Off on his left, sunlight was just spilling over the dazzling snowcapped peaks of the Sangre de Cristo range. It lit steep slopes carpeted with gold-leafed aspens, towering firs, ponderosa pines, and oaks. Farther down, at the foot of the mountains, the shorter piñon pines, junipers, and clumps of sagebrush surrounding the Institute's thick sand-colored adobe walls were still cloaked in shadow.

Some of the protesters camped out along the road crawled out of their sleeping bags to watch his car go by. A handful waved handmade signs demanding STOP KILLER SCIENCE, NO TO NANOTECH, or LET LAZARUS LEAD. Most stayed put, unwilling to face the chilly October dawn. Santa Fe was at seven thousand feet and the nights were growing cold.

Smith felt a momentary twinge of sympathy for them. Even with the heater in his rental car going, he could feel the cold through his brown leather bomber jacket and sharply creased khakis.

At the gate, a gray-uniformed security guard waved him to a stop. Jon rolled down his window and handed over his U.S. Army ID for inspection. The photo on his identity card showed a fit man in his early forties – a man whose high cheekbones and smooth, dark hair gave him the look of a haughty Spanish cavalier. In person, the twinkle in Smith's dark blue eyes shattered the illusion of arrogance.

'Good morning, Colonel,' said the guard, an ex-Army Ranger staff sergeant named Frank Diaz. After scrutinizing the ID, he leaned forward, peering through the car windows to make sure that Smith was alone. His right hand hovered warily near the 9mm Beretta pistol holstered at his side. The flap on the holster was unsnapped – freeing the Beretta for a quick draw if necessary.

Smith raised an eyebrow at that. Security at the Teller Institute was usually more relaxed, certainly not up to the level of the top-secret nuclear labs at nearby Los Alamos. But the president of the United States, Samuel Adams Castilla, was scheduled to visit the Institute in three days. And now a huge anti-technology protest rally had been organized to coincide with his speech. The demonstrators outside the gate this morning were just the first wave of thousands more who were expected to pour in from all over the world. He jerked a thumb over his shoulder. 'Are you catching flak from those people, Frank?'

'Not much so far,' Diaz admitted. He shrugged. 'But we're keeping a close eye on them anyway. This rally has the folks in Admin spooked. The FBI says there are some real hard-core troublemakers heading this way – the kind who get their kicks tossing Molotov cocktails and breaking windows.'

Smith frowned. Mass protests were a lure for anarchists with a taste for violence and property destruction. Genoa, Seattle, Cancun, and half a dozen other cities around the world had already seen their streets turned into battlegrounds between masked rioters and the police.

Chewing that over, he sketched a rough salute to Diaz and drove toward the parking lot. The prospect of being caught in a riot was not especially appealing. Not when he was in New Mexico on what was supposed to be a vacation.

Strike that, Smith told himself with a lopsided grin. Make that a *working* vacation. As a military medical doctor and expert in molecular biology, he spent most of his time assigned to the U.S. Army Medical Research Institute of Infectious Diseases (USAMRIID) at Fort Detrick, Maryland. His affiliation with the Teller Institute was only temporary.

The Pentagon's Office of Science and Technology had sent him to Santa Fe to observe and report on the work being done in the Institute's three nanotechnology labs. Researchers around the world were locked in a fierce competition to develop practical and profitable nanotech applications. Some of the best were right here at Teller, including teams from the Institute itself, Harcourt Biosciences, and Nomura PharmaTech. Basically, Smith thought with satisfaction, the Defense Department had given him an all-expenses-paid ringside seat to scope out the century's most promising new technologies.

The work here was right up his alley. The word *nanotech* carried an incredibly wide range of meanings. At its most basic, it meant the creation of artificial devices on the smallest of imaginable scales. A nanometer was just one-billionth of a meter, about ten times the size of an atom. Make something ten nanometers across and you were still looking at a construct that was only one ten-thousandth of the diameter of a single human hair. Nanotechnology was engineering on the molecular level, engineering that involved quantum physics, chemistry, biology, and supercomputing.

Popular science writers painted glowing word-pictures of robots only a few atoms across prowling through the human body – curing diseases and repairing internal injuries. Others asked their readers to imagine information storage units one-millionth the size of a grain of salt yet able to hold all human knowledge. Or dust motes that were actually hypercapable atmosphere miners, drifting silently through polluted skies while scrubbing them clean.

Smith had seen enough during his weeks at the Teller Institute to know that a few of those seemingly impossible imaginings were already hovering right on the edge of reality. He squeezed his car into a parking space between two behemoth SUVs. Their windshields were covered in frost, evidence that the scientists or technicians who owned them had been in the labs all night. He nodded appreciatively. These were the guys who were working the real miracles, all on a diet of strong black coffee, caffeinated soda, and sugar-laced vending machine snacks.

He got out of the rental car, zipping his jacket up against the brisk morning air. Then he took a deep breath, catching the faint smell of cooking fires and cannabis on the wind wafting across from the protest camp. More minivans, Volvo station wagons, chartered buses, and hybrid gas-electric cars were arriving in a steady stream, turning off Interstate 25 and heading up the access road toward the Institute. He frowned. The promised multitudes were assembling.

Unfortunately, it was the potential dark side of nanotechnology that fed the terrified imaginations of the activists and Lazarus Movement zealots gathering outside the chain-link fence. They were horrified by the idea of machines so small they could freely penetrate human cells and so powerful that they could reshape atomic structures. Radical civil libertarians warned about the dangers of 'spy molecules' hovering unseen in every public and private space. Crazed conspiracy theorists filled Internet chat rooms with rumors of secret miniaturized killing machines. Others were afraid that runaway nanomachines would endlessly replicate themselves, dancing across the world like an endless parade of *Sorceror's Apprentice* enchanted brooms – finally devouring the Earth and everything on it.

Jon Smith shrugged his shoulders. You could not match wild hyperbole with anything but tangible results. Once most people got a good close look at the honest-to-God benefits of nanotechnology, their irrational fears should begin to subside. Or so he hoped. He spun sharply on his heel and strode toward the Institute's main entrance, eager to see what new wonders the men and women inside had cooked up overnight.

Two hundred meters outside the chain-link fence, Malachi MacNamara sat cross-legged on a colorful Indian blanket laid out in the shade of a juniper tree. His pale blue eyes were open, but he sat calmly, without moving. The Lazarus Movement followers camped close by were convinced that the lean, weather-beaten Canadian was meditating – restoring his mental and physical energies for the struggle ahead. The retired Forest Service biologist from British Columbia had already won their admiration by forcefully demanding 'immediate action' to achieve the Movement's goals.

'The Earth is dying,' he told them grimly. 'She is drowning, crushed beneath a deluge of toxic pesticides and pollution. Science will not save her. Technology will not save her. They are her enemies, the true source of horror and contagion. And we must act against them. Now. Not later. Now! While there is still time . . .'

MacNamara hid a small smile, remembering the sight of the glowing faces fired by his rhetoric. He had more talent as an orator or an evangelist than he ever would have imagined.

He observed the activity around him. He had carefully chosen this vantage point. It overlooked the large green canvas tent set up as a command center by the Lazarus Movement. A dozen of its top national and international activists were busy inside that tent – manning computers linked to its worldwide Web sites, registering new arrivals, making banners and signs, and coordinating plans for the upcoming rally. Other groups in the TechStock coalition, the Sierra Club, Earth First!, and the like, had their own headquarters scattered throughout the sprawling camp, but MacNamara knew he was in precisely the right place at precisely the right time.

The Movement was the real force behind this protest. The other environmental and anti-technology organizations were only along for the ride, trying desperately to stem a steady decline in their numbers and influence. More and more of their most committed members were abandoning them to join Lazarus, drawn by the clarity of the Movement's vision and by its courage in confronting the world's most powerful corporations and governments. Even the recent slaughter of its followers in Zimbabwe was acting as a rallying cry for Lazarus. Pictures of the massacre at Kusasa were being offered as proof of just how much the 'global corporate rulers' and their puppet governments feared the Movement and its message.

The craggy-faced Canadian sat up just a bit straighter.

Several tough-looking young men were heading toward the drab green tent, making their way purposefully through the milling crowds. Each carried a long duffel bag slung over his shoulder. Each moved with the wary grace of a predator.

One by one, they arrived at the tent and ducked inside.

'Well, well, well,' Malachi MacNamara murmured to himself. His pale eyes gleamed. 'How very interesting.'

CHAPTER TWO

The White House, Washington, D.C.

The elegant eighteenth-century clock along one curved wall of the Oval Office softly chimed twelve o'clock noon. Outside, ice-cold rain fell in sheets from a dark gray sky, spattering against the tall windows overlooking the South Lawn. Whatever the calendar said, the first portents of winter were closing in on the nation's capital.

Overhead lights glinted off President Samuel Adams Castilla's titanium-frame reading glasses as he paged through the top-secret Joint Intelligence Threat Assessment he had just been handed. His face darkened. He looked across the big ranch-style pine table that served him as a desk. His voice was dangerously calm. 'Let me make sure I understand you gentlemen correctly. Are you *seriously* proposing that I cancel my speech at the Teller Institute? Just three days before I'm scheduled to deliver it?'

'That is correct, Mr. President. To put it bluntly, the risks involved in your Santa Fe trip are unacceptably high,' David Hanson, the newly confirmed Director of Central Intelligence, said coolly. He was echoed a moment later by Robert Zeller, the acting director of the FBI.

Castilla eyed both men briefly, but he kept his attention focused on Hanson. The head of the CIA was the tougher and more formidable of the pair – despite the fact that he looked more like a bantam-weight mild-mannered college professor from the 1950s, complete with the obligatory bow tie, than he did a fire-breathing advocate of clandestine action and special operations.

Although his counterpart, the FBI's Bob Zeller, was a decent man, he was way out of his depth in Washington's sea of swirling political intrigue. Tall and broad-shouldered, Zeller looked good on television, but he should never have been moved up from his post as the senior U.S. attorney in Atlanta. Not even on a temporary basis while the White House staff looked for a permanent replacement. At least the ex-Navy linebacker and longtime federal prosecutor knew his own weaknesses. He mostly kept his mouth shut in meetings and usually wound up backing whoever he thought carried the most clout.

Hanson was a completely different case. If anything, the Agency veteran was too adept at playing power politics. During his long tenure as chief of the CIA's Operations Directorate, he had built a firm base of support among the members of the House and Senate intelligence committees. A great many influential congressmen and senators believed that David Hanson walked on water. That gave him a lot of maneuvering room, even room to buck the president who had just promoted him to run the whole CIA.

Castilla tapped the Threat Assessment with one blunt forefinger. 'I see a whole lot of speculation in this document. What I do not see are hard facts.' He read one sentence aloud. ' "Communications intercepts of a nonspecific but significant nature indicate that radical elements among the demonstrators at Santa Fe may be planning violent action – either against the Teller Institute or against the president himself." '

He took off his reading glasses and looked up. 'Care to put that in plain English, David?'

'We're picking up increased chatter, both over the Internet and in monitored phone conversations. A number of troubling phrases crop up again and again, all in reference to the planned rally. There's constant talk about "the big event" or "the action at Teller," ' the CIA chief said. 'My people have heard it overseas. So has the NSA. And the FBI is picking up the same undercurrents here at home. Correct, Bob?'

Zeller nodded gravely.

'*That's* what has your analysts in such a lather?' Castilla shook his head, plainly unimpressed. 'People e-mailing each other about a political protest?' He snorted. 'Good God, any rally that might draw thirty or forty thousand people all the way out to Santa Fe is a pretty damned big event! New Mexico is my home turf and I doubt half that many ever showed up for any speech I ever made.'

'When members of the Sierra Club or the Wilderness Federation talk that way, I don't worry,' Hanson told him softly. 'But even the simplest words can have very different meanings when they are used by certain dangerous groups and individuals. Deadly meanings.'

'You're talking about these so-called "radical elements"?'

'Yes, sir.'

'And just who are these dangerous folks?'

'Most are allied in one way or another with the Lazarus Movement, Mr. President,' Hanson said carefully.

Castilla frowned. 'This is an old, old song of yours, David.'

The other man shrugged. 'I'm aware of that, sir. But the truth doesn't become any less true just because it's unpalatable. When viewed as a whole, our recent intelligence on the Lazarus Movement is extremely alarming. The Movement is metastasizing and what was once a relatively peaceful political and environmental alliance is rapidly altering itself into something far more secretive, dangerous, and deadly.' He looked across the table at the president. 'I know you've seen the relevant surveillance and communications intercept reports. And our analysis of them.'

Castilla nodded slowly. The FBI, CIA, and other federal intelligence agencies kept tabs on a host of groups and individuals. With the rise of global terrorism and the spread of chemical, biological, and nuclear weapons technology,

17

no one in Washington wanted to take any more chances on being blindsided by a previously unrecognized enemy.

'Then let me speak bluntly, sir,' Hanson went on. 'Our judgment is that the Lazarus Movement has now decided to attain its objectives through violence and terrorism. Its rhetoric is increasingly vicious, paranoid, and full of hatred aimed at those whom it considers enemies.' The CIA chief slid another piece of paper across the pine table. 'This is just one example.'

Castilla put his glasses back on and read it in silence. His mouth curved down in disgust. The sheet was a glossy printout of a page from a Movement Web site, complete with grotesque thumbnail photos of mangled and muti-lated corpses. The banner headline across the top screamed: INNOCENTS BUTCHERED AT KUSASA. The text between the pictures blamed the massacre of an entire village in Zimbabwe on either corporate-funded 'death squads' or 'mercenaries armed by the U.S. government.' It claimed the killings were part of a secret plan to destroy the Lazarus Movement's efforts to revitalize organic African farming – lest they threaten the American monop-oly on genetically modified crops and pesticides. The page ended by calling for the destruction of those who would 'destroy the Earth and all who love her.'

The president dropped it back on the table. 'What a load of horseshit.'

'True.' Hanson retrieved the printout and slid it back into his briefcase. 'It is, however, highly effective horseshit – at least for its target audience.'

'Have you sent a team into Zimbabwe to find out what really happened at this Kusasa place?' Castilla asked.

The director of the CIA shook his head. 'That would be extremely difficult, Mr. President. Without permission from the government there, which is hostile to us, we'll have to go in covertly. Even then, I doubt we'll find much. Zimbabwe is a total basket case. Those villagers could have been murdered by anyone – all the way from government troops on down to rampaging bandits.'

'Hell,' Castilla muttered. 'And if our people get caught snooping there without permission, everyone will assume we *were* involved in this massacre and that we're only trying to cover our tracks.'

'That is the problem, sir,' Hanson agreed quietly. 'But whatever really took place at Kusasa, one thing is quite clear: The leadership of the Lazarus Movement is using this incident to radicalize its followers, to prepare them for more direct and violent action against our allies and us.'

'Damn, I hate to see this happening,' Castilla growled. He leaned forward in his chair. 'Don't forget, I knew many of the men and women who founded Lazarus. They were respected environmental activists, scientists, writers . . . even a couple of politicians. They wanted to save the Earth, to bring it back to life. I disagreed with most of their agenda, but they were good people. Honorable people.'

'And where are they now, sir?' the head of the CIA asked quietly. 'There were nine original founders of the Lazarus Movement. Six of them are dead, either from natural causes or in suspiciously convenient accidents. The other three have vanished without a trace.' He looked carefully at Castilla. 'Including Jinjiro Nomura.'

'Yes,' the president said flatly.

He glanced at one of the photographs clustered on a corner of his desk. Taken during his first term as governor of New Mexico, it showed him exchanging bows with a shorter and older Japanese man, Jinjiro Nomura. Nomura had been a prominent member of the Diet, Japan's parliament. Their friendship, founded on a shared taste for single-malt Scotch and straight talk, had survived Nomura's retirement from politics and his turn toward more strident environmental advocacy.

Twelve months ago, Jinjiro Nomura had disappeared while traveling to a Lazarus-sponsored rally in Thailand. His son, Hideo, the chairman and chief executive officer of Nomura PharmaTech, had begged for American help in finding his father. And Castilla had reacted quickly. For weeks a special task force of CIA field officers had combed the streets and back alleys of Bangkok. The president had even pressed the NSA's ultra-secret spy satellites into service in the hunt for his old friend. But nothing had ever turned up. No ransom demand. No dead body. Nothing. The last of the original founders of the Lazarus Movement had vanished without a trace.

The photo stayed on Castilla's desk as a reminder of the limits of his power.

Castilla sighed and turned his gaze back to the two somber men seated in front of him. 'Okay, you've made your point. The leaders I knew and trusted either are dead or have dropped off the face of the earth.'

'Precisely, Mr. President.'

'Which brings us again to the issue of just who *is* running the Lazarus Movement *now*,' Castilla said grimly. 'Let's cut to the chase here, David. After Jinjiro disappeared, I approved your special interagency task force on the Movement – despite my own misgivings. Are your people any closer to identifying the current leadership?'

'Not much closer,' Hanson admitted reluctantly. 'Not even after months of intense work.' He spread his hands. 'We're fairly certain that ultimate power is vested in one man, a man who calls himself Lazarus – but we don't know his real name or what he looks like or where he operates from.'

'That's not exactly satisfying,' Castilla commented drily. 'Maybe you should stop telling me what you don't know and stick to what you do know.' He looked the shorter man in the eye. 'It might take less time.'

Hanson smiled dutifully. The smile stopped well short of his eyes. 'We've devoted a huge amount of resources, both human and satellite, to the effort. So have MI6, the French DGSE, and several other Western intelligence agencies, but over the past year the Lazarus Movement has deliberately reconfigured itself to defeat our surveillance.'

'Go on,' Castilla said.

'The Movement has organized itself as a set of ever-tighter and more secure concentric circles,' Hanson told him. 'Most of its supporters fall into the outer ring. They operate out in the open – attending meetings, organizing demonstrations, publishing newsletters, and working for various Movement-sponsored projects around the world. They staff the various Movement offices around the world. But each level above that is smaller and more secretive. Few members of the upper echelons know one another's real names, or meet in person. Leadership communications are handled almost exclusively through the Internet, either by encrypted instant messaging . . . or by communiqués posted on any one of the several Lazarus Web sites.'

'In other words, a classic cell structure,' Castilla said. 'Orders move freely down the chain, but no one outside the group can easily penetrate to the inner core.'

Hanson nodded. 'Correct. It's also the same structure adopted by any number of very nasty terrorist groups over the years. Al-Qaeda. Islamic Jihad. Italy's Red Brigades. Japan's Red Army. Just to name a few.'

'And you haven't had any luck in gaining access to the top echelons?' Castilla asked.

The CIA chief shook his head. 'No, sir. Nor have the Brits or the French or anyone else. We've all tried, without success. And one by one, we've lost our best existing sources inside Lazarus. Some have resigned. Others have been expelled. A few have simply vanished and are presumed dead.'

Castilla frowned. 'People seem to have a habit of disappearing around this bunch.'

'Yes, sir. A great many.' The CIA director left that uncomfortable truth hanging in the air.

Fifteen minutes later, the Director of Central Intelligence strode briskly out of the White House and down the steps of the South Portico to a waiting black limousine. He slid into the rear seat, waited while a uniformed Secret Service officer closed the car door behind him, and then punched the intercom. 'Take me back to Langley,' he told his driver.

Hanson leaned back against the plush leather as the limousine accelerated smoothly down the drive and turned left onto Seventeenth Street. He looked at the stocky, square-jawed man sitting in the rear-facing jump seat across from him. 'You're very quiet this afternoon, Hal.'

'You pay me to catch or kill terrorists,' Hal Burke said. 'Not to play courtier.'

Amusement flickered briefly in the CIA chief's eyes. Burke was a senior officer on the Agency's counterterrorism staff. Right now he was assigned to lead the special task force on the Lazarus Movement. Twenty years of clandestine fieldwork had left him with a bullet scar down the right side of his neck and a permanently cynical view of human nature. It was a view Hanson shared.

'Any luck?' Burke asked finally.

'None.'

'Shit.' Burke stared moodily out the limousine's rain-streaked windows. 'Kit Pierson's going to throw a fit.'

Hanson nodded. Katherine Pierson was Burke's FBI counterpart. The pair had worked closely together to prepare the intelligence assessment he and Zeller had just shown the president. 'Castilla wants us to push our investigation of the Movement as hard as possible, but he will not cancel his trip to the Teller Institute. Not without clearer evidence of a serious threat.'

Burke looked away from the window. His mouth was set in a thin, grim line. 'What that really means is that he doesn't want *The Washington Post*, *The New York Times*, and Fox News calling him gutless.'

'Would you?'

'No,' Burke admitted.

'Then you have twenty-four hours, Hal,' the CIA chief

said. 'I need you and Kit Pierson to dig up something solid that I can take back to the White House. Otherwise, Sam Castilla is flying to Santa Fe to confront those protesters head-on. You know what this president is like.'

'He's one stubborn son of a bitch,' Burke growled.

'Yes, he is.'

'So be it,' Burke said. He shrugged. 'I just hope it doesn't get him killed this time.'

CHAPTER THREE

Teller Institute for Advanced Technology

Jon Smith took the wide, shallow steps to the Institute's upper floor two at a time. Running up and down its three main staircases was pretty much the only exercise he had time for now. The long days and occasional nights he spent in the various nanotechnology labs were cutting into his usual workout routine.

He reached the top and paused for a moment, pleased to note that both his breathing and his heart rate were perfectly normal. The sun slanting through the stairwell's narrow windows felt comfortably warm on his shoulders. Smith glanced at his watch. The senior researcher for Harcourt Biosciences had promised him 'one seriously cool demonstration' of their most recent advances in five minutes.

Up here, the routine hum from below – phones ringing, keyboards clicking and clattering, and people talking – fell away to a cathedral-like hush. The Teller Institute kept its administrative offices, cafeteria, computer center, staff lounges, and science library on the first floor. The upper level was reserved for the lab suites allotted to different research teams. Like its rivals from the Institute itself and Nomura PharmaTech, Harcourt had its facilities in the North Wing.

Smith turned right into a wide corridor that ran the whole length of the I-shaped building. Polished earth brown floor tiles blended comfortably with off-white adobe walls. At regular intervals, *nichos*, small niches with rounded tops, displayed paintings of famous scientists – Fermi, Newton, Feynman, Drexler, Einstein, and others – commissioned from local artists. Between the *nichos* stood tall ceramic vases filled with brilliant yellow chamisa and pale purple aster wildflowers. If you ignored the sheer size of this place, Smith thought, it looked just like the hall of a private Santa Fe home.

He came to the locked door outside the Harcourt lab and swiped his ID card through the adjacent security station. The light on top flashed from red to green and the lock clicked open. His card was one of the relatively few coded for access to all restricted areas. Rival scientists and technicians were not permitted to stray into one another's territory. While trespassers were not shot, they were issued immediate one-way tickets out of Santa Fe. The Institute took its obligation to protect intellectual property rights very seriously.

Smith stepped through the door and immediately entered a very different world. Here the polished wood and textured adobe of courtly old Santa Fe gave way to the gleaming metal and tough composite materials of the twenty-first century. The elegance of natural sunlight and recessed lighting surrendered to the glare of overhead fluorescent strip lights. These lights had a very high ultraviolet component – just to kill surface germs. A small breeze tugged at his shirt and whispered through his dark hair. The nanotech laboratory suites were kept under positive pressure to minimize the risk of any airborne contaminants from the public areas of the building. Ultraefficient particulate air – or 'ULPA' – filters fed in purified air at a constant temperature and humidity.

The Harcourt lab suite was arranged as a series of 'clean rooms' of increasing rigor. This outer rim was an office area, crammed full of desks and workstations piled high with reference books, chemical and equipment catalogs, and paper printouts. Along the east wall, blinds were drawn across a floor-to-ceiling picture window, obscuring what would otherwise be a spectacular view of the Sangre de Cristo Mountains.

Farther inside the suite came a control and sample preparation area. Here were black-topped lab benches, computer consoles, the awkward bulk of two scanning tunneling electron microscopes, and the other equipment needed to oversee nanotech design and production processes.

The true 'holy of holies' was the inner core: visible only through sealed observation windows on the far wall. This was a chamber full of mirror-bright stainless steel tanks; mobile equipment skids loaded with pumps, valves, and sensor devices; vertically mounted disk frames for osmotic filters; and stacked Lucite cylinders packed with various grades of purification gels, all connected with looping lengths of clear, silastic tubing.

Smith knew that the core could be reached only through a succession of air locks and gowning rooms. Anyone working inside the production chamber had to wear fully sterile coveralls, gloves and boots, and an air-displacement breather helmet. He smiled wryly. If the Lazarus Movement activists camped outside ever saw anyone wearing that alien-looking getup, it would confirm all their worst fears about mad scientists toying with deadly toxins.

In truth, of course, the real situation was exactly the reverse. In the world of nanotechnology, humans were the source of danger and contamination. A falling flake of skin, a hair follicle, the wafted particles of moisture breathed out in casual conversation, and the shotgun blast of a sneeze all could wreak havoc on the nanoscale, releasing oils, acids, alkalines, and enzymes that could poison the manufacturing process. Humans were also a rich source of bacteria: fast-growing organisms that would consume production broths, clog filters, and even attack the developing nanodevices themselves.

Fortunately, most of the necessary work could be done remotely from outside the core and the control and sample preparation chambers. Robotic manipulators, computer-controlled motorized equipment skids, and other innovations greatly reduced the need for humans to enter the 'clean rooms.' The incredible level of automation in its lab suites was one of the Teller Institute's most popular innovations, since it gave scientists and technicians far more freedom of movement than at other facilities.

Smith threaded through the maze of desks in the outer room, making his way toward Dr. Philip Brinker, the senior scientist for Harcourt Biosciences. The tall, pale, rail-thin researcher had his back to the entrance, so intently studying the image relayed from a scanning electron microscope that he didn't catch Jon's cat-quiet approach.

Brinker's chief assistant, Dr. Ravi Parikh, was more alert. The shorter, darker molecular biologist looked up suddenly. He opened his mouth to warn his boss, then closed it with a shy smile when Smith winked at him and motioned for silence.

Jon stopped just two feet behind the two researchers and stood at ease.

'Damn, that looks nice, Ravi,' Brinker said, still peering at the image on the screen in front of him. 'Man, I bet our favorite DoD spook is gonna bow down before us when he sees this.'

This time Smith did not bother hiding his grin. Brinker always called him a spook – a spy. The Harcourt scientist meant it as a joke, a kind of running gag about Smith's role as an observer for the Pentagon, but Brinker had no clue as to just how close that was to the truth.

The fact was that Jon was more than just an Army officer and scientist. From time to time he took on missions for Covert-One, a top-secret intelligence outfit reporting directly to the president. Covert-One worked in the shadows, so far back in the shadows that no one in Congress or the official military-intelligence bureaucracy even knew it existed. Fortunately, Jon's work here at the Institute was purely scientific in nature.

Smith leaned forward, looking right over the senior Harcourt scientist's shoulder. 'So what is it exactly that's going to make me worship the ground you walk on, Phil?'

Startled, Brinker jumped six inches in the air. 'Jesus Christ!' He spun round. 'Colonel, you pull that ghost act on me just one more time and I swear to God I'm gonna drop dead right in front of you! Then how would you feel?'

Smith laughed. 'Sorry, I guess.'

'Sure you would,' Brinker grumbled. Then he brightened. 'But since I'm not dead, despite your best efforts, you can take a look at what Ravi and I have cooked today. Feast your eyes on the not-yet-patented Mark Two Brinker-Parikh nanophage, guaranteed to zap cancer cells, dangerous bacteria, and other internal nasties . . . most of the time, anyway.'

Smith moved closer and studied the hugely magnified black-and-white image on the monitor. It showed a spherical semiconductor shell packed with an assortment of complex molecular structures. A scale indicator on one side of the screen told him he was looking at an assembly that was just two hundred nanometers in diameter.

Smith was already familiar with the Harcourt research team's general concept. Brinker and Parikh and the others were focused on creating medical nanodevices – their 'nanophages' – that would hunt down and kill cancer cells and disease-causing bacteria. The interior of the sphere he was examining should be loaded with the biochemical substances – phosphatidylserine and other costimulator molecules, for example – needed either to trick the target cells into committing suicide or to mark them for elimination by the body's own immune system.

Their Mark I design had failed in early animal testing because the nanophages themselves were destroyed by the immune system before they could do their work. Since then Jon knew the Harcourt scientists had been evaluating different shell configurations and materials, trying hard to find a combination that would be effectively invisible to the body's natural defenses. And for months the magic formula had eluded them.

He glanced up at Brinker. 'This looks almost identical to your Mark One configuration. So what have you changed?'

'Take a closer look at the shell coating,' the blond-haired Harcourt scientist suggested.

Smith nodded and took over the microscope controls. He tapped the keypad gently, slowly zooming in on a section of the outer shell. 'Okay,' he said. 'It's bumpy, not smooth. There's a thin molecular coating of some kind.' He frowned. 'The structure of that coating looks hauntingly familiar . . . but where have I seen it before?'

'The basic idea came to Ravi here in a flash,' the tall, blond-haired researcher explained. 'And like all great ideas it's incredibly simple and freaking obvious . . . at least after the fact.' He shrugged. 'Think about one particularly bad little mother of a bacterium – resistant *staphylococcus aureus*. How does it hide from the immune system?'

'It coats its cell membranes in polysaccharides,' Smith said promptly. He looked at the screen again. 'Oh, for Pete's sake . . .'

Parikh nodded complacently. 'Our Mark Twos are essentially sugar-coated. Just like all the best medicines.'

Smith whistled softly. 'That is brilliant, guys. Absolutely brilliant!'

'With all due modesty, you are right about that,' Brinker admitted. He laid one hand on the monitor. 'That beautiful Mark Two you see here should do the trick. In theory, anyway.'

'And in practice?' Smith asked.

Ravi Parikh pointed toward another high-resolution display – this one the size of a wide-screen television. It showed a double-walled glass box secured to a lab table in an adjoining clean room. 'That is just what we are about to find out, Colonel. We have been working almost nonstop for the past thirty-six hours to produce enough of the new design nanophages for this test.'

Smith nodded. Nanodevices were not built one at a time with microscopic tweezers and drops of subatomic glue. Instead, they were manufactured by the tens of millions or hundreds of millions or even billions, using biochemical and enzymatic processes precisely controlled by means of pH, temperature, and pressure. Different elements grew in different chemical solutions under different conditions. You started in one tank, formed the basic structure, washed away the excess, and then moved your materials to a new chemical bath to grow the next part of the assembly. It required constant monitoring and absolutely precise timing.

The three men moved closer to the monitor. A dozen white mice occupied the clear double-walled container. Half of the mice were lethargic, riddled with lab-induced tumors and cancers. The other six, a healthy control group, scampered here and there, looking for a way out. Numbered and color-coded tags identified each mouse. Video cameras and a variety of other sensors surrounded the box, ready to record every event once the experiment began.

Brinker pointed to a small metal canister attached to one end of the test chamber. 'There they are, Jon. Fifty million Mark Two nanophages all set to go, plus or minus five million either way.' He turned to one of the lab techs hovering close by. 'Have our little furry friends had their shots, Mike?'

The technician nodded. 'Sure thing, Dr. Brinker. I did it myself just ten minutes ago. One good jab for each of them.'

'The nanophages go in inert,' Brinker explained. 'Their internal ATP power cell only lasts so long, so we surround that section with a protective sheath.'

Smith understood the reason for that. ATP, adenosine triphosphate, was a molecule that provided energy for most metabolic processes. But ATP would begin releasing its energy as soon at it came in contact with liquid. And all living creatures were mostly liquid. 'So the injection is a kick start?' he asked.

'That's right,' Brinker confirmed. 'We inject a unique chemical signal into each test subject. Once a passive sensor on the nanophage detects that signal, the sheath opens, and the surrounding liquid activates the ATP. Our little machines light up and off they go on the hunt.'

'Then your sheath also acts as a fail-safe,' Smith realized. 'Just in case any of the Mark Twos wind up where they aren't supposed to be – say inside one of you, for example.'

'Exactly,' Brinker agreed. 'No unique chemical signature . . . no nanophage activation.'

Parikh was less certain about that.

'There is a small risk,' the shorter molecular biologist warned. 'There is always a certain error rate in the nanophage build process.'

'Which means sometimes the sheath doesn't form properly? Or the sensor is missing or set to receive the wrong signal? Or maybe you wind up with the wrong biochemical substances stored inside the phage shell?'

'Stuff like that,' Brinker said. 'But the error percentage is very small. Ridiculously tiny. Heck, almost nil.' He shrugged. 'Besides, these things are programmed to kill cancer cells and nasty bacteria. Who really cares if a few strays go wandering around inside the wrong target for a couple of minutes?'

Smith raised a skeptical eyebrow. Was Brinker serious? Low risk or not, the senior Harcourt scientist's attitude seemed just a bit too cavalier. Good science was the art of taking infinite pains. It did not mean writing off potential safety hazards, no matter how small.

The other man saw his expression and laughed. 'Don't sweat it, Jon. I'm not crazy. Well, not completely, anyway. We keep our nanophages on a damned tight leash.

They're well and truly contained. Besides, I've got Ravi here to keep me on the straight and narrow. Okay?'

Smith nodded. 'Just checking, Phil. Chalk it up to my suspicious spook-like nature.'

Brinker shot him a quick, wry smile. Then he glanced at the technicians standing by at various consoles and monitors. 'Everybody set?'

One by one, they each gave him a thumbs-up.

'Right,' Brinker said. His eyes were bright and excited. 'Mark Two nanophage live subject trial numero uno. On my mark . . . three, two, one . . . now!'

The metal canister hissed.

'Nanophages released,' one of the technicians murmured, watching a readout from the canister.

For several minutes nothing seemed to happen. The healthy mice moved here and there, seemingly at random. The sick mice stayed put.

'ATP power cycle complete,' another technician announced at last. 'Nanophage life span complete. Live subject trial complete.'

Brinker breathed out. He glanced up at Smith in triumph. 'There we go, Colonel. Now we'll anesthetize our furry friends, open them up, and see what percentage of their various cancers we just nailed. Me, I'm betting we're talking close to one hundred percent.'

Ravi Parikh was still watching the mice. He frowned. 'I think we may have a runaway, Phil,' he said quietly. 'Take a look at test subject five.'

Smith bent down to get a closer view. Mouse Five was one of the healthy ones, a member of the control group. It was moving erratically, repeatedly stumbling headlong into its fellows, mouth opening and closing rapidly. Suddenly it fell on its side, writhed in apparent agony for a few seconds – and then lay still.

'Crap,' Brinker said, staring blankly at the dead mouse. 'That's sure as hell not supposed to happen.'

Jon Smith frowned, suddenly resolving to recheck

Harcourt Bioscience's containment and safety procedures. They had better be as thorough as Parikh and Brinker claimed, so that whatever had just killed a perfectly healthy mouse stayed locked away inside this lab.

It was nearly midnight.

A mile to the north, the lights of Santa Fe cast a warm yellow glow into the clear, cold night sky. Ahead, the upper-floor windows of the Teller Institute glowed behind drawn blinds. Arc lights mounted on the roof cast long black shadows across the Institute's grounds. Along the northern edge of the perimeter fence, small stands of pine and juniper trees were wholly submerged in darkness.

Paolo Ponti slithered closer to the fence through the tall, dry grass. He hugged the dirt, careful to stay in the shadows where his black sweatshirt and dark jeans made him almost invisible. The Italian was twenty-four, slender, and athletic. Six months ago, tired of his life as a part-time university student on the dole, he had joined the Lazarus Movement.

The Movement offered his life meaning, a sense of purpose and excitement beyond anything else he had ever imagined. At first, the secret oaths he had sworn to protect Mother Earth and to destroy her enemies had seemed melodramatic and silly. Since then, however, Ponti had embraced the tenets and creeds of Lazarus with a zeal that surprised everyone who knew him, even himself.

Paolo glanced over his shoulder, seeing the faint shape wriggling along in his wake. He had met Audrey Karavites at a Lazarus rally in Stuttgart the month before. The twenty-one-year-old American woman had been traveling through Europe, a college graduation gift from her parents. Bored by museums and churches, she had gone to the rally on a whim. That whim had changed her whole life when Paolo swept her right off her feet, into his bed, and into the Movement.

The Italian turned back, still smiling smugly to himself.

Audrey was not beautiful, but she had curves where a woman should. More important, her rich, naive parents gave her a generous allowance – an allowance that had bought her and Paolo's plane tickets to Santa Fe to join this protest against nanotechnology and corrupt American capitalism.

Paolo crawled cautiously right up to the fence, so close his fingertips brushed lightly against the cold metal. He looked through the mesh. The cacti, clumps of sagebrush, and native wildflowers planted there as drought-resistant landscaping should provide good cover. He checked the luminous dial of his watch. The next patrol by the Institute's security guards should not pass this point for more than an hour. Perfect.

The Italian activist touched the fence again, this time curling his fingers around its metal links to test their strength. He nodded, pleased by what he found. The bolt cutters he had brought along would do the trick quite easily.

There was a loud crack behind him – a dry, sharp sound like that of a thick twig being snapped by strong hands. Ponti frowned. Sometimes Audrey moved with all the grace of an arthritic hippo. He looked back over his shoulder, planning to reprimand her with an angry glare.

Audrey Karavites lay curled on her side in the tall weeds. Her head flopped at a sickening angle. Her eyes were wide open, forever frozen in a look of horror. Her neck had been broken. She was dead.

Stunned, Paolo Ponti sat up, unable at first to comprehend what he saw. He opened his mouth to cry out . . . and an enormous hand gripped his face, shoving it back, muffling his screams. The last thing the young Italian felt was the terrible pain as an ice-cold blade plunged deep into his exposed throat.

The tall auburn-haired man tugged his fighting knife out of the dead man's neck, then wiped it clean on a fold of Ponti's black sweatshirt. His green eyes shone brightly.

He looked over to where the girl he had murdered lay

sprawled. Two black-clad shapes were busy rummaging through the duffel bag she had been dragging behind her. 'Well?'

'What you expected, Prime,' the hoarse whisper came back. 'Climbing gear. Cans of fluorescent spray paint. And a Lazarus Movement banner.'

The green-eyed man shook his head, amused. 'Amateurs.'

Another of his men dropped to one knee beside him. 'Your orders?'

The giant shrugged. 'Sanitize this site. Then dump the bodies somewhere else. Somewhere they will be found.'

'Do you want them found sooner? Or later?' the man asked calmly.

The big man bared his teeth in the darkness. 'Tomorrow morning will be soon enough.'

CHAPTER FOUR

Wednesday, October 13

'Preliminary analysis shows no contamination in the first four chemical baths. Temperature and pH readouts were also all well within the expected norms. . . .'

Jon Smith sat back, rereading what he had just typed. His eyes felt gritty. He had spent half of last night reviewing biochemical formulas and nanophage build procedures with Phil Brinker, Ravi Parikh, and the rest of their team. So far the error that had wrecked the first Mark II nanophage trial had eluded them. The Harcourt Biosciences researchers were probably still hard at it, he knew, poring over reams of computer printouts and test data. With the president of the United States scheduled to laud their work – and that of the other Teller Institute labs – in a little less than forty-eight hours, the pressure was on. No one at Harcourt's corporate headquarters was going to want the media to show pictures of their 'lifesaving' new technology killing mice.

'Sir?'

Jon Smith swung away from his computer monitor, fighting down a sudden surge of irritation at being interrupted. 'Yes?'

A sturdy, serious-looking man wearing a dark gray suit, button-down shirt, and pale red tie stood in the open door to his small office. He checked a photocopied list. 'Are you Dr. Jonathan Smith?'

'That's me,' Smith said. He sat up straighter, noticing the faint bulge of a shoulder holster under the other man's suit coat. That was odd. Only uniformed security personnel were licensed to carry firearms on Institute grounds. 'And you are?'

'Special Agent Mark Farrows, sir. U.S. Secret Service.'

Well, that explained the concealed weapon. Smith relaxed a bit. 'What can I do for you, Agent Farrows?'

'I'm afraid I have to ask you to leave your office for a short time, Doctor.' Farrows smiled warily, anticipating his next question. 'And no, sir, you are not under arrest. I'm with the Protective Division. We're here to conduct an advance security sweep.'

Smith sighed. Scientific institutions prized presidential visits because they often meant a higher national profile and added congressional funding. But there was no getting around the fact that they were also highly inconvenient. Security checks like this one, presumably scouting for explosive devices, potential hiding places for would-be assassins, and other dangers, always disrupted any lab's normal routine.

On the other hand, Smith knew that it was the responsibility of the Secret Service to protect the president's life. For the agents involved, shepherding the nation's chief executive safely through a massive facility crammed full of toxic chemicals, pressurized high-temperature vats, and enough high-voltage electricity to run a small city would be a waking nightmare.

The word had already come down from the Institute's hierarchy to expect a thorough inspection by the Secret Service. The betting had been that it would happen tomorrow – closer to the president's arrival. The growing army of protesters outside must have prodded the Secret Service into acting earlier.

Smith stood up, took his jacket off the back of his chair, and followed Farrows into the hallway. Dozens of scientists, technicians, and administrative staff were streaming past, most of them carrying files or laptops to work on until the Secret Service unit gave them permission to return to their labs and offices.

'We're asking Institute personnel to wait in the cafeteria, Doctor,' Farrows said politely, indicating the direction. 'Our sweep really shouldn't take long. Not more than an hour, we hope.'

It was nearly eleven in the morning. Somehow the prospect of sitting jammed in the cafeteria with the others was not very appealing to Smith. He had already been stuck inside for far too long, and one could only breathe recycled air and drink stale coffee for so many hours without going crazy. He turned to the agent. 'If it's all the same to you, I want to grab some fresh air instead.'

The Secret Service agent put out a hand to stop him. 'I'm sorry, sir, but it's not the same to me. My orders are very clear. All Institute employees report to the cafeteria.'

Smith eyed him coolly. He did not mind letting the Secret Service men do their job, but he would be damned if he would let them ride roughshod over him for no good reason. He stood still, waiting until the other man let go of the sleeve of his leather jacket. 'Then your orders don't apply to me, Agent Farrows,' he said calmly. 'I'm not a Teller Institute employee.' He flipped open his wallet to show his military ID.

Farrows scanned it quickly. One eyebrow lifted. 'You're an Army light colonel? I thought you were one of these scientist-types.'

'I'm both,' Smith told him. 'I'm here on detached duty from the Pentagon.' He nodded at the list the other man still held. 'Frankly, I'm surprised that little piece of information isn't on your roster.'

The Secret Service agent shrugged. 'Looks like somebody in D.C. fouled up. It happens.' He tapped the radio receiver in his ear. 'Just let me clear this with my SAIC, okay?'

Smith nodded. Each Secret Service detail was commanded by a SAIC – a special-agent-in-charge. He waited patiently while Farrows explained the situation to his superior.

At last, the other man waved him through. 'You're good

to go, Colonel. But don't stray too far. Those Lazarus Movement goofballs out there are in a really bad mood right now.'

Smith walked past him and came out into the Institute's large front lobby. To his left, one of the building's three staircases led up to the second floor. Doors on either side led to various administrative offices. Across the lobby, a waist-high marble railing enclosed the visitors' registration and information desks. To the right, two enormous wood-paneled doors stood open to the outside.

From there a shallow set of wide sand-colored steps led down to a broad driveway. Two big black SUVs with U.S. government license plates were parked along the edge of the drive, right at the foot of those steps. A second plain-clothes Secret Service agent stood in the doorway, keeping an eye on both the lobby and the vehicles parked outside. He wore sunglasses and cradled a deadly-looking 9mm Heckler & Koch MP5 submachine gun. His head swiveled briefly to watch Smith walk past him, but then he turned back to his sentry duty.

Outside, Smith stopped at the top of the steps and stood quietly for a moment, enjoying the feel of the sun on his lean, tanned face. The air was warming up and puffs of white cloud moved lazily across a brilliant azure sky. It was a perfect autumn day.

He took a deep breath, trying to wash the accumulated fatigue toxins out of his system.

'LET LAZARUS LEAD! NO TO NANOTECH! LET LAZARUS LEAD! NO TO NANOTECH! LET LAZARUS LEAD!'

Smith frowned. The rhythmic, singsong slogans hammered at his ears, shattering the momentary illusion of peace. They were much louder and angrier than they had been the day before. He eyed the mass of chanting protesters pressed up close against the perimeter fence. There were a lot more of them here today, too. Maybe even as many as ten thousand.

A sea of bloodred and bright green banners and plac-ards rose and fell in time with each roar from the crowd. Protest organizers roamed back and forth on a portable stage set up near the Institute security booth, shouting into microphones – whipping the demonstrators into a frenzy.

The main gate was closed. A small squad of gray-uniformed security guards stood behind the gate, nervous-ly facing the chanting throng. Outside, much farther down the access road, Smith could see a few patrol cars – a couple in the black-and-white markings of the New Mexico State Police, the rest in the white, light blue, and gold stripes of the Santa Fe County Sheriff's Office.

'This is shaping up to be one hell of a mess, Colonel,' a familiar voice said grimly from behind him.

Frank Diaz came forward from his post by the door. Today the ex-Ranger noncom was wearing a bulky bullet-proof vest. He had a riot helmet dangling from one hand and a twelve-gauge Remington pump-action shotgun slung over the other shoulder. A bandolier held a mixed assortment of CS (tear gas) shells and solid slugs for the shotgun.

'What has these people so revved up?' Smith asked. 'President Castilla and the media aren't due here until the day after tomorrow. Why all the outrage now?'

'Somebody offed a couple of Lazarus Movement–types last night,' Diaz said. 'The Santa Fe PD found two bodies stuffed into a Dumpster. Down behind that big outlet mall on Cerrillos Road. One was stabbed, and the other had a broken neck.'

Smith whistled softly. 'Damn.'

'No kidding.' The Army veteran hawked and spat. 'And those fruitcakes over there are blaming us.'

Smith turned to look more closely at him. 'Oh?'

'Apparently the dead guys were planning to cut through our fence last night,' Diaz explained. 'For some big act of civil-fricking-disobedience. Naturally the radicals claim we must have caught the two of them and slaughtered 'em. Which is all bullshit, of course. . . .'

'Of course,' Smith agreed absently. He ran his eyes over the stretch of chain-link fence in sight. It seemed perfectly intact. 'But they're still dead, and you're the designated bad guys, right?'

'Hell, Colonel,' the ex-Ranger noncom said. He sounded almost aggrieved. 'If I knocked off a couple of punk-ass, eco-freak infiltrators, do you think I'd be stupid enough to just dump them in some trash bin behind a goddamned shopping mall?'

Smith shook his head. He could not stop a quick grin from flashing across his face. 'No, Staff Sergeant Diaz. I really do not believe you would be that stupid.'

'Damned straight.'

'Which still leaves me wondering, who *was* that stupid?'

Ravi Parikh kept his attention focused closely on the highly magnified image on his monitor. The semiconducting sphere he was looking at seemed well within its design specs. He zoomed in even closer, scanning the front half of the nanophage. 'I cannot find a problem with this sensor array, Phil,' he told Brinker. 'Everything is just where it should be.'

Brinker nodded wearily. 'Which makes ninety-nine out of the last hundred.' He rubbed at his eyes. 'And the one flawed build we've found so far didn't form a sensor array at all, which means the onboard power source would never have gone active.'

Parikh frowned thoughtfully. 'That is a nonfatal error.'

'Yeah, for the host, at least.' Brinker stared into the monitor gloomily. 'But whatever ran wild in Mouse Five was pretty damned fatal.' He fought off a yawn. 'Man, Ravi, this gig is like looking for a single needle in a haystack the size of Jupiter.'

'Perhaps we will get lucky?' Parikh suggested.

'Yeah, well, we've got . . . oh, say . . . forty-seven hours and thirty-two minutes to do it in.'

Brinker swiveled around in his chair. Not far away stood the head of the Secret Service team assigned to secure their lab ahead of the president's visit. He was a big man, well over six-foot-six and probably weighing 250 pounds, most of it in muscle. Right now he was busy watching two members of his unit carefully place what they called 'anti-bugging' and 'hazard detection' devices at various points in the lab.

The scientist snapped his fingers, trying to remember the agent's name. Fitzgerald? O'Connor? Something Irish anyhow. 'Uh, Agent Kennedy?'

The tall auburn-haired man turned his head. 'The name is O'Neill, Dr. Brinker.'

'Oh, right. Sorry.' Brinker shrugged. 'Well, I just wanted to thank you again for letting Ravi and me stay here while your guys do their stuff.'

O'Neill smiled back. The smile did not reach his bright green eyes. 'No thanks are necessary, Dr. Brinker. None at all.'

'LET LAZARUS LEAD! NO TO DEATH! NO TO NANOTECH! LET LAZARUS LEAD!'

Malachi MacNamara stood close to the speakers' platform, near the very heart of the angry, shouting throng. Like those around him, he rhythmically jabbed his fist in the air in rage. Like those around him, he joined each deafening chant. But all the while his pale blue eyes were busy scanning the crowd.

Now Lazarus Movement volunteers were moving through the mass of protesters, handing out new signs and posters. Eager hands grabbed at them. MacNamara pushed and shoved his way through the jostling, agitated mob to get one for himself. It carried a much-enlarged and hurriedly color-copied photo of Paolo Ponti and Audrey Karavites – a picture that must have been taken very recently

42

indeed, because they stood silhouetted against the white peaks of the Sangre de Cristo Mountains. Scrawled above their young, smiling faces in bold red letters were the words: THEY WERE MURDERED! BUT LAZARUS LIVES!

Still chanting, the pale-eyed man nodded to himself. Clever, he thought coldly. Quite clever.

'Jesus Christ, Colonel,' Diaz murmured, listening to the sound of raw hatred spreading through the mob outside. 'It's like feeding time at the goddamned zoo!'

Smith nodded, tight-lipped. For a moment he wished he was armed. Then he shook the thought away. If things turned ugly, fifteen 9mm rounds in a Beretta clip were not going to save his life. Nor had he joined the U.S. Army to shoot unarmed rioters.

The sight of flashing lights out on the access road attracted his attention. A small convoy of black SUVs and sedans was moving slowly up the access road, steadily forcing its way through the swelling crowds. Even at this distance, Jon could see angry fists being shaken at the vehicles. He looked over at Diaz. 'You expecting reinforcements, Frank?'

The security guard shook his head. 'Not really. Hell, barring the National Guard, we've already got every unit available within fifty miles.' He peered closely at the oncoming vehicles. The lead car had just pulled up outside the gate. 'And that sure ain't the National Guard out there.'

The Army veteran's tactical radio squawked suddenly, loud enough for Smith to hear it.

'Sarge?' a voice said. 'This is Battaglia, at the gate.'

'Go ahead,' Diaz snapped. 'Make your report.'

'I've got some more Feds here. But I think there's something really screwy going on. . . .'

'Like what?'

'Well, like these guys say *they're* the Secret Service advance team. The only one,' the other guard stammered.

'And there's a Special Agent O'Neill down here who's madder than spit because I won't open the gate for him.'

Diaz lowered his radio slowly. He stared at Smith in utter confusion. 'Two Secret Service teams? How the hell can there be two goddamned Secret Service teams?'

A shiver ran down Jon's spine. 'There can't.'

He fumbled through the inner pocket of his leather jacket and tugged out his cell phone. It was a special model, and all transmissions to and from the phone were highly encrypted. He punched a single button, triggering an auto-dial emergency sequence.

The phone on the other end rang once – just once. 'Klein here,' a quiet voice said calmly. The voice belonged to Nathaniel Frederick Klein, the reclusive head of Covert-One. 'What can I do for you, Jon?'

'Can your people patch into the Secret Service's internal communications system?' Smith demanded.

There was a brief pause. 'Yes,' Klein replied. 'We can.'

'Then do it now!' Smith said urgently. 'I need to know the *exact* location of the presidential advance team for the Teller Institute!'

'Wait one.'

Smith cradled the phone between his shoulder and his ear, temporarily freeing both of his hands. He looked at Frank Diaz, who was watching him with a strange expression of disbelief. 'Did your boss give that first Secret Service unit your tactical radio frequencies?'

'Yeah. Naturally.'

'Well, then, Staff Sergeant,' Smith said coolly, 'I'm going to need a weapon.'

The former noncom nodded slowly. 'Sure thing, Colonel.' He handed over his Beretta. He saw Smith check the pistol's magazine, slap it back in, pull back its slide to chamber a round, and then flip the decocking lever to safely lower the hammer, all in a series of smooth, fast motions. Both Diaz's eyebrows went up. 'I guess I should have figured out that you were more than just a doctor.'

Fred Klein came back. 'The advance team headed by SAIC Thomas O'Neill is presently just outside the Institute's main gate. They report that the security personnel there have refused to admit them.' The head of Covert-One hesitated. 'What precisely is happening out there, Jon?'

'I don't have time to explain in detail,' Smith told him. 'But we're looking at a Trojan Horse situation. And the damned Greeks are already inside the gates.'

Then suddenly he and Diaz had even less time than he had imagined.

The fake Secret Service agent he had seen guarding the main doors was moving out into the open. And he was already swinging the muzzle of his submachine gun toward them.

Smith reacted instantly, diving to one side. He landed flat on the steps with the Beretta already extended in both hands and on-target. Diaz threw himself the other way.

For a split second the gunman hesitated, trying to pick out the biggest threat. Then he swung the MP5 toward the uniformed guard.

Big mistake, Smith thought coldly. He flipped the safety catch off and squeezed the trigger. The Beretta bucked upward in his hands. He forced the pistol back on-line and fired again.

Both 9mm rounds slammed home, tearing flesh and shattering bone. Hit twice in the chest, the gunman went down in a heap. His submachine gun clattered to the pavement and a widening rivulet of blood trickled down the steps.

Smith heard a car door open behind him. He looked back.

Another dark-suited man had climbed out of one of the two black SUVs parked along the drive. This man had his SIG-Sauer pistol out and it was aimed squarely at Jon's head.

Smith swung round in a frantic attempt to bring his

own weapon to bear, knowing that it was no use. He was too slow, too far out of position, and the dark-suited man's finger was already tightening on the trigger. . . .

Frank Diaz fired his shotgun at point-blank range. The blunt-tipped CS gas round struck the second gunman right under the chin and ripped his head off. Tumbling now, the tear gas shell bounced off the SUV and exploded high in the air – sending a puff of gray mist drifting east, away from the building.

'Shit,' Diaz murmured. 'Nonlethal ammunition, my ass.' The ex-Ranger noncom quickly reloaded his shotgun, this time with solid slugs. 'Now what, Colonel?'

Smith lay flat for several seconds longer, scanning the Institute's wide doorway for more enemies. There were no signs of movement. 'Cover me.'

Diaz nodded. He knelt, aiming at the door.

Smith belly-crawled up the steps to where the first dead gunman lay. His nose twitched at the hot, coppery smell of blood and the uglier stench of voided bowels. Ignore it, he told himself grimly. Win first. Regret taking life later. He put the Beretta on safety and shoved it into his belt, at the small of his back. Moving fast, he scooped up the MP5.

The sentry's surveillance radio gear caught his eye. It would be very useful to know what the bad guys were up to, he decided. He stripped the lightweight radio set off the other man's belt and fitted the tiny receiver into his own ear.

'Delta One? Delta Two? Reply, over,' a harsh voice said.

Smith held his breath. This was the sound of the enemy. But who the hell were these people?

'Delta Section? Reply, over,' the voice repeated. Then it spoke again, issuing an order. 'This is Prime. Delta One and Two are off-line. All sections. ComSec enable. Mark. Mark. Now – '

Abruptly the voice vanished, replaced by static. Smith knew what had just happened. Once they realized their communications were compromised, the intruders inside the building had switched to a new channel, following a preset plan and rendering this radio useless to him.

Smith whistled softly to himself. Whatever the hell was going on here, one thing was absolutely clear: He and Diaz were up against a force of stone-cold professionals.

CHAPTER FIVE

Inside the quiet, clean confines of the Harcourt Biosciences Lab, the tall, auburn-haired man frowned. The early arrival of the real Secret Service advance unit was a possibility he had anticipated in his mission plan. Losing the two men he had left guarding the Institute's main entrance was a somewhat more serious complication. He spoke quietly into the small radio mike attached to his suit coat lapel. 'Sierra One, this is Prime. Cover the stairs. Now.'

He turned to the men under his direct command. 'How much longer?'

The senior technician, short and stocky, with pronounced Slavic features, looked up from the large metal cylinder he was wiring into a remote-control circuit. He had clamped the cylinder to a desk next to the lab's floor-to-ceiling picture window. 'Two more minutes, Prime.' He murmured into his own mike and listened intently. 'Our sections in the other labs confirm they, too, are almost finished,' he reported.

'Is there a problem, Agent O'Neill?'

The green-eyed man swung round to find Dr. Ravi Parikh staring at him. His colleague Brinker was still engrossed in his analysis of the failed nanophage trial, but the Indian molecular biologist looked suspicious now.

The big man donned a reassuring smile. 'There's no problem, Doctor. You can go on with your work.'

Parikh hesitated. 'What is that piece of equipment?' he asked at last, pointing to the bulky cylinder beside which the technician crouched. 'It does not look much like a "hazardous materials detector" or whatever else you have said you are placing in our lab.'

'My, my, my, Dr. Parikh . . . you are a very observant fellow,' the green-eyed man said carefully. He stepped closer and then, almost casually, chopped down hard on the scientist's neck with the edge of his right hand.

Parikh crumpled to the floor.

Startled by the sudden noise, Brinker spun around. He stared down at his assistant in shock. 'Ravi? What the – '

Still moving, the big man pivoted and kicked out with tremendous force. His heel slammed into the blond-haired researcher's chest, hurling him back against his desk and computer monitor. Brinker's head snapped forward. He slid to the floor and lay still.

Smith twisted a control knob on the captured radio set, running through as many different frequencies as he could as fast as he could. He listened attentively. Static hissed and popped. There were no voices. No orders he could intercept and interpret.

With a frown, he yanked the receiver out of his ear and set the now-useless radio gear aside. It was time to get moving. Sitting out here any longer meant surrendering the initiative to the enemy. That would be dangerous enough against amateurs. Against a trained force it was likely to be catastrophic. Right now those fake Secret Service agents were methodically running through some kind of very nasty scheme inside the Teller Institute. But what was their game? he wondered. Terrorism? Hostage taking? High-risk industrial espionage? Sabotage?

He shook his head. There was no real way to know. Not yet. Still, whatever the enemy was doing, this was the time to press them, before they could react. He rose to one knee, checking the shadowed entrance to the Institute.

'Where are you going, Colonel?' Diaz whispered.

'Inside.'

The security guard's eyes widened in disbelief. 'That's crazy! Why not wait here for help? There are at least ten more of those bastards in there.'

Smith risked a quick glance behind him, toward the perimeter fence and the gate. The angry crowd down there was spiraling out of control – pushing and shoving against the fence and hammering furiously on the hoods and roofs of the stalled Secret Service convoy. Unwilling to provoke the enraged mob any further, the real federal agents had retreated inside their locked vehicles. And even if the Teller Institute security guards opened the gate to let them in, the protesters would pour through at the same time. He swore softly. 'Take a look, Frank. I don't think the cavalry is coming. Not this time.'

'Then let's hold here,' Diaz argued. He jerked a thumb at the SUVs parked behind them. 'That's their line of escape. Let's make 'em come through us to get away.'

Smith shook his head. 'Too risky. First, these guys may be dead-enders who don't plan to leave. Second, they know we're out here by now. These guys are pros. They must have alternate escape routes, and there are just too many other ways for them to get away – maybe a helo landing on that big flat roof up there, or more vehicles waiting outside the fence. Third, these weapons' – he nodded at both the MP5 submachine gun he had captured and Diaz's shotgun – 'don't give us enough firepower to stop a determined attack. If we let the bad guys run a set-piece battle, they're going to roll right over us.'

'Ah, crap,' the Army veteran sighed, rechecking the loads for his Remington. 'I hate this John Wayne shit. They don't pay me enough to be a hero.'

Smith bared his teeth in a tight, fierce grin. 'Me, neither. But we're it. So I suggest you shut up and soldier, Sergeant.' He breathed out. 'Are you ready?'

Grim-faced but determined, Diaz gave him a thumbs-up.

Cradling the MP5, Smith sprinted for the right side of

the Institute's huge main doors. His stomach muscles tensed, expecting the sudden, tearing agony of a bullet fired from inside the main lobby. There was only silence. Breathing fast, he flattened himself against the sun-warmed adobe wall.

Diaz joined him a second later.

Smith rolled around the corner of the door, moving the submachine gun through a steady, controlled arc as he sighted along the barrel. Nothing. The huge room appeared empty. Half-crouched, he moved forward and took cover behind a stretch of waist-high marble railing. Caught in a gentle breeze from the open doors, papers fluttered off the Institute's registration and information desks and swirled lazily across the tiled floor.

He started to poke his head over the railing.

'Get down!' Diaz roared.

Smith sensed a shape moving in the corridor off to his left. He threw himself flat just as the gunman opened up – firing rapid aimed shots at him with a 9mm pistol. Rounds hammered the marble right over his head, sending jagged chips of shattered stone flying through the air. One sharp-edged fragment sliced a thin red line across the back of his right hand.

Lying prone, with the stock of the MP5 braced against his shoulder, Jon fired back, shooting in controlled three-round bursts. From the open doorway Diaz began firing solid slugs from his twelve-gauge shotgun. Each slug tore huge chunks out of the Institute's adobe walls.

Smith rolled out from behind the railing. A pistol bullet cracked right past his head. Damn. He rolled faster and then stopped himself suddenly, lying prone again – but this time with a clear view right down the corridor.

Jon could see the gunman staring straight at him. They were less than fifty feet apart. It was the sturdy, serious-looking man who had said his name was Farrows. The supposed Secret Service agent was down on one knee, with a SIG-Sauer pistol extended in a two-handed shooting grip, still firing steadily. Another bullet punched into the floor close by Smith's head, spraying small bits and pieces of broken tile across the side of his face.

He ignored the stinging impacts and breathed out. The MP5's forward sight steadied on the gunman. He squeezed the trigger. The submachine gun stuttered three times. Two rounds missed. The third hit Farrows in the face, blowing a hole right out the back of his skull.

Smith scrambled to his feet and raced to the foot of the U-shaped staircase leading up to the Institute's second floor. Three of the enemy down so far, he thought. But how many more to go?

Diaz sprinted through the lobby and went prone not far away, covering the first flight of stairs with his shotgun. 'Where to now, Colonel?' he called softly.

That was a good question, Smith thought grimly. Much depended on what the intruders intended. If they were set on holding the research staff as hostages, most of them would be holed up in the Institute cafeteria – not far down the corridor from where Farrows lay dead. But if this was a hostage situation, charging in headlong was likely to get far too many innocent people killed.

Somehow, though, Smith doubted hostage taking was the goal here. This whole operation was too elaborate and too precisely timed for something so simple and low-tech. Coming in disguised as Secret Service agents on a bomb sweep seemed aimed primarily at gaining unimpeded access to the labs.

He made his decision and pointed to the ceiling.

Diaz nodded.

Moving in alternate bounds, with one man always ready to provide covering fire while the other went forward, Jon Smith and the Institute security guard began climbing the central staircase.

'LAZARUS LIVES! NO TO NANOTECH! LAZARUS LIVES! NO TO DEATH MACHINES! LAZARUS LIVES!'

Malachi MacNamara was jostled ever closer to the Institute's perimeter fence, borne along by the shouting, chanting mob. He scowled. He was a man who disdained displays of wild, unreasoning emotion – a man who felt far happier alone in the wilderness than trapped like this in a sea of his fellow humans. For now, though, he knew he could only move with this maddened tide. If he tried to stand against the pressure for too long, he would only be swept off his feet and trampled to death.

Still, he thought icily, that did not mean he had to play the utterly passive puppet.

He swung his elbows through a series of short, vicious arcs, hammering at the ribs of those closest to him. Frightened by his cold rage, they fell back – giving him just enough room to risk a look back at the protest stage. It was deserted. His pale eyes narrowed in sudden calculation. The Lazarus Movement radicals who had whipped this mass of more than ten thousand demonstrators into uncontrolled wrath had vanished.

Where were they?

Even this deep in the mob, the lean, weather-beaten Canadian was tall enough to see past the outer fringes of the crowd. Two of the Secret Service vehicles were edging slowly back down the access road. Dented hoods and car roofs, crumpled fenders, and smashed windshields testified to the fury of the human storm through which they had passed. There were also small knots of worried-looking New Mexico State Police troopers and Santa Fe County sheriffs, most backing slowly away to avoid triggering an all-out riot. Lured by the prospect of shooting dramatic footage they could feed to the national and international networks, several local TV crews were much closer to the stamping and shouting protesters.

MacNamara turned his gaze away. His eyes hunted through the angry crowd for a glimpse of the Movement activists he sought. They were nowhere to be found. Curiouser and curiouser, he thought coolly. Rats deserting a sinking ship? Or predators slipping away to make a new kill somewhere else?

The pressure of the mob along the fence was growing. At places the barrier bulged inward, stretching dangerously under the impact of so many bodies. The gray-uniformed security guards behind the fence were already edging backward, retreating toward the relative safety of the Institute's main building. The Canadian nodded to himself. That was not terribly surprising. No one but a fool would expect a small force of part-time policemen to face a rampaging crowd of ten thousand out in the open. Doing so would be choosing a particularly pathetic form of suicide.

He stiffened suddenly, spotting several men moving with grim, determined purpose through the press of hate-filled faces, red and green banners and placards, and up-raised fists. They were the young toughs he had seen arriving the day before, each carrying the same long duffel bag slung over his shoulder.

Shielded from police scrutiny by the crowd, the young men reached the fence. Down went their duffels and out came long-handled bolt cutters. They started slicing through metal link after metal link, cutting from top to bottom with practiced speed and efficiency. Soon whole sections of the Institute's security fence tore away and came crashing down. Hundreds and then thousands of demonstrators poured through the gaps, loping across the open ground toward the huge sand-colored science building.

'LAZARUS LIVES! LAZARUS LIVES! LAZARUS LIVES!' they clamored. 'NO TO NANOTECH! NO TO DEATH MACHINES!'

Unable to do anything else, the pale, blue-eyed man named Malachi MacNamara ran wildly with them, howling like all the rest.

Smith advanced north along one side of the Teller Institute's second-floor corridor with the MP5 submachine gun cradled against his shoulder, ready to fire. Frank Diaz moved up the other side.

They came to a heavy metal door, one of several opening onto this broad central hallway. The light above the adjacent security station glowed red. A sign identified this as the lab assigned to VOSS LIFE SCIENCES – HUMAN GENOME DIVISION. Diaz gestured at the door with his shotgun. He mouthed a question. 'Do we go in?'

Smith shook his head quickly. The Institute was home to more than a dozen different technology R&D efforts, all of them highly advanced and all of them enormously expensive and potentially valuable. There was no way that he and Diaz could realistically comb through every lab and office on this upper floor.

So Smith had decided to play a hunch. The president's scheduled trip to Santa Fe was intended to highlight the nanotech research conducted by Harcourt, Nomura PharmaTech, and an independent Institute-affiliated group. By disguising themselves as a Secret Service advance unit, the intruders had guaranteed themselves access to those same labs. All in all, Smith thought it was a pretty safe bet that whatever they were up to involved the facilities in the North Wing.

Still gliding silently down the central corridor, he and Diaz came to a T-shaped intersection at the far end of the building. Another staircase to the ground floor lay straight ahead of them. Beyond the head of those stairs was a stainless steel door leading into the laboratory leased by Nomura PharmaTech. Turning right would take them to the suite occupied by the Institute's own nanotech team. The Harcourt Biosciences Lab run by Phil Brinker and Ravi Parikh was down the hallway to the left.

Smith hesitated briefly. Which way should they go now?

Suddenly, the warning light on the Nomura lab security station flashed from red to green. 'Down!' Jon hissed. He and Diaz each dropped to one knee, waiting.

The door slid open. Three men stepped out into the hallway. Two of them, one fair-haired, the other bald, wore blue technicians' coveralls. They were bowed under the weight of the equipment cases slung over their shoulders. The third, taller and prematurely gray, wore a dark-colored jacket and khaki slacks. He carried a small Uzi submachine gun.

Smith could feel his pulse accelerating. He and Diaz could cut these men down with a couple of short bursts. No doubt that would be the safest and simplest course of action. But if they were dead, they could not tell him what was going on inside the Teller Institute. He sighed inside. Though it meant taking added risks, he needed prisoners to interrogate a lot more than he needed three silent corpses.

He rose to his feet, covering the intruders with his MP5. 'Drop your weapons!' he barked. 'And then put your hands up!'

Caught completely by surprise, they froze.

'Do what the man says,' Frank Diaz told them calmly, sighting down the barrel of his pump-action shotgun. 'Before I splatter you all over that nice shiny door.'

Still visibly stunned by this sudden reversal of fortune, the two men in coveralls carefully lowered their equipment cases and raised their hands. Scowling, the Uzi-armed man also obeyed. His weapon clattered onto the tiles.

'Now come here,' Smith said. 'Slowly. One at a time. You first!' he said, jabbing the muzzle of the MP5 at the one he suspected was their leader, the taller, gray-haired man. The intruder hesitated.

Intending to hurry him along, Jon stepped out into the intersecting corridor. There was a tiny flicker of movement off to his left. He swung round, his finger already starting to squeeze the trigger. But there was no one to shoot. Instead he saw a small olive-drab metal sphere arcing toward him through the air. It bounced off the nearest wall and rolled back out into the intersection. For a frozen moment of time Smith could not believe what he was seeing. But then years of training, combat-tested reflexes, and raw animal fear kicked in.

'Grenade!' he roared in warning. He hit the floor, curled up, and buried his head in his arms.

The grenade went off.

The thunderous blast tore at his clothes and sent him skittering across the floor. White-hot fragments hissed overhead – smashing jagged holes in the adobe walls and shattering lights.

Nearly deafened by the explosion, with his ears still ringing, Smith uncurled and slowly sat up, amazed to find himself unhurt. His submachine gun lay close by. He grabbed it. There were raw gouges along the plastic stock and hand guard, but it seemed otherwise undamaged.

His ears were clearing. He could hear high-pitched screams now. They were coming from across the corridor, by the door to the Nomura lab. Flayed by dozens of razor-edged steel splinters, the two men wearing coveralls writhed in agony – smearing blood across the tiled floor. The third man, luckier or blessed with quicker reactions, was unwounded. And he was reaching for the Uzi he had dropped.

Smith shot him three times. The gray-haired man fell forward onto his face and lay still.

Then Jon looked over at Diaz. He was dead. The bulletproof vest he was wearing had stopped most of the grenade fragments – but not the one jagged shard that had torn open his throat. Smith swore softly, angry with himself for dragging the other man into this fight and angry at the fates.

Another grenade bounced across the corridor and rolled toward the head of the stairs. This one did not explode. Instead it hissed and sputtered, spewing thick, coiling tendrils of red smoke into the air. In seconds, the two intersecting corridors were blanketed in billowing smoke.

Smith peered down the barrel of his MP5, looking for any sign of movement in the smoke. Firing blind would only give away his position. He needed a target.

From somewhere ahead, deep in that red, roiling cloud, two Uzis stuttered on full automatic, spraying a hail of bullets down the hall. Copper-jacketed 9mm rounds punched new holes in walls or ricocheted off steel doors. Ceramic vases shattered. Shredded pieces of yellow and purple wildflowers swirled madly in the bullet-torn air. Smith fell prone, desperately hugging the floor while the Uzi rounds ripped right over his head.

The shooting stopped abruptly, leaving only an eerie silence in its wake.

He waited a moment longer, listening. Now he thought he could hear feet clattering down the smoke-filled staircase, growing ever fainter. He grimaced. The bad guys were falling back. That fusillade of submachine-gun fire had been meant to keep his head down while they escaped. Worst of all, it had worked.

Smith scrambled upright and went forward into the blinding red cloud. He strained to see what was ahead of him. His feet sent spent shell casings tinkling across the tile floor and crunched on powdered bits of adobe. The top of the stairs loomed up out of the smoke.

He crouched, peering down the stairwell. If the intruders had left someone behind to guard their retreat, those stairs would be a death trap. But he did not have time to run all the way back to the central staircase. He had to either chance it – or stay here and cower.

With his submachine gun held ready, he started down the wide, shallow steps. Behind him, blinding white light suddenly flared across the corridor. The whole stairwell swayed violently from side to side, rocked by a series of powerful explosions rippling through the

Nomura PharmaTech and Institute nanotech labs.

Reacting instinctively, Smith threw himself down the stairs, rolling and tumbling head over heels while the building above him erupted in flame.

CHAPTER SIX

Dr. Ravi Parikh swam slowly upward through darkness, blearily trying to regain full consciousness. His eyes fluttered open. He was lying with his face pressed against the floor. The cool brown tiles bucked and jolted beneath him – shuddering as carefully placed demolition charges systematically smashed the other North Wing lab complexes into splintered, flaming ruins. The molecular biologist groaned, fighting down a stomach-churning wave of nausea and pain.

Sweating with the effort, he forced himself up onto his hands and knees. He raised his head slowly. He was looking at the floor-to-ceiling picture window that ran the whole length of the Harcourt lab's outer-office area. The blinds, usually drawn tight, were wide open.

Close to his head, the strange metal cylinder he had wondered about was still clamped to a desk facing the window. A blinking digital readout attached to one end of the cylinder flickered through a series of numbers, counting down: 10 . . . 9 . . . 8 . . . 7 . . . 6 . . . 5 . . .

Small shaped charges attached to the picture window detonated in a rapid-fire succession of orange and red flashes. Instantly the glass shattered into thousands of tiny shards and blew outward. The sudden change in pressure sucked dozens of scraps of loose paper into the air. They were wafted out through the jagged opening.

Still dazed and sick, Parikh stared after them in utter, uncomprehending bewilderment. He drew a single deep, shuddering breath.

3 . . . 2 . . . 1. The blinking digital readout went dead. A relay valve clicked and cycled inside the cylinder. And then, with a quiet, snake-like hiss, the nanophage canister began releasing its highly compressed and deadly contents into the outside world.

The cloud of Stage II nanophages drifted silently and invisibly through the shattered window. There were tens of billions of them, each still inert – each still waiting for the signal that would bring it to life. Pushed outward by the Harcourt lab's own air pressure system, the vast mass of microscopic phages gradually dispersed and then slowly, ever so slowly, slid downward through the air.

Still spreading, this unseen mist settled onto the thousands of stunned Lazarus Movement protesters watching in horror as explosions ripped through the upper floor of the Teller Institute. Millions of nanophages were drawn with each breath and carried down into their lungs. Millions more entered through the porous membranes of their noses or filtered through the soft tissues around their eyes.

For several seconds these nanophages stayed inactive, spreading outward through blood vessels and cell walls by natural processes. But one out of every hundred thousand or so, larger and of a more sophisticated design than its companions, went active immediately. These control phages prowled the host body under their own power, hunting for one of the various biochemical signatures that their sensor arrays were able to recognize. Any positive reading triggered the immediate release of coded streams of unique messenger molecules.

The nanophages themselves, still floating silently through the body, carried only a single sensor of their own, a sensor able to detect those coded molecules, even when they were diluted to the level of a few parts per billion. Its creators coldly referred to this aspect of their nanophage design as the 'shark receptor,' since it mimicked the uncanny ability of great white sharks to sniff out even the tiniest drop of blood drifting amid the vast depths of the sea. But the comparison was cruelly apt in yet another way. Each nanophage reacted to this faint whiff of the messenger molecule exactly as though it were a shark scenting fresh blood in the water.

Trapped in the middle of the mob, the lean, weather-beaten man was the first to recognize the true horror descending on them. Like all the rest, he had stopped chanting and now stood in grim silence, watching the bombs going off one after another. Most were detonating on the Teller Institute's north and west sides – sending huge pillars of flame and debris soaring high into the air. But Malachi could also hear other, smaller charges exploding deep inside the massive building.

The woman pressed next to him, a young hard-faced blonde wearing a surplus army-issue jacket with the sleeves rolled up, suddenly groaned. She fell to her knees and began retching, quietly at first and then uncontrollably. MacNamara glanced down at her, noting the needle tracks scarring her arms. Those higher up were livid, still raw.

A heroin addict, he realized, feeling a mixture of pity and disgust. Probably lured to the Lazarus Movement rally by the promise of thrills and the chance to take part in something bigger and more important than her drab everyday life. Was the young fool overdosing here and now? He sighed and knelt down to see if there was anything he could do to help her.

Then he saw the grotesque web of red-rimmed fissures spreading swiftly across her terrified face and her needle-scarred arms, and he knew that this was something infinitely more terrible. She moaned again, sounding more like an animal than a human being. The fissures widened. Her skin was sloughing away, rapidly dissolving into a kind of translucent slime.

To his own horror, MacNamara saw that the connective tissues beneath her skin – the muscles, tendons, and ligaments – were dissolving, too. Her eyes liquefied and slid dripping out of their sockets. Bright red blood welled up within those terrible wounds. Beneath the mask of blood that was now her face he could see the pale white of bone.

Blind now, the young woman reached out desperately with clawed hands. More red-tinged slime poured out of the shapeless cavity that had once been her mouth. Sickened and ashamed of his own fear, he backed away. Her hands and fingers dissolved, falling apart in a welter of disconnected bones. She fell forward and lay twitching on the ground. Even as he watched, her fatigue jacket and jeans sagged inward, stained dark by the blood and other fluids pouring out of her disintegrating body.

For what seemed an eternity, MacNamara stared at her in unbelieving dread, unable to look away. It was as though this woman were being eaten alive from within. At last, she lay still, already more a jumble of bones and slime-soaked clothing than an identifiable human corpse.

He scrambled upright, now hearing a gruesome chorus of tormented howls and groans and wailing rising from the tightly packed crowd around him. Hundreds of other protesters were reeling now, clawing and clutching at themselves as their flesh was consumed from the inside out.

For a long-drawn-out moment, the thousands of Lazarus Movement activists still unaffected stayed motionless, rooted to the ground by shock and sheer mind-numbing fear. But then they broke and fled, scattering in all directions – trampling the dead and dying in a mad, panicked rush to escape whatever new plague had escaped from the explosion-shattered labs of the Teller Institute.

And again Malachi MacNamara ran with them, this time with his pulse hammering in his ears as he wondered just how much longer he might have to live.

*

Lieutenant Colonel Jon Smith lay in a tangled heap at the foot of the North Wing staircase. For a few tortured seconds he could not force himself to move. Every bone and muscle in his body felt twisted, bruised, or scraped in some painful and unnatural way.

The Teller Institute swayed, rocked by yet another enormous explosion somewhere on its upper floor. A hail of dust and broken bits of adobe pattered down the stairs. Scraps of paper set alight by the blast spun lazily through the air, each a tiny flaring torch drifting downward.

Time to go, Smith told himself. It was either that or stay and get crushed when the bomb-damaged building finally collapsed in on itself. Gingerly he uncurled himself and stood up. He winced. The first fifteen feet of his rolling, tumbling dive down the stairs had been the easy part, he thought wryly. Everything after that had been one long, bone-jarring nightmare.

He eyed his surroundings. The last wisps of red mist from the smoke grenade were dissipating, but clouds of thicker, darker smoke were beginning to roll through the ground-floor corridors. There were fires raging throughout the building. He glanced up at the ceiling. The sprinkler heads there were bone-dry, meaning that the Institute's fire suppression system must have been knocked out by one of the bomb blasts.

Smith pursed his lips, frowning. He was willing to bet that was deliberate. This was not a case of industrial espionage gone wrong or of simple sabotage; this was cold-blooded, ruthless terrorism.

He limped over to where his submachine gun lay. By some miracle the weapon hadn't gone off accidentally when it tumbled with him down the stairs, but the curved thirty-round ammo magazine was twisted and bent at an awkward angle. He hit the release catch and tugged hard on the damaged magazine. It was jammed tight.

He laid the submachine gun down and drew the 9mm Beretta. The pistol seemed unharmed, but the pain he felt made Smith sure he was going to have a Beretta-shaped bruise on the small of his back the next morning.

If you live to see the next morning, he reminded himself coldly.

Holding the pistol ready, he set off to make his way out through the burning, bomb-damaged building. It was easy enough to follow the path taken by the retreating intruders. They had left a trail of corpses behind them.

Smith passed a number of bodies huddled in the smoke-filled corridor. Most were people he knew, at least by sight, and some were men or women he knew well, among them Takashi Ukita, the chief scientist for Nomura PharmaTech's lab. He had been shot twice in the head. Jon shook his head in regret.

Dick Pfaff and Bill Corimond lay dead not far away in that same hallway. Both of them had been shot multiple times at point-blank range. They had been the senior researchers in the Institute's own nanotech group. Their work had been aimed at developing small self-replicating devices that would consume oil spills without further damage to the environment.

The farther he walked, the more coldly furious Smith became. Parikh, Brinker, Pfaff, Corimond, Ukita, and the others had all been dedicated scientists and truth seekers. Their research would have yielded enormous benefits for the whole world. So now some terrorist sons of bitches had killed them and destroyed years of hard work? Well, then, he decided icily, he would do his damnedest to make sure those same terrorists paid dearly for their crimes.

He picked up the pace – trotting now. His eyes were narrow slits. Somewhere ahead there were men he needed to kill or capture.

He passed more corpses. The smoke was thicker now. The acrid stench stung his eyes and left his throat raw. He could feel the glowing heat from the uncontrolled fires raging in offices on both sides of the corridor. Some of the wood doors were starting to smolder. Smith ran faster.

At last he came to a side door that had been left propped half-open. He knelt quickly, checking for any tripwires that could trigger a booby trap. Seeing none, he eased through the doorway and stepped out into the open air.

Before him lay a scene that might have been one of the grotesque paintings of hell and devils and damnation so favored by medieval Christians. Thousands of terrified Lazarus Movement activists were streaming away from the Institute, scrambling wildly through its rock gardens of cactus, sagebrush, and wildflowers. Some staggered, reeled, and then dropped to their knees with loud, despairing wails. One by one they folded in on themselves. Smith stared at them in utter horror, appalled by what he saw happening before his very eyes. Hundreds of people were literally falling apart, dissolving into a reddish liquid sludge. Hundreds more had already been reduced to sad heaps of stained clothing and scraps of whitened bone.

For a moment he fought against an almost overpowering urge to turn and flee himself. There was something so awful, so inhuman, in what he saw happening to those people that it stirred every primitive fear he had thought long buried by training, discipline, and willpower. No one should die like that, he thought desperately. No man should have to watch himself rotting away while still alive.

With an effort, Smith tore his eyes away from the rotting flesh and mangled corpses strewn outside the Teller Institute. Pistol in hand, he scanned the panicked mob fleeing toward the perimeter fence, trying to pick out those who showed no fear – those whose movements were disciplined and sure. He spotted a group of six men walking steadily toward the fence. They were more than a hundred meters ahead of him. Four were clad in blue coveralls and lugged heavy equipment cases. Smith nodded to himself. Those had to be the specialists who had planted the bombs inside the Institute. The two remaining men, striding a few yards behind the others, wore identical charcoal gray suits. Each was armed with a short-nosed Uzi submachine gun. The shorter of the two was about Jon's own height, with short-cropped black hair. But the one who really caught his attention, the powerfully built auburn-haired man who seemed to be giving the orders, was at least a head taller than his comrades.

Smith started running again. He loped across the open ground, dodging the pathetic remains scattered here and there, closing rapidly on the retreating terrorists. He was within fifty meters or so when their chief, turning his head for a last satisfied look at the bomb-gutted and burning Teller Institute, saw him coming.

'Action! Rear!' the giant shouted, warning his men. He was already swinging to face Smith with his submachine gun gripped in both hands. He opened fire instantly, walking short bursts across the sand and scrub toward the running American.

Jon threw himself to the right, rolling on his shoulder. He came back up on one knee with the Beretta aimed in the right general direction. Without waiting for the sights to settle on his target, he squeezed off two shots. Neither came that close, but at least they forced the big man to drop behind a clump of sagebrush.

Another Uzi burst pulverized the ground right behind Smith, kicking up huge dirt clods. He swiveled. The black-haired gunman was coming up on his flank, firing as he ran.

Jon swung the Beretta through a wide arc, leading the other man by just a hair. He breathed out calmly and fired three times. His first shot missed. The second and third shattered the terrorist's leg and smashed his right shoulder.

Screaming in pain, the black-haired man stumbled and went down. Two of the men in coveralls dropped their equipment cases and ran to help him. Immediately the tall auburn-haired man popped up from behind the sagebrush and began shooting again.

Smith felt an Uzi round punch through the lining of his leather bomber jacket. The superheated air trailing the near miss tore a searing line of fire across his ribs.

He rolled again, trying frantically to throw off the big man's aim. More bullets clipped the sand and dry vegetation all around him. Expecting to get hit any second, he fired back with the Beretta while rolling, snapping off several unaimed shots in a desperate bid to force the other man back into cover.

Still rolling, Smith landed behind a large rock half-buried in a patch of tall wheatgrass. He went prone. Submachine-gun fire hammered the small boulder.

The noise of a powerful engine roared above the sound of gunfire. Warily Jon raised his head for a quick look. He saw a mammoth dark green Ford Excursion accelerating through one of the gaps in the fence. The SUV veered left, heading straight for the skirmish. Hundreds of panicked protesters ducked out of its path as it bounced over the broken ground at high speed.

Brakes squealing, the vehicle slewed round and skidded to a stop next to the small band of terrorists. The cloud of dust thrown by its tires hung low in the air, drifting slowly downwind. Protected by the SUV's bulk, the four explosives experts tossed their equipment cases into the back, shoved the wounded gunman into one of the rear seats, and scrambled inside themselves. Still firing short aimed bursts in Smith's direction, the auburn-haired giant backed away slowly toward the getaway vehicle. He was smiling now, his eyes alight with pleasure.

That murderous son of a bitch! Jon's cold fury suddenly flared into white-hot rage, erasing any instinct for self-preservation. Without stopping to think more clearly, he stood straight up, bracing the Beretta in a target shooter's grip.

Surprised by his boldness, the tall man stopped shooting controlled bursts and went to full auto. The Uzi chattered wildly, climbing higher with every round it fired.

Smith felt bullets ripping the air close to his head. He ignored them, choosing instead to focus entirely on his target. Fifty meters was near the outside edge of his effective pistol range, so concentration was vital. The Beretta's sights slid down on the big man's massive chest and stayed there.

He squeezed the trigger rapidly, firing as many shots as quickly as he could without spoiling his aim. His first bullet punched a hole in the front passenger side door, just inches from the auburn-haired giant's hip. The second smashed the window next to his elbow.

Jon frowned. The Beretta was pulling to the left. He shifted his aim slightly and fired again. This 9mm round smashed the Uzi out of the terrorist leader's hands, sending it flying into the scrub far out of his reach. The bullet ricocheted off the SUV's hood in a shower of sparks.

Unnerved by the gunfire hammering his vehicle, the getaway driver stomped down hard on the accelerator. The Excursion's tires spun futilely for a second and then found some traction. The dark green SUV peeled out, skidded through another tight turn, and roared away toward the fence, leaving the tall auburn-haired man behind in a drifting spray of sand and dust.

For a moment the giant stood motionless, with his head cocked to watch his comrades abandon him. Then, to Smith's astonishment, he simply shrugged his massive shoulders and turned back to face the American. His face was now utterly devoid of any expression.

Jon moved closer, still aiming the Beretta at him. 'Get your hands up!'

The other man just stood there, waiting.

'I said get your hands up!' Smith snapped. He kept walking, closing the range. He stopped about fifteen meters away, well inside the zone where he knew he could put every 9mm round exactly where he wanted it.

The auburn-haired giant said nothing. His bright green eyes narrowed. The look in them reminded Jon of one he had seen in a caged tiger padding back and forth past human prey it could not reach.

'And what will you do if I refuse? Kill me?' the tall man said at last.

His voice was softer than Smith expected and his English was perfect, utterly without trace of an accent.

Smith nodded coldly. 'If I have to.'

'Then do it,' the other man told him. Without waiting any longer, he took a long stride forward, moving with a predator's lithe grace. His right hand darted inside his coat and came out gripping a razor-edged fighting knife.

Smith squeezed the Beretta's trigger. It bucked upward, and recoil slammed the slide back, ejecting the spent shell casing. But this time the slide locked to the rear. He swore under his breath. He had just fired the last of the fifteen rounds in the pistol's magazine.

The 9mm bullet hit the auburn-haired giant high up on his left side. For a brief instant the impact rocked him back. He looked down at the small red-rimmed hole in his coat. Blood pulsed in the wound, spilling slowly out across the dark fabric. Then he flexed the fingers of his left hand and waggled the fighting knife in his right. His lips twisted into a cruel grin. He shook his head in mock pity. 'Not good enough. As you see, I still live.'

Still grinning, the green-eyed man slowly moved in for the kill, sweeping his knife back and forth in a sinuous, almost hypnotic, arc. The deadly-looking blade glinted in the sun.

Desperately Smith hurled the now-useless Beretta at him.

The big man ducked under it and attacked. He struck with unbelievable speed, aiming for the American's throat.

Smith jerked aside. The knife blade flashed past less than an inch from his face. He backed away fast, breathing hard.

The green-eyed man came after him. He lunged again, this time lower.

Jon spun to one side and chopped down hard, trying to break the other man's right wrist. It was like hitting a piece of high-quality steel. His hand went numb. He fell back again, shaking his fingers, trying frantically to work some life back into them. What the hell was he fighting?

The big man came prowling after him a third time, grinning even wider now, plainly enjoying himself. This time he feinted with the knife in his right hand and then punched Smith in the ribs with his left – striking with pile-driving force.

The massive jolt knocked the air out of Jon's lungs. He stumbled backward, gasping, panting – fighting now just to stay on his feet and conscious.

'Perhaps you should have saved that last bullet for yourself,' the green-eyed man suggested politely. He held up the fighting knife. 'It would have been quicker and less painful than this will be.'

Smith kept backing away, looking for something, any-thing, he could use as a weapon. There was nothing, just sand and hard-packed soil. He felt himself starting to panic. Hold it together, Jon, he told himself. If you freeze in front of this bastard, you are as good as dead. Hell, you may be dead anyway, but at least you can make a fight of it.

Somewhere off in the distance, he thought he could hear the sound of police sirens – sirens drawing nearer. But still the green-eyed man stalked after him, eager to make his kill.

CHAPTER SEVEN

Two hundred meters away, on the edge of a small thicket of piñon pines and juniper trees, three men lay concealed in the tall, dry grass. One of them, much bigger than his companions, focused a pair of high-powered binoculars on the corpse-littered grounds of the Institute, watching the hand-to-hand combat between the lean dark-haired American and his taller, far more powerful opponent. He frowned, weighing his options. Beside him, a sniper kept one eye glued to the telescopic sight of an odd-looking rifle, slowly and steadily adjusting his aim.

The third man, a signals expert, lay in a tangle of sophisticated communications gear. He listened intently to the urgent, static-riddled voices in his headphones. 'The authorities are starting to respond more effectively, Terce,' he said flatly. 'Additional police, ambulance, and fire units are all converging rapidly on this location.'

'Understood.' Terce, the man with the binoculars, shrugged his shoulders. 'Prime has made a regrettable error.'

'His driver reacted improperly,' murmured the sniper beside him.

'The driver will be disciplined,' the man agreed. 'But Prime knew the mission requirements. This fight is pointless. He should have left when given the chance, but he is allowing his lusts to override his better judgment. He may kill this man he hunts, but he is unlikely to escape.' He made a decision. 'So be it. Mark him.'

'And the other, too?' the sniper asked.

'Yes.'

The sniper nodded. He looked through the scope, adjusting his aim one last time. 'Target acquired.' He pulled the trigger. The odd-looking rifle coughed quietly. 'Target marked.'

Smith ducked under another deadly slash from the green-eyed man's knife. He backpedaled again, knowing that he was running out of time and maneuvering room. Sooner or later, this maniac would nail him.

Suddenly the auburn-haired man slapped irritably at his neck – almost as if he were crushing a wasp. He took another step forward and then stopped, staring down at his hand with a look of absolute horror. His mouth fell open and he half-turned – looking back over his shoulder at the silent woods behind him.

And then, while Smith watched in growing terror, the tall green-eyed man began to come apart. A web of red cracks snaked rapidly across his face and hands, growing ever wider. In seconds, his skin fell away, dissolving into translucent red-tinged ooze. His green eyes melted and slid down his face. The big man shrieked aloud in inhuman agony. Screaming and writhing, the giant toppled to the ground – clawing wildly at what little was left of his body in a futile effort to fight off whatever was eating him alive.

Jon could not bear to see any more. He turned, stumbled, and fell to his knees, retching uncontrollably. In that moment, something hissed past his ear and buried itself in the earth in front of him.

Instinct taking over, Smith threw himself sideways and then he crawled rapidly toward the nearest cover.

In the grove of trees, the sniper slowly lowered his odd-looking rifle. 'The second target has gone to ground. I have no shot.'

'It does not matter,' the man with the binoculars said

coldly. 'One man more or less is of no real consequence.' He turned to the signaler. 'Contact the Center. Inform them that Field Two is under way and seems to be proceeding according to plan.'

'Yes, Terce.'

'What about Prime?' the sniper asked quietly. 'How will you report his death?'

For a moment, the man with binoculars sat still, pondering the question. Then he asked, 'Do you know the legend of the *Horatii*?'

The sniper shook his head.

'It is an old, old story,' Terce told him. 'From the days of the Romans, long before their empire. Three identical brothers, the *Horatii*, were sent to duel against the three champions of a neighboring city. Two fought bravely, but they were killed. The third of the *Horatii* triumphed – not through sheer force of arms alone but through stealth and cunning.'

The sniper said nothing.

The man with the binoculars turned his head and smiled coldly. A stray shaft of sunlight fell on his auburn hair and lit his strikingly green eyes. 'Like Prime, I am one of the *Horatii*. But unlike Prime, I plan to survive and to win the reward I have been promised.'

PART TWO

CHAPTER EIGHT

The Hoover Building, Washington, D.C.

FBI Deputy Assistant Director Katherine ('Kit') Pierson stood at the window of her fifth-floor office, frowning down at the rain-slick surface of Pennsylvania Avenue. There were just a few cars waiting at the nearest traffic lights and only a small scattering of tourists scurrying along the avenue's broad sidewalks beneath bobbing umbrellas. The usual evening mass exodus of the city's federal workforce was still a couple of hours away.

She resisted the urge to check the time again. Waiting for others to act had never been one of her strengths.

Kit Pierson glanced up from the street and caught a faint glimpse of her reflection in the tinted glass. For a brief instant she studied herself dispassionately, wondering again why the slate gray eyes gazing back at her so often seemed those of a stranger. Even at forty-five, her ivory white skin was still smooth, and her short dark brown hair framed a face that she knew most men considered attractive.

Not that she gave them many chances to tell her so, she thought coolly. A failed early marriage and a bitter divorce had proved to her that she could not successfully mix romance with her career in the FBI. The national interests of the Bureau and the United States always came first – even those interests her superiors were sometimes too afraid to recognize.

Pierson was aware that the agents and analysts under her command called her the Winter Queen behind her back. She shrugged that off. She drove herself much harder than she ever drove them. And it was better to be thought a bit cold and distant than to be seen as weak or inefficient. The FBI's Counter-Terrorism Division was no place for clock-punching nine-to-fivers whose eyes were fixed on their pensions rather than on the nation's ever-more dangerous enemies.

Enemies like the Lazarus Movement.

For several months now she and Hal Burke over at the CIA had warned their superiors that the Lazarus Movement was becoming a direct threat to the vital interests of the United States and those of its allies. They had zeroed in on all the signs that the Movement was escalating its rhetoric and moving toward violent action. They had presented policy papers and analysis and every scrap of evidence they could lay their hands on.

But no one higher up the ladder had been willing to act forcefully enough against the growing threat. Burke's boss, CIA Director David Hanson, talked a good game, but even he fell short in the end. Many of the politicians were worse. They looked at Lazarus and saw only the surface camouflage, the do-gooder environmental organization. It was what lay beneath that camouflage that Kit Pierson feared.

'Imagine a terrorist group like al-Qaeda, but run instead by Americans and Europeans and Asians – by people who look just like you or me or those nice neighbors down Maple Lane,' she often reminded her staff. 'What kind of profiling can we run against a threat like that?'

Hanson, for one, understood that the Lazarus Movement was a clear and present danger. But the CIA director insisted on fighting this battle within the law and within the bounds set down by politics. In contrast, Pierson and Burke and others around the world knew that it was too late to play by 'the rules.' They were committed to destroying the Movement by aggressive action – using whatever means were necessary.

The phone on her desk rang. She turned away from the window and crossed her office in four long, graceful strides to pick it up on the second ring. 'Pierson.'

'Burke here.' It was the call she had been expecting, but her stocky, square-jawed CIA counterpart sounded uncharacteristically edgy. 'Is your line secure?' he asked.

She toggled a switch on the phone, running a quick check for any sign of electronic surveillance. The FBI spent a lot of time and taxpayer money making sure its communications networks were untapped. An indicator light glowed green. She nodded. 'We're clear.'

'Good,' Burke said, in a flat, clipped tone. There were sounds of traffic in the background. He must be calling on his car phone. 'Because something's fouled up in New Mexico, Kit. It's bad, real bad. Worse than we expected. Turn on any one of the cable news stations. They practically have the pictures on continuous loop.'

Puzzled, Pierson leaned over her desk and hit the keys that would display TV signals on her computer monitor. For a long moment she stared in shocked silence as the live footage shot earlier outside the Teller Institute flickered across her high-resolution screen. Even as she watched, new explosions erupted inside the burning building. Thick columns of smoke stained the clear blue New Mexico sky. Outside the Institute itself, thousands of Lazarus Movement demonstrators fled in terror, trampling one another in their frenzy to escape. The camera zoomed in, showing nightmarish images of human beings melting like bloodstained wax.

She drew a short, sharp breath, fighting for composure. Then she gripped the phone tighter. 'Good God, Hal. What happened?'

'It's not clear, yet,' Burke told her. 'First reports say the demonstrators broke through the fence and they were swarming the building when all hell broke loose inside – explosions, fires, you name it.'

'And the cause?'

'There's speculation about some kind of toxic release from the nano-tech labs,' Burke said. 'A few sources are calling it a tragic accident. Others are blaming sabotage by as-yet-unidentified perps. The smart money is on sabotage.'

'But no confirmation either way?' she asked sharply. 'No one's been taken into custody?'

'No one so far. I don't have contact with our people yet, but I expect to hear something soon. I'm heading out there myself, pronto. There's an Air Force emergency flight taking off from Andrews in thirty minutes – and Langley wangled me a seat on the plane.'

Pierson shook her head in frustration. 'This was not the plan, Hal. I thought we had this situation locked down tight.'

'Yeah, so did I,' Burke said. She could almost hear him shrug. 'Something always goes wrong at some point in every operation, Kit. You know that.'

She frowned. 'Not this wrong.'

'No,' agreed Burke coldly. 'Not usually.' He cleared his throat. 'But now we have to play the cards we're dealt. Right?'

'Yes.' Pierson reached out and shut down the TV link on her computer. She did not need to see any more. Not now. She suspected those images would haunt her dreams for a very long time.

'Kit?'

'I'm here,' she said softly.

'You know what has to happen next?'

She nodded, forcing herself to focus on the immediate future. 'Yes, I do. I have to lead the investigative team in Santa Fe.'

'Will that be a problem?' the CIA officer asked. 'Arranging it with Zeller, I mean.'

'No, I don't think so. I'm sure he'll jump at the chance to assign the job to me,' Pierson said carefully, thinking it through out loud. 'I'm the Bureau expert on the Lazarus

Movement. The acting director understands that. And one thing is going to be very clear to everyone, from the White House all the way on down the chain of command. Somehow, somewhere, in some way, this atrocity must be linked to the Movement.'

'Right,' Burke said. 'And in the meantime, I'll keep pushing TOCSIN from my end.'

'Is that wise?' Pierson asked sharply. 'Maybe we should pull the plug now.'

'It's too late for that,' Burke told her bluntly. 'Everything is already in motion, Kit. We either ride the wave, or we get pulled under.'

CHAPTER NINE

The White House

The members of the president's national security team who were gathered around the crowded conference table in the White House Situation Room were in a somber, depressed mood. As they damned well should be, thought Sam Castilla grimly. The first accounts of the Teller Institute disaster had been bad enough. Each new report was even worse.

He glanced at the nearest clock. It was much later than he had thought. In the confines of this small artificially lit underground room, the passage of time was often distorted. Several hours had already passed since Fred Klein first flashed him the news of the horror unfolding in Santa Fe.

Now the president looked around the table in disbelief. 'You're telling me that we still don't have a firm estimate of casualties – either inside the Teller Institute itself, or outside among the demonstrators?'

'No, Mr. President. We don't,' Bob Zeller, the acting director of the FBI, admitted. He sat miserably hunched over in his chair. 'More than half of the Institute's scientists and staff are listed as missing. Most of them are probably dead. But we can't even send in search-and-rescue teams until the fires are out. As for the protesters . . .' Zeller's voice trailed away.

'We may never know exactly how many of them were killed, Mr. President,' his national security adviser, Emily Powell-Hill, interrupted. 'You've seen the pictures of what happened outside the labs. It could take months to identify what little is left of those people.'

'The major networks are saying there are at least two thousand dead,' said Charles Ouray, the White House chief of staff. 'And they're predicting the count could go even higher. Maybe as high as three or four thousand.'

'Based on what, Charlie?' the president snapped. 'Spitballing and raw guesswork?'

'They're going with claims made by Lazarus Movement spokesmen,' Ouray said quietly. 'Those folks have more credibility with the press – and the general public – than they used to. More credibility than we do right now.'

Castilla nodded. That was true enough. The first terrifying TV footage had gone out live and unedited over several news network satellite feeds. Tens of millions of people in America and hundreds of millions around the world had seen the gruesome images with their own eyes. The networks were now showing more discretion, carefully blurring the more graphic scenes of terrified Lazarus Movement protesters being eaten alive. But it was too late. The damage was done.

All the wild, lurid claims made by the Lazarus Movement about the dangers posed by nanotechnology seemed vindicated. And now the Movement seemed determined to push an even more sinister and paranoid story. This theory was already showing up on their Web sites and on other major Internet discussion groups. It claimed that the Teller labs were developing secret nanotech war weapons for the U.S. military. Using eerily similar photos of the ravaged dead in both places, it connected the horror in Santa Fe to the earlier massacre at Kusasa in Zimbabwe. Those pushing the story were arguing that these pictures proved that 'elements within the American government' had wiped out a peaceful village as a first test of those nanotech weapons.

Castilla grimaced. In the prevailing hysteria, no one was going to pay any attention to calm technical rebuttals by leading scientists. Or to reassuring speeches by politicians like him, the president reminded himself. Pressured by frightened constituents, many in Congress were already demanding an immediate federal ban on nanotech research. And God only knew how many other governments around the world were going to buy into the Movement's wild-eyed claims about America's secret 'nanotech weapons program.'

Castilla turned to David Hanson, sitting at the far end of the table. 'Anything to add, David?'

The CIA director shrugged. 'Beyond the observation that what happened at the Teller Institute is almost certainly an act of coldly calculated terrorism? No, Mr. President, I do not.'

'Aren't you jumping the gun just a bit?' Emily Powell-Hill asked curtly. There was no love lost between the former Army brigadier general and the Director of Central Intelligence. She thought Hanson was far too eager to apply extreme solutions to national security problems.

Privately, the president agreed with her assessment. But the uncomfortable truth was that Hanson's wilder predictions often hit the mark, and most of the clandestine operations he pushed forward were successful. And in this case, the CIA chief's assertion tied in perfectly with what Castilla had already heard from Fred Klein at Covert-One.

'Am I speculating in advance of all the facts? Clearly, I am,' Hanson admitted. He peered condescendingly over the rims of his tortoiseshell glasses at the national security adviser. 'But I don't see that we need to waste much time on alternate theories, Emily. Not unless you honestly believe that the intruders who broke into the Teller Institute had nothing to do with the bombs that exploded less than an hour later. Frankly, that seems a bit naive to me.'

Emily Powell-Hill flushed bright red.

Castilla intervened before the dispute could get out of

hand. 'Let's assume you're right, David. Say this disaster is an act of terrorism. Then who are the terrorists?'

'The Lazarus Movement,' said the CIA director bluntly. 'For precisely the reasons I outlined when we discussed the Joint Intelligence Threat Assessment, Mr. President. We wondered then what the "big event" in Santa Fe was supposed to be.' He shrugged his narrow shoulders. 'Well, now we know.'

'Are you seriously suggesting the leaders of the Lazarus Movement arranged the deaths of more than two thousand of their own supporters?' Ouray asked. The chief of staff was openly skeptical.

'Deliberately?' Hanson shook his head. 'I don't know. And until we get a better sense of exactly what killed those people, we won't know. But I am quite sure that the Lazarus Movement was involved in the terrorist attack itself.'

'How so?' Castilla asked.

'Consider the timing, Mr. President,' the CIA director suggested. He began making his points, ticking them off with the precision of a professor presenting a much-loved thesis to a particularly slow freshman class. 'One: Who organized a mass demonstration outside the Teller Institute? The Lazarus Movement. Two: Why were the Institute's security guards outside the building when the counterfeit Secret Service team arrived – and not able to intervene against them? Because they were pinned down by that same protest. Three: Who prevented the real Secret Service agents from entering the building? Those same Lazarus Movement demonstrators. And finally, four: Why couldn't the Santa Fe police and sheriffs intercept the intruders as they left the Institute? Because they were tied down handling the chaos outside the Institute.'

Almost against his will, Castilla nodded. The case the CIA chief made was not airtight, but it was persuasive.

'Sir, we cannot go public with an unsupported allegation like that against the Lazarus Movement!' Ouray broke in. 'It would be political suicide. The press would crucify us for even suggesting it!'

'Charlie's absolutely right, Mr. President,' Emily Powell-Hill said. The national security adviser shot a quick glare at the head of the CIA before continuing. 'Blaming the Movement for this would play straight into the hands of every conspiracy theorist around the world. We can't afford to give them more ammunition. Not now.'

A gloomy silence fell around the Situation Room conference table.

'One thing is certain,' David Hanson said coldly, breaking the hush. 'The Lazarus Movement is already profiting from the public martyrdom of so many of its followers. Around the world, hundreds of thousands of new volunteers have added their names to its e-mail lists. Millions more have made electronic donations to its public bank accounts.'

The CIA chief looked straight at Castilla. 'I understand your reluctance to act against the Lazarus Movement without proof of its terrorist activities, Mr. President. I know the politics involved. And I earnestly hope that the FBI probe at the Teller Institute produces the evidence you require. But it is my duty to warn you that delay could have terrible consequences for this nation's security. With every passing day, this Movement will grow stronger. And with every passing day, our ability to confront it successfully will diminish.'

Lazarus Mobile Command Center

The man called Lazarus sat alone in a small but elegantly furnished compartment. The window shades were pulled down, shutting out any glimpse of the larger world outside. Images flickered across the computer screen set before him, televised images of the carnage outside the Teller Institute.

He nodded to himself, coolly satisfied by what he saw. His plans, so carefully and patiently prepared over the course of several years, were at last coming to fruition. Much of the work, like that involved in selectively pruning the Movement's former leadership, had been difficult and painful and full of risk. The *Horatii*, physically powerful, precisely trained in the arts of assassination, and infinitely cruel, had served him well in that effort.

For a moment a trace of sorrow crossed his face. He genuinely regretted the need to eliminate so many men and women he had once admired – people whose only fault had been a reluctance to see the need for sterner measures to accomplish their shared dreams. But then Lazarus shrugged. Personal regrets aside, events were proving the correctness of his vision. In the past twelve months, under his sole leadership, the Movement had accomplished more than in all the prior years of halfhearted conventional activism combined. Restoring the purity of the world required bold, decisive action, not dreary oratory and weak-kneed political protests.

In fact, as the name of the Movement suggested, it meant bringing new life out of death itself.

His computer chimed softly, signaling the arrival of another encrypted report relayed to him from the Center itself. Lazarus read through it in silence. Prime's death was an inconvenience, but the loss of one of his three *Horatii* was far outweighed by the results from the attack on the Teller Institute and the resulting slaughter of his own followers. Gulled by the information he had fed them, information that confirmed their own worst fears, officials in the American CIA and FBI and those of other allied intelligence services had trapped themselves in an act of mass murder. What must seem to those poor fools to have been a terrible error was, in fact, intended from the beginning. They were guilty and he would use their guilt against them for his own purposes.

Lazarus smiled coldly. With a single deadly stroke he had made it virtually impossible for the United States, or for any other Western government, to act decisively against the Movement. He had turned their own strength against them – just as would any master of jujitsu. Though his enemies did not yet realize it, he controlled the essential levers of power. Any action they took against the Movement would only strengthen his grip and weaken them in the same moment.

Now it was time to begin the process of setting once-loyal allies at one another's throats. The world was already suspicious of America's military and scientific power and of Washington's motives. With the right prodding and media manipulation, the world would soon believe that America, the sole superpower, was tinkering with the building blocks of creation, creating new weapons on a nanoscale – all in pursuit of its own cruel and selfish aims. The globe would begin to divide between those who sided with Lazarus and those who did not. And governments, pressured by their own people, would increasingly turn against the United States.

The resulting confusion, chaos, and disorder would serve him well. It would buy the time he needed to bring his grand design to completion – a design that would transform the Earth forever.

CHAPTER TEN

Night was falling fast across the high desert country around Santa Fe. To the northwest, the highest peaks of the Jemez Mountains shone crimson, lit by the last rays of the setting sun. The lower lands to the east were already immersed in the gathering darkness. Just south of the city itself, tongues of fire still danced eerily amid the twisted and broken ruins of the Teller Institute, flickering orange and red and yellow as the flames fed on broken furniture and supporting beams, spilled chemicals, bomb-mangled equipment, and the bodies of those trapped inside. The rank, acrid smell of smoke hung heavy in the cool evening air.

Several fire engine companies were on the scene, but they were being held outside the area cordoned off by local police and the National Guard. There was no longer any real hope of finding any survivors inside the burning building, so no one wanted to risk exposing more men to the runaway nanomachines that had killed so many Lazarus Movement activists.

Jon Smith stood stiffly near the outside edge of the cordon, watching the fires burn out of control. His lean face was haggard and his shoulders were slumped. Like many soldiers, he often experienced a feeling of melancholy in the aftermath of intense action. This time it was worse. He was not accustomed to losing. Between them, he and Frank Diaz must have killed or wounded half of the terrorists who had attacked the Teller Institute, but the bombs they had planted had still gone off. Nor could

Smith forget the horror of seeing thousands of people reduced to slime and bone fragments.

The encrypted cell phone in his inner jacket pocket vibrated suddenly. He pulled the phone out and answered. 'Smith.'

'I need you to brief me in more detail, Colonel,' Fred Klein said abruptly. 'The president is still meeting with his national security team, but I expect another call from him in the not-too-distant future. I've already passed your preliminary report to him, but he'll want more. I need you to tell me exactly what you saw and exactly what you think happened there today.'

Smith closed his eyes, suddenly exhausted. 'Understood,' he said dully.

'Were you injured, Jon?' the head of Covert-One asked, sounding concerned. 'You didn't say anything earlier and I assumed – '

Smith shook his head. The abrupt movement set every bruise and torn muscle on fire. 'It's nothing serious,' he said, wincing. 'A few cuts and scrapes, that's all.'

'I see.' Klein paused, plainly doubtful. 'I suspect that means you are not actively bleeding at this moment.'

'Really, Fred, I'm all right,' Smith told him, irritated now. 'I'm a doctor, remember?'

'Very well,' Klein said carefully. 'We'll proceed. First, are you still convinced that the terrorists who hit the Institute were professionals?'

'No question about it,' Smith said. 'These guys were smooth, Fred. They had Secret Service procedures, weapons, and ID all down cold. If the real Secret Service team hadn't shown up early, the bad guys could have been in and out without anyone batting an eye.'

'Right up to the moment the bombs went off,' Klein suggested.

'Until then,' Smith agreed grimly.

'Which brings us to the protesters who died,' the head of Covert-One said. 'The common assumption seems to be that the explosions released something from one of the labs – either a toxic chemical substance or more likely a nanotech creation that went wild. You were assigned out there to review the labs and their research. What do you think happened?'

Smith frowned. Ever since the shooting and screaming had stopped, he had been racking his brains, trying to piece together a plausible answer to that question. What could possibly have killed so many demonstrators outside the Institute so quickly and so cruelly? He sighed. 'Only one lab was working on anything directly connected to human tissues and organs.'

'Which one?'

'Harcourt Biosciences,' Smith said. Speaking rapidly, he sketched in the work Brinker and Parikh had been doing with their Mark II nanophages – including their last experiment, the one that had killed a perfectly healthy mouse. 'And one of the major bomb blasts went off inside the Harcourt lab,' he concluded. 'Both Phil and Ravi are missing, and presumed dead.'

'That's it, then,' Klein said, sounding faintly relieved. 'The bombs were set deliberately. But the deaths outside must have been unintended, basically a kind of high-tech industrial accident.'

'I don't buy it,' Smith said bluntly.

'Why not?'

'For one thing, the mouse I saw die showed no signs of cellular degeneration,' Smith answered, thinking it through. 'There was nothing remotely resembling the wholesale disintegration I watched this afternoon.'

'Could that be the difference between the effects of these nanophages inside a mouse and inside human beings?' Klein asked carefully.

'That's highly unlikely,' Smith told him. 'The whole reason for using lab mice for preliminary tests is their biological similarity to humans.' He sighed. 'I can't swear to it, Fred, not without further study, anyway. But my gut feeling is that the Harcourt nanophages could not have been responsible for those deaths.'

There was silence on the other end of the phone for a long moment. 'You realize what that would mean,' Klein said at last.

'Yeah,' Smith agreed heavily. 'If I'm right and nothing inside the Institute could have killed all those people, then whatever did came in with the terrorists and was set deliberately – as part of some cold-blooded plan to massacre thousands of Lazarus Movement activists. And that doesn't seem to make any sense.'

He closed his eyes for a moment. He swayed, feeling the fatigue he had been holding at bay gaining the upper hand.

'Jon?'

With an effort, Smith forced himself back upright. 'I'm still here,' he said.

'Wounded or not, you sound all in,' Klein told him. 'You need a chance to rest and recover. What's your situation there?'

Despite his exhaustion, Smith could not help smiling wryly. 'Not great. I'm not going anywhere soon. I've already given my statement, but the local Feds are holding every single Institute survivor who can still walk and talk right here, pending the arrival of their great white chief from D.C. And she's not due in until sometime early tomorrow morning.'

'Not surprising,' Klein said. 'But not good, either. Let me see what I can do. Hold on.' His voice faded.

Smith looked out into the darkness, watching rifle-armed men in camouflage fatigues, Kevlar helmets, and body armor patrolling the cordon between him and the burning building. The National Guard had deployed a full company to seal off the area around the Teller Institute. The troops had been issued shoot-to-kill orders to stop anyone trying to break through their perimeter.

From what Smith heard, more National Guard units were tied up in Santa Fe itself, protecting state and federal offices and trying to keep the highways open for emergency traffic. One of the local sheriffs had told him that several thousand people from the city were evacuating, fleeing to Albuquerque or even up into the mountains around Taos in search of safety.

The police also had their hands full keeping tabs on survivors from the Lazarus Movement rally. Many had already fled the area, but a few hundred dazed activists were wandering aimlessly through the streets of Santa Fe. Nobody was sure if they were really in shock or if they were only waiting to cause more trouble.

Fred Klein came back on the line. 'It's all arranged, Colonel,' he said calmly. 'You have clearance to leave the security zone – and a ride back to your hotel.'

Smith was deeply grateful. He understood why the Bureau wanted to secure the area and maintain control over its only dependable witnesses. But he had not been looking forward to spending a long, cold night on a cot in a Red Cross tent or huddled in the back of some police squad car. As so often before, he wondered briefly just how Klein – a man who operated only in the shadows – could pull so many strings without blowing his cover. But then, as always, he filed those questions away in the back of his mind. To Smith, the important thing was that it worked.

Twenty minutes later, Smith was riding in the back of a State Police patrol car heading north on Highway 84 through the center of Santa Fe. There were still long lines of civilian autos, pickups, minivans, and SUVs inching slowly south toward the junction with Interstate 25, the main road to Albuquerque. The message was clear. Many locals were not buying the official line that any danger was limited to a relatively small zone around the Institute.

Smith frowned at the sight, but he could not blame people for being scared to death. For years they had been assured that nanotechnology was absolutely, positively safe – and then they turned on their TV sets and watched screaming Lazarus Movement protesters being torn to shreds by tiny machines too small to be seen or heard.

The patrol car turned east off Highway 84 onto the Paseo de Peralta, the relatively wide avenue ringing Santa Fe's historic center. Smith spotted a National Guard Humvee blocking an intersection to the right. More vehicles, troops, and police were in position along every road heading into the downtown area.

He nodded to himself. Those responsible for law and order were making the best use of their limited resources. If you had to pick just one place to defend against looting or lawlessness, that area was it. There were other beautiful museums, galleries, shops, and homes scattered around the rest of the city, but the heart and soul of Santa Fe was its historic center – a maze of narrow one-way streets surrounding the beautiful tree-lined Plaza and the four-centuries-old Palace of the Governors.

The streets of the old city followed the winding trace of old wagon roads like the Santa Fe and Pecos Trails, not an antiseptic ultra-modern grid. Many of the buildings lining those roads were a blend of old and new in the Spanish-Pueblo revival style, with earth-toned adobe walls, flat roofs, small, deep-set windows, and protruding log beams. Others, like the federal courthouse, displayed the brick facades and slender white columns of the Territorial style – dating back to 1846 and the U.S. conquest during the Mexican-American War. Much of the history, art, and architecture that made Santa Fe so unique an American city lay within that relatively small district.

Smith frowned as they drove past the darkened, deserted streets. On most days, the Plaza was bustling with tourists taking photos and browsing through the wares of local artists and craftsmen. Native Americans sat in the shade of the *portal*, the covered walkway, outside the

Palace, selling distinctive pottery and silver and turquoise jewelry. He suspected that those places would be eerily abandoned in the coming morning, and possibly for many days to come.

He was staying just five blocks from the Plaza, at the Fort Marcy Hotel Suites. Back when he was first assigned as an observer at the Teller Institute, it had amused him to check into a hotel with a military-sounding name. But there was nothing Army-issue or drab about the Fort Marcy suites themselves. Eighty separate units occupied a series of one- and two-story buildings set on a gentle hillside with views of the city or the nearby mountains. All of them were quiet, comfortable, and elegantly furnished in a mix of modern and traditional Southwestern styles.

The state trooper dropped him off at the front of the hotel. Smith thanked him and limped along the walkway to his room, a one-bedroom suite nestled in among shade trees and landscaped gardens. Few lights were on in any of the neighboring buildings. He suspected that many of his fellow guests were long gone – heading for home as fast as they could.

Jon fumbled through his wallet for the room card key, found it, and let himself in. With the door firmly closed, he felt himself starting to relax for the first time in hours. He carefully shrugged out of his bullet-ripped leather jacket and made his way into the bathroom. He splashed some cold water on his face and then looked in the mirror.

The eyes that stared back at him were haunted, weary, and full of sadness.

Smith turned away.

More out of habit than of real hunger, he checked the refrigerator in the suite's kitchen. None of the tinfoil-wrapped restaurant leftovers inside looked appealing. Instead, he took out an ice-cold Tecate, twisted off the cap, and set the beer bottle out on the dining room table.

He looked at it for a long moment. Then he swung

away and sat staring blindly out the windows, seeing only the horrors he had witnessed earlier replaying over and over in his exhausted mind.

CHAPTER ELEVEN

Malachi MacNamara paused just inside the doors of Cristo Rey Church. He stood quietly for some moments, surveying his surroundings. Pale moonlight filtered in through windows set high up in massive adobe walls. A large high-ceilinged nave stretched before him. Far ahead, at the altar, he could see a large screen, a *reredos*, composed of three large sections of white stone. Carvings of flowers, saints, and angels covered the stone screen. Groups of weary men and women sat slumped here and there among the pews. Some were weeping openly. Others sat silent, staring into nothingness, still numbed by the horrors they had witnessed.

MacNamara moved slowly and unobtrusively down one of the side aisles, watching and listening to those around him. He suspected the men he was hunting were not here, but it was best to make sure of that before moving on to the next possible sanctuary. His feet ached. He had already spent several hours walking the meandering streets of this city, tracking down several of the dispersed groups of Lazarus Movement survivors. It would have been faster and more efficient with a car, of course. But terribly out of character, he reminded himself – and bloody damn obvious. The vehicle he had brought with him to New Mexico would have to stay hidden for a while longer.

A middle-aged woman with a pleasant, friendly face hurried up to him. She must be one of the parishioners who had opened their church to those they saw in need, he realized. Not everyone in Santa Fe had panicked and run for the hills. He could see the concern in her eyes. 'Can I help you?' she asked. 'Were you at the rally outside the Institute?'

MacNamara nodded somberly. 'I was.'

She put her hand on his sleeve. 'I am so sorry. It was frightening enough to watch from a distance, on the television, I mean. I can't imagine how it must feel to have . . .' Her voice died away. Her eyes widened.

He suddenly became aware that his expression had grown cold, infinitely forbidding. The horrors he had seen were still too close. With an effort, he pushed away the dreadful images rising in his mind. He sighed. 'Forgive me,' he said gently. 'I didn't intend to frighten you.'

'Did you lose . . .' The woman hesitated. 'That is . . . are you looking for someone? Someone in particular?'

MacNamara nodded. 'I *am* searching for someone. For several people, in fact.' He described them for her.

She listened attentively, but in the end she could only shake her head. 'I'm afraid there's no one here like that.' She sighed. 'But you might try at the Upaya Buddhist temple, farther up Cerro Gordo Road, back in the hills. The monks there are also offering shelter to survivors. If you like, I can give you directions to the temple.'

The lean blue-eyed man nodded appreciatively. 'That would be most kind.' He pulled himself upright. There are many more miles to go before you sleep, he told himself grimly. And quite probably in vain, too. The men he was after had undoubtedly already gone to ground.

The woman looked down at his scuffed, dust-smeared boots. 'Or I could give you a ride,' she suggested hesitantly. 'If you've been walking all day, you must be just about worn-out.'

Malachi MacNamara smiled for the first time in days. 'Yes,' he said softly. 'I am extremely tired. And I would be very glad of a lift.'

Outside Santa Fe

The safe house secured by the TOCSIN action team was high up in the foothills of the Sangre de Cristo Mountains, not far off the road leading to the Santa Fe Ski Basin. A narrow drive blocked by a chain and a large KEEP OUT sign wound uphill between gold-leafed aspens, oak trees covered in copper-red foliage, and towering evergreens.

Hal Burke turned off the main road and rolled down the window of the Chrysler LeBaron he had rented immediately after arriving at Albuquerque's international airport. He sat waiting, careful to keep his hands in plain sight on the steering wheel.

A shadowy figure moved out from the shelter of one of the big trees. The dim glow of the car's headlights revealed a narrow, hard-edged, suspicious face. One hand hovered conspicuously near the 9mm Walther pistol holstered at his hip. 'This is a private road, mister.'

'Yes, it is,' Burke agreed. 'And I am a private man. My name is Tocsin.'

The sentry drew nearer, reassured by Burke's use of the correct recognition code. He flashed a penlight across the CIA officer's face and then into the backseat of the Chrysler, making sure Burke was alone. 'Okay. Show me some ID.'

Burke carefully fished his CIA identity card out of his jacket pocket and handed it over.

The sentry scrutinized the picture. Then he nodded, handed back the ID card, and undid the chain blocking the drive. 'You can go ahead, Mr. Tocsin. They're waiting for you up at the house.'

The house, a quarter-mile up the narrow road, was a large half-timbered Swiss-style chalet, with a steeply pitched roof designed to shed large masses of accumulated snow. In an average winter, well over a hundred inches fell on this part of the Sangre de Cristo range – and the winter often took shape in late October. Twice that much snow usually accumulated at the ski areas on the higher slopes.

Burke parked on a weather-cracked concrete pad close to a set of stairs leading up to the chalet's front door. Against the darkness, lights shone yellow behind drawn window blinds. The woods surrounding the house were silent and perfectly still.

The front door of the chalet opened before he even finished getting out of the car. The sentry below must have radioed ahead. A tall auburn-haired man stood there, looking down at him with bright green eyes.

'You made good time, Mr. Burke.'

The CIA officer nodded, staring up at the bigger man. Which one of the strange trio who called themselves the *Horatii* was this? he wondered uneasily. The three big men were not brothers by birth. Instead, their identical appearance, enormous strength and agility, and wide range of skills were said to be the result of years of painstaking surgery, elaborate physical conditioning, and intensive training. Burke had selected them as section leaders for TOCSIN at their creator's urging but could not entirely suppress a feeling of mingled fear and awe whenever he saw one of the *Horatii*. Nor could he tell them apart.

'I had every reason to hurry, Prime,' he replied, guessing at last.

The green-eyed man shook his head. 'I am Terce. Unfortunately, Prime is dead.'

'Dead? How?' Burke asked sharply.

'He was killed in the operation,' Terce told him calmly. He stepped aside, ushering Burke into the chalet. Carpeted stairs led up to the second floor. A long stone-flagged hall paneled in dark pine led deeper into the house. Bright light spilled out through an open door at the back. 'In fact, you have arrived just in time to help us decide a small matter connected with Prime's death.'

The CIA officer followed the big man through the open door and into a large glass-enclosed porch running the width of the house. The gently sloping concrete floor, a metal drain in the middle, and the racks on the walls told him this room was normally used as a storage and drying room for snow-encrusted outdoor gear – heavy boots, cross-country skis, and snowshoes. Now, though, the chalet's new owners were using it as a holding cell.

A small stoop-shouldered man with olive skin and a neatly trimmed mustache perched uneasily on a stool set squarely in the middle of the room – right above the drain. He was gagged and his hands were tied behind him. His feet were bound to the legs of the stool. Above the gag, a pair of dark brown eyes were wide open, staring frantically at the two men who had just entered.

Burke turned his head toward Terce. He raised a single eyebrow in an unspoken question.

'Our friend there, Antonio, was the assault team's backup driver,' the bigger man said quietly. 'Unfortunately, he panicked during the extraction phase. He abandoned Prime.'

'Then you were forced to eliminate Prime?' Burke asked. 'To prevent his capture?'

'Not quite. Prime was . . . *consumed*,' Terce told him. He shook his head grimly. 'You should have warned us about the plague our bombs would release, Mr. Burke. I earnestly hope your failure to do so was only an oversight – and not intentional.'

The CIA officer frowned, hearing the implicit threat in the other man's voice. 'No one knew how dangerous those damned nanomachines really were!' he said quickly. 'Nothing in the classified reports I studied from Harcourt, Nomura, or the Institute suggested anything like that could happen!'

Terce studied him for a few moments. Then he nodded. 'Very well. I accept your assurances. For now.' The second of the *Horatii* shrugged. 'But the mission has backfired. The Lazarus Movement will be stronger now, not weaker. Given that, do you wish to proceed further? Or should we fold our tents and steal away while there is still time?'

Burke scowled. He was in too far to back out now. If anything, it was more imperative than ever to arrange the destruction of the Movement. He shook his head decisively. 'We keep going. Is your team ready to activate the cover plan?'

'We are.'

'Good,' the CIA officer said flatly. 'Then we still have a fighting chance to pin what happened at the Institute on Lazarus. Trigger the cover – tonight.'

'It will be done,' Terce agreed quietly. He indicated the bound man. 'In the meantime, we need to resolve this disciplinary problem. What do you suggest we do with Antonio here?'

Burke eyed him closely. 'Isn't the answer obvious?' he said. 'If this man broke once under pressure, the odds are that he will break again. We can't afford that. TOCSIN is already risky enough. Just finish him and dump the body where it won't be found for a few weeks.'

The driver moaned softly behind his gag. His shoulders slumped.

Terce nodded. 'Your reasoning is impeccable, Mr. Burke.' His green eyes were amused. 'But since it is *your* reasoning and *your* verdict, I think you should carry out the sentence yourself.' He offered the CIA officer a long-bladed fighting knife, pommel first.

This was a test, Burke realized angrily. The big man wanted to see how far he would go in binding himself to the dirty work he ordered. Well, riding herd on a group of black ops mercenaries was never easy, and he had killed men before to prove himself on other operations – murders he had carefully concealed from his deskbound superiors. Hiding his distaste, the CIA officer shrugged out of his jacket and hung it over one of the ski clamps. Then he rolled up his shirtsleeves and took the dagger.

Without pausing for further reflection, Burke stepped behind the stool, yanked the bound driver's head back, and drew the blade of the fighting knife hard across his throat.

Blood sprayed through the air, scarlet under the bright bulb of the overhead light.

The dying man thrashed wildly, kicking and tugging at the ropes holding him down. He toppled over, still tied to the stool, and lay twitching, bleeding his life away onto the concrete floor.

Burke turned back to Terce. 'Satisfied?' he snapped. 'Or do you want me to dig his grave, too?'

'That will not be necessary,' the other man said calmly. He nodded toward a large roll of canvas in the far corner of the porch. 'We already have a grave for poor Joachim over there. Antonio can share it with him.'

The CIA officer suddenly realized he was looking at another corpse, this one rolled up in a tarp.

'Joachim was wounded while retreating from the Institute,' Terce explained. 'He was hit in the shoulder and leg. His injuries were not immediately life-threatening, but they would soon have required significant medical attention. I did what was necessary.'

Burke nodded slowly, understanding. The tall green-eyed man and his comrades would not risk their own security by seeking medical treatment for anyone hurt too badly to keep up. The TOCSIN action team would kill anyone who threatened its mission, even its own members.

CHAPTER TWELVE

Thursday, October 14
The White House

It was after midnight and the heavy red-and-yellow Navajo drapes were drawn tight, sealing off the Oval Office from any prying eyes. No one outside the White House West Wing needed to know that the president of the United States was still hard at work – or with whom he was meeting.

Sam Castilla sat at his big pine table in his shirtsleeves, steadily reading through a sheaf of hastily drafted emergency executive orders. The heavy brass reading lamp on one corner of his desk cast a circular pool of light across his paperwork. From time to time, he jotted rough notes in the margin or crossed out a poorly worded phrase.

At last, with a quick stroke of his pen, he slashed his signature across the bottom of the several different marked-up orders. He could sign clean copies for the national archives later. Right now the important thing was to get the ponderous wheels of government turning somewhat faster. He glanced up.

Charles Ouray, his chief of staff, and Emily Powell-Hill, his national security adviser, sat slumped in the two big leather chairs drawn up in front of his desk. They looked weary, worn down by long hours spent shuttling back and forth between the White House complex and the various cabinet offices to get those orders ready for his signature. Trying to broker agreements among half-a-dozen different executive branch departments, each with its own competing views and pet agendas, was never easy.

'Is there anything else I need to know now?' Castilla asked them.

Ouray spoke up first. 'We're getting our first look at the morning papers from Europe, Mr. President.' His mouth turned down.

'Let me guess,' Castilla said sourly. 'We're getting hammered?'

Emily Powell-Hill nodded. Her eyes were worried. 'By most of the major dailies in every European nation – France, Germany, Italy, the UK, Spain, and all the others. The general consensus seems to be that no matter what went wrong *inside* the Teller Institute, the carnage *outside* is largely our responsibility.'

'On what grounds?' the president asked.

'There's a lot of wild speculation about some kind of secret nanotech weapons program gone awry,' Ouray told him quietly. 'The European press is playing that angle hard, with all the sensational claims front and center and our official denials buried way down near the end.'

Castilla grimaced. 'What are they doing? Running Lazarus Movement press releases verbatim?'

'For all practical purposes,' Powell-Hill said bluntly. She shrugged. 'Their story has all the plot elements Europeans love: a big, bad, secretive, and blundering America running roughshod over a peaceful, plucky, Mother Earth-loving band of truth-telling activists. And, as you can imagine, every foreign policy mistake we've made over the past fifty years is being raked up all over again.'

'What's the political fallout likely to be?' the president asked her.

'Not good,' she told him. 'Of course, some of our "friends" in Paris and Berlin are always looking for a chance to stick it to us. But even our real European friends and allies will have to play this one very carefully. Siding with the world's sole superpower is never very popular and a lot of those governments are shaky right now. It wouldn't take much of a swing in public opinion to bring them down.'

Ouray nodded. 'Emily's right, Mr. President. I've talked to the folks over at the State Department. They're getting very worried back-channel questions from Europe, and from the Japanese, too. Our friends want some firm assurances that these stories are false – and just as important, that we can *prove* that they're false.'

'Proving a negative?' Castilla shook his head in frustration. 'That's not an easy thing to do.'

'No, sir,' Emily Powell-Hill agreed. 'But we're going to have to do our best. Either that, or watch our alliances begin crumbling, and see Europe pull even further away from us.'

For several minutes after his two closest advisers left, Castilla sat behind his desk mulling over different ways to reassure European public and elite opinion. His face darkened. Unfortunately, his options were very limited. No matter how many of its federal labs and military bases the U.S. opened to public inspection, it could never hope to completely calm the tempest of Internet-fed hysteria. Crackpot rumors, damning exaggerations, doctored photos, and outright lies could circle the globe with the speed of light, far outpacing the truth.

He looked up at the sound of a light tap on his open door. 'Yes?'

His executive secretary poked her head in. 'The Secret Service just called, Mr. President. Mr. Nomura has arrived. They're bringing him in now.'

'Discreetly, I hope, Estelle,' Castilla reminded her.

The faint trace of a smile crossed her normally prim and proper face. 'They're coming through the kitchens, sir. I trust that is discreet enough.'

Castilla chuckled. 'Should be. Well, let's just hope none of the night-shift press corps folks are foraging there for a midnight snack.' He stood up, straightened his tie, and pulled on his suit coat. Being ushered into the White House past the kitchen trash cans was a far cry from the impressive ceremony that usually accompanied a visit to the American president, so the least he could do was greet Hideo Nomura with as much formality as possible.

His secretary, Mrs. Pike, opened the door for the head of Nomura PharmaTech just a minute or two later. Castilla advanced to meet him, smiling broadly. The two men exchanged quick, polite bows in the Japanese manner and then shook hands.

The president showed his guest to the big leather couch set squarely in the middle of the room. 'I'm very grateful you could come at such short notice, Hideo. You flew in from Europe this evening, I hear?'

Nomura smiled back civilly. 'It was no great trouble, Mr. President. The benefits of owning a fast corporate jet. In fact, it is I who should express my thanks. If your staff had not contacted me, I would be the one begging for a meeting.'

'Because of the catastrophe out at the Teller Institute?'

The younger Japanese man nodded. His black eyes flashed. 'My company will not soon forget this cruel act of terrorism.'

Castilla understood his anger. The Nomura Pharma-Tech Lab inside the Institute had been completely destroyed and the immediate financial loss to the Tokyo-based multinational company was staggering, close to $100 million. That didn't include the cost to replicate the years of research wiped out along with the lab, and the human cost was even higher. Fifteen of the eighteen highly skilled scientists and technicians working in the Nomura section were missing and presumed dead.

'We're going to find and punish those responsible for this attack,' Castilla promised the other man. 'I've ordered our national law-enforcement and intelligence agencies to make it their top priority.'

'I appreciate that, Mr. President,' Nomura said quietly. 'And I am here to offer what little help I can.' The Japanese industrialist shrugged. 'Not in the hunt for the terrorists, of course. My company lacks the necessary expertise. But we can provide other assistance that might prove useful.'

Castilla raised a single eyebrow. 'Oh?'

'As you know, my company maintains a rather substantial medical emergency response force,' Nomura reminded him. 'I can have aircraft en route to New Mexico in a matter of hours.'

The president nodded. Nomura PharmaTech spent huge sums annually on charitable medical work around the world. His old friend Jinjiro began the practice when he founded the company back in the 1960s. After he retired and entered the political world, his son had continued and even expanded its efforts. Nomura money now funded everything from mass vaccination and malaria control programs in Africa to water sanitation projects in the Middle East and Asia. But the company's disaster relief work was what really caught the public eye and generated headlines.

Nomura PharmaTech owned a fleet of Soviet-made An-124 Condor cargo aircraft. Bigger than the mammoth C-5 transports flown by the U.S. Air Force, each Condor could carry up to 150 metric tons of cargo. Operating from a central base located in the Azores Islands, they were used by Nomura to ferry mobile hospitals – complete with operating rooms and diagnostics labs – to wherever emergency medical care was needed. The company boasted that its hospitals could be up and running in twenty-four hours at the scene of any major earthquake, typhoon, disease outbreak, wildfire, or flood, anywhere in the world.

'That's a generous offer,' Castilla said slowly. 'But I'm afraid there were no injured survivors outside the Institute. These nanomachines killed everyone they attacked.

There's no one left alive for your medical personnel to treat.'

'There are other ways in which my people could assist,' Nomura said delicately. 'We do possess two mobile DNA analysis labs. Perhaps their use might speed the sad work of – '

'Identifying the dead,' Castilla finished for him. He thought about that. FEMA, the Federal Emergency Management Agency, was estimating it could take months to put names to the thousands of partial human remains left outside the ruined Teller Institute. Anything that could accelerate that slow, mournful effort was worth trying, no matter how many legal and political complications it might add. He nodded. 'You're absolutely right, Hideo. Any help along those lines would be most welcome.'

Then he sighed. 'Look, it's late and I'm tired, and it's been a rotten couple of days. Frankly, I could use a good stiff drink. Can I get you one?'

'Please,' Nomura replied. 'That would be most welcome.'

The president moved to a sideboard near the door to his private study. Earlier, Mrs. Pike had set a tray holding a selection of glasses and bottles there. He picked up one of the bottles. It was full of a rich amber liquid. 'Scotch all right with you? This is the twenty-year-old Caol Ila, a single malt from Islay. It was one of your father's favorites.'

Nomura lowered his eyes, apparently embarrassed by the emotions stirred by this offer. He inclined his head in a quick bow. 'You honor me.'

While Castilla poured, he carefully eyed the son of his old friend, noting the changes since they had last seen each other. Though Hideo Nomura was nearly fifty, his short-cropped hair was still pitch-black. He was tall for a Japanese man of his generation, so tall that he could easily look most Americans and Europeans squarely in the face. His jaw was firm and there were just a few tiny furrows around the edges of his eyes and mouth. From a distance,

Nomura might easily pass for a man fully ten or fifteen years younger. It was only up close that one could discern the wearing effects of time and hidden grief and suppressed rage.

Castilla handed one of the glasses to Nomura and then sat down and sipped at his own. The sweet, smoky liquid rolled warmly over his tongue, carrying with it just a bare hint of oak and salt. He noticed that the younger man tasted his without any evident sense of enjoyment. The son is not the father, he reminded himself sadly.

'I had another reason for asking you here tonight,' Castilla said at last, breaking the awkward silence. 'Though I think it may be related in some way to the tragedy at the Institute.' He chose his words carefully. 'I need to ask you about Jinjiro ... and about Lazarus.'

Nomura sat up straighter. 'About my father? And the Lazarus Movement? Ah, I see,' he murmured. He set his glass to one side. It was almost full. 'Of course. I will tell you whatever I can.'

'You opposed your father's involvement in the Movement, didn't you?' Castilla asked, again treading cautiously.

The younger Japanese nodded. 'Yes.' He looked straight at the president. 'My father and I were never enemies. Nor did I hide my views from him.'

'Which were?' Castilla wondered.

'That the goals of the Lazarus Movement were lofty, even noble,' Nomura said softly. 'Who would not want to see a planet purified, free of pollution, and at peace? But its proposals?' He shrugged. 'Hopelessly unrealistic at best. Deadly lunacy at worst. The world is balanced on a knife-edge, with mass starvation, chaos, and barbarism on one side and potential utopia on the other. Technology maintains this delicate balance. Strip away our advanced technologies, as the Movement demands, and you will

110

surely hurl the entire planet into a nightmare of death and destruction – a nightmare from which it might never awaken.'

Castilla nodded. The younger man's beliefs paralleled his own. 'And what did Jinjiro say to all of that?'

'My father agreed with me at first. At least in part,' Nomura said. 'But he thought the pace of technological change was too fast. The rise of cloning, genetic manipulation, and nanotechnology troubled him. He feared the speed of these advances, believing that they offered imperfect men too much power over themselves and over nature. Still, when he helped found Lazarus, he hoped to use the Movement as a means of slowing scientific progress – not of ending it altogether.'

'But that changed?' Castilla asked.

Nomura frowned. 'Yes, it did,' he admitted. He picked up his glass, stared into the smoky amber liquid for a moment, and then set it down again. 'The Movement began to change him. His beliefs grew more radical. His words became more strident.'

The president stayed silent, listening intently.

'As the other founders of the Movement died or disappeared, my father's thoughts grew darker still,' Nomura continued. 'He began to claim that Lazarus was under attack . . . that it had become the target of a secret war.'

'A war?' Castilla said sharply. 'Who did he say was waging this secret war?'

'Corporations. Certain governments. Or elements of their intelligence services. Perhaps even some of the men in your own CIA,' the younger Japanese said softly.

'Good God.'

Nomura nodded sadly. 'At the time, I thought these paranoid fears were only more evidence of my father's failing mental health. I begged him to seek help. He refused. His rhetoric became ever more violent, ever more deranged.

'Then he vanished on the way to Thailand.' His face was somber. 'He vanished without any word or trace. I do not know whether he was abducted, or whether he disappeared of his own free will. I do not know whether he is alive or dead.'

Nomura looked up at Castilla. 'Now, however, after seeing those peaceful protesters murdered outside the Teller Institute, I have another concern.' He lowered his voice. 'My father talked of a covert war being waged against the Lazarus Movement. And I laughed at him. But what if he was right?'

Later, once Hideo Nomura had gone, Sam Castilla walked to the door of his private study, knocked once, and went into the dimly lit room.

A pale, long-nosed man in a rumpled dark gray suit sat calmly in a high-backed chair placed right next to the door. Bright, highly intelligent eyes gleamed behind a pair of wire-rimmed glasses. 'Good morning, Sam,' said Fred Klein, the head of Covert-One.

'You heard all that?' the president asked.

Klein nodded. 'Most of it.' He held up a sheaf of papers. 'And I've read through the transcript of last evening's NSC meeting.'

'Well?' Castilla asked. 'What do you think?'

Klein sat back in his chair and ran his hands through his rapidly thinning hair while he considered his old friend's question. Every year it seemed as though his hairline receded another inch. It was the price of the stress involved in running the most secret operation in the whole U.S. government. 'David Hanson is no fool,' he said finally. 'You know his record as well as I do. He has a nose for trouble and he's bright and pushy enough to follow that nose wherever it leads him.'

'I know that, Fred,' said the president. 'Hell, that's why I nominated him as DCI in the first place – over Emily

Powell-Hill's vigorous and often-expressed objections, I might add. But I'm asking you for your opinion of his latest brainstorm: Do *you* think this mess in Santa Fe is really the work of the Lazarus Movement itself?'

Klein shrugged. 'He makes a fairly strong case. But you don't need me to tell you that.'

'No, I don't.' Castilla walked over heavily and dropped into another chair, this one next to a fireplace. 'But how does the CIA's theory track with what you've learned from Colonel Smith?'

'Not perfectly,' the head of Covert-One admitted. 'Smith was very clear. Whoever these attackers were, they were professionals – well-trained, well-equipped, and well-briefed professionals.' He fiddled with the briarwood pipe tucked in his coat pocket and fought off the temptation to light up. The whole White House was a no-smoking area these days. 'Frankly, that does not seem to square with what little we know about the Lazarus Movement . . .'

'Go on,' the president said.

'But it's not impossible,' Klein finished. 'The Movement has money. Maybe it hired the pros it needed. God knows that there are enough special ops-rained mercenaries kicking around idle these days. These people could have been ex-Stasi from the old East Germany, or ex-KGB or Spetsnaz-types from Russia. Or they might be from other commando units in the old Warsaw Pact, the Balkans, or the Middle East.'

He shrugged. 'The real kicker is Smith's claim that none of the nanotechnology being developed at the Institute could have killed those protesters. If he's right, then Hanson's theory goes right out the window. Of course, so does every other reasonable alternative.'

The president sat staring into the empty fireplace for a long moment. Then he shook himself and growled, 'It feels a bit too damned convenient, Fred, especially when you consider what Hideo Nomura just told me. I just don't like the way both the CIA and the FBI are zeroing in on one particular theory of what took place in Santa Fe, to the exclusion of every other possibility.'

'That's understandable,' Klein said. He tapped the NSC transcript. 'And I'll admit I have the same qualms. The worst sin in intelligence analysis comes when you start pounding square facts into round holes just to fit a favorite hypothesis. Well, when I read this, I can hear both the Bureau and the Agency banging away on pegs – whatever their shape.'

The president nodded slowly. 'That's exactly the problem.' He looked across the shadowed room at Klein. 'You're familiar with the A-Team/B-Team approach to analysis, aren't you?'

The head of Covert-One shot him a lopsided grin. 'I'd better be. After all, that's one of the justifications for my whole outfit.' He shrugged. 'Back in 1976, the then-DCI, George Bush Sr., later one of your illustrious predecessors, wasn't completely satisfied with the in-house CIA analysis of Soviet intentions he was getting. So he commissioned an outside group – the B-Team – made up of sharp-eyed academics, retired generals, and outside Soviet experts to conduct its own independent study of the same questions.'

'That's right,' Castilla said. 'Well, starting right now, I want you to form your very own B-Team to sort through this mess, Fred. Don't get in the way of the CIA or the FBI unless you have to, but I want somebody I can trust implicitly checking the shape of those pegs they're hammering.'

Klein nodded slowly. 'That can be arranged.' He tapped the unlit pipe on his knee for a few seconds, thinking. Then he looked up. 'Colonel Smith is the obvious candidate. He's already on the scene and he knows a great deal about nanotechnology.'

'Good.' Castilla nodded. 'Brief him now, Fred. Figure

out what authorizations he'll need to do this, and I'll make sure they land on the right desks first thing in the morning.'

CHAPTER THIRTEEN

In the Cerrillos Hills, Southwest of Santa Fe

An old, often-dented red Honda Civic drove south along County Road 57, trailing a long cloud of dust. Unbroken darkness stretched for miles in every direction. Only a faint glow cast by the sliver of the moon lit the rugged hills and steep-sided gulches and arroyos east of the unpaved dirt-and-gravel road. Inside the cramped, junk-filled car, Andrew Costanzo sat hunched over the steering wheel. He glanced down at the odometer periodically, lips moving as he tried to figure out just how far he had come since leaving Interstate 25. The instructions he had been given were precise.

Few people who knew him would have recognized the strange look of mingled exhilaration and dread on his pallid, fleshy face.

Ordinarily, Costanzo seethed with frustration and accumulated resentments. He was plump, forty-one years old, unmarried, and trapped in a society that did not value either his intellect or his ideals. He had worked hard to earn an advanced degree in environmental law and American consumerism. His doctorate should have opened doors for him into the academic elite. For years he had dreamed of working for a Washington, D.C.-based think tank, single-handedly drafting the blueprints for essential social and environmental reforms. Instead he was just a part-time clerk in a chain bookstore, a crummy dead-end job that barely paid his share of the rent on a shabby, run-down ranch house in one of Albuquerque's poorest neighborhoods.

But Costanzo had other work, secret work, and it was the only part of his otherwise miserable life he found meaningful. He licked his lips nervously. Being asked to join the inner circles of the Lazarus Movement was a great honor, but it also carried serious risks. Watching the news this afternoon had made that even clearer. If his superiors in the Movement had not given him strict orders to stay home, *he* would have been at the Teller rally. *He* would have been one of the thousands slaughtered so viciously by the corporate death machines.

For an instant, he felt a deep-seated rage boiling up inside him, overwhelming even the everyday petty grudges he usually savored. His hands tightened on the wheel. The Civic swerved to the right, nearly running off the rough road and into the shoulder of soft sand and dead brush banked up on that side.

Sweating now, Costanzo breathed out. Pay attention to what you're doing now, he told himself sharply. The Movement would take vengeance on its enemies in good time.

The Honda's odometer clicked through another mile. He was close to the rendezvous point. He slowed down and leaned forward, staring through the windshield at the heights looming on his left. There it was!

Setting the Civic's turn signal blinking out of habit, Costanzo swung off the county road and drove cautiously into the mouth of a small canyon snaking deeper into the Cerrillos Hills. The Honda's tires crunched across a wash of small stones carried down by periodic flash floods. Tiny clumps of stunted trees and sagebrush clung precariously to the arroyo's sheer slopes.

A quarter-mile off the road, the canyon twisted north. Narrower gulches fed into the arroyo at this place, winding in from several directions. There were more withered trees here, springing up between weathered boulders and low mounds of loose gravel. Steep rock walls soared high on either side – striped with alternating layers of buff-colored sandstone and red mudstone.

Costanzo turned off the ignition. The air was silent and perfectly still. Was he too early? Or too late? The orders he had been given had stressed the importance of promptness. He drew his shirtsleeve across his forehead, mopping away the droplets of sweat that were stinging his shadowed, bloodshot eyes.

He scrambled out of the Honda, dragging a small suitcase with him. He stood awkwardly, waiting, not sure of what he should do next.

Headlights suddenly speared out from one of the narrow side canyons. Surprised, Costanzo swung toward the lights, shading his eyes in a desperate attempt to see through the blinding glare. He couldn't make out anything but the vague outline of a large vehicle and two or three shapes that might be men standing beside it.

'Put the bag down,' a voice ordered loudly, speaking through a bullhorn. 'Then step away from your car. And keep your hands where we can see them!'

Shaking now, Costanzo obeyed. He walked forward stiffly, feeling sick to his stomach. He stuck his hands high in the air, with their palms out. 'Who are you?' he asked plaintively.

'Federal agents, Mr. Costanzo,' the voice said more quietly, without the bullhorn now.

'But I haven't done anything wrong! I haven't broken any laws!' he said, hearing the shrill quaver in his voice and hating it for revealing his fear so plainly.

'No?' the voice suggested. 'Aiding and abetting a terrorist organization is a crime, Andrew. A serious crime. Didn't you realize that?'

Costanzo licked his lips again. He could feel his heart pounding wildly. The sweat stains under his arms were spreading.

'Three weeks ago, a man fitting your description ordered two Ford Excursions from two separate auto dealers in Albuquerque. Two black Ford SUVs. He paid for them in cash. Cash, Andrew,' the voice said. 'Care to tell me how someone like you had nearly one hundred thousand dollars in spare cash lying around?'

'It wasn't me,' he protested.

'The car salesmen involved can identify you, Andrew,' the voice reminded him. 'All cash transactions of more than ten thousand dollars have to be reported to the federal government. Didn't you know that?'

Dumbfounded, Costanzo stood with his mouth hanging open. He should have remembered that, he realized dully. The cash-reporting requirement was part of the nation's drug laws, but really it was just another way for Washington to monitor and squelch potential dissent. Somehow, in all the excitement of being given a special mission for the Lazarus Movement, he had forgotten about it. How could he have been so blind? So stupid? His knees shook.

One of the shapes moved forward slowly, taking on the firmer outline of a remarkably tall and powerfully built man. 'Face the facts, Mr. Costanzo,' he said patiently. 'You were set up.'

The Lazarus Movement activist stood miserably rooted in one place. That was true, he thought bleakly. He had been betrayed. Why should he be so surprised? It had happened to him all of his life – first at home, then in school – and now it was happening again. 'I can identify the man who gave me the money,' he said frantically. 'I have a very good memory for faces – '

A single 9mm bullet hit him right between the eyes, tore through his brain, and exploded out the back of his head.

Still holding his silenced pistol, the tall auburn-haired member of the *Horatii* looked down at the dead man. 'Yes, Mr. Costanzo,' Terce said quietly. 'I am quite sure of that.'

Jon Smith was running, running for his life. He knew that much, though he could not remember why it was so. Others ran beside him. Over their terrified screams he heard a harsh buzzing noise. He glanced over his shoulder and saw a vast swarm of flying insects descending on them, coming on fast and gaining. He turned and ran faster, heart pounding in time with his feet.

The buzzing grew louder, ever more insistent and menacing. He felt something flutter onto his neck and tried frantically to brush it off. Instead, it clung to his palm. He stared down at the winged thing in dismay. It was a large yellow jacket.

Suddenly the wasp changed, transforming itself, altering its shape and structure into an artificial creature made of steel and titanium – a creature equipped with needle-tipped drills and diamond-edged saws. The robot wasp slowly turned its triangular head toward him. Its crystalline multi-faceted eyes gleamed with an eerie hunger. He stood transfixed, watching with mounting horror as the wasp's drills and saws blurred into motion and started boring deep into his flesh –

He jolted awake and sat bolt upright in bed, still panting hard and fast in reaction. Acting on reflex, he slid his hand under the pillow, automatically reaching for his 9mm SIG-Sauer pistol. Then he stopped. A dream, he thought edgily. It was only a dream.

His cell phone buzzed again, sounding from the nightstand where he had placed it before at last dropping off to sleep. Numbers on the digital clock beside the phone faintly glowed red, showing that it was just after three in the morning. Smith grabbed the phone before it could go off again. 'Yes. What is it?'

'Sorry to wake you, Colonel,' Fred Klein said, without sounding noticeably apologetic. 'But something's come up that I think you need to see . . . and hear.'

'Oh?' Smith swung his legs off the bed.

'The mysterious Lazarus has surfaced at long last,' the head of Covert-One said. 'Or so it appears.'

Smith whistled softly. *That* was interesting. His briefing on the Lazarus Movement had stressed that no one in the

CIA, the FBI, or any other Western intelligence agency knew who really directed its operations. 'In person?'

'No,' Klein said. 'It'll be easier to show you what we've got. Do you have your laptop handy?'

'Hold on.' Smith put the phone down and flipped on the lights. His portable computer was still in its case near the closet. Moving quickly, he slipped the machine out onto the bed, plugged the modem into a wall jack, and booted it up.

The laptop hummed, clicked, and whirred to life. Smith tapped in the special security code and password needed to connect with the Covert-One network. He picked up the phone. 'I'm online.'

'Wait a moment,' Klein told him. 'We're downloading the material to your machine now.'

The laptop's screen lit up – showing first a jumble of static, then random shapes and colors, and then finally clearing to show the stern, handsome face of a middle-aged man. He was looking straight into the camera.

Smith leaned forward, closely studying the figure before him. That face was somehow strangely familiar. Everything about it, from the faintly curly brown hair with just the right touch of gray at the temples to the open blue eyes, classically straight nose, and firm, cleft chin, conveyed an impression of enormous strength, wisdom, intelligence, and controlled power.

'I am Lazarus,' the figure said calmly. 'I speak for the Lazarus Movement, for the Earth, and for all of humanity. I speak for those who have died and for those as yet unborn. And I am here today to speak truth to corrupt and corruptible power.'

Smith listened to the perfectly pitched, sonorous voice as the man who called himself Lazarus delivered a short, powerful speech. In it, he called for justice for those killed outside the Teller Institute. He demanded an immediate ban on all nanotechnology research and development. And he called on all members of the Movement to take whatever actions were necessary to safeguard the world from the dangers posed by this technology.

'Our Movement, a gathering of all peoples, of all races, has warned for years of this growing threat,' Lazarus said solemnly. 'Our warnings have been ignored or mocked. Our voices have been silenced. But yesterday the world saw the truth – and it was a terrible and deadly truth. . . .'

The screen faded back to a neutral background once the speech ended. 'Pretty damned effective propaganda,' Smith said quietly over the phone.

'Extremely effective,' Klein agreed. 'What you just saw was a feed to every major television network in the United States and Canada. The NSA pulled it down off a communications satellite two hours ago. Every agency in Washington has been analyzing it ever since.'

'We can't stop the tape from being broadcast, I suppose,' Smith mused.

'After yesterday?' Klein snorted. 'Not in a million years, Colonel. This Lazarus message is going to run as the lead on every morning show and on every newscast for the whole day – maybe longer.'

Smith nodded to himself. No news director in his or her right mind was going to pass up the chance to feature a statement by the leader of the Lazarus Movement, especially since there was so much mystery surrounding him. 'Can the NSA track the source of the transmission?'

'They're working on it, but it's not going to be easy. This footage came in as a highly compressed, highly encrypted blip piggybacked somewhere on any one of a host of other signals. Once it was up on the satellite, the signal uncoiled and decoded itself and started feeding down to New York, Los Angeles, Chicago . . . you name the major city and there it went.'

'Interesting,' Smith said slowly. 'Doesn't that seem like a strangely sophisticated method of communication for a group that claims it's opposed to advanced technology?'

'Yes, it does,' Klein agreed. 'But we know that the Lazarus

Movement relies heavily on computers and various Web sites to handle its internal communications. Perhaps we shouldn't be surprised that it uses the same methods to speak to the world at large.' He sighed. 'And even if the NSA does succeed in pinpointing the origin of this transmission, I suspect we will learn that it arrived as an anonymous DVD at a small independent studio somewhere, along with a substantial cash payment for the technicians involved.'

'At least now we can put a face to this guy,' Smith said. 'And with that, we can pin down his real identity. Run those pictures through all of our databases – and those of our allies. Somebody, somewhere, will have a file on whoever that is.'

'You're jumping the gun a bit, Colonel,' Klein said. 'That wasn't the only satellite feed the NSA intercepted this morning. Take a look. . . .'

The screen showed an older Asian man – a man with thin white hair, a high, smooth forehead, and dark, almost ageless eyes. His appearance reminded Smith of paintings he had seen of ancient sages, full of wisdom and knowledge. The older man began speaking, this time in Japanese. A simultaneous translation into English crawled across the screen below. 'I am Lazarus. I speak for the Lazarus Movement, for the Earth, and for all of humanity. . . .'

The next image was of an African elder, another man with all the power and force of an ancient king or a shaman of great power. He spoke in full, resonant Swahili, but they were the same words, conveying the same message. When he finished, the handsome middle-aged Caucasian reappeared, this time speaking in perfect, idiomatic French.

Smith sat back in stunned silence, watching a parade of different Lazarus images – each one delivering the same powerful message fluently, in more than a dozen major languages. When the display at last flickered through static and faded into gray emptiness, he whistled softly again. 'Man, now there's a clever trick! So maybe three-quarters of the world population is going to hear this same Lazarus Movement speech? And all from people who look like them and speak languages they understand?'

'That appears to be their plan,' the head of Covert-One agreed. 'But the Movement is even cleverer than that. Take another look at that first Lazarus.'

The image came up on Smith's computer and froze just before it began speaking. He stared at the handsome middle-aged face. Why did it seem so damned familiar? 'I'm looking, Fred,' he said. 'But what I am looking for?'

'That is not a real face, Colonel,' Klein told him flatly. 'Nor are any of the other Lazarus images.'

Smith raised a single eyebrow. 'Oh? Then what are they?'

'Computer constructs,' the other man told him. 'A blend of artificially generated pixels and bits and pieces of hundreds, perhaps thousands, of real people all mixed to create a set of different faces. The voices are all computer-generated, too.'

'So we have no way to identify them,' Smith realized. 'And still no way to know whether the Movement is run by one man – or by many.'

'Exactly. But it goes beyond that,' Klein said. 'I've seen some of the CIA's analysis. They're convinced those im-ages and voices are very specially crafted – that they repre-sent archetypes, or idealized figures, for the cultures to whom the Lazarus Movement is delivering its message.'

That would certainly explain why he had reacted so fa-vorably to the first image, Smith realized. It was a varia-tion on the ancient Western ideal of the just and noble hero-king. 'These people are awfully damned good at what they're trying to do,' he said grimly.

'Indeed.'

'In fact, I'm beginning to think that the CIA and FBI may be right on-target in fingering these guys for what happened yesterday.'

'Perhaps. But skill with propaganda and secrecy doesn't necessarily reveal terrorist intentions. Try to keep an open mind, Colonel,' the other man warned. 'Remember that Covert-One is the B-Team on this investigation. Your job is to play devil's advocate, to make sure evidence isn't overlooked just because it doesn't conveniently fit the preconceived theory.'

'Don't worry, Fred,' Smith said reassuringly. 'I'll do my best to poke and prod and pry to see what breaks.'

'Discreetly, please,' Klein reminded him.

'Discretion is my middle name,' said Smith with a quick grin.

'Is it?' the head of Covert-One said tartly. 'Somehow I never would have guessed.' Then he relented. 'Good luck, Jon. If you need anything – access, information, backup, anything – we'll be standing by.'

Still grinning, Smith disconnected his phone and computer and began preparing himself for the long day ahead.

CHAPTER FOURTEEN

Emeryville, California

Once a sleepy little town full of dilapidated warehouses, rusting machine shops, and artists' studios, Emeryville had suddenly blossomed as one of the centers of the Bay Area's booming biotech industry. Multinational pharmaceutical corporations, genetic engineering startups, and venture capital-funded entrepreneurs pursuing new opportunities like nanotechnology all vied for office and lab space along the busy Interstate 80 corridor between Berkeley and Oakland. Rents, taxes, and living costs were all exorbitant, but most corporate executives seemed to focus instead on Emeryville's proximity to top-notch universities and major airports and, perhaps most important of all, its spectacular views of San Francisco, the Bay, and the Golden Gate.

Telos Corporation's nanoelectronics research facility took up a whole floor of one of the new glass-and-steel high-rises looming just east of the approaches to the Bay Bridge. Interested more in profiting from its multi-million-dollar investment in equipment, materials, and personnel than it was in publicity, Telos maintained a comparatively low profile. No expensive and flashy logo on the building advertised its presence inside. School groups, politicians, and the press were not offered time-consuming tours. A single guard station just inside the main doors provided security.

Pacific Security Corporation deputy Paul Yiu sat behind the marble-topped counter of the security station, skimming through a paperback mystery. He flipped a page, idly noting the death of yet another suspect he had fingered as the killer. Then he yawned and stretched. Midnight had long since come and gone, but he still had two hours to go on his shift. He shifted uncomfortably on his swivel chair, readjusted the butt of the pistol holstered at his side, and went back to his book. His eyelids drooped.

A light tapping on the glass doors roused him. Yiu looked up, fully expecting to see one of the half-crazy homeless bums who sometimes wandered down here from Berkeley by mistake. Instead, he saw a petite redhead with a worried expression on her face. Fog had rolled in from the Bay and she looked cold in her tight blue skirt, white silk blouse, and stylish black wool coat.

The security guard slid off his chair, straightened his own khaki uniform shirt and tie, and went to the door. The young woman smiled in relief when she saw him and tried the door. It rattled but stayed locked.

'I'm sorry, ma'am,' he called through the glass. 'This building's closed.'

Her worried look came back. 'Please, I just need to borrow a phone to call Triple A,' she said plaintively. 'My car broke down just up the street, and now my cell phone's gone dead, too!'

Yiu thought about that for a moment. The rules were quite clear. No unauthorized visitors after business hours. On the other hand, none of his bosses ever had to know that he had decided to play the Good Samaritan for this frantic young woman. Call it my good deed for the week, he decided. Besides, she was pretty cute, and he had always had an unrequited passion for redheads.

He took the building key card out of his shirt pocket and swiped it through the lock. It buzzed once and clicked open. He pulled the heavy glass door back with a welcoming smile. 'Here you go, ma'am. The phone's just – '

The mace blast caught Yiu right in the eyes and open mouth. He doubled over, blinded, gagging, and helpless. Before he could even try to fumble for his weapon, the door slammed wide open – hurling him backward onto the slick tiled floor. Several people burst through the open door and into the lobby. Strong arms grabbed him, pinioned his arms behind his back, and then secured his wrists using his own handcuffs. Someone else yanked a cloth hood over his head.

A woman bent down to whisper in his ear. 'Remember this! Lazarus lives!'

By the time Yiu's relief arrived to set him free, the intruders were long gone. But the Telos nanotech lab was a total wreck – full of smashed glassware, burned out electron-scanning microscopes, punctured steel tanks, and spilled chemicals. The Lazarus Movement slogans spray-painted across the walls, doors, and windows left little doubt about the loyalties of those responsible.

Zurich, Switzerland

As the weak autumn sun climbed toward the zenith, thousands of protesters already clogged the steep tree-lined hill overlooking Zurich's Old Town and the River Limmat. They blockaded every street around the twin campuses of the Swiss Federal Institute of Technology and the University of Zurich. Scarlet and green Lazarus Movement flags waved above the crowds, along with signs demanding a ban on all Swiss-based nanotechnology research projects.

Squads of riot police holding truncheons and clear Plexiglas shields waited at parade rest some blocks away from the mass of protesters. Armored cars with water cannons and tear gas grenade launchers were parked nearby. But the police did not appear to be in any real hurry to move in and clear the streets.

Dr. Karl Friederich Kaspar, the head of one of the labs now under peaceful siege, stood just behind the police barricades, close to the upper station of the Zurich Polybahn, the funicular railway built more than a century before to serve both the university and the Institute. He checked his watch again and ground his teeth together in frustration. Fuming, he sought out the highest-ranking police official he could find. 'Look, why all the delay? Without a permit, this demonstration is illegal. Why don't you put your troops in and break it up?'

The police officer shrugged. 'I follow my orders, Herr Professor Direktor Kaspar. At the moment, I have no such orders.'

Kaspar hissed in disgust. 'This is absurd! I have staff waiting to go to work. We have many very valuable and expensive experiments to conduct.'

'That is a pity,' said the policeman carefully.

'A pity!' Kaspar growled. 'It's more than a pity; it's a disgrace.' He eyed the other man angrily. 'I might almost think you have sympathy for these ignorant dunderheads.'

The police officer turned to face him, meeting Kaspar's furious gaze without flinching. 'I am not a member of the Lazarus Movement, if that is what you are suggesting,' he said quietly. 'But I saw what happened in America. I do not wish such a catastrophe to occur here in Zurich.'

The lab director turned bright red. 'Such a thing is impossible! Utterly impossible! Our work is completely different from anything the Americans and Japanese were doing at the Teller Institute! There is no comparison!'

'That is excellent news,' the policeman said, with the faint hint of a sardonic smile. He made a show of offering Kaspar a bullhorn. 'Perhaps if you assured the protesters of this truth, they might see the error of their ways and disperse?'

Kaspar could only stare back at him, dismayed to find so much ignorance and insolence in a fellow public servant.

CHAPTER FIFTEEN

Albuquerque International Airport, New Mexico

With the sun rising red behind it, the huge An-124 Condor thundered low over the airport's inner beacon line and dropped heavily onto Runway Eight. Its four large pylon-mounted turbofans howled as the pilot reversed thrust. Decelerating, the Condor bounced and rolled down the nearly thirteen-thousand-foot-long landing strip, chasing its own lengthening shadow. In seconds, it lumbered past the hangars and revetments holding F-16s that belonged to New Mexico's 150th Air National Guard Fighter Wing. Still slowing, it passed camouflaged concrete-and-steel ordnance bunkers, which had been used to store strategic and tactical nuclear weapons during the Cold War.

Near the western end of the tarmac, the enormous Russian-made Antonov cargo aircraft turned off onto a freight apron and rolled ponderously to a complete stop beside a much smaller corporate jet. The shrill noise of its engines died away. Seen up close, the Nomura Pharma-Tech-owned plane dwarfed the group of reporters and cameramen waiting to record its arrival.

The An-124's sixty-foot-high rear cargo ramp whined open, settling heavily on the oil- and jet fuel-stained concrete. Two crewmen in flight suits walked down the ramp, shading their eyes against the bright sunlight. Once on the ground, they turned and began using hand signals to guide the drivers slowly backing a convoy of vehicles out of the Condor's cavernous cargo bay. The mobile DNA analysis labs promised by Hideo Nomura had arrived.

Nomura himself stood among the journalists, watching his support crews and medical technicians quickly and calmly preparing to make the short drive to Santa Fe. Their efficiency pleased him.

When he judged that the media had all the footage they needed, he signaled for their attention. It took some time for them to refocus their cameras and make sound checks. He waited patiently until they were ready.

'I have one other major decision to announce, ladies and gentlemen,' Nomura began. 'It is not one I have made lightly. But I think it is the only sensible decision, especially in view of the terrible tragedy we all witnessed yesterday.' He paused for dramatic effect. 'Effective immediately, Nomura PharmaTech will suspend its nanotechnology research programs – both those in our own facilities and those we fund in other institutions around the world. We will invite outside observers into our labs and factories to confirm that we have halted all our activities in this scientific field.'

He listened politely to the frenzied clamor of questions aroused by this sudden announcement, answering those that seemed best suited to his purposes. 'Was my decision prompted by the demands made earlier this morning by the Lazarus Movement?' He shook his head. 'Absolutely not. Though I respect their motives and ideals, I do not share the Movement's bias against science and technology. This temporary halt is prompted by simple prudence. Until we know exactly what went wrong at the Teller Institute, it would be foolish to put other cities at risk.'

'What about your competitors?' one of the reporters asked bluntly. 'Other corporations, universities, and governments have already invested billions of dollars in medical nanotech. Should they follow your company's lead and halt their work, too?'

Nomura smiled blandly. 'I will not presume to dictate what steps others should take. That is a matter for their best scientific judgment, or perhaps more appropriately, for their consciences. For my part, I can only assure you that Nomura PharmaTech will never put its own profits ahead of innocent human life.'

Boston, Massachusetts
Big, bullheaded James Severin, the chief executive officer of Harcourt Biosciences, watched the CNN tape of Hideo Nomura's interview come to an end. 'That sly, shrewd Japanese son of a bitch,' he murmured, half in grudging admiration and half in outrage. His eyes blinked angrily behind the thick lenses of his black-framed glasses. 'He knows his company's nanotech projects are way behind everybody else's work – so far behind that they've got no real chance of catching up!'

His senior aide, just as tall but about one hundred pounds lighter, nodded. 'From what we can tell, Nomura's people lag our researchers by at least eighteen months. They're still sorting out basic theory, while our lab teams are developing real-world applications. This is a race PharmaTech can't win.'

'Yeah,' Severin growled. 'We know that. And our friend Hideo there knows it. But who else is going to see what he's up to? Not the press, that's for sure.' He frowned. 'So he gets to pull the plug on failing projects that have been costing his company an arm and a leg while masquerading as a selfless corporate white knight! Sweet, isn't it?'

The head of Harcourt Biosciences shoved his chair back, pushed himself heavily to his feet, and went over to stare moodily out the floor-to-ceiling windows of his office. 'And that little stunt by Nomura just revved up the public and political pressure on the rest of us. We're already catching enough hell over that mess out in Santa Fe. Now it's going to get worse.'

'We could buy some relief by going along with PharmaTech's self-imposed moratorium,' his aide suggested cautiously. 'Just until we can prove our Teller lab wasn't at fault for the disaster.'

Severin snorted. 'How long will that take? Months? A year? Two years? You really think we can afford to keep a bunch of bright-eyed scientists sitting around twiddling their thumbs for that long?' He leaned forward against the thick glass. Far below, the waters of Boston Harbor were a frigid-looking green-gray. 'Don't forget that a lot of people in Congress and in the press would claim we were practically admitting fault by suspending our other nano-tech projects.'

His aide said nothing.

Severin swung away from the windows. He clasped his hands behind his back. 'No. We're not going to play No-mura's game. We're going to tough it out. Get out a press release right away. Say that Harcourt Biosciences flatly re-jects the demands made by the Lazarus Movement. We will not give in to threats made by a secretive and extrem-ist organization. And let's arrange some special media tours of our other nanotech labs. We need to show people that we have absolutely nothing to hide – and they have nothing to fear.'

CHAPTER SIXTEEN

The Teller Institute

Wearing a thick plastic protective suit, gloves, a sealed hood with its own oxygen supply, and a blue hard hat, Jon Smith stepped cautiously through the shattered ruins of the Institute's first floor. He ducked sideways under a large charred beam hanging down from the torn ceiling, taking care to avoid ripping his suit on any of the nails protruding from the blackened wood. No one knew if the nanomachines that had butchered thousands of protesters were still active. So far no one had tried to find out the hard way. Small fragments of crumbled adobe and shards of broken glass crunched under his thick-soled boots.

He came out into a more open area that had once been the employee cafeteria. This room was mostly intact, but there were signs of bomb damage along two of the four walls, and chalked outlines on the broken tile floor showed where bodies had been removed.

The FBI task force investigating the disaster was using the cafeteria as a rallying point and on-site tactical command center. Two portable computers were up and running on tables near the middle of the room, though it was clear that the agents trying to use them were having trouble entering data in their thick gloves.

Smith made his way over to where a man wearing a black hard hat was bent over one of the salvaged dining tables, studying a set of blueprints. The tag on the agent's protective suit read LATIMER, C.

The agent looked up at his approach. 'Who are you?' he asked. The protective hood muffled his voice.

'Dr. Jonathan Smith. I'm with the Pentagon.' Smith lightly tapped his blue hard hat for emphasis. Blue was the color assigned to observers and outside consultants. 'I have a watching brief – with orders to provide whatever help I can.'

'Special Agent Charles Latimer,' the other man introduced himself. He was slender, fair-haired, and had a strong Southern accent. He was openly curious now. 'Just what kind of help can you offer us, Doctor?'

'I have a decent working knowledge of nanotechnology,' Smith said carefully. 'And I know the layout of the labs pretty well. I was stationed here on a temporary assignment when the terrorists hit this place.'

Latimer stared hard at him. 'That makes you a witness, Doctor – not an observer.'

'Last night and earlier this morning I was a witness,' Smith said with a wry grin. 'Since then I've been promoted to independent consultant.' He shrugged. 'I know that's not exactly by the book.'

'No, it's not,' the FBI agent agreed. 'Look, have you cleared this with my boss?'

'I'm sure all the necessary authorizations and clearances are somewhere on Deputy Assistant Director Pierson's desk right now,' Smith said mildly. The last thing he wanted to do was start out by barging in at the top of the FBI's chain of command. He had not met Kit Pierson before, but he strongly suspected she was not going to be pleased to find someone outside her control hovering around her investigation.

'Meaning, no, you haven't talked this over with her,' Latimer said. He shook his head in disbelief. Then he shrugged. 'Swell. Well, nothing else in this screwy place is running by the book.'

'It's a tough site to work in,' Smith agreed.

'Now there's an understatement,' said the FBI agent

with a lopsided smile of his own. 'Trying to hunt through all this bomb and fire damage is hard enough. Having to shield ourselves against these nanophages, or whatever they are, makes the job almost impossible.'

He pointed to the protective clothing they both wore. 'Between the limited oxygen supply and avoiding heat prostration, we only get three hours of wear out of these moon suits. And we have to waste a whole half hour of that in decontamination. So our work is moving at a crawl, right at a time when Washington is screaming for fast results. Plus, we face a classic catch-22 on every piece of evidence we gather.'

Smith nodded sympathetically. 'Let me guess: You can't take anything out of the building for lab analysis until it's been decontaminated. And if you decontaminate it, there's probably nothing left to analyze.'

'Peachy, isn't it?' Latimer said acidly.

'The risk of contamination may not be that high,' Smith pointed out. 'Most nanodevices are designed for very specific environments. They should start to break down fairly rapidly after being exposed to atmosphere, pressure, or temperature conditions outside their parameters. We might be perfectly safe right now.'

'Sounds like a nice theory, Doctor,' the FBI agent said. 'You volunteering to be the first one to take a good deep breath in here?'

Smith grinned. 'I'm a medical man, not a lab rat. But ask me again in about twenty-four hours and I just might try it.'

He looked down at the set of blueprints the other man had been inspecting. They showed the layout of the Institute's first and second floors. Red circles of varying sizes dotted the blueprints. Most were clustered in and around the nanotech lab suites in the North Wing, but others were scattered throughout the building. 'Bomb detonation points?' he asked the other man.

Latimer nodded. 'Those we've identified so far.'

Smith examined the blueprints carefully. What he saw there confirmed his earlier impressions of the remarkable precision used by the terrorists in making their attack. Several explosive charges had completely smashed the security office, wiping out all the archived images from the external and internal security cameras. Another bomb had disabled the fire suppression system. Other demolition charges had been set in the computer center – destroying everything from personnel files to the records of equipment and materials deliveries made to scientists working at the Institute.

At first glance, the bombs placed inside the nanotech labs seemed to show the same determination to inflict maximum damage. Concentric circles covered the floor plans for the Nomura and Institute complexes. He nodded to himself. Those charges were clearly set to obliterate every single piece of major equipment in both labs, all the way from the biochemical vats in their inner cores to their desktop computers. But something about the detonation patterns he observed in the Harcourt lab bothered him.

Smith bent forward over the table. So what was wrong? He traced the array of circles with one gloved forefinger. The explosives rigged around the lab's inner core were far less likely to have caused as much damage. They seemed set to blow holes in the containment around the Harcourt nanophage-manufacturing tanks – not to completely destroy the tanks themselves. Was that an error? he wondered. Or was it deliberate?

He glanced up to ask Latimer whether he had noticed the same pattern. But the FBI agent was looking away, listening closely to someone talking over his radio headset.

'Understood,' Latimer said crisply into his mike. 'Yes, ma'am. I'll make sure he gets the message and complies. Out.' The fair-haired man turned back to Smith. 'That was Pierson. It seems your paperwork finally caught her attention. She wants to see you at the primary command center outside.'

'As in immediately?' Smith guessed.

Latimer nodded. 'Even sooner than that, if possible,' he said with a twisted smile. 'And I'd be lying if I said you were going to get a warm welcome.'

'How truly wonderful,' Jon said drily.

The FBI agent shrugged his shoulders. 'Just watch your step when you talk to her, Dr. Smith. The Winter Queen is damned good at her job, but she's not exactly what you might call a people person. If she thinks you're going to screw up this investigation in any way, she's liable to find a hole somewhere and drop you into it for the duration. Oh, she might call it "preventive detention" or "protective custody," but it still won't be real comfortable . . . or very easy to get out of.'

Smith studied Latimer's face, sure that he must be exaggerating for effect. To his dismay, the other man seemed perfectly serious.

The safe house sat high on the crest of a rise overlooking the southern reaches of Santa Fe. From the outside, it appeared to be a classic Pueblo-style adobe built around a shaded courtyard. Inside, the decor and furnishings were absolutely modern, a study in gleaming chrome, blacks, and whites. Small satellite dishes were mounted discreetly in one corner of the building's flat roof.

Several of the home's west-facing windows had a direct line of sight to the Teller Institute, about two miles away. The rooms behind these windows were now filled with an array of radio and microwave receivers, video and still cameras fitted with powerful telephoto, infrared (IR), and thermal-imaging lenses, a bank of networked computers, and secure satellite communications gear.

A six-man surveillance team ran all this equipment, monitoring the comings and goings inside the cordoned-off area outside the Institute. One of them, young and olive-skinned with sad brown eyes, sat perched on a chair at one of the computer workstations, humming tunelessly while listening to a pair of headphones plugged into the various receivers.

Suddenly the young man sat up straighter. 'I have a signal tone,' he reported calmly while simultaneously entering a series of commands on his keyboard. The monitor in front of him lit up and began filling with scrolling data – a complex and bewildering montage of numbers, graphs, scanned photographs, and text.

His team leader, much older, with short-cropped white hair, studied the monitor for several seconds. He nodded in satisfaction. 'Excellent work, Vitor.' He turned to one of his other men. 'Contact Terce. Inform him that Field Two appears complete and that we now have access to all of the investigative data being gathered. Report also that we are relaying this information to the Center.'

Sweating inside his protective suit now, Jon Smith submitted himself to the rigorous decontamination procedures required for anyone leaving the cordoned-off area around the Institute. Doing so meant entering one end of a chain of connected trailers and moving through a series of high-pressure chemical showers, electrically charged aerosol sprays, and high-powered vacuum suction systems. The equipment, borrowed from Air Force and Homeland Security WMD defense units, was designed to treat nuclear, chemical, and biological contamination. No one was really sure that it would neutralize the nanomachines that everyone now feared. But it was the best system anyone had been able to come up with in the limited time available. And since no one had died yet, Smith was willing to bet that either the decon procedures worked – or there were no active nanomachines left inside the cordon.

If nothing else, the painstaking process gave him plenty of time to think about what he had seen inside the Teller Institute. And that, in turn, gave him time to formulate a very ugly hypothesis about what had happened – one that might just knock the stuffing out of a lot of the pet theories floating around inside the FBI and the CIA.

Finished at last, Smith stripped off the heavy gear, dumped it in a sealed hazardous materials bin, and put his own clothes back on. He retrieved his shoulder holster and SIG-Sauer pistol from the worried-looking National Guard corporal manning a final checkpoint and stepped outside.

It was the middle of the afternoon. The wind was kicking up a bit, blowing down out of the forested mountains to the east. Jon took a deep breath of the pine-scented air, clearing the last lingering reek of harsh chemicals out of his nose and lungs.

A trim, efficient-looking young man in a conservatively cut charcoal-gray suit came straight up to him. He had the wooden, expressionless demeanor so prized by recent FBI Academy graduates. 'Dr. Smith?'

Jon nodded pleasantly. 'That's right.'

'Deputy Assistant Director Pierson is waiting for you at the command center,' the young man said. 'I'll be happy to escort you there.'

Smith hid a wry grin. Clearly, the woman he had heard called the Winter Queen had decided not to take any chances with him. He was not going to be allowed to bunk off without hearing what the FBI thought of having another government agency, the Pentagon in his case, meddling in its patch.

Remembering Fred Klein's admonition to act discreetly, he followed the other man without kicking up a fuss. They crossed through a growing assembly of trailers and large tents. Power and fiber-optic cables connected the temporary working quarters. Satellite dishes and microwave relays were set up around the outside. Portable generators hummed close by, supplying auxiliary and backup power.

Smith was impressed despite himself. This command center was nearly as big as some of the divisional HQs he had seen in Desert Storm and running a lot more smoothly. Kit Pierson might not score high marks in the warmth and charm department, but she obviously knew how to organize an efficient operation.

She had her own work area in a small tent near the outer rim. It was sparsely furnished with a table and a single chair, power for her personal laptop, a secure phone, an electric lantern, and a folding cot.

Smith hastily suppressed his surprise when he registered that last item. Was she really serious?

'Yes, Dr. Smith,' said Pierson drily, noticing the almost imperceptible flicker of his eyes. 'I do plan to sleep here.' A thin, humorless smile crossed a pale face that he might have found appealing if it had a bit more life in it. 'It may be Spartan, but it is also absolutely inaccessible to the press – which I count as a blessing of the first magnitude.'

She spoke over his shoulder to the young agent hovering near the open tent flap. 'That will be all, Agent Nash. Lieutenant Colonel Smith and I will have our little chat in private.'

Here we go, Jon realized, noting her deliberate shift to his military rank. He decided to try preempting her objections to his presence at the site. 'First of all, I want you to know that I'm not here to horn in on your investigation.'

'Really?' Pierson asked. Her gray eyes were ice-cold. 'That seems unlikely . . . unless you're here as some kind of a military tourist. In which case your presence is equally unwelcome.'

So much for the pleasantries, Smith thought, gritting his teeth. This sounded like it was going to be more a duel than a discussion. 'You've read my orders, and my clearances, ma'am. I'm here simply to observe and assist.'

'With all due respect, I don't need help from the Joint Chiefs of Staff or Army Intelligence – or whoever really issued your orders,' Pierson told him bluntly. 'Frankly, I can't think of anyone more likely to cause trouble I do *not* need.'

Smith reined in his temper, but only by the narrowest of margins. 'Really? In what way?'

'Just by existing,' she said. 'Maybe you've missed it, but the Internet and the tabloids are crammed full of rumors that Teller was the center of a secret military program to create nanotech-based weapons.'

'And those rumors are crap,' Smith said forcefully.

'Are they?'

Smith nodded. 'I saw all the research here myself. No one at Teller was working on anything that could possibly have had any immediate military application.'

'Your presence at the Institute is precisely my problem, *Colonel* Smith,' Pierson said coldly. 'How do you propose that we explain your assignment to monitor these nano-tech projects?'

Smith shrugged. 'Easy. I'm a doctor and a molecular biologist. My interests here in New Mexico were purely medical and scientific.'

'*Purely* medical and scientific? Don't forget that I've read both your witness statement and your Bureau file,' she shot back. 'For a doctor, you certainly know how to kill easily and efficiently. Weapons training and unarmed combat skills are a little out of the usual medical school curriculum, aren't they?'

Smith kept his mouth shut, wondering just how much Kit Pierson really knew about his career. Everything he had ever done for Covert-One was buried beyond her reach, but his Army Intelligence work would have left some traces she could sniff out. So had the part he had played in resolving the Hades Factor crisis.

'More to the point,' she continued, 'maybe one out of every three people in this country will be bright enough to understand your medical connection. Everybody else, especially the crazies, will only see that nice little Army uniform jacket you keep in the closet – the one with the silver oak leaves on its shoulder straps.'

Pierson tapped him on the chest with one long finger.

'And *that*, Colonel Smith, is why I don't want you anywhere near this investigation. If just one nosy reporter zeroes in on you, we're going to have real trouble on our hands. This case is tricky enough,' she said. 'I don't intend to provoke another Lazarus riot on top of everything else.'

'Neither do I,' Smith assured her. 'Which is why I plan to keep a low profile.' He indicated his civilian clothes, a lightweight gray windbreaker, green Polo shirt, and khakis. 'While I'm here, I'm just plain Dr. Smith . . . and I don't talk to journalists. Not ever.'

'That's not good enough,' she replied adamantly.

'It will have to be,' Jon told her quietly. He would bend a bit to placate Kit Pierson's natural irritation at finding an outsider poaching in her province, but he would not shirk his duty. 'Look,' he said. 'If you want to complain to Washington, that's fine. In the meantime, though, you're stuck with me . . . so why not take me up on my offer to help?'

Her eyes narrowed dangerously. For a second Smith wondered whether he was heading for that 'preventive detention' hole Agent Latimer had warned him about. Then she shrugged. The gesture was so slight that he almost missed it. 'All right, Dr. Smith,' she said coolly. 'We'll play this your way, for the moment. But the instant I get permission to sling you out of here, off you go.'

He nodded. 'Fair enough.'

'Then, if that's all, I'm sure you can find your own way out,' she suggested, pointedly checking her watch. 'I have work to do.'

Smith decided to push her just a bit further. 'I need to ask just a couple of questions first.'

'If you must,' Pierson said levelly.

'What do your people think about the odd way the demolition charges were set inside the Harcourt lab?' he asked.

She raised a single perfect eyebrow. 'Go on.' She listened carefully to his conjecture that the bombs there were only intended to breach the lab's containment – not to wreck it completely. When he finished, she shook her head in icy amusement. 'So you're an explosives expert, too, Doctor?'

'I've seen them used,' he admitted. 'But no, I'm not an expert.'

'Well, let's assume your hunch is correct,' Pierson said. 'You're suggesting the slaughter outside was deliberate – that the terrorists planned all along to release these Harcourt nanophages on anyone in reach. Which means the Lazarus Movement came here intending to make its own martyrs.'

'Not quite,' Smith corrected her. 'I'm suggesting the people who pulled this off wanted to make it seem that way.' He shook his head. 'But I've been thinking hard about this, and there's no way that the nanodevices Brinker and Parikh created were responsible for what happened. No way at all. It's completely impossible.'

Pierson's face froze. 'You'll have to explain that to me,' she said stiffly. 'Impossible, how?'

'Each Harcourt nanophage carried biochemical substances intended to eliminate specific cancerous cells, not to break down all living tissues,' Smith said. 'Plus, each individual phage was infinitesimally small. It would take millions of them, maybe tens of millions, to inflict the kind of damage I saw on any single human being. Multiply that by the number of people killed, and you're talking about billions of nanophages, possibly even tens of billions. That's far beyond the number the Harcourt folks could possibly have manufactured with their equipment. Don't forget, they were focused entirely on the design, engineering, and testing of what they hoped would be a medical miracle. They were not set up for mass production.'

'Can you prove that?' Pierson asked. Her face was still an unreadable mask.

'Without the computer records?' Smith shook his head. 'Maybe not solidly enough to suit a court of law, I guess.

But I was in that lab almost every day and I know what I saw – and what I didn't see.' He looked curiously at the pale, dark-haired woman to see whether or not she would arrive at the same damning conclusion he had.

Instead, she said nothing. Her mouth was a tight, thin line. Her gray eyes seemed fixed on a distant point somewhere far beyond the narrow confines of her tent.

'You understand what that means, don't you?' Smith said urgently. 'It means these terrorists came to Teller with their own nanodevices already prepared – nanodevices that were engineered from the start to butcher thousands. Whoever those people were, they sure as hell weren't part of the Lazarus Movement, not unless you think the Movement maintains its own sophisticated nanotech labs!'

At last, Pierson swung her gaze back toward him. A muscle on the right side of her face twitched. She frowned. '*If* your suppositions are correct, that may well be true, Doctor.' Then she shook her head. 'But that is a very big *if*, and I'm not yet prepared to overlook all the other evidence of Lazarus Movement involvement.'

'What other evidence?' Smith asked sharply. 'Do you have solid IDs for those terrorists Sergeant Diaz and I killed yet? They have to be in some agency's files. Those guys were professionals. What's more, they were pros who had access to very high-level Secret Service planning and procedures. People like that don't hang around street corners looking for work.'

Again, Pierson said nothing.

'Okay, what about their vehicles?' Jon pressed her. 'Those big black SUVs they drove up in. The ones left parked outside the building. Have your agents been able to trace them yet?'

She smiled icily. 'I conduct investigations in an organized fashion, Colonel Smith. That means I do not run around prematurely reporting the results of every separate inquiry. Now, until I persuade the powers-that-be to yank you out of here, you're welcome to attend all relevant briefings. When I have facts to share with you, that is where you will hear them. Until then, I strongly suggest that you exercise the virtue of patience.'

After Smith left her tent, Kit Pierson stood next to her desk, considering the wild claims he had made. Was the self-assured Army officer right? Could Hal Burke's operatives have deliberately released their own plague of killing machines? She shook her head abruptly, pushing the thought away. That was impossible. It *had* to be impossible. The deaths outside the building were completely unintended. Nothing more.

And the deaths inside the building? her conscience asked. What about them? Casualties of war, she answered herself coldly, trying hard to believe it. There was nothing to be gained by wasting time wrestling with feelings of guilt or regret. She had more immediate problems to deal with, chief among them Lieutenant Colonel Jonathan Smith. He did not strike her as a man who would be content to stand aside, no matter how many warnings she gave him.

Pierson frowned. Everything depended on her ability to maintain sole control over this investigation. Having someone like Smith running around pushing theories that contradicted her official line was unacceptable – and dangerous, to her, to Hal Burke, and to the whole TOCSIN operation.

Nor did Pierson believe for a minute that Smith was working solely as a scientific observer and liaison officer for either USAMRIID or the Joint Chiefs. He had too many unusual skills, too wide a range of experiences. There were also some very odd gaps in the FBI file she had examined. So who were Smith's real bosses? The Defense Intelligence Agency? Army Intelligence? Or one of the half-dozen other government cloak-and-dagger outfits?

She picked up her secure phone and dialed a seven-digit cell number.

'Burke here.'

'This is Kit Pierson,' she said. 'We have a problem. I want you to run a detailed background check on a Lieutenant Colonel Jonathan Smith, U.S. Army.'

'That name rings an unpleasant bell,' her CIA counterpart said sourly.

'It should,' she told him. 'He's the so-called doctor who managed to kill half your handpicked assault team.'

CHAPTER SEVENTEEN

**Hidden Nanotechnology Production Facility,
Inside the Center**

Nothing from the outside world was allowed to easily penetrate the secure areas of the Center. While they were working inside, no one could smell the salt tang of the nearby ocean or hear the noise of jets revving up as they prepared for takeoff. Everything was pristine, silent, and utterly sterile.

Even in the outer areas of the huge concealed lab complex, technicians and scientists moved with careful precision – wearing surgical scrubs under sterile coveralls, masks covering the entire nose, mouth, and chin, safety glasses, and polyester head covers that resembled the chain-mail hoods of Frankish knights. They spoke in hushed tones. All written work was handled electronically. No paper notes or reference books were allowed inside any of the clean areas. The risk of airborne particulate contamination was deemed too high.

Each move closer to the Class-10 environment in the production core itself involved ever-stricter gowning and sterilization procedures. Air locks and elaborate filtration systems connected each chamber. Checklists were posted at each outer air lock door, along with armed guards ordered to make sure that each step was followed and in the proper order. No one wanted to risk contaminating the nanophage production tanks. The developing phages were too delicate, too vulnerable to the slightest change in their rigidly controlled environment. Nor was anyone in the secret lab complex willing to risk unprotected exposure to the nanophages in their finished form.

Three men sat at a conference table in one of the outer rooms. They were going over the operational and experimental data gathered so far from the 'events' in Zimbabwe and New Mexico. Two were nanotechnology specialists, among the most brilliant molecular scientists in the world. The third, much taller and broad-shouldered, had a very different set of skills. This man, the third of the *Horatii*, called himself Nones.

'Preliminary reports from Santa Fe indicate our Stage Two devices activated inside roughly twenty to thirty percent of those exposed,' the first scientist commented. His gloved fingers fluttered over a keypad, pulling up a graph on the plasma screen display before them. 'As you can see, that exceeds our initial projections. I think we can safely assume that our control-phage design modification is fundamentally sound.'

'True,' his colleague agreed. 'It's also clear that the Stage Two biochemical loads were far better balanced than those used at Kasusa – achieving a significantly higher rate of tissue and bone dissolution.'

'But can you increase the kill ratio?' the tall man named Nones asked harshly. 'You know our employer's requirements. They are absolute. A weapon which devours fewer than a third of its intended victims will not meet them.'

Behind their masks, the two scientists frowned in distaste at his inelegant choice of words. They preferred to think of themselves as surgeons engaged in an essential, though admittedly unpleasant, operation. Crude reminders that their work ultimately involved murder on a massive scale were neither necessary nor welcome.

'Well?' Nones demanded. His vivid green eyes glinted behind his acrylic safety glasses. He knew how much these men disliked focusing on the deadly results of their scientific efforts. It amused him from time to time to rub their ivory tower noses in the muck and the mud of their mission.

'We expect our design for the Stage Three phages and their controls to produce much higher efficiencies,' the senior molecular scientist assured him. 'The Stage Two sensor arrays were limited in number and type. By adding additional sensors configured for different biochemical signatures, we can greatly expand the number of potential targets.'

The green-eyed man nodded his understanding.

'We have also been able to boost the yield of each nanophage's internal power source,' the second scientist reported. 'We expect a matching increase in their effective life span and operational range.'

'What about the field contamination problem?' Nones asked. 'You've seen the safety precautions being taken outside the Teller Institute.'

'The Americans are being overcautious,' the first scientist said dismissively. 'By now, most of the Stage Two nanophages should have deteriorated beyond usefulness.'

'Their fears are not relevant,' the green-eyed man told him coldly. 'Our employer's demands are. You were asked to produce a reliable self-destruct mechanism for the Stage Three phages, were you not?'

The second scientist nodded hastily, hearing the implied threat in the bigger man's voice. 'Yes, of course. And we've succeeded.' He began clicking keys, flipping rapidly through different design sketches on the screen. 'Finding the necessary space inside the shell was a difficult problem, but in the end, we were able to – '

'Spare me the technical details,' the third member of the *Horatii* said drily. 'But you may transmit them to our employer if you wish. I concern myself solely with practical matters. If the weapons you are creating for us kill quickly, efficiently, and reliably, I don't feel any need to know exactly how they work.'

CHAPTER EIGHTEEN

Chicago, Illinois

Bright arc lights turned night into imitation day along much of the western edge of the University of Chicago's Hyde Park campus. They were set to illuminate the tan-and-gray stone facade of the newly built Interdivisional Research Building (IRB), a mammoth five-story structure containing 425,000 square feet of lab and research space. Construction trailers still blocked most of the sidewalks and green spaces along the south side of 57th Street and the east side of Drexel Boulevard. Lights were also on throughout the huge building, as electricians, carpenters, ironworkers, and others worked around-the-clock to finish the enormous project.

Scientists from the University of Chicago had played crucial roles in the major scientific and technological advances of the twentieth century – in everything from the development of carbon-14 dating to the advent of controlled nuclear power. Now the university was determined to maintain its competitive edge in the new sciences of the twenty-first century. The IRB was the cornerstone of that effort. When it was fully up and running, biological and physical scientists would share the building's state-of-the-art facilities. The hope was that working side by side would help them transcend the narrow and increasingly artificial boundaries between the two traditional disciplines.

Nearly $1 billion in corporate and individual donations had been raised to pay for construction, purchase the necessary high-tech materials, and guarantee funding for the first wave of new projects. One of the largest corporate grants came from Harcourt Biosciences, to pay for a cutting-edge nanotech complex. Now, in the wake of the destruction of its Teller Institute facility, the company's senior management saw the IRB lab as an urgently needed replacement – and a signal of its continued determination to pursue nanotechnology. Inside the lab suite, technicians and work crews were busy installing computers, scanning microscopes, remote manipulators, filter and air pressure systems, chemical storage, and other equipment.

Jack Rafferty came on-shift with a grin and a spring in his step. The short, skinny electrician had spent the commute from his suburban La Grange home adding up how much the overtime on this project was going to put in his pocket. He figured he could pay off the twins' parochial school tuition and still have enough left over to buy the Harley motorcycle he had been eyeing for more than a year.

The grin faded as soon as he walked inside the lab. Even from the door, he could see that someone had been screwing around with the wiring he had finished putting in just yesterday. Wall panels were left hanging open, exposing disarranged bundles of color-coded cables. Untidy coils and loops of insulated electrical wire dangled from jagged holes cut in the brand-new ceiling tiles.

Rafferty swore under his breath. He stormed over to the shift supervisor, a genial bear of a man named Koslov. 'Tommy, what exactly is all this junk? Did someone change the specs on us again?'

The supervisor checked his clipboard and shook his head. 'Not that I know of, Jack.'

Rafferty frowned. 'Then maybe you can tell me why Levy dinked around with my work – and left all this goddamned mess?'

Koslov shrugged. 'It wasn't Levy. Someone said he called in sick. A couple of new guys were filling in for him.' He looked around the room. 'I saw 'em both maybe fifteen minutes ago. I guess they knocked off early.'

The electrician rolled his eyes. 'Nice. Probably non-union goons. Or maybe they're just connected.' He hitched up his tool belt and settled the hard hat squarely on his narrow head. 'It's gonna take me half my shift just to clean this up, Tommy. So I don't want to hear any bitching about being off-schedule.'

'You won't hear any from me,' Koslov promised, conspicuously crossing his heart with one beefy paw.

Satisfied for the moment, Rafferty got to work, trying first to untangle the rat's nest of cabling Levy's substitutes had left behind the walls. He peered into one of the open panels, shining a flashlight into a narrow space filled with bundled wiring, pipes, and conduits of all sizes and types.

One strand of loose green wire caught his eye. What was that supposed to be? He tugged gently on it. There was a weight on the other end. Slowly, he reeled the wire in, maneuvering it through the maze, using his long, thin fingers to guide it past obstructions. One end of the wire came into view. It was plugged into a solid block of what looked like some sort of gray moldable compound.

Puzzled, Rafferty stared down at the block for several seconds, wondering what it could possibly be. Then it clicked in his mind. He turned pale. 'Jesus . . . that's plastic explosive – '

The six bombs planted in and around the lab complex exploded simultaneously. Searing white light ripped through the walls and ceiling. The first terrible shock wave tore Rafferty, Koslov, and the other workers inside the lab to shreds. A wall of flame and superheated air roared through the corridors of the half-finished building – incinerating everything and everyone in its path. The enormous force of the blast rippled outward, shattering steel-and-concrete structural supports, snapping them like matchsticks.

Slowly at first, and then with increasing speed, one whole side of the IRB shuddered, folded in on itself in a shrieking cacophony of wrenching, tearing steel, and then collapsed. Masses of broken stone and twisted metal cascaded down into the Science Quad. A thick, choking cloud of smoke, pulverized concrete, and dust billowed skyward, lit eerily from within by the surviving construction lights.

An hour later and ten blocks away, the three leaders of a Chicago-based Lazarus Movement action cell met hurriedly inside the top-floor apartment of a Hyde Park brownstone. Still visibly shaken, the two men and one woman – all in their mid-twenties – stood staring at a television in the living room, watching the frantic reports being broadcast live on every local and national news channel.

Sets of construction company coveralls, hard hats, tool kits, and fake ID cards they had laboriously assembled over four months of intensive planning were heaped on a table in the adjoining dining room behind them. A manila folder sat on top of the pile. It contained IRB floor plans downloaded from the University of Chicago Web site. Tightly capped jars of foul-smelling liquids, cans of spray paint, and folded Movement banners were packed in boxes on the hardwood floor next to the table.

'Who would do that?' Frida McFadden asked out loud in confusion. She chewed nervously on the ends of her straight mop of green-dyed hair. 'Who would blow up the IRB? It couldn't have been any of our own people. Our orders came straight from the top, from Lazarus himself.'

'I don't have any idea,' her boyfriend answered grimly. Bill Oakes was busy buttoning up the shirt he had thrown on when their phone first rang with the terrible news. He shook his long fair hair out of his eyes impatiently. 'But I do know one thing: We've got to dump all the stuff we were planning to use for our own mission. And soon. Before the cops come pounding on our doors.'

'No shit,' muttered their heavyset companion, the third member of their action cell. Rick Avery scratched at his beard. 'But where can we get rid of the gear safely? The lake?'

'It would be found there,' said a quiet mocking voice from behind them. 'Or you would be seen throwing your materials into the water.'

Startled, the three Lazarus Movement activists spun around. None of them had heard the locked front door open or close. They found themselves staring at a very tall and very powerfully built man gazing back at them from the central hall separating the living and dining rooms. He was wearing a heavy wool coat.

Oakes recovered first. He stepped forward, with his jaw thrust out belligerently. 'Who the hell are you?'

'You may call me Terce,' the green-eyed man said calmly. 'And I have something to give you – a gift.' His hand came smoothly out of the pocket of his coat. He pointed the silenced 9mm Walther pistol straight at them.

Frida McFadden cried out softly in fear. Avery stood frozen, with his fingers still tangled in his beard. Only Bill Oakes had the presence of mind to speak. 'If you're a cop,' he stammered, 'show us your warrant.'

The tall man smiled politely. 'Alas, I am not a policeman, Mr. Oakes.'

Oakes felt a shiver run through him in the last second before the Walther coughed. The bullet hit him in the forehead and killed him instantly. He fell back against the television.

The second member of the *Horatii* swung his pistol slightly to the left and fired again. Avery groaned once and went to his knees, clutching futilely at the blood pumping out of his torn throat. The big auburn-haired man squeezed the trigger a third time, putting this round squarely into the bearded young activist's head.

White-faced with horror, Frida McFadden turned and tried to run for the nearest bedroom. The tall man shot her in the back. She stumbled, fell awkwardly across a futon sofa, and lay moaning, writhing in pain. He shoved the pistol back in his coat pocket, stepped forward, cradled her head in two powerful arms – and then yanked hard, twisting sharply at the same time. Her neck snapped.

The green-eyed man named Terce surveyed the three bodies for several seconds, checking them for any signs of life. Satisfied, he went back to the front door and pulled it open. Two of his men were waiting out on the landing. Each carried a pair of heavy suitcases.

'It's done,' the big man told them. He stood back and let them past. Neither wasted any time looking at the corpses. Anyone who worked closely with one of the *Horatii* soon grew used to the sight of death.

Working fast, they began unpacking, setting out blocks of plastic explosives, detonators, and timers on the dining room table. One of them, a short, stocky man with Slavic features, indicated the clothing, maps, chemicals, and paint stacked on the table or packed in boxes on the hardwood floor. 'What about these things, Terce?'

'Pack them up,' ordered the green-eyed man. 'But leave the coveralls, helmets, and their false identity cards. Dump those in with the bomb-making materials you're leaving.'

The Slav shrugged. 'The ruse will not fool the police for very long, you realize. When the American authorities run tests, they will not find chemical residues on any of those you killed.'

The tall man nodded. 'I know.' He smiled coldly. 'But then again, time is on our side – not on theirs.'

The lights in the bar at O'Hare International Airport were turned down very low, in sharp contrast to the blinding fluorescent strips in the corridors and departure lounges just outside. Even this late at night, it was fairly crowded – as jet-lagged and sleep-deprived travelers sought solace in peace, relative quiet, and large doses of alcohol.

Hal Burke sat moodily at a corner table, sipping at the rum-and-Coke he had ordered half an hour before. His flight for Dulles was set to begin boarding soon. He looked up when Terce slid into the chair across from him. 'Well?'

The bigger man showed his teeth, plainly quite pleased with himself. 'There were no problems,' he said. 'Our information was accurate in every detail. The Chicago Lazarus cell is now leaderless.'

Burke smiled sourly. Their creator's high-level sources inside the Movement had been one of his chief motivations for bringing the eerie, almost inhuman, *Horatii* into TOCSIN. Though it galled Burke to admit it, those sources were better than any network he had ever been able to develop.

'The Chicago police will see what they expect to see,' Terce went on. 'Plastic explosives. Detonators. And false identity papers.'

'Plus three dead bodies,' the CIA officer pointed out. 'The cops might wonder a bit about that little detail.'

The other man lifted his shoulders in a quick, dismissive shrug. 'Terrorist movements often cannibalize themselves,' he said. 'The police may believe the dead were perceived as weak links by their comrades. Or they may suspect that there was a falling-out among different factions within the Movement.'

Burke nodded. Once again, the big auburn-haired man was right. 'Hell, it happens,' he agreed. 'You put a bunch of radical nutcases with weapons in the same tight space under serious pressure . . . Well, if some of them snap and go ape-shit on the others, I guess that's not exactly news.'

He took another sip of his drink. 'Anyway, at least it will look like the IRB bomb attack was in the works for months,' he muttered. 'That should help persuade Castilla that the Teller Massacre was a Lazarus put-up job, from start to finish. That it was a go code for these bastards – a way to radicalize their base of support and tie us down politically at the same time. With luck, the president will finally designate the whole Movement as a terrorist organization.'

The second of the *Horatii* smiled dubiously. 'Perhaps.'

Burke gritted his teeth. The old scar on the side of his neck turned white as his face tightened. 'We have another, more immediate problem,' he said. 'Out in Santa Fe.'

'A problem?' Terce asked.

'Lieutenant Colonel Jonathan Smith, M.D.,' the CIA officer told him. 'He's rattling cages and asking some very inconvenient questions.'

'We still have a security element in New Mexico,' Terce said carefully.

'Good,' Burke downed the last of his rum-and-Coke. He stood up. 'Let me know when they're ready to move. And make it soon. I want Smith dead before anyone higher up the chain of command starts paying attention to him.'

CHAPTER NINETEEN

Friday, October 15
Santa Fe

The early-morning sun was slanting through the windows of his hotel suite when Jon Smith's cell phone buzzed. He set his coffee cup down on the kitchen counter. 'Yes?'

'Check the news,' Fred Klein suggested.

Smith pushed the plate with his half-eaten breakfast Danish on it out of the way, spun his laptop around, and tapped into the Internet. He read through the headlines scrolling across the screen in growing disbelief. The story was the lead on every major news organization's Web site. FBI MASSACRE PROBE NAILS LAZARUS! blared one. LAZARUS ACTIVIST BOUGHT GETAWAY SUVS! shouted another.

Every article was pretty much the same. Top-level sources within the FBI investigation of the Teller Massacre confirmed that a longtime Lazarus Movement activist from Albuquerque had purchased the vehicles used by the phony Secret Service agents – using roughly one hundred thousand dollars in cash. Then, only a few hours after the Institute was attacked, Andrew Costanzo was seen by his neighbors driving away from his home with a suitcase in the back of his car. File pictures of Costanzo and his description were being circulated to every federal, state, and local law-enforcement agency.

'Interesting, isn't it?' the head of Covert-One said in Smith's ear.

'That's one word for it,' Smith told him wryly. 'At least yours is printable.'

'I assume then this is the first you've heard about this remarkable break in the case?' Klein murmured.

'You assume correctly,' Smith said, frowning. He thought back to the FBI briefings he had attended. Neither Pierson nor her closest aides had mentioned anything so potentially incendiary. 'Is this a real leak or some reporter's fantasy?'

'It appears to be genuine,' Klein told him. 'The Bureau isn't even bothering to deny the story.'

'Any word on the source? Was it someone out here in Santa Fe? Or back in D.C.?' Smith asked.

'No idea,' the head of Covert-One said. He hesitated briefly. 'I will say that no one here in Washington seems especially sorry to see this development go public.'

'I'll bet.' Judging by Kit Pierson's eagerness to ignore his disquieting questions yesterday, Smith knew how pleased the FBI must be to come up with hard evidence that linked the destruction of the Teller Institute to the Lazarus Movement. That would be even truer after the overnight terrorist attacks in California and Chicago. Finding out about this guy Costanzo must have seemed like manna raining down from heaven.

'What do you think, Colonel?' Klein asked.

'I don't buy it,' Smith said, shaking his head. 'At least, not completely. It's just too darned convenient. Besides, nothing in this Costanzo story explains how the Movement could get its hands on nanophages designed to kill – or why it would deliberately release them, especially on its own supporters.'

'No, it doesn't,' Klein agreed.

Smith fell silent for a moment, reading through one of the most recent articles. This piece paid more attention to what the Lazarus Movement representative, a woman named Heather Donovan, had to say about Andrew Costanzo. Smith considered her claims carefully. If even half of what she said was true, the FBI could be haring off down a false trail, one deliberately laid as a distraction. He nodded to himself. It was worth checking out.

'I'm going to try talking to this Movement spokes-woman,' he told Klein. 'But I'll need a temporary cover of some kind, probably as a journalist. With some fake ID that'll stand up to scrutiny. No one from the Lazarus organization is going to talk freely to an Army officer or a scientist.'

'When will you need it by?' Klein asked.

Smith thought about that. His day was already booked solid. Late last night, some members of the FBI investigative team had finally risked working without their heavy protective gear. They were still alive. As a result, medical teams from the local hospitals and Nomura PharmaTech were beginning to retrieve bodies and parts of bodies from the site. He wanted to sit in on some of the pathology work they were planning – hoping he might learn the answers to some of the questions that still troubled him.

'Sometime this evening,' he decided. 'I'll try to arrange a meeting at a downtown restaurant or bar. The panic's mostly over out here now and folks are coming back to town.'

'Tell this Ms. Donovan that you're a freelance journalist,' Klein suggested. 'An American stringer for *Le Monde* and a few other smaller European papers, most of them shading to the left.'

'Sounds good,' Smith said. He knew Paris very well, and *Le Monde* and its European counterparts were generally viewed as being sympathetic to the environmental, anti-technology, and anti-globalization line pushed by the Lazarus Movement.

'I'll have a courier deliver a package with a *Le Monde* press card in your name to the hotel by this afternoon,' Klein promised.

FBI Deputy Assistant Director Kit Pierson sat at the folding table that served as her desk, paging through the 'eyes-only' CIA file faxed to her by Hal Burke. Langley had only a little more information on this Jonathan Smith than did the Bureau. But there were occasional and cryptic references to him in mission reports or cables from the Agency's case officers – usually in connection with some developing crisis or existing hot spot.

Her eyes narrowed as she ran through the long and worrying list. Moscow. Paris. Shanghai. And now here he was in Santa Fe. Oh, there was always some plausible excuse for Smith's sudden appearance on the scene, whether it was checking up on an injured friend, attending a routine medical conference, or simply doing the work he was trained for. On the surface, he was just what he claimed to be – a military scientist and doctor who occasionally wound up in the wrong place at the wrong time.

Pierson shook her head. There were entirely too many 'coincidental' meetings, too many plausible excuses, for her to swallow. What she saw was a pattern, and it was a pattern she did not like at all. Although USAMRIID cut Smith's paycheck, he seemed to have extraordinary latitude in his duty assignments and in his ability to take personal leaves of absence. She was sure now that he was a clandestine operator, one who worked at a very high level. But what worried her most was that she still could not pin down his real employer. Every serious inquiry about him through official channels vanished into a bureaucratic never-never land. It was as though someone very high up somewhere had stamped a big NO TRESPASSING sign across the full life and career of Lieutenant Colonel Jonathan Smith, M.D.

And that made her nervous – very nervous. That was why she had a two-man team keeping a close eye on him. The minute the good doctor stepped across the lines she had laid out, she planned to run him right out of the investigation, tarred, feathered, and on a rail if necessary.

She slid the CIA file into a portable shredder and watched the tiny crosscut strips of paper rain down into a wastebasket marked *Burn Material*. The secure phone on her desk beeped before they stopped falling.

'This is Burke,' a voice on the other end growled. 'Are your people still tailing Smith?'

'They are,' Pierson confirmed. 'He's out at St. Vincent's Hospital, working in their pathology lab.'

'Call them off,' Burke said flatly.

She sat bolt upright in her chair, surprised by the request. 'What?'

'You heard me,' her CIA counterpart said. 'Pull your agents off Smith's back. Right now.'

'Why?'

'Trust me on this, Kit,' Burke told her coldly. 'You do *not* want to know.'

When the phone went dead, Pierson sat in frozen silence, wondering again whether there was any way she could escape the trap she felt closing around her.

Jon Smith came through the swinging doors into the small locker room next to the hospital's pathology lab. It was deserted. Yawning, he sat down on a bench and peeled off his gloves and mask. He tossed them into a receptacle already full to the brim. His set of green surgical scrubs came off next. He had almost finished donning his street clothes when Fred Klein called.

'Is your interview with Ms. Donovan set?' the head of Covert-One asked.

'Yes,' Smith said. He leaned over, putting on his shoes. 'I'm meeting her at nine tonight. At a little café in the Plaza Mercado.'

'Good,' Klein said. 'Now, how are the autopsies going? Any new developments?'

'A few,' Smith told him. 'But I'm damned if I know yet what they mean.' He sighed. 'Understand that we have very few intact body parts to study. Almost all that's left of most of the dead is a weird sort of organic soup.'

'Go on.'

'Well, there are some odd patterns emerging from the autopsies we've been able to conduct,' Smith reported. 'It's too soon and the sample sizes are too small to say anything definite, but I suspect the trends we're seeing will hold up over the long haul.'

'Such as?' Klein prompted.

'Significant indications of systemic drug use or serious chronic illness among those who were killed,' Smith said, standing up from the bench and grabbing his windbreaker. 'Not in all cases. But in a very large percentage – far higher than the statistical norm.'

'Do you know yet what killed those people?'

'Precisely? No.'

'Give me your best guess, Colonel,' Klein prodded gently.

'A guess is all I've got,' said Smith wearily. 'But I'd say that most of the damage was done by chemicals distributed by these nanophages to break up peptide bonds. Do that enough times to enough different peptides and you wind up with the kind of organic goo we're finding.'

'But these devices don't kill everybody they infest,' Klein commented. 'Why not?'

'My bet is that the nanophages are triggered by different biochemical signals –'

'Like those you'd find in someone who uses drugs. Or who suffers from heart disease. Or perhaps some other illness or chronic condition,' Klein realized suddenly. 'Without those signals, these devices would lie dormant.'

'Bingo.'

'That doesn't explain why that big green-eyed fellow you were fighting suddenly succumbed,' the other man pointed out. 'Both of you ran through the cloud of these nanophages without at first being affected.'

'The guy was tagged, Fred,' Smith said grimly. He closed his eyes, willing away the terrible memories of his enemy dissolving in front of him. 'I'm pretty sure that somebody hit him with a needle tipped with a substance that triggered the nanophages he'd breathed in earlier.'

'Which means his own side betrayed him to prevent his possible capture,' Klein said.

'That's the way I see it,' Smith agreed. He grimaced, suddenly remembering the sound of that cold, deadly hiss right past his ear. 'And I guess they tried to hit me with one of those same damned needles, too.'

'Watch your step, Jon,' Klein said abruptly. 'We still don't know precisely who the enemy here is, and we certainly don't understand their plans yet. Until we do, you should consider anyone, including Ms. Donovan, a potential threat.'

Surveillance Team Safe House, on the Outskirts of Santa Fe

Two miles east of the Teller Institute, all was quiet inside the house occupied by the covert surveillance team. Computers softly hummed and clicked and whirred, gathering data from the various sensors focused on the zone around the Institute. The two men assigned to this shift sat silently monitoring radio transmissions while simultaneously keeping an eye on the information streaming in.

One of them listened intently to the voices in his radio headset. He turned toward his team leader, an older white-haired Dutchman named Willem Linden. 'The action team is reporting. Smith has just entered the Plaza Mercado.'

'Alone?'

The younger man nodded.

Linden smiled broadly, showing a mouthful of tobacco-stained teeth. 'That is excellent news, Abrantes. Signal the team to stand by. Then contact the Center and inform them that everything is going according to plan. Tell them we will report the moment Smith is eliminated.'

Abrantes looked worried. 'Are you sure it will be that simple? I've read this American's file. He could be very dangerous.'

'Don't panic, Vitor,' the white-haired man said soothingly. 'If you put a bullet or a knife blade in the right place, any man will die.'

CHAPTER TWENTY

Smith paused in the doorway of the Longevity Café, briefly surveying the patrons clustered at several of its small round tables. They seemed a somewhat eclectic bunch, he thought with hidden amusement. Most of them, usually those seated as couples, looked ordinary enough – a mix of nicely dressed, health-conscious professionals and earnest college kids. Others sported an eye-catching variety of tattoos and body piercings. A few wore turbans or long blond dreadlocks. Several customers turned toward the door, plainly curious about him as well. The vast majority carried on with their own intense conversations.

The café itself occupied much of the Plaza Mercado's second floor, with large windows looking down onto West San Francisco Street. Walls painted in striking bright reds, burnt orange, and yellows and floors in vivid blue and bleached wood were matched by unusual pieces of artwork – many based on Asian, Hindu, or Zen themes.

Smith headed straight for the table occupied by a woman sitting alone, one of those who had turned to study him. That was Heather Donovan. Fred Klein had included her photo and a brief bio in the packet with Smith's forged credential from *Le Monde*. The local spokesperson for the Lazarus Movement was in her mid-thirties, with a slender, boyish figure, an unruly mop of strawberry blond curls, sea green eyes, and a light dusting of freckles across the bridge of her nose.

She watched him walk toward her with a bemused expression on her face. 'Can I help you?' she asked.

'My name is Jon Smith,' he said quietly, politely doffing his black Stetson. 'I believe you're here waiting for me, Ms. Donovan.'

One finely sculpted reddish gold eyebrow went up. 'I expected a journalist, not a cowboy,' she murmured in perfect French.

Smith grinned and looked down at his tan corduroy jacket, bolo string tie, jeans, and boots. 'I try to adapt myself to local customs,' he replied, in the same language. 'After all, when in Rome . . .'

She smiled and switched to English. 'Please sit down, Mr. Smith.'

He set his hat down on the table, pulled a small notepad and a pen out of his jeans, and took the chair opposite hers. 'I appreciate your meeting me like this, so late, I mean. I know you've already had a long day.'

The Lazarus Movement spokeswoman nodded slowly. 'It *has* been a long day. Several long days, in fact. But before we start this interview, I would like to see some identification – just as a formality, of course.'

'Of course,' Smith said evenly. He handed her the forged press card, watching closely as she held it up to the light. 'Are you always so careful around journalists, Ms. Donovan?'

'Not always,' she told him. She shrugged. 'But I'm learning to be a bit less trusting these days. Seeing several thousand people murdered by your own government will do that.'

'That's understandable,' Smith said calmly. According to her Covert-One dossier, Heather Donovan was a relatively recent recruit to the Lazarus Movement. Before joining up with Lazarus, she had worked the state capital lobbying circuit for the more mainstream environmental groups, the Sierra Club and the World Wildlife Federation among them. She was rated as tough, smart, and politically savvy.

'Okay, you seem on the level,' she said finally, sliding his press card back.

'What can I get you folks?' a languid voice interrupted. One of the waiters, a willowy young man with pierced eyebrows, had drifted over to their table and now stood patiently hovering over them.

'A cup of gunpowder green tea,' the Lazarus Movement spokeswoman told him.

'And a glass of red wine for me,' Smith said. He saw the pitying look in her eyes. 'No wine? Then how about a beer?'

She shook her head apologetically, a gesture repeated by the waiter. 'Sorry, they don't serve alcohol here,' she said. Her lips twitched upward in the hint of another smile. 'Maybe you should try one of the Longevity's elixirs.'

'Elixirs?' he asked dubiously.

'They're a blend of traditional Chinese herbal recipes and natural fruit juices,' the waiter said, showing some enthusiasm for the first time. 'I recommend the Virtual Buddha. It's quite stimulating.'

Smith shook his head. 'Maybe some other time.' He shrugged. 'Then I'll have the same as Ms. Donovan – just a cup of green tea.'

When the waiter sidled off to get their drinks, Smith turned back to the Lazarus Movement spokeswoman. He held up his small notebook. 'So, now that we've established my status as a bona fide reporter – '

'You can ask your questions,' Heather Donovan finished for him. She eyed him carefully. 'Which I understand revolve around the FBI's grotesque suggestion that the Movement is somehow responsible for destroying the Teller Institute, and for killing so many innocent people.'

Smith nodded. 'That's right. I read the other papers this morning, and what you said about this Andrew Costanzo intrigued me. From the sound of it, I have to admit the guy doesn't strike me as someone I'd pick as a secret conspirator.'

'He isn't.'

'That's pretty definite,' he said. 'Care to elaborate?'

'Andy is a talker, not a doer,' she told him. 'Oh, he never misses a Movement meeting, and he always has plenty to say, or at least to complain about. The thing is, I've never seen him actually *do* anything! He'll filibuster for hours, but show him envelopes that need to be stuffed or flyers that need to be distributed and suddenly he's too busy or too sick. He thinks he's the original philosopher-king, the man whose visions lie beyond the reach of mere mortals like the rest of us.'

'I know the type,' Smith said with a quick grin. 'The unappreciated Plato of the bookstore stockroom.'

'That's Andy Costanzo all over,' Heather agreed. 'Which is why the FBI claim is so absurd. We all tolerated him, but nobody in the Movement would ever trust Andy with anything serious – let alone with more than a hundred thousand dollars in cash!'

'Somebody did,' he pointed out. 'The identifications by those Albuquerque car dealers are airtight.'

'I know that!' She sounded frustrated. 'I believe that someone gave Andy the money to buy those SUVs. And I even believe he was stupid enough, or arrogant enough, to actually go ahead and do what they asked. But the money could not possibly have come from the Movement! We're not exactly poor, but we're certainly not rolling in that kind of cash!'

'So you think Costanzo was set up?'

'I'm sure of it,' she said firmly. 'As a means of smearing Lazarus and all we stand for. The Movement is completely committed to nonviolent protest. We would never condone murder or terrorism!'

Smith was tempted to point out that smashing up lab equipment automatically crossed the line into violence, but he kept his mouth shut. He was here to learn the answers to certain questions, not to spark a political debate. Besides, he now felt sure this woman was telling the truth – at least about those elements of the Lazarus Movement with which she was familiar. On the other hand, she was only a mid-level activist, the equivalent of an Army captain or a major. How much could she really know about any secret moves made by the higher levels of her organization?

The arrival of their tea gave her time to regain her composure.

She took a cautious sip and then eyed him warily over the rim of her steaming cup. 'You're wondering whether or not the money might have come from somewhere higher up inside the Movement, aren't you?'

Smith nodded. 'No offense, Ms. Donovan. But you folks have drawn a remarkably tight veil of secrecy around the top leadership of the Lazarus Movement. It's only natural to wonder what's hidden behind it.'

'This veil of secrecy, as you call it, is purely a defensive measure, Mr. Smith,' she said levelly. 'You know what happened to our original founders. They lived open, public lives. And then, one by one, they were killed or kidnapped. Either by corporations they had angered or by governments doing the bidding of those corporations. Well, the Movement will not allow itself to be so easily beheaded again!'

Smith decided to let her wilder claims pass without comment. She was starting to recite preset talking points.

To his surprise, she smiled suddenly, a smile that lit up her vivid green eyes. 'Okay, I admit that's partly rhetoric. Heartfelt rhetoric, to be sure, but I agree it's not the most persuasive argument I've ever made.' She took another sip of her tea and then set the cup down on the table between them. 'I'll try logic instead: Let's say I'm totally wrong. That I'm a dupe, and that there are people in the Movement who've decided to use clandestine violence to achieve our goals. Well, think about that. If *you* were running a top-secret operation whose disclosure could destroy everything you've ever worked for . . . would you use someone like Andy Costanzo as your agent?'

'No, I wouldn't,' Smith agreed. 'Not unless I wanted to get caught.'

And that was what had bothered him from the beginning, from the first moment he read those leaked stories from the FBI. Now, after hearing her, he was even more convinced that the whole SUV angle stank to high heaven. Relying on an overeducated goofball like Costanzo to buy the getaway vehicles for a terrorist attack was asking for big trouble. It was the kind of boneheaded mistake that just did not jibe with the ruthless, calculating professionalism he had witnessed during the attack on the Institute. Which meant that somebody was manipulating this investigation.

One block west of the Plaza Mercado, Malachi MacNamara waited patiently, concealed in the shadows of a covered sidewalk. It was growing late, and the streets of downtown Santa Fe were nearly deserted.

The lean, weather-beaten man carefully raised his Kite handheld night-vision scope and peered through it with one pale blue eye. Rather a useful gadget, he thought. The British-made monocular was sturdy, very lightweight, and produced a crisp, clear image magnified by four times. He painstakingly scanned the surrounding area, checking the movements of his chosen quarry yet again.

He focused first on the man standing motionless in the recessed doorway of an art gallery about fifty yards away. The shaven-headed fellow wore jeans, heavy work boots, and a surplus U.S. Army field jacket. Whenever a car drove by, his eyes narrowed to preserve his night vision. Otherwise, he stayed put despite the growing cold. A young tough, MacNamara thought critically, but very fit and reasonably well disciplined.

Three more watchers were posted at different points along the street, for a total of four. Two of them were stationed to the west of the Plaza Mercado. Two lurked to the east. All of them were positioned in good cover, well out of sight to anyone but a trained observer with light-intensifier gear.

They were part of the group MacNamara had been hunting since the catastrophe outside the Teller Institute. He had lost them in the immediate aftermath of the nanomachine slaughter, but they had reappeared as soon as the Lazarus Movement regrouped and set up camp outside the National Guard cordon. Earlier tonight, not long after sunset, these four had moved north on foot, making their way deeper into old Santa Fe's narrow streets.

He had followed them at a safe distance. The short trek had taught him much about his quarry. These men were not mere street thugs or anarchist ruffians lured by the Movement rally, as he had first thought. Their movements were too precise, too well planned, and too well executed. They had slipped right past the FBI and police surveillance around the Lazarus camp. And more than once he had been forced to hurriedly go to ground to avoid being spotted by one of their number hanging back as a rear guard.

Trailing them had been like stalking big game – or tracking a patrol of elite enemy commandos scouting unknown territory. In some ways, MacNamara found the challenge exhilarating. It was a high-stakes game of wits and skill that he had played many times before, in many different parts of the world. At the same time, he was conscious now of an underlying sense of fatigue, a slight dulling of his perceptions and reflexes. Perhaps the strains of the past several months had taken a higher toll on his nerves and endurance than he had first reckoned.

The shaven-headed man he was observing suddenly straightened up, going fully alert. The man whispered a few words into a tiny radio mike fixed to his collar, listened carefully to the reply, and then leaned forward to peer cautiously around the edge of the doorway.

MacNamara rapidly shifted his view to the other watchers, noticing the same unmistakable signs of increased readiness. He shifted his own stance and breathed out gently, tamping down the first surge of adrenaline as his body prepared itself for action. The vague feeling of weariness fell away. Ah, he thought, here we go. The prolonged period of waiting motionless in the cold and dark was almost over.

Still peering through the night-vision scope, he panned across the front of the Plaza Mercado. A man and a woman had just come out of the building. They were standing together on the sidewalk out front, carrying on an animated conversation. He recognized the slender, attractive woman straightaway. He had seen her bustling around the Lazarus camp. Her name was Heather Donovan. She was the local activist who handled press inquiries for the Movement.

But who was the dark-haired man she was talking to? The clothing, boots, and cowboy hat all suggested he was a local, but somehow MacNamara doubted that was really the case. Something about the way the tall, broad-shouldered man moved and held himself was oddly familiar.

The dark-haired man swung around, pointing toward the concrete parking garage off down the street to the west. For that brief instant, his face was plainly visible. Then he turned away again.

Malachi MacNamara slowly lowered his night-vision scope. His pale blue eyes were both amused and surprised. 'Bloody hell,' he muttered under his breath. 'The good colonel certainly has a talent for popping up wherever and whenever one least expects him.'

CHAPTER TWENTY-ONE

Brick paths curved through Santa Fe's central Plaza, circling the various monuments and winding under a spreading canopy of trees – towering American elms and cottonwoods, firs, maples, honey locusts, and others. Wrought-iron park benches painted white were set out at intervals along the walkways. A thin scattering of fallen leaves lay on patches of grass and hard-packed earth.

Surrounded by a low iron railing, an obelisk commemorating the Civil War battles in New Mexico stood in the very center of the square. Few people remembered that the bloody war between the North and South had spread this far to the west. In some spots, thin rays of light filtered through the trees, cast by the street lamps surrounding the Plaza, but otherwise this centuries-old expanse was a place of darkness and dignified silence.

Jon Smith glanced at the slender, pretty woman walking beside him. Shivering, Heather Donovan hugged her black cloth coat tightly around herself. Whenever they crossed the broken streaks of pale light between the shadows he saw her breath steaming in the chilly night air. With the sun long gone, the temperature was dropping fast. It was not uncommon for Santa Fe's daytime highs and nighttime lows to vary by as much as thirty or forty degrees.

After they finished their tea at the Longevity Café, he had volunteered to escort her to her car, which was parked on a side street not far from the Palace of the Governors. Though plainly surprised by this old-fashioned act of chivalry, she had also accepted his offer with evident relief. Santa Fe was ordinarily a very safe city, she had explained, but she was still feeling a little jittery after seeing the horrors outside the Teller Institute.

They were just a few yards away from the Civil War obelisk when Smith stopped abruptly. Something was wrong, he thought. His senses were sending him a warning signal. And now that they had stopped walking, he heard others – two or three men, he judged – moving quietly up the path at their backs. He could just make out the faint crunch of heavy boots on the brick pavement. In the same moment, he noticed two more vague shapes slipping through the shadows under the trees ahead, drawing steadily nearer.

The Lazarus Movement spokeswoman noticed the figures closing on them in that same instant. 'Who are those men?' she asked, clearly startled.

For a split second Smith stood still, hesitating. Were these guys FBI agents sent by Kit Pierson? He had been sure that he was under surveillance earlier that afternoon. But when he had checked for tags before heading to the Longevity Café he had come up empty-handed. Had he missed them earlier?

Just then one of the men moving in from the front strayed into a small pool of light. He had a shaved head and wore an Army fatigue jacket. Smith's eyes narrowed at the sight of the silenced pistol the man held out and ready. So much for the FBI, he thought coldly.

They were being surrounded – boxed in on the open ground in the middle of the Plaza. His instincts kicked into gear. They had to break out of this trap before it was too late.

Reacting quickly, Smith grabbed Heather Donovan's arm and tugged her with him to the right, around the curve of the obelisk. At the same time, he drew his own pistol from the shoulder holster concealed by his corduroy jacket. 'This way!' he muttered. 'Come on!'

'What are you doing?' she protested loudly, too shocked by his sudden action to pull away. 'Let go of me!'

'If you want to live, come with me!' Smith snapped, still drawing her away from the open space around the Civil War monument and toward the darkness under the surrounding trees.

One of the two men who had been coming up behind them stopped, aimed quickly, and opened fire. *Phut*. The silencer on his pistol reduced the sound of the shot to that of a muffled cough. The bullet tore past Smith's head and smacked into the trunk of a tall cottonwood tree not far away. *Phut*. Another round shattered a low-hanging branch. Splinters and falling leaves rained down on them.

He pushed the Movement spokeswoman to the ground. 'Stay down!'

Smith dropped to one knee, swung his SIG-Sauer pistol toward the shooter, and squeezed the trigger. The weapon barked once, a loud crack that echoed back from the buildings surrounding the Plaza.

His shot, fired hurriedly and on the move, missed. But the sound of gunfire drove three of the four attackers he could see to the ground. They went prone and began shooting back at him, firing rapidly.

Heather Donovan screamed piercingly, pressing herself flat against the hard, unyielding earth.

Pistol rounds whined close by, either thudding into the trees on either side or spanging off a nearby park bench in showers of sparks, torn bits of metal, and pulverized white paint. Smith ignored the near misses, concentrating instead on the one gunman who was still moving.

It was the shaven-headed man he had first spotted. Hunched over in a crouch, the gunman was sidling off to the right, trying to make it back into the shelter of the trees and then come up on his flank.

Jon squeezed off three shots in rapid succession.

The bald man stumbled. His silenced pistol tumbled to the ground. Slowly he fell forward onto his hands and knees. Blood poured out of his mouth. Black in the dim light, it spilled across the brick pavement in a widening pool.

More bullets ripped past Smith as the wounded man's comrades kept shooting. One round punched through the broad felt brim of his brand-new Stetson and tore it right off his head. The hat sailed off into the shadows. They were getting way too close, he thought grimly – starting to zero in on him.

He threw himself prone and fired three more shots with his SIG-Sauer, trying to keep their heads down or at least shake their aim. Then he rolled quickly over to where Heather Donovan lay with her face pressed to the earth. She had stopped screaming, but he could see her shoulders shaking as terrified sobs wracked her whole body.

The three unhurt gunmen had spotted his movement. They were shooting lower now, taking the time to aim. Nine-millimeter pistol rounds tore at the earth all around Jon and the Movement spokeswoman. Others, slightly wider off the mark, sent shattered bits of brick flying.

Smith grimaced. They needed to get out of here, and fast. He put his hand gently on the back of the frightened woman's head. She quivered but stayed down. 'We've got to keep moving,' he said urgently. 'Come on! Crawl, damn it! Head for that big cottonwood tree over there. It's only a few yards away.'

She turned her head toward him. Her eyes were wide in the darkness. He wasn't sure she had even heard him.

'Let's go!' he told her again, louder this time. 'If you stay low, you can make it.'

She shook her head desperately, smudging her cheek against the ground. She was frozen, he realized, paralyzed with fear.

Smith grimaced. If he left her and scrambled into cover behind that tree, she was dead. If he stayed with her out here in the open, they were probably both dead. The smart move was to leave her. But if he ran for it, he doubted the gunmen would leave her alone. They did not seem like the kind who believed in letting potential witnesses live. There were limits to what he could stomach – and abandoning this woman to save his own skin would blow right through them.

Instead, he raised his pistol and began firing back at the barely visible gunmen. The SIG-Sauer's slide locked open. Thirteen rounds expended. He hit the release catch, dumped the empty magazine out, and slapped in his second and last clip.

Smith saw that two of the gunmen were in motion, edging rapidly to the left and right while staying low. They were trying to outflank him. Once they were in position, they could nail him with a murderous crossfire. The trees here were too widely spaced to provide cover from all angles. Meanwhile, the third man was still shooting steadily to keep Jon's head down – covering the pincers movement by his teammates.

Smith swore silently. He had waited too long. Now he was pinned down.

Well then, he would just have to fight it out here and see how many of the enemy he could take with him. Another bullet slammed into the ground within inches of his head. Jon spat out bits of torn grass and dirt and took aim, trying to draw a bead on the attacker swinging around his right flank.

More shots suddenly rang out, echoing across the Plaza. The gunman moving to his right screamed in agony. He went down, moaning loudly and clutching at his mangled shoulder. His comrades stared at him in shock for a moment and then whirled around – frantically looking toward the shadowy mass of trees along the square's southern edge.

Smith's eyes opened wide in astonishment. He had not fired those shots. And the bad guys were using silenced weapons. So who else had just joined this fight?

The new gunfire continued, hammering the ground

and trees around the two unwounded gunmen. This unexpected counterattack must have been too much for them. They fell back rapidly, retreating north toward the street fronting the Palace of the Governors. One of them dragged the wounded man to his feet and helped him hobble away. The other made a sudden dash toward the man Jon had hit, but more bullets lashed the pavement at his feet – driving him back into the concealing shadows.

Smith saw movement at the edge of the trees to his right. A lean gray-haired man came out into the open, advancing steadily while firing the pistol he held in a two-handed shooting grip. He slipped into the cover provided by the Civil War obelisk and reloaded his weapon, a 9mm Browning Hi-Power.

Silence again fell across the Plaza.

The newcomer looked across toward Smith. He shrugged apologetically. 'Very sorry about the delay, Jon,' he called softly. 'It took longer to work my way around behind those fellows than I anticipated.'

It was Peter Howell. Smith stared in utter amazement at his old friend. The former British Special Air Service officer and MI6 agent wore a heavy sheepskin coat over a faded red-and-green flannel shirt and a pair of denims. His thick gray hair, normally cropped short, was now a long, curling mane that framed a pair of pale blue eyes and a deeply lined face weathered by years of exposure to the wind, sun, and other elements.

Both men heard the sound of a car suddenly racing along the north edge of the square. Brakes squealed as it stopped briefly and then roared off into the night – heading east along Palace Avenue toward the ring road of the Paseo de Peralta.

'Damnation!' Peter growled. 'I should have realized those lads would have backup and a quick way out if things went pear-shaped for them. As they have.' He hefted his Browning. 'Keep watch here, Jon, while I conduct a quick recce.'

Before Smith could say anything, the older man loped forward and vanished into the shadows.

The Lazarus Movement spokeswoman raised her head warily. Tears ran down her face, trickling through the dirt streaking her pale skin. 'Is it over?' she whispered.

Smith nodded. 'I certainly hope so,' he told her, still scanning the darkness around them – making sure no one else was out there.

Slowly, shakily, the slender woman sat up. She stared at Jon and at the pistol in his hand. 'You aren't really a reporter, are you?'

'No,' he said softly. 'I'm afraid not.'

'Then who – '

Peter Howell's return cut short her question. 'They've done a bunk,' he said irritably. His gaze fell on the shaven-headed man Smith had shot. He nodded in satisfaction. 'But at least they had to leave this one behind.'

He knelt down and rolled the body over. Then he shook his head. 'Poor fellow's deader than Judas Iscariot,' Peter announced coolly. 'You hit him twice. Fairly good marksmanship for a simple country doctor, I'd say.'

He rummaged through the dead man's pockets, looking for a wallet or papers that might help identify him.

'Anything?' Smith asked.

Peter shook his head. 'Not so much as a matchbook.' He looked up at the American. 'Whoever hired this poor sod made sure he was clean before sending him off to kill you.'

Jon nodded. The would-be assassin had been stripped of anything that could link him to those who had issued his orders. 'That's too bad,' he said, frowning.

'It is a pity when the opposition thinks ahead,' Peter agreed. 'But all is not yet lost.'

The former SAS officer pulled a small camera out of one of his coat pockets and snapped several close-up photos of the dead man's face. He was using super-high-speed film, so there was no flash. Then he tucked the camera

181

away and tugged out another small gadget – this one about the size of a paperback book. It had a flat clear screen and several control buttons on the side. He noticed Smith staring at it in fascination.

'It's a digital fingerprint scanner,' Peter explained. 'Does the trick with nice clean electrons, instead of all that messy old ink.' His teeth gleamed white in the darkness. 'Whatever will the boffins dream up next, eh?'

Working quickly, he pressed the dead man's hands to the surface of the scanner, first the right and then the left. It flashed, hummed, and whirred – storing the images of all ten fingerprints in its memory card.

'Collecting mementos for your old age, are you?' Smith asked pointedly, knowing full well that his friend must be working for London again. Ostensibly retired, Peter was periodically pressed back into service, usually by MI6, the British secret intelligence service. He was a maverick who preferred working alone, a throwback to the eccentric, sometimes piratical, English adventurers who had long ago helped build an empire.

Peter only smiled.

'I don't mean to rush you,' Smith said. 'But shouldn't we be making tracks ourselves? Unless you really want to try explaining all this to the Santa Fe police, that is.' He waved a hand at the body on the ground and the bullet-pocked trees.

The Englishman eyed him carefully. 'Curious thing, that,' he said, rising to his feet. He tapped the tiny radio receiver in his ear. 'This is set to the police frequency. And I can tell you that the local constabulary has been very busy over these past several minutes – responding to emergency calls in all directions . . . and always on the very farthest outskirts of the city. The nearest patrol car is still at least ten minutes away.'

Smith shook his head in disbelief. 'Good grief! These people don't mess around, do they?'

'No, Jon,' Peter said quietly. 'They do not. Which is

why I strongly suggest you find a new place to stay tonight. Somewhere discreet and unobserved.'

'Oh, my God,' said a small voice from behind them.

Both men turned. Heather Donovan was standing there, staring down in horror at the dead man at their feet.

'Do you know him?' Smith asked gently.

She nodded unwillingly. 'Not personally. I don't even know his name. But I've seen him around the Movement camp and at the rally.'

'And in the Lazarus command tent,' Peter said sternly. 'As you well know.'

The slender woman blushed. 'Yes,' she admitted. 'He was part of a band of activists our top organizers brought in . . . for what they said were "special tasks." '

'Like cutting through the Teller Institute's fence when the rally turned ugly,' Peter reminded her.

'Yes, that's true.' Her shoulders slumped. 'But I never imagined they were carrying guns. Or that they would try to kill anyone.' She looked at them with eyes that were haunted and full of shame. 'Nothing was supposed to happen this way!'

'I rather suspect there are a number of things about the Lazarus Movement you never imagined, Ms. Donovan,' the gray-haired Englishman told her. 'And I think you've had a very narrow and very lucky escape.'

'She can't go back to the Movement camp, Peter,' Smith realized. 'It would be too dangerous.'

'Perhaps it might,' the older man agreed. 'Our guntoting friends have run off for now, but there may well be others who would not be happy to see Ms. Donovan looking so hale and hearty.'

Her face whitened.

'Do you have somewhere you can stay out of sight for a while, with family or friends? With people who aren't in the Lazarus Movement?' Smith asked. 'Preferably somewhere far away?'

She nodded slowly. 'I have an aunt in Baltimore.'

'Good,' said Smith. 'I think you should fly out there straightaway. Tonight, if possible.'

'Leave this to me, Jon,' Peter told him. 'Your face and name are rather too well known to these people now. If you arrive at the airport with Ms. Donovan, you might as well paint a target on her back.'

Smith nodded.

'You were at the rally, too!' she suddenly said, looking more closely at Peter Howell's face. 'But you said your name was Malachi. Malachi MacNamara!'

He nodded with a slight smile creasing his deeply lined face. 'A *nom de guerre*, Ms. Donovan. A regrettable deception, perhaps, but a necessary one.'

'Then who are you people really?' she asked. She looked from the lean, weather-beaten Englishman to Smith and then back again. 'CIA? FBI? Someone else?'

'Ask us no more questions and we'll tell you no more lies,' Peter said. His pale blue eyes twinkled. 'But we *are* your friends. Of that you may be sure.' His expression darkened. 'Which is far more than I can say for some of your former comrades in the Movement.'

CHAPTER TWENTY-TWO

Saturday, October 16
CIA Headquarters, Langley, Virginia

Shortly after midnight, Director of Central Intelligence David Hanson walked briskly into his gray-carpeted seventh-floor office suite. Despite the rigors of what had become an eighteen-hour workday, he was still immaculately dressed in a well-tailored suit, with a crisp, clean shirt and a perfectly knotted bow tie. He turned his careful gaze on the rumpled, tired-looking man waiting for him.

'We need to talk, Hal,' he said tightly. 'Privately.'

Hal Burke, head of the CIA's Lazarus Movement task force, nodded. 'Yes, we do.'

The CIA director led the way into his inner office and tossed his briefcase onto one of the two comfortably upholstered chairs in front of his desk. He waved Burke into the other. Then Hanson folded his hands together and rested his elbows on the bare surface of his large desk. He studied his subordinate over the tips of his fingers. 'I've just come from the White House. As you can imagine, the president is not especially happy with us or with the FBI right now.'

'We warned him about what would happen if the Lazarus Movement ran wild,' Burke said bluntly. 'The Teller Institute, the Telos lab out in California, and this bomb blast in Chicago were just the opening rounds. We've got to stop pussyfooting around. We have to hit the Movement hard *now*, before it digs in any deeper. Some of its mid-level activists are still out in the open. If we can haul those people in and break them open, we still have a shot at penetrating to the inner core. That's our best hope for pulling Lazarus apart from the inside out.'

'I've made that point very strongly,' Hanson told him. 'And I'm not the only one. Castilla is getting an earful from senior Senate and House leaders – from both parties.'

Burke nodded. The word inside the CIA was that Hanson had been making the rounds on Capitol Hill for most of the day, privately meeting with the heads of the Senate and House intelligence committees and with the majority and minority leaders in both chambers. As a result, his powerful congressional allies were demanding that President Castilla officially designate the Lazarus Movement as a terrorist organization. Once that happened, the gloves could come off and federal law-enforcement and intelligence agencies would be free to act forcefully against the Movement – going after its leaders, bank accounts, and public communications channels.

By making an end run around the president to Congress, however, Hanson was playing with fire. CIA directors were not supposed to use politics to manipulate the policies of the president they served. But Hanson had always been willing to take chances when the stakes were high, and he obviously thought his support in the House and Senate was strong enough to protect him from Castilla's anger.

'Any luck?' Burke asked.

Hanson shook his head. 'Not so far.'

Burke scowled. 'Why the hell not?'

'Ever since the Teller Massacre, Lazarus and his followers have been riding a huge wave of public sympathy and support. Especially in Europe and Asia,' the CIA director reminded him. He shrugged. 'These latest acts of violence might dent that a bit, but too many people are going to buy the Lazarus line that the Telos and Chicago attacks were faked to discredit their cause. So governments around the world are putting serious diplomatic pressure on us to back off the Movement. They're telling the president that aggressive action against Lazarus could trigger violent anti-American unrest in their own countries.'

Burke snorted in disgust. 'Are you telling me that Castilla is willing to let Paris or Berlin or some other two-bit foreign power hold a veto over our counterterrorism policy?'

'Not a veto precisely,' Hanson said. 'But he won't move openly – not until we produce rock-solid evidence that the Lazarus Movement is pulling the strings on these terrorist acts.'

For several seconds Burke sat silently staring back at his superior. Then he nodded. 'That can be arranged.'

'Genuine evidence, Hal,' the head of the CIA warned. 'Facts that will stand up to the closest scrutiny. Do you understand me?'

Again, Burke nodded. Oh, I understand you, David, he thought – and maybe better than you do yourself. Inside his mind he was working furiously on new ways to retrieve the situation that had begun spiraling out of his control at the Teller Institute.

Rural Virginia, Outside the Beltway

Three hours before dawn, bands of cold rain swept in succession across the Virginia countryside, drenching the already-sodden fields and woods below. Autumn was usually a time of drier weather, especially after the humid, tropical thunderstorms of the summer months, but the weather patterns were off-kilter this year.

Roughly forty miles southwest of Washington, D.C., a small farmhouse sat on a low rise overlooking a few sparse stands of trees, a stagnant pond, and forty acres of patchy grassland now mostly choked with weeds and dense thickets of brambles. The roofless, blackened ruins of an old barn stood close to the house. The remnants of a fence surrounded the farm's empty, overgrown fields, but most of the wooden fence rails and posts either were split or lay rotting in the tall grass, briars, and weeds. A rutted gravel track ran up the rise from the paved county road paralleling the fence. It ended at an oil-stained concrete slab just outside the front door of the farmhouse.

At first glance, the small satellite dish on the roof and a microwave relay tower on a nearby hill were the only pieces of evidence that this tumbledown farm had any ties whatever to the modern age. In reality, a state-of-the-art alarm system secured the farmhouse, which was furnished inside with the latest in CIA high-tech computer and electronics gear.

Hal Burke sat at the desk in his study, listening to the rain beat down on the roof of what he sardonically termed his 'occasional weekend country retreat.' One of his great-uncles had farmed this piss-poor patch of land for decades before the constant toil and frustration finally killed him. After his death, it had passed through the hands of several slow-witted cousins before it landed in the CIA officer's lap ten years ago as partial repayment of an old family debt.

He had neither the money nor the time to put in any crops, but he valued the seclusion the farm offered. No uninvited guests ever came knocking on his door out here – not even the local Jehovah's Witnesses. It was so far off the beaten track that even the fast-growing tentacles of the northern Virginia suburbs had passed it by. When the weather was clear, Burke could walk outside at night and see the sickly orange glow made by the lights of Washington, D.C., and its sprawling bedroom communities. They stained the sky in a vast arc to the north, northeast, and east, a constant reminder of the hive culture and the bogged-down bureaucracy he so despised.

Over the poor backcountry roads and traffic-clogged highways, travel to and from Langley was often long and torturous, but an array of secure communications equipment – installed at federal expense – allowed him to work from the farm should any sudden crisis arise. The gear functioned well enough for official CIA use. More advanced pieces of hardware and software, supplied by others, made it possible for him to control the far-flung elements of TOCSIN in greater security. He had come straight here after his midnight meeting with Hanson. Events were moving fast now and he needed to stay in close touch with his agents.

His computer chimed, signaling the arrival of an encrypted situation report from the security unit working in New Mexico. He frowned. They were late.

Burke rubbed at his eyes and typed in his password. The jumble of seemingly random characters, letters, and numbers instantly changed shape, forming coherent words and then whole sentences as the decoding program did its job. He read through the message with increasing alarm.

'Damn it,' he muttered. 'Who the hell *is* this bastard?' Then he picked up the secure phone next to his computer and dialed his FBI counterpart. 'Kit, listen up,' he said urgently. 'There's a situation I need you to handle. A corpse has to disappear. Permanently and pronto.'

'Colonel Smith?' Pierson asked levelly.

Burke scowled. 'I wish.'

'Fill me in,' she said. He could hear rustling in the background as she threw on her clothes. 'And no evasions this time. Just the facts.'

The CIA officer briefed her rapidly on the failed ambush. Pierson listened in icy silence. 'I'm growing rather tired of cleaning up the messes left by your private army, Hal,' she said bitterly after he finished.

'Smith had backup,' Burke snapped. 'That was something we didn't anticipate. We all thought he was operating as a lone wolf.'

'Any description of this other man?' she asked.

'No,' the CIA officer admitted. 'It was too dark for my people to get a good look at him.'

'Wonderful,' Pierson said coldly. 'This just gets better

and better, Hal. Now Smith will be sure there's something fishy about the terrorist SUV buy I've linked to the Movement. Why don't you just go ahead and paint a big, fat bull's-eye on my forehead?'

Burke resisted the urge to slam the phone down. 'Constructive suggestions would be more welcome, Kit,' he said finally.

'Shut TOCSIN down,' she told him. 'This whole operation has been a disaster right from the start. And with Smith still alive and sniffing around my heels, I don't have the maneuvering room I need to push this investigation toward Lazarus.'

He shook his head. 'I can't do that. Our people already have their next orders. We're in more danger if we try to abort now than we are if we go ahead.'

There was a long silence.

'Let's be clear about one thing, Hal,' Pierson said tightly. 'If TOCSIN comes apart at the seams, I'm not going to be the only one taking the fall, understand?'

'Is that a threat?' Burke asked slowly.

'Call it a statement of fact,' she replied. The phone went dead.

Hal Burke sat staring at his screen for several minutes, considering his next move. Was Kit Pierson losing her nerve? He hoped not. He had never really liked the dark-haired woman, but he had always respected her courage and her will to win at all costs. Without them, she would be only a liability – a liability TOCSIN could not afford.

He made a decision and began typing fast, composing a new set of instructions to the remnants of the unit in New Mexico.

Lazarus Movement Secure Videoconference
Around the world, small groups of men and women of every color and race gathered in secret. They met in front of satellite-linked monitors and video cameras. They were the elite of the Lazarus Movement, the leaders of its most

important action cells. All of them appeared on-edge, straining at the leash – eager to launch the operations they had been planning for many months.

The man called Lazarus stood at ease in front of a huge display, one that showed him the pictures relayed from each assembled group. He knew that none of them would see his real face or hear his real voice. As always, his advanced computer systems and software were busy constructing the different, idealized images fed to each Movement cell. Equally sophisticated software provided simultaneous language translation.

'The time has come,' Lazarus said. He smiled slightly, seeing the shiver of anticipation ripple through each of his distant audiences. 'Millions of people in Europe, Asia, Africa, and the Americas are flocking to our cause. The political and financial strength of our Movement is increasing by leaps and bounds. In short order, whole governments and corporations will tremble before our growing power.'

His confident statement drew nods of approval and murmurs of excitement from the watching Movement leaders.

Lazarus held up a hand in warning. 'But do not forget that our enemies are also on the move. Their secret war against us has failed. So now the open war I have long predicted has begun. The slaughters in Santa Fe and in Chicago are surely only the first of many atrocities they plan.'

He stared directly into the cameras, knowing that it would appear to each of the widely dispersed cells that his eyes were focused solely on them. 'The war has begun,' he repeated. 'We have no choice. We must strike back, swiftly and surely and without remorse. Wherever possible, your operations should avoid taking innocent life, but we must destroy these nanotech laboratories – the breeding vats of death – before our enemies can unleash more horrors on the world, and on us.'

'What about the facilities of Nomura PharmaTech?'

the head of the Tokyo cell asked. 'After all, this corporation, alone among all the others, has already agreed to our demands. Their research work is at an end.'

'Spare Nomura PharmaTech?' Lazarus said coldly. 'I think not. Hideo Nomura is a shrewd young man – too shrewd. He bends when the wind is strong, but does not break. When he smiles, it is the smile of a shark. Do not be taken in by Nomura. I know him far too well.'

The leader of the Tokyo cell bowed his head, accepting the reproof. 'It shall be as you command, Lazarus.'

When at last the conference screens went dark, the man called Lazarus stood alone, savoring his moment of triumph. Years of planning and preparation were coming to fruition. Soon the hard and dangerous work of reclaiming the world would begin. And soon the harsh, but necessary, sacrifices he had made would be redeemed.

His eyes clouded over briefly, full of remembered pain. Softly he recited the poem, a haiku, that often lingered close to the edge of his waking mind:

> *'Sorrow, like mist, falls*
> *On a father forsaken*
> *By his faithless son.'*

CHAPTER TWENTY-THREE

North of Santa Fe

The morning sun, rising ever higher in a cloud-streaked azure sky, seemed to set the big, flat-topped hill looming above the Rancho de Chimayó aflame. Piñon pines and junipers along its crest stood starkly outlined against the dazzling golden light. Sunshine spread down steep slopes and threw long shadows across the old hacienda's sprawling apple orchards and terraced patios.

Still wearing his jeans, boots, and corduroy jacket, Jon Smith walked through the crowded dining rooms of the ancient adobe house and out onto a stone-flagged patio. Set in the foothills roughly twenty-five miles north of Santa Fe, the Rancho de Chimayó was one of the oldest restaurants in New Mexico. Its owners traced their lineage back to the original wave of Spanish colonists in the Southwest. Their family had first settled at Chimayó in 1680, during the long and bloody Pueblo Indian revolt against Spanish rule.

Peter Howell was seated there already, waiting for him at one of the patio tables. He waved his old friend into the empty chair across from him. 'Take a pew, Jon,' he said kindly. 'Damned if you don't look all in.'

Smith shrugged, resisting the temptation to yawn. 'I had a long night.'

'Any serious trouble?'

Jon shook his head. Collecting his laptop and other gear from the Fort Marcy suites had proved unexpectedly easy. Wary at first of FBI or terrorist surveillance, he had used every trick he knew to flush any tail – without spotting anyone. But doing that right took time, and lots of it. Which meant he had not checked into his new digs, a cheap fleabag motor lodge on the outskirts of Santa Fe, until close to dawn. Then he had phoned Fred Klein and told him about the unsuccessful attempt on his life. All in all, he had scarcely had time to close his eyes before Peter called to set this clandestine rendezvous.

'And no one followed you? Then or now?' the Englishman asked after listening intently to Smith's account of his actions.

'Not a soul.'

'Most curious,' Peter said, arching a shaggy gray eyebrow. He frowned. 'And more than a little worrying.'

Smith nodded. Try as he might, he could not understand why the FBI had been so eager to track his movements all yesterday – and then seemingly called off its team only hours before four gunmen tried to kill him. Maybe Kit Pierson's agents had simply assumed he was in his suite to stay and packed it in for the night, but that seemed uncharacteristically sloppy.

'What about you and Heather Donovan?' he asked. 'Did you have any trouble getting her away safely?'

'Not a bit,' Peter said easily. He checked his watch. 'By now the lovely Ms. Donovan is winging her way across America – bound for her aunt's home on the shores of the Chesapeake.'

'You never thought she was in serious danger, did you?' Smith asked quietly.

'Once the shooting stopped, you mean?' the older man said. He shrugged. 'No, not really, Jon. *You* were the primary target, not her. Ms. Donovan is just what she seems – a somewhat naive young woman with a good heart and a decent brain. Since she has no real knowledge of whatever it is that the upper echelons of the Lazarus Movement are planning, I doubt very much that they will view her as a serious threat. So long as the young lady stays well away from you, she ought to be perfectly safe.'

'And there you have the story of my love life,' Smith said with a twisted smile.

'Occupational hazard, I'm afraid,' Peter said lightly. He grinned. 'I mean, of the medical life, naturally. Perhaps you should try intelligence work instead. I understand spies are all the rage this season.'

Smith ignored the gentle tweak. He knew the Englishman was sure he worked for one of the various U.S. intelligence agencies, but Peter made it a point of professional courtesy never to pry too deeply. Just as he tried to avoid asking too many inconvenient questions about the older man's occasional work for Her Majesty's government.

Peter looked up as a smiling waitress in a frilled white blouse and long flowing skirt approached, bearing a large tray crowded with plates and a pot of hot, fresh coffee. 'Ah, the grub,' he said happily. 'Hope you don't mind, but I took the liberty of ordering for both of us.'

'Not at all,' Smith said, suddenly aware that he was desperately hungry.

For several minutes the two men ate rapidly – feasting on eggs cooked with slices of chorizo sausage, black beans, and spicy *pico de gallo*, a salsa made with red and green chilies, tomatoes, onions, cilantro, and small dollops of sour cream. To help tame the fiery taste of the salsa, the restaurant provided a basket of homemade *sopaipillas*, light pillows of puffy fried bread best served warm with drizzled honey and melted butter poked through a hole on top.

When they finished, Peter sat back with a contented look on his craggy face. 'In some parts of the world, a prodigious belch right now would be considered a compliment to the chef,' he said. His eyes twinkled. 'But for the moment, I'll refrain.'

'Believe me, I'm grateful,' Smith told him drily. 'I'd actually like to be able to eat here again sometime.'

'To business, then,' Peter said. He pointed to the mass

of long gray hair on his head. 'No doubt you've been wondering about my changed appearance.'

'Just a bit,' Smith admitted. 'You look sort of like an Old Testament prophet.'

'I do rather,' the Englishman agreed complacently. 'Well, look your last upon this hoary mane of mine and weep, for like Samson I shall soon be shorn.' He chuckled. 'But it was all in a good cause. Some months ago, an old acquaintance asked me to poke my long nose into the inner workings of the Lazarus Movement.'

For 'old acquaintance' read MI6, the British Secret Intelligence Service, Smith thought.

'Well, that sounded like a bit of fun, so I grew the old locks somewhat shaggy, changed my name to something appropriately biblical and impressive-sounding, and drifted into the outer ranks of the Movement – posing as a retired Canadian forestry official with a radical grudge against science and technology.'

'Did you have any luck?' Smith asked.

'In penetrating the Movement's inner core? No, alas,' Peter said. His expression turned more serious. 'The leadership is damned fanatical about its security. I never quite managed to break through its safeguards. Still, I learned enough to worry me. Most of these Lazarus followers are decent enough, but there are some very hard-edged types manipulating them from behind the scenes.'

'Like the guys who tried to nail me last night?'

'Perhaps,' Peter said reflectively. 'Though I would characterize them as more brawn than brains. I had my eye on them for several days before they attacked you – ever since they first arrived at the Lazarus rally, in fact.'

'Any particular reason?'

'At first, simply the way they moved,' Peter explained. 'Those fellows were like a pack of wolves gliding through a flock of grazing sheep. You know what I mean. Too careful, too controlled . . . too aware of their surroundings at all times.'

'Kind of like us?' Smith suggested with a thin smile.

Peter nodded. 'Precisely.'

'And were your "friends" in London able to make anything out of the material you sent them?' Jon asked, remembering the digital photos and fingerprints Howell had taken of the shaven-headed gunman he had killed.

'I'm afraid not,' Peter said regretfully. 'So far my inquiries have drawn a complete blank.' He reached into the pocket of his sheepskin coat and then slid a computer disk across the table toward Smith. 'Which is why I thought you might care to take your own stab at identifying the fellow you so efficiently put down last night.'

Smith looked steadily back at him. 'Oh?'

'There's no need to play coy, Jon,' Peter told him with a hint of amusement. 'I'm quite sure you have your own friends – or friends of friends – who can run those pictures and prints through their databases . . . as a personal favor to you, of course.'

'It may be possible,' Smith admitted slowly. He took the disk. 'But I'll have to find a connection for my computer first.'

The older man smiled openly now. 'Then you'll be pleased to hear that our hosts have access to a wireless Internet node. This charming hacienda may date back to the seventeenth century, but its owners' business sense is very firmly rooted in our modern age.' Peter pushed his chair back and stood up. 'And now I'm sure you'd like some privacy, so like a good little guard dog I'll go and prowl around the rest of the grounds.'

Jon watched him go, shaking his head in hopeless admiration at the Englishman's ability to get what he wanted from almost anybody. 'Peter Howell could con a tribe of cannibals into turning vegetarian,' CIA officer Randi Russell, a mutual friend of theirs, had once told him. 'And probably persuade them to pay him for the privilege.'

Still amused, Smith dialed Fred Klein's number on his encrypted cell phone.

'Yes, Colonel,' the head of Covert-One said.

Smith relayed Peter's request for help in identifying the dead gunman. 'I've got the disk with the photos and fingerprints right here,' he finished.

'What does Howell know?' Klein asked.

'About me? He hasn't asked,' Smith said forcefully. 'Peter is sure that I'm working for Army Intelligence, or one of the other Pentagon outfits, but he's not pushing for specifics.'

'Good,' Klein said. He cleared his throat. 'All right, Jon, send me the files, and I'll see what we can dig up. Can you stay on where you are? This could take a while.'

Smith looked around the quiet, restful terrace. The sun was high enough now to provide some real warmth. And the sweet scent of flowers hung in the fresh air. He signaled the waitress for another pot of coffee. 'No sweat, Fred,' he said into the phone with an easy, relaxed drawl. 'I'll just sit here and suffer.'

The head of Covert-One called back within the hour. He didn't waste time in pleasantries. 'We have a serious problem, Colonel,' he said grimly.

Smith saw Peter Howell hovering around the door out onto the patio and motioned him over. 'Go ahead,' he told Klein. 'I'm all ears.'

'The man you shot was an American, a man named Michael Dolan. He was ex-U.S. Army Special Forces. A decorated combat veteran. He left the service as a captain five years ago.'

'Shit,' Jon said softly.

'Oh, it gets worse, Colonel,' Klein cautioned him. 'Once he got out of the Army, Michael Dolan applied for admission to the FBI Academy at Quantico. They turned him down outright.'

'Why?' Smith wondered aloud. Ex-military officers were often in high demand by the FBI, which valued their skills, physical fitness, and disciplined outlook on life.

'He failed the Academy psychological evaluation,' Klein told him quietly. 'Apparently, he showed clear traces of sociopathic tendencies and attitudes. The Bureau profilers noted a distinct willingness to kill, without significant compunction or remorse.'

'Not exactly someone you would really want carrying a law-enforcement badge and a weapon, I guess,' Smith said.

'No,' Klein agreed.

'Okay, the FBI didn't want him,' Smith pressed. 'Then who did take him on? How did he wind up involved in the Lazarus Movement?'

'There we begin to come to the heart of our serious problem,' the head of Covert-One said slowly. 'It appears that the late and unlamented Mr. Dolan worked for the CIA.'

'Jesus.' Smith shook his head in disbelief. 'Langley hired this guy?'

'Not officially,' Klein replied. 'The Agency rather wisely seems to have kept him at arm's length. On paper, Dolan was employed as an independent security consultant. But his paychecks were funneled through a number of CIA fronts. He's worked for them on and off since leaving the Army, mostly conducting high-risk counterterror operations, usually in Latin America or Africa.'

'Cute. So Langley could always deny that he was one of theirs if an op went sour,' Smith realized, frowning.

'Exactly,' Klein said.

'And was Dolan on the CIA payroll last night?' Smith asked tightly, wondering just how much trouble they were in right now. Was that firefight last night the result of some total foul-up – a horrible incident of friendly fire between two clandestine outfits operating in the same area without adequate communication?

'No, I don't think so,' the head of Covert-One told him. 'My best guess is that his last paid contract from the

Agency ended a little more than six months ago.'

Smith felt the rigid muscles of his face relax a tiny bit. He breathed out. 'I'm glad to hear that. Damned glad.'

'There is more, Colonel,' Fred Klein warned. He cleared his throat. 'The information I've just relayed comes from our own Covert-One database – a set of files I've built up using highly classified material siphoned from the CIA, the FBI, the NSA, and other agencies. Without their knowledge, of course.'

Smith nodded to himself. Klein's ability to pull together information from the several competing factions in the U.S. intelligence community was one of the reasons President Castilla put such a high value on Covert-One's work.

'As a cross-check, I ran the pictures and fingerprints you sent me through both the CIA and the FBI databases,' Klein went on. His voice was flat and cold. 'But both searches came back empty-handed. So far as Langley and the Bureau are concerned, Michael Dolan never took the FBI exam and never worked for the CIA. In fact, their records do not mention him at all.'

'What?' Smith exclaimed suddenly. He saw Peter raise an eyebrow in surprise and hurriedly lowered his voice. 'That's impossible!'

'Not impossible,' Klein told him quietly. 'Merely improbable. And very frightening.'

'You mean the CIA and FBI files have been scrubbed,' Smith realized. He felt a shiver run down his spine. 'Which is something that could only be done by people operating at a very high level. People in our own government.'

'I'm afraid so, Colonel,' Klein agreed. 'Clearly, someone has taken enormous risks to erase those records. So now the questions we have to ask are, Why? And who?'

Hidden Nanotechnology Production Facility, Inside the Center

The technicians working inside the nanophage production core wore full protective suits, each with its own self-contained air supply. Thick gloves and the heavy suits slowed every movement and robbed them of much of their dexterity. Nevertheless, harsh training and intensive practice helped each man perform the delicate task of loading hundreds of billions of fully formed Stage III nanophages into four small, thick-walled metal cylinders.

As the cylinders were filled, they were slowly and carefully disconnected from the stainless steel production vats. Technicians working in pairs clamped the cylinders onto robotic carts designed to ferry them through a narrow tunnel – sealed at both ends by massive air locks – and out into another sealed chamber. There another team of technicians wearing masks, gloves, and coveralls took charge of the deadly cargo.

One by one, the nanophage-filled canisters were loaded into larger hollow metal tanks, which were carefully sealed and then welded shut. Once this work was finished, these larger metal tanks were stacked in a foam-padded heavy-duty shipping crate. As a last step, large white and red labels were stuck all over the crate: APPROVISION-NEMENTS MÉDICAUX DE L'OXYGÈNE. AVERTISSEMENT: CONTENU SOUS PRESSION!

The tall, powerfully built man who called himself Nones stood outside the production core, watching through the multiple layers of a sealed observation window as the loading proceeded. He turned his head toward the much shorter senior scientist beside him. 'Will this new delivery system of yours yield the increased effectiveness our employer demands?'

The scientist nodded emphatically. 'Absolutely. We have designed the Stage Three nanophages with a longer life span and for a much wider range of external conditions. Our new method takes advantage of those design improvements – allowing us to conduct this next field test from much higher altitudes and in more variable weather. Our computer modeling predicts significantly more efficient dispersion of the nanophages as a result.'

'And substantially higher kill rates?' Nones, the third of the *Horatii*, asked bluntly.

The scientist nodded reluctantly. 'Of course.' He swallowed hard. 'I doubt that very many people in the target area will survive.'

'Good.' The green-eyed man smiled coldly. 'After all, that is the point of all this new technology of yours, isn't it?'

PART THREE

CHAPTER TWENTY-FOUR

Shinjuku Ward, Tokyo
As a multinational corporation worth nearly $50 billion, Nomura PharmaTech owned factories, laboratories, and warehouse facilities all around the world, but it still retained a substantial presence in Japan. The company's Tokyo-based complex occupied a forty-acre campus located in the very heart of the sprawling city's Shinjuku Ward. Three identical skyscrapers held administrative offices and science labs for Nomura's thousands of dedicated employees. At night, Tokyo's vivid, shimmering neon lights were reflected by each tower's mirrored facade – turning them into jeweled pillars on which the city's night sky rested. But the rest of the campus was a peaceful rural setting of forested parkland, flowing streams, and restful pools. During his tenure as CEO and chairman, Jinjiro Nomura, Hideo's father, had insisted on creating an oasis of natural beauty, peace, and tranquillity around his corporate headquarters – no matter how much it cost his company or its shareholders.

Three main gates controlled access to the walled compound. From each gate tree-lined paths and service roads fed pedestrian, auto, and truck traffic to one of the three towers.

Mitushara Noda had worked for Nomura PharmaTech for all of his adult life. Over the course of twenty-five years, the short, spare man with a passion for order and routine had risen steadily, if unspectacularly, from the post of junior nightshift watchman to that of Gate Three security supervisor. The work was equally steady and equally unspectacular. Apart from making sure his guards checked employee badges, Noda's day consisted largely of making sure that shipments of food, office supplies, and lab chemicals arrived on time and were directed to the proper loading dock. Before beginning any shift, he always arrived early just so he could spend the time he needed to memorize the scheduled arrivals, departures, and loads for every vehicle slated to pass through his gate during the next eight hours.

That was why the unexpected sound of a heavy tractor-trailer truck shifting its gears noisily as it turned off the main road brought Mitsuhara Noda rushing out of his small office at the gatehouse. By his calculations, no shipments of any kind were due to arrive for at least another two hours and twenty-five minutes. The little man's black brows were furrowed as he watched the huge rig draw nearer, engine roaring as it steadily picked up speed.

Behind him, several of the other security guards whispered nervously to one another, wondering aloud what they should do. One unsnapped the holster at his side, readying his pistol for a quick draw.

Noda's eyes narrowed. The access road through Gate Three led directly to the tower dedicated to Nomura PharmaTech's nanotechnology research efforts. Several security circulars were posted in his office warning all company employees about the threats made by the Lazarus Movement. And there were no corporate markings on either the trailer or the cab of this fast-approaching truck.

He made a decision. 'Lower the gate!' he snapped. 'Hoshiko, phone the main office and report a possible security incident.'

Noda stepped right out into the road, signaling the driver of the oncoming truck to stop. Behind him, a solid steel pole swung down with a shrill electrical whine and locked in place. The other guards fumbled for their weapons.

But the truck kept coming. Its gears screamed as the big engine revved higher, accelerating to more than forty miles an hour. Unable for a moment to believe what he was seeing, the little gate supervisor stood his ground, still frantically waving his arms as he shouted for the big rig to halt.

Through the tinted windshield he caught a momentary glimpse of the man behind the wheel. There was no expression on the driver's face, no sign of recognition in his glassy, unseeing eyes. A kamikaze! Noda realized in horror.

Far too late, he turned to run.

The front end of the huge truck slammed into him with lethal force, shattering every bone in his upper body. Unable even to force a scream out of his ruptured lungs, he was hurled backward against the steel pole. The impact snapped his spine in half. Noda was already dead when the truck crashed straight through the gate amid the high-pitched shriek of rending metal.

Two of the shocked security guards reacted fast enough to open fire. But their pistol shots only ricocheted off the big rig's improvised armor plating and bulletproof windows. The truck kept going, roaring deeper into the wooded Nomura complex, racing straight for the tall mirrored tower containing the company's Tokyo nanotech research facility.

Scarcely one hundred yards from the skyscraper's main entrance, the speeding tractor-trailer crashed head-on into a row of massive steel-and-concrete barriers hurriedly deployed by the company after the terrorist attack on the Teller Institute. Huge pieces of broken concrete flew away from the point of impact, but the barriers held.

The big rig jackknifed and then exploded.

An enormous orange and red fireball roared high into the air. The shock wave smashed windows all across the front of the lab complex. Knife-edge shards of glass cascaded onto the pavements and lawns far below. Bomb-mangled pieces of the truck and trailer were blown through a wide arc – tearing jagged holes in the steel fabric of the building and toppling trees in the surrounding groves.

The nanotech labs themselves, however, unoccupied and sealed under Japanese government supervision, were largely untouched. Casualties, aside from the suicide-bomb driver and the unfortunate Mitsuhara Noda, were remarkably low.

Thirty minutes later, an e-mail message issued by the Lazarus Movement arrived at the offices of every major Tokyo media outlet. In it, the Movement's Japan-based wing took credit for what it called 'a mission of heroic self-sacrifice in defense of the planet and all humanity.'

Surveillance Team Safe House, on the Outskirts of Santa Fe

Two large panel vans were parked close to the front entrance of the secluded hilltop house. Their rear doors stood wide open, revealing an assortment of boxes and equipment cases crammed into the back of each vehicle. Five men were gathered near the vans, waiting for their leader.

The older, white-haired Dutchman named Linden was inside, going from room to room to make sure they were leaving nothing suspicious or incriminating behind. What he saw, or rather didn't see, pleased him. The safe house had been stripped and sanitized. Apart from a few tiny holes drilled in the walls, there were no longer any traces of the large array of cameras, radio and microwave receivers, computers, and communications gear they had installed to eavesdrop on every facet of the Teller investigation. Every smooth surface and piece of wood or metal furniture gleamed, scrubbed clean of all fingerprints and other traces of recent human habitation.

He came out of the house and stood blinking in the dazzling sunshine. He crooked a finger at one of his men, beckoning him over. 'Is everything packed, Abrantes?'

The younger man nodded. 'We're ready.'

'Good, Vitor,' Linden said. The surveillance team leader checked his watch. 'Then let's go. We have planes to catch.' He showed his tobacco-stained teeth in a quick, humorless smile. 'Center's timetable for this new mission is very tight, but it will be good to leave this high and arid desert behind and return to Europe.'

CHAPTER TWENTY-FIVE

Santa Fe

The Santa Fe Municipal Police Department had its head-quarters on the Camino Entrada, out on the western edge of the city – not far from the county jail, and next to the city courthouse. Half an hour after first setting foot in the building, Jon Smith found himself sitting in the office of the ranking policeman on duty. Several photographs showing a pretty wife and three young children were hung on two of the plain white walls. A watercolor depicting one of the nearby pueblos took up part of another. Case files in manila folders were neatly organized on one corner of a plain desk, right next to a computer. A background buzz of ringing phones, conversations, and busy keyboards drifted in through an open door to the adjoining squad room.

Lieutenant Carl Zarate looked down at Smith's U.S. Army identity card and then back up with a puzzled frown. 'Now what is it exactly that I'm supposed to do for you, Colonel?'

Smith kept his tone casual. He'd been bucked up to Zarate by a profusely sweating desk sergeant who had been made very uneasy by his questions. 'I'm looking for some information, Lieutenant,' he said calmly. 'A few facts about the gun battle somebody fought in the Plaza late last night.'

Zarate's narrow, bony face went blank. 'What gun battle was that?' he asked carefully. His dark brown eyes were wary.

Smith cocked his head to one side. 'You know,' he said,

at last. 'I was sort of surprised when the press didn't run wild with speculation about all the shooting going on right in the heart of the city. Then I thought that maybe someone leaned on the local papers and the TV and radio stations to keep the lid on – just for a while, just while an investigation was going on. With things so tense after the Teller disaster, that'd be natural, I guess. But I'd be very surprised to learn that you folks at the Santa Fe police department were playing the same game.'

The police officer eyed him for a moment longer. Then he shrugged. 'If there were a gag order in effect, Colonel Smith, I'm damned if I know why I'd break the rules for you.'

'Maybe because these rules don't apply to me, Lieutenant Zarate?' Jon suggested easily. He handed the police officer the sheaf of investigative authorizations Fred Klein had arranged for him. He nodded toward them. 'Those orders require me to observe and report on every aspect of the Teller investigation. *Every* aspect. And if you look at the last page there, you'll see the signature of the Chairman of the Joint Chiefs of Staff. Now, do you really want to get caught in a pissing match between the Pentagon and the FBI, especially since we're all supposed to be on the same side in this mess?'

Zarate flipped rapidly through the papers, with his frown growing even deeper. He slid them back across the desk with a snort of disgust. 'There are times, Colonel, when I damned well wish the federal government would keep its big, fumbling paws out of my jurisdiction.'

Smith nodded sympathetically. 'There are people in D.C. with all the grace and tact of a five-hundred-pound gorilla and the common sense of your average two-year-old.'

Zarate grinned suddenly. 'Strong words, Colonel. Maybe you'd better watch your mouth around the red-tape boys and girls. I hear they don't much care for soldiers who won't toe the line.'

'I'm a doctor and scientist first and foremost and an Army officer second,' Smith said. He shrugged. 'I doubt I'm on anybody's short list to make general.'

'Uh-huh,' the police lieutenant said skeptically. 'That's why you're running around with personal orders signed by the head of the JCS.' He spread his hands. 'Unfortunately, there's really not much I can tell you. Yeah, there was some kind of shoot-out in the Plaza last night. One guy got himself killed. There may have been others who were hit. We were still checking blood trails when my forensics team was called off.'

Smith pounced on that. 'Your team was called off?'

'Yeah,' Zarate said flatly. 'The FBI swooped in and took over. Said it was a matter of national security and that it fell within their jurisdiction.'

'When was that?' Jon asked.

'Maybe an hour after we first arrived on the scene,' the police officer told him. 'But they didn't just kick us off the ground, they also confiscated every spent shell casing, every piece of paperwork, and every crime scene photo. They even took the tapes of dispatcher calls to and from units responding to the scene!'

Smith whistled softly in surprise. This was more than a simple dispute over jurisdiction. The FBI had made a clean sweep of every scrap of official evidence. 'On whose authority?' he asked quietly.

'Deputy Assistant Director Katherine Pierson signed the orders,' Zarate answered. His mouth tightened. 'I won't pretend I'm happy about tucking my tail in and complying, but nobody in the mayor's office or on the city council wants to rock the boat with the Feds right now.'

Jon nodded his understanding. With a major disaster right on its doorstep, Santa Fe would be depending heavily on federal aid money and assistance. And local pride and turf consciousness would naturally take a backseat to urgent necessity.

'Just one more question,' he promised Zarate. 'You said there was a corpse. Do you know what happened to the body? Or who's handling the autopsy?'

The police lieutenant shook his head in confusion. 'That's where this whole screwy situation gets *very* weird.' He scowled. 'I made a few phone calls to the various coroners and hospitals, just checking around for my own edification. And as far as I can tell nobody did anything at all to try to identify the stiff. Instead, it looks like the FBI slid the dead guy right into an ambulance and shipped him off to a mortuary way down in Albuquerque for immediate cremation.' He looked straight at Smith. 'Now what the hell do you make of that, Colonel?'

Jon fought for control over his face and won, maintaining a stony, impassive expression. Exactly what was Kit Pierson doing out here in Santa Fe? he wondered. Who was she covering up for?

It was a little before noon when Smith left the Santa Fe police department and walked out onto the Camino Entrada. His eyes flickered briefly to the left and right, checking the street in both directions, but otherwise he revealed no great interest in his surroundings. Instead, still apparently deep in thought, he climbed into his rented dark gray Mustang coupe and drove away. A few quick turns on surface streets led him into the crowded parking lot surrounding the city's indoor shopping center, the Villa Linda Mall. Once there, he threaded through several rows of parked cars, acting as though he was simply looking for an open space. Finally, he drove away from the mall, crossed the encircling Wagon Road, and parked under the shade of some trees growing next to a shallow ravine marked on his map as the Arroyo de las Chamisos.

Two minutes later, another car, this one a white four-door Buick, turned in right behind him. Peter Howell got out and stretched while carefully checking the environment. Satisfied that they were unobserved, he sauntered up, pulled open the Mustang's passenger-side door, and then slid into the bucket seat next to Smith.

In the hours since they had met for breakfast, the Englishman had found time to have his hair cut fashionably short. He had also changed his clothes, abandoning the faded denims and heavy flannel shirt he had worn as Malachi MacNamara in favor of a pair of khaki slacks, a solid blue button-down shirt, and a herringbone sports coat. The fiery Lazarus Movement fanatic was gone, replaced by a lean, sun-browned British expatriate apparently out for an afternoon's shopping.

'Spot anything?' Jon asked him.

Peter shook his head. 'Not so much as a suspiciously turned head. You're clean.'

Smith relaxed slightly. The other man had been operating as his distant cover, hanging back while he went into the police headquarters and then keeping an eye on his tail to spot anyone following him when he came out.

'Were you able to learn anything yourself?' Peter asked. 'Or did your pointed questions fall on stony ground?'

'Oh, I learned a fair amount,' Jon said grimly. 'Maybe even more than I bargained for.'

Peter raised an inquiring eyebrow but otherwise stayed quiet, listening carefully while Smith filled him in on what he had learned. When he heard that Dolan's body had been cremated, he shook his head, sourly amused. 'Well, well, well . . . ashes to ashes and dust to dust. And no fingerprints or inconvenient dental impressions left for anyone to match up with any embarrassing personnel files. I suppose no matter how thoroughly the CIA and FBI databases were scrubbed, somebody, somewhere, would have been bound to recognize the fellow.'

'Yep.' Jon's fingers drummed on the steering wheel of his car. 'Nifty, isn't it?'

'It does raise a number of intriguing questions,' Peter agreed. He ticked them off on his own fingers. 'Who are these secret operations lads like the late and unlamented

Michael Dolan really working for? The Lazarus Movement, as they seem to be on the surface? Or some other organization, sub rosa? Perhaps even your very own CIA? All very confusing, wouldn't you say?'

'One thing's certain,' Smith told him. 'Kit Pierson must be in this mess up to her neck. She probably has the authority to take over the Plaza crime scene. But there's no way she can justify cremating Dolan's body, not under standard FBI practice and procedure.'

'Could she be doubling for Lazarus?' Peter asked quietly. 'Working to sabotage the FBI's investigation from within?'

'Kit Pierson as a Lazarus mole?' Jon shook his head firmly. 'I can't see it. If anything, she's been pushing far too hard to blame everything that happened at the Institute on the Movement.'

Peter nodded. 'True. So if she's not working for Lazarus, she must be working against them – which suggests she's covering for an off-the-books anti-Movement operation run by the FBI, or the CIA, or both.'

Smith looked at him. 'You think they're really running an operation that sensitive without the president's approval?'

Peter shrugged. 'It happens, Jon, as you well know.' He smiled drily. 'Remember poor old Henry the Second? He gets a bit pissed one night and roars out, "Will no one rid me of this turbulent priest?" Then, practically before he can sober up, there's blood spilled all over the floor of Canterbury Cathedral. Thomas Becket's suddenly a sainted martyr. And the sad, sorry, hung-over king is down for a round of scourging, hair shirts, and public penitence.'

Smith nodded slowly. 'Yeah, I know. Intelligence outfits sometimes exceed their authority. But it's a damned dangerous game to be playing.'

'Of course it is,' Peter said. 'Careers can be wrecked. And even high-ranking officials can be sent to prison. That's precisely why they might have decided to kill you.'

Jon frowned. 'I can understand a CIA/FBI covert operation designed to wreck the Lazarus Movement from within. It would be stupid and completely illegal, but I can understand it. And I can see a Movement attempt to sabotage the Institute labs. But what I can't make fit into either scenario is the nanophage release that slaughtered all those protesters.'

'Yes,' Peter said slowly, with his eyes full of remembered horror. 'That is the one piece which remains stubbornly outside the puzzle. And a bloody awful piece it is, too.'

Nodding, Smith sat back from the steering wheel and pulled out his phone. 'Maybe it's time we stopped pissing around on the outside.' He punched in a number. It was answered on the first ring. 'This is Colonel Jonathan Smith, Agent Latimer,' he said sharply. 'I want to speak to Deputy Assistant Director Pierson. Right now.'

'Bearding the lioness in her den?' Peter murmured. 'Not very subtle even for you, is it, Jon?'

Smith grinned at him over the phone. 'I'll leave subtlety to you Brits, Peter. Sometimes you've just got to fix bayonets and launch a good old-fashioned frontal assault.' Then, as he listened to the voice on the other end, his grin slowly faded. 'I see,' he said quietly. 'And when was that?'

He hung up.

'Trouble?' Peter asked.

'Maybe.' Smith frowned. 'Kit Pierson is already on her way back to Washington for certain urgent and unspecified consultations. She's catching an executive jet out of Albuquerque a little later this afternoon.'

'So the bird is on the wing, eh? Interesting timing, isn't it?' Peter said with a sudden gleam in his eye. 'I begin to suspect that Ms. Pierson just received a rather disturbing call from the local police.'

'You're probably right,' Smith agreed, remembering the nervous looks he had gotten from the policeman who had passed him up the chain to Zarate. The desk sergeant must have tipped off the FBI that an Army lieutenant colonel named Jonathan Smith was digging into an incident the Bureau was trying to bury. He glanced at the Englishman. 'Are you up for a quick trip to D.C.? I know it's outside your current area of operations, but I could sure use some help. Kit Pierson is the one solid lead I've got and I don't plan to just watch her walk away.'

'Count me in,' Peter replied with a slow, predatory grin. 'I wouldn't miss this for the world.'

CHAPTER TWENTY-SIX

The White House

'I understand you very well, Mr. Speaker,' President Samuel Adam Castilla growled into the phone. He looked up and saw Charles Ouray, his chief of staff, poke his head into the Oval Office. Castilla motioned him inside with a wave and then turned back to the phone. 'Now it's time for you to understand me. I will not be stampeded into any executive action I think unwise. Not by the CIA or the FBI. Not by the Senate. And not by you. Is that clear? Very well, then. Good day to you, sir.'

Castilla hung up, resisting the urge to slam the phone down in its cradle. He rubbed a big hand over his weary face. 'They say Andrew Jackson once threatened to horsewhip a fellow off the White House grounds. I used to think that was just Old Hickory on a wild-eyed tear, letting his famous temper get the better of him. But now I'm mighty tempted to follow his example.'

'Are you receiving more helpful advice from Congress?' Ouray asked drily, nodding toward the phone.

The president grimaced. 'That was the Speaker of the House,' he said. 'Graciously suggesting that I immediately sign an executive order naming the Lazarus Movement a terrorist organization.'

'Or?'

'Or the House and Senate will enact legislation on their own initiative,' Castilla finished.

Ouray raised an eyebrow. 'By a veto-proof majority?'

The president shrugged. 'Maybe. Maybe not. Either

way, we lose. Politically. Diplomatically. You name it.'

His chief of staff nodded soberly. 'I guess it doesn't matter much whether an anti-Lazarus bill ever really becomes law. If it passes the Congress, our increasingly shaky international alliances will take another serious hit.'

'Too true, Charlie,' Castilla said, sighing. 'Most people around the world will see a law like that as more proof that we're overreacting, turning paranoid and panicked. Oh, I suppose a few of our friends, the ones worried by those bombs in Chicago and Tokyo, might cheer quietly, but most folks will only think we're making matters worse. That we're pushing an otherwise peaceful group toward violence – or that we're covering up our own crimes.'

'It's a terrible situation,' Ouray agreed.

'Yes, it is.' Castilla sighed. 'And it's about to get much worse.' Feeling trapped behind his desk, he stood up and crossed over to the windows. For a short time he stared out across the South Lawn, noting the squads of heavily armed guards in helmets and body armor now patrolling openly around the grounds. After the Lazarus Movement attack in Tokyo, the Secret Service had insisted on tightening security around the White House.

He looked back over his shoulder at Ouray. 'Before the Speaker dropped his little legislative ultimatum on me, I had another call – this one from Ambassador Nichols at the UN.'

The White House chief of staff frowned. 'Is something up inside the Security Council?'

Castilla nodded. 'Nichols just got wind of a resolution some of the nonaligned countries on the Council are going to propose. Basically, they're going to demand that we open all of our nanotech research facilities – both public and private – to full international inspection, including an examination of all their proprietary processes. They say it's the only way they can be sure that we're not running a secret nanotech weapons program. And Nichols says he thinks the nonaligned bloc has enough Council votes lined up for passage.'

Ouray grimaced. 'We can't allow that to go through.'

'No, we can't,' Castilla agreed heavily. 'It's basically a license to steal every nanotech development we've made. Our companies and universities have spent billions on this research. I can't let all of that work go down the drain.'

'Can we persuade one of the other permanent members to veto this resolution for us?' Ouray asked.

Castilla shrugged. 'Nichols says Russia and China are ready to stick it to us. They want to know how far we've gone in nanotechnology. We'll be lucky if the French decide to abstain. That leaves just the British. And I'm not sure how far the prime minister can go right now to give us political cover. His control over Parliament is tenuous at best.'

'Then we'll have to veto it ourselves,' Ouray realized. His jaw tightened. 'And that will look bad. Really bad.'

Castilla nodded grimly. 'I can't imagine anything more likely to confirm the world's worst fears about what we're doing. If we veto a Security Council resolution on nanotech, we'll immediately lend credibility to the Lazarus Movement's most outrageous claims.'

Kirtland Air Force Base, Albuquerque, New Mexico

Still driving his rented Mustang, Smith pulled away from the Truman Gate guardhouse and headed south through the sprawling air base, passing Little League baseball fields crowded with teams and cheering parents on the right. It was near the end of the season, and the local championships were in full swing.

Following the directions the Air Force security police had given him, he made his way through the maze of streets and buildings and arrived at a small parking lot near the flight line. Peter Howell's white Buick LeSabre pulled in next to him.

Smith climbed out of the Mustang and slung his laptop

and a small travel bag over one shoulder. He tossed the keys onto the front seat and left the door unlocked. He saw Peter following his example. After they were gone, one of Fred Klein's occasional couriers would arrange for the safe return of the two rental cars.

Commercial passenger aircraft in bright colors thundered low overhead, taking off and landing at precisely regulated intervals. Kirtland shared its runways with Albuquerque's international airport. Heat waves shimmered out on the concrete, and the sharp tang of jet fuel hung in the hot air.

A large C-17 Globemaster transport in pale gray U.S. Air Force camouflage sat on the tarmac with its engines already spooling over. Jon and Peter walked toward the waiting jet.

The loadmaster, a senior Air Force noncom with a square, hard face and permanently furrowed brows, came to meet them. 'Is one of you guys Lieutenant Colonel Jonathan Smith?' he asked after looking down at the clipboard in his hand to make sure he got the name and rank right.

'That's me, Sergeant,' Jon told him. 'And this is Mr. Howell.'

'Then if you'll both follow me, sir,' the loadmaster said, after a long, dubious look at Smith's civilian clothes. 'We've only got a five-minute window for takeoff, and Major Harris says he ain't disposed to lose his spot and wind up sitting in line behind a goddamned bunch of airborne buses full of tourists.'

Smith hid a rueful grin. He strongly suspected the C-17 pilot had said considerably more than that on hearing that he was making an unscheduled cross-country flight – solely to ferry one Army light colonel and a foreign-born civilian to the Washington, D.C., metropolitan area. Once again, Fred Klein had waved Covert-One's magic wand, this time working through contacts inside the Pentagon's bureaucracy. He and Peter followed the C-17 crewman into the aircraft's cavernous cargo bay and then up onto the flight deck.

The pilot and co-pilot were waiting for them in the cockpit, already running through their last preflight checklist. Both had active heads-up displays, HUDs, fixed in front of them. On the control console below the windshield four large multi-function computer displays flashed through a variety of modes, showing the status of the engines, hydraulics, avionics, and other controls.

Major Harris, the pilot, turned his head when they came in. 'Are you gentlemen ready to go?' he asked through gritted teeth, emphasizing the word 'gentlemen' to make plain that was not the word he would have preferred to use.

Smith nodded apologetically. 'We're set, Major,' he said. 'And I'm sorry about the short notice. If it's any consolation, this is a genuinely critical mission – not just a glorified VIP jaunt.'

Slightly mollified, Harris jerked a thumb at the two observer seats right behind him. 'Well, strap yourselves in.' He leaned across to his co-pilot. 'Let's get this crate moving, Sam. We're on the clock now.'

The two Air Force officers busied themselves with the controls and brought the big plane rumbling out onto the apron, taxiing slowly toward the main runway. The roar of the C-17's four turbofan engines grew even louder as Harris pushed the throttles forward with his left hand.

After Jon and Peter buckled themselves in, the loadmaster handed them each a helmet with a built-in radio headset. 'Air-to-ground transmissions are pretty much it as far as in-flight entertainment goes,' he told them, raising his voice over the howl of the engines.

'What? You mean there are no stewardesses, champagne, or caviar?' Peter asked with a horrified look.

Almost against his will, the C-17 crewman grinned back. 'No, sir. Just me and my coffee, I'm afraid.'

'Fresh-brewed, I trust?' the Englishman asked.

'Nope. Instant decaf,' the Air Force sergeant replied, smiling even more broadly. He vanished, heading for his own seat down in the aircraft's cavernous cargo bay.

'Good lord! The sacrifices I make for queen and country,' Peter murmured with a quick wink at Smith.

The jet swung through a sharp turn, lining up with the long main runway. Ahead, a Southwest Airlines 737 lifted off and banked north. 'Air Force Charlie One-Seven, you are cleared for immediate takeoff,' the tower air traffic controller's voice crackled suddenly through Smith's radio earphones.

'Roger, Tower,' Harris replied. 'Charlie One-Seven is rolling now.' He shoved the four engine throttles all the way forward.

The C-17 accelerated down the runway, gaining speed fast. Jon felt himself pressed back against the padding of his seat. Less than a minute later, they were airborne, climbing steeply over the patchwork of houses, freeways, and parks of Albuquerque.

They were flying at thirty-seven thousand feet somewhere over West Texas when the co-pilot leaned back and tapped Smith on the knee. 'There's a secure transmission for you, Colonel,' he said. 'I'll switch it to your headset.'

Smith nodded his thanks.

'I have a situation update, Colonel,' Fred Klein's familiar voice said. 'Your target is also aloft and heading east for Andrews Air Force Base. She's approximately four hundred miles ahead of your aircraft now.'

Jon worked that out in his head. The C-17 had a cruise speed of roughly five hundred knots, which meant Kit Pierson's FBI executive jet would touch down at Andrews at least forty-five minutes before he and Peter could hope to arrive there. He frowned. 'Any chance of delaying her? Maybe have the FAA put her plane in a parking orbit until we can get down?'

'Alas, no,' Klein said crisply. 'Not without tipping our

hand entirely. Arranging this flight was tricky enough.'

'Damn it.'

'The situation may not be as dire as you think,' Klein told him. 'She has a confirmed meeting at the Hoover Building first and there's an official car standing by to take her straight there. Whatever else she plans isn't likely to take place until later, which should give you time to pick up her trail in D.C.'

Smith thought about that. The head of Covert-One was probably right, he decided. Although he was pretty sure that Kit Pierson's real purpose in returning to Washington went far beyond simply delivering a personal high-level briefing for her Bureau superiors, she was going to have to play the game as though it were.

'What about the vehicles and gear I requested?' he asked.

'They'll be waiting for you,' Klein promised. His voice sharpened. 'But I still have some very serious misgivings about involving Howell so closely with this operation, Colonel. He's a bright fellow . . . maybe too bright, and his fundamental loyalties lie outside this country.'

Smith glanced at Peter. The Englishman was staring out the cockpit side windows, seemingly wrapped up in watching the vast panorama of drifting cloud masses and seemingly endless flat brown countryside over which they were flying. 'You'll have to trust me on this one,' he told Klein softly. 'Back when you signed me on to this show, you told me you needed mavericks, self-starters who didn't quite fit into everybody else's neat little tables of organization. People who were willing to buck the system for results, remember?'

'I remember,' Klein said. 'And I meant it.'

'Well, I'm bucking the system right now,' Smith said firmly. 'Peter is already basically focused on the same problem we are. Plus, he's got skills and instincts and brainpower we can use to our advantage.'

There was silence on the other end for several seconds

while Klein digested that. 'Cogently argued, Colonel,' he said at last. 'All right, cooperate with Howell as closely as you can, but remember: He must never learn about Covert-One. Never. Is that understood?'

'Cross my heart and hope to die, Chief,' Smith answered.

Klein snorted. 'Fair enough, Jon.' He cleared his throat. 'Let me know once you're on the ground, all right?'

'Will do,' Smith replied. He leaned forward to check the navigation display, which showed their position, distance from Andrews, and current airspeed. 'It looks like that should be sometime around nine P.M., your time.'

CHAPTER TWENTY-SEVEN

La Courneuve, Near Paris

The grim, soulless high-rise housing projects of the Parisian slums, the *cités*, rose black against the night. Their design – massive, oppressively ugly, and intentionally sterile – was a monument to the grotesque ideals of the Swiss architect Le Corbusier, who thought solely in cold, utilitarian terms. The projects were also a testament to the penny-pinching of French bureaucrats – who wanted only to cram as many of their nation's unwanted immigrants, most of them Muslims, into the smallest possible spaces.

Few lights shone around the graffiti-smeared concrete bulk of the *Cité des Quatre Mille*, the 'city of four thousand,' a notorious haven for thieves, thugs, drug dealers, and Islamic radicals. The honest poor were trapped in a de facto prison essentially run by the criminals and terrorists among them. Most of the street lamps were either burned out or broken. The charred wrecks of stripped cars littered the potholed streets. The few stores in the neighborhood were either barricaded behind steel bars or else reduced to looted, blackened rubble.

Ahmed ben-Belbouk drifted through the night, a shadow among other shadows. He wore a long black raincoat against the night air and a kufi cap to cover his head. He was a little less than six feet tall, and he cultivated a full beard that masked some of the acne scars that pockmarked his round, soft face. By birth French, by heritage Algerian, and by faith a follower of radical Islam, ben-Belbouk was a recruiter for the jihad against America and the decadent

West. He operated out of a backroom office in one of the local mosques, quietly and carefully screening those who heeded the call to holy war. Those he judged the most promising were given false passports, cash, and plane tickets and sent outside France for advanced training.

Now, after a long day, he was at last returning to the bleak, grimy welfare apartment graciously provided for him by the state. Counting the secret funds at his disposal, he had money enough to live someplace better, but ben-Belbouk believed it was better to live among those whose loyalty he sought. When they saw him sharing their hardships and their hopelessness, they were more willing to listen to his sermons of hatred and his calls for vengeance on their Western oppressors.

Suddenly the terrorist recruiter noticed movement along the darkened avenue ahead. He stopped. That was odd. These were the hours when the streets of this district were usually deserted. The timid and honest were already cowering at home behind their locked doors, and the criminals and drug dealers were usually either still asleep or too busy indulging their vicious habits to be out and about.

Ben-Belbouk slipped into the darkened door of a burnt-out bakery and stood watching. He slipped his right hand into the pocket of his raincoat and felt the butt of the pistol he carried, a compact Glock 19. The street gangs and other petty criminals who preyed on the residents of the *Cité* usually steered a wide berth around men like him, but he preferred the option of providing for his own security.

From his place of concealment he watched the activity with growing suspicion. There was a van parked near the base of one of the smashed street lamps. Two men in coveralls were outside the vehicle, holding a ladder for a third technician working on something up near the top of the dark metal pole. Was this supposed to be a crew from the state-run electricity company? Sent here on some quixotic mission to again repair the streetlights already destroyed ten times over by the local residents?

The bearded man's eyes narrowed, and he spat silently to one side. The very thought was ridiculous. Representatives of the French government were despised in this district. Policemen were mobbed on sight. BAISE LA POLICE, 'screw the police,' was the single most popular graffiti. The coarse, obscene phrase was spray-painted on every building in sight. Even the firemen sent in to put out the frequent arson blazes were greeted with barrages of Molotov cocktails and rocks. They had to be escorted by armored cars. Surely no electrician in his right mind would dare to set foot in La Courneuve? Not after dark – and certainly not without a detachment of heavily armed riot police to guard him.

So who were these men, and what were they really doing? Ben-Belbouk looked more carefully. The technician on the ladder seemed to be installing a piece of equipment – a small gray rectangular plastic box of some kind.

He ran his gaze along the other street lamps in sight. To his surprise, he noticed identical gray boxes mounted on several of them at precise, regular intervals. Though it was difficult to be sure in the dim light, he thought he could make out dark round openings on the boxes. Were those camera lenses? His suspicions hardened into certainty. These *cochons*, these pigs, were setting up something – a new surveillance system, perhaps – that would tighten the government's grip on this lawless zone. He could not allow that to pass without resistance.

For a moment he debated whether or not to slip away and rouse the local Islamic brotherhoods. Then he thought better of it. In the inevitable delay these spies could easily finish their work and vanish. Besides, they were unarmed. It would be safer and more satisfying to handle them himself.

Ben-Belbouk drew the small Glock pistol out of his coat pocket and moved out into the open, holding the weapon unobtrusively at his side. He stopped a few paces away from the trio of technicians. 'You there!' he called out. 'What are you doing here?'

Startled, the two holding the ladder turned toward him. The third man, busy tightening screws on the clamps holding the box to the utility pole, kept working.

'I said, what are you doing here?' ben-Belbouk demanded again, louder this time.

One of the pair at the ladder shrugged. 'Our work is none of your business, *m'sieur*,' he said dismissively. 'Go on your way and leave us in peace.'

The bearded Islamic extremist saw red. His thin lips turned downward in a fierce scowl, and he brought the Glock out into plain sight. 'This,' he snarled, jabbing the pistol at them, 'makes it my business.' He moved closer. 'Now answer my question, filth, before I lose my patience!'

He never heard the silenced shot that killed him.

The 7.62mm rifle round hit Ahmed ben-Belbouk behind the right ear, tore through his brain, and blew a large hole in the left side of his skull. Pieces of pulverized bone and brain matter sprayed across the pavement. The terrorist recruiter fell in a heap, already dead.

Secure in the concealing shadows of a trash-strewn alley some distance away, the tall, broad-shouldered man who called himself Nones tapped his sniper lightly on the shoulder. 'That was a decent shot.'

The other man lowered his Heckler & Koch PSG-1 rifle and smiled gratefully. Words of praise from any of the *Horatii* were rare.

Nones keyed his radio mike, speaking to the pair of observers he had posted on nearby rooftops to watch over his technicians. 'Any further sign of movement?'

'Negative,' they both replied. 'Everything is quiet.'

The green-eyed man nodded to himself. The incident was unfortunate but evidently not a serious threat to his operational security. Murders and disappearances were relatively common occurrences in this part of La Courneuve. One more meant little or nothing. He switched to the technicians' frequency. 'How much longer?' he demanded.

'We're almost finished,' their leader reported. 'Two more minutes.'

'Good.' Nones turned back to the sniper. 'Stay ready. Shiro and I will dispose of the body.' Then he looked back at the much shorter man crouching behind him. 'Come with me.'

About one hundred meters from the place where Ahmed ben-Belbouk now lay dead, a slender woman stayed prone, hidden beneath the stripped and burnt-out chassis of a little Renault sedan. She was dressed from head to foot in black, with a black cotton jumpsuit for her torso, arms, and legs, black gloves, black boots, and a black watch cap to conceal her golden hair. She stared at the image in her night-vision binoculars. 'Son of a bitch!' she swore under her breath. Then she spoke softly into her own radio. 'Did you see that, Max?'

'Oh, I saw it,' confirmed her subordinate, posted farther back in the shelter of a small copse of dead trees. 'I'm not sure I believe it, but I definitely saw it.'

CIA officer Randi Russell focused her binoculars on the three men grouped around the street lamp. She watched silently while two more men – one very tall, with auburn hair, the other an Asian – crossed the street and joined the others. Working swiftly, the two newcomers rolled ben-Belbouk's corpse up in a black plastic sheet and lugged it away.

Randi gritted her teeth. With the dead man went the fruits of several months of hard, concentrated research, complicated planning, and risky covert surveillance. That was how long her section of the CIA's Paris Station had been tasked with tracking the recruitment of would-be

Islamic terrorists in France. Zeroing in on ben-Belbouk had been like finding the pot of gold at the end of a rainbow. By monitoring his contacts they were beginning to build comprehensive files on a host of very nasty characters, just the sorts of sick bastards who would get a thrill out of murdering thousands of innocents.

And now her whole operation was wiped out – well and truly wrecked by a single silenced shot.

She rubbed at her perfectly straight nose with one gloved finger, furiously thinking. 'Who the hell are those guys?' she muttered.

'Maybe DGSE? Or GIGN?' Max speculated aloud, naming both the French foreign intelligence service and the country's counterterrorist specialists.

Randi nodded to herself. That was possible. The French intelligence services and counterterror units were known for playing rough – very rough. Had she just witnessed a piece of government-sanctioned 'wet work' designed to rid France of a security threat without the inconvenience and expense of an arrest and a public trial?

Maybe, she thought coldly. If so, though, it was a remarkably stupid thing to do. While alive, Ahmed ben-Belbouk had been a window straight into the deadly underground world of Islamic terrorism – a world that was almost impossible for U.S. and other intelligence services to penetrate. Dead, he was useless to everybody.

'They're pulling out, boss,' Max's voice said in her ear.

Randi watched closely while the three men in overalls folded their ladder, shoved it into the back of their van, and drove away. Moments later, two cars, a dark blue BMW and a smaller Ford Escort, pulled onto the darkened avenue and followed the van. 'Did you jot down the license plates on those vehicles?' she asked.

'Yeah, I got 'em,' Max replied. 'They were all local numbers.'

'Good, we'll run them through the computer once we're finished here. Maybe that'll give us some idea of which jackasses just kicked us in the teeth,' she said grimly.

Randi lay motionless for a while longer, now focusing her binoculars on the small gray boxes fixed to a number of lampposts up and down the avenue and on the nearby side streets. The more she studied the boxes, the odder they seemed. They looked very much like containers for a variety of sensors, she decided – complete with several apertures for cameras, intakes for air sampling devices, and short, stubby data relay antennae on top.

Weird, she thought. Very weird. Why would anyone waste money setting up a whole network of expensive scientific instruments in a crime-ridden slum like La Courneuve? The boxes were reasonably unobtrusive, but they weren't invisible. Once the locals noticed them, their life span and that of the equipment they contained would be measured in minutes at most. So why kill ben-Belbouk just because he was starting to raise a fuss? She shook her head in frustration. Without more of the pieces to this puzzle, nothing she had seen tonight made much sense.

'You know, Max, I think we ought to take a closer look at what those guys were installing,' she told her subordinate. 'But we're going to have to come back with a ladder to do it.'

'Not tonight, we're not,' the other man warned. 'The crazies, druggies, and jihad boys are due out on the streets any minute now, boss lady. We need to git while the gittin' is good.'

'Yeah,' Randi agreed. She tucked her binoculars away and slithered gracefully backward out from under the charred Renault. Her mind was still working fast. The more she thought about it, the less likely it seemed that killing ben-Belbouk had been the primary aim of the men installing those strange sensor arrays. Maybe his murder was just a piece of unintended collateral damage. Then who were they, she wondered, and what were they really up to?

CHAPTER TWENTY-EIGHT

Sunday, October 17
Rural Virginia

FBI Deputy Assistant Director Kit Pierson saw the weathered signpost caught in the high beams of her green Volkswagen Passat. HARDSCRABBLE HOLLOW – ¼ MILE. That was her next landmark. She tapped the brakes, slowing down. She did not want to risk missing the turnoff to Hal Burke's run-down farm.

The rolling Virginia countryside was covered in almost total darkness. Only the quarter moon cast a faint glow through the solid layer of clouds high overhead. There were a few other farms and homes scattered through these low wooded hills, but it was already past midnight and their inhabitants were long since asleep. With chores and early morning Sunday church services awaiting them, most people in this part of the state went to bed early.

The rutted gravel drive to her CIA counterpart's weekend retreat appeared just ahead, and she slowed further. Before turning onto it, though, she glanced again in the rearview mirror. Nothing. There were no other headlights in sight along this desolate stretch of county road. She was still alone.

Partly reassured by that, Pierson turned her Passat onto the track and followed it uphill to the house. The lights were on, spilling out onto the weed-and bramble-choked hillside through partly drawn curtains. Burke was expecting her.

She parked next to his car, an old Mercury Marquis,

and walked quickly to the front door. It opened before she could even knock. The stocky, square-jawed CIA officer stood there in his shirtsleeves. He looked weary and rumpled, with shadowed, bloodshot eyes.

Burke took one suspicious look around, making sure that she was by herself, and then stepped back to let her come into the narrow front hall. 'Did you have any trouble?' he asked harshly.

Kit Pierson waited for him to close the door before replying. 'On my way here? No,' she said coolly. 'At my meeting with the director and his senior staff? Yes.'

'What kind of trouble?'

'They weren't especially pleased to see me in D.C. instead of still out in the field,' she said flatly. 'In fact, there were several rather pointed suggestions that my preliminary report was entirely too "thin" to justify coming back in person.'

The CIA officer shrugged. 'That was your call, Kit,' he reminded her. 'We didn't need to meet here in person. We could have worked through this problem on the phone if you'd just sat tight.'

'With Smith starting to breathe right down my neck?' she snapped back. 'Not likely, Hal.' She shook her head. 'I don't know how much he knows yet, but he's getting too close. Shutting down the Santa Fe police probe was a mistake. We should have just let the local cops go ahead and try to identify your man's body.'

Burke shook his head. 'Too risky.'

'Our files were scrubbed,' Pierson said stubbornly. 'There's no way this Dolan character could have been linked to either of us. Or even to the Agency or the Bureau as a whole.'

'Still too risky,' he told her. 'Other agencies have their own databases – databases over which we have no control. The Army has its own files, for that matter. Hell, Kit, you're the one who's so panicked about Smith and his mysterious employers! You know as well as I do that anyone pegging Dolan as an ex-Special Forces officer would be bound to start asking some goddamned tough questions.'

Burke showed her into his study. The small dark-paneled room was crowded with a desk, a monitor and keyboard, two chairs, several bookcases, a television, and racks full of computer and communications equipment. An open half-empty bottle of Jim Beam whiskey and a shot glass sat on the desk, right next to the computer keyboard. A faint stale whiff of sweat, unwashed dishes, mildew, and general neglect hung in the air.

Pierson wrinkled her nose in distaste. The man was disintegrating under the pressure as TOCSIN collapsed around them, she thought coldly.

'Want a drink?' Burke growled, dropping heavily into the swivel chair in front of his desk. He waved her into the other chair, a battered armchair with lumpy, fraying upholstery.

She shook her head and then sat watching while he poured one for himself. The whiskey sloshed over the rim and left a wet ring on his desk. He ignored the spill, instead downing his drink in one swift gulp. He set the glass down with a thump and looked up at her. 'Okay, Kit, why exactly are you here?'

'To persuade you to shut TOCSIN down,' she said without hesitating.

One corner of the CIA officer's mouth turned down in an irritated frown. 'We've gone through this before. My answer is still the same.'

'But the situation is not the same, Hal!' Pierson said forcefully. Her lips thinned. 'And you know it. The Teller attack was supposed to force President Castilla to act against the Lazarus Movement before it was too late – to act as a relatively bloodless wake-up call. It wasn't supposed to make Lazarus stronger. And it certainly wasn't supposed to trigger a worldwide spree of bombings and murders we can't stop!'

'Wars always have unintended consequences,' Burke said through clenched teeth. 'And we *are* in a war against the Movement. Maybe you've forgotten what's at stake in this matter.'

She shook her head. 'I haven't forgotten anything. But TOCSIN is only a means to an end – not the end itself. The whole damned operation is unraveling faster than you can stitch it back together. So I say we cut our losses while we still can. Call off your action teams now. Tell them to abort any ongoing missions and drop back into cover. Then, once that's done, we can plan our next move.'

To buy himself some time before replying, Burke picked up the whiskey bottle and poured another drink. But this time he left the glass untouched. He looked closely at her. 'You can't run from this one, Kit. It's gone too far for that. Even if we shut TOCSIN down right now and pull in our horns, your little friend Dr. Jonathan Smith is still going to be out there asking questions we do *not* want answered.'

'I know that,' she said bitterly. 'Trying to kill Smith was a mistake. Failing to kill him was a disaster.'

'What's done is done,' Burke said, shrugging both shoulders. 'One of my security units is hunting the colonel. Once they pinpoint him, they'll nail him.'

Pierson looked at him in exasperation. 'Which means you have absolutely no idea where he is right now.'

'He's gone to ground again,' Burke admitted. 'I sent people to the Santa Fe PD after you called to let me know Smith was snooping there, but he disappeared before they arrived.'

'Wonderful.'

'The nosy bastard can't run far, Kit,' the CIA officer said confidently. 'I have agents watching the airport terminals in both Santa Fe and Albuquerque. And I have a contact in Homeland Security running his name through every commercial flight manifest. The moment he surfaces, we'll know it. And when he does, our guys will close in.' He smiled thinly. 'Trust me on this, okay? For all practical purposes, Smith is nothing but a dead man walking.'

Along the county road below, the drivers of the two dark-colored automobiles traveling slowly without any head-lights turned off their ignitions and coasted to a stop, pulling off to the side not far from the gravel track heading uphill. Still wearing the U.S. Army-issue AN/PVS 7 night-vision goggles he'd been using to drive without lights, Jon Smith stiffly climbed out of the second car and walked forward to the vehicle in front.

Peter Howell unrolled his window as Smith came up. Below his own set of goggles, the Englishman's teeth flashed white in the near-total darkness. 'Rather an excit-ing ride, wasn't it, Jon?'

Smith nodded wryly. 'Perfectly delightful.' He rolled his neck and shoulders from side to side, hearing tense muscles and joints crack and pop. The last fifteen minutes of driving had been nerve-racking.

The night-vision equipment was top-of-the-line gear, but even so the images these third-generation goggles produced were not perfect – they were monochromatic, with a slight green tint, and they were a tiny bit grainy. You could drive without lights while wearing them, but it took real effort and serious concentration to avoid drifting off the road or colliding with the vehicle ahead of you.

In contrast, following the government sedan taking Kit Pierson from the FBI's Hoover Building to her own home in Upper Georgetown had been a piece of cake. Even late on Saturday night, Washington's streets were packed with cars, trucks, minivans, and taxis. It had been easy enough to hang two or three car lengths back without being no-ticed.

Neither Jon nor Peter had been surprised when Pier-son took off only minutes later, this time using her own car. Both had been sure from the beginning that this sudden briefing for her superiors was only a blind, a way to cover her real reason for flying back so abruptly from New Mexico. But again, the task of following her discreetly was comparatively easy – at least at first. It had only gotten really difficult once she turned off the highway onto a succession of smaller side roads where traffic was sporadic at best. And Kit Pierson was no fool. She would have been bound to grow suspicious if she saw the same two pairs of headlights gleaming in her rearview mirror through mile after mile of darkened, nearly empty countryside.

That was when both Smith and Peter Howell had been forced to slip on their night-vision goggles and switch off their lights. Even so, they had been forced to hang back farther from her Passat than they would have preferred – always hoping they would not miss whichever turnoff or crossroads she finally took to make her rendezvous.

Smith looked up the gravel track. He could just make out a small house on the crest of a low hill. The lights were on, and he could see two cars parked outside. This looked like it could be the place they were hunting.

'What do you think?' he asked Peter quietly.

The Englishman pointed to the U.S. Geological Survey 1:20,000-scale map open on the seat beside him. It was part of the set included in the equipment left for them at Andrews Air Force Base. The IR illuminators on their goggles allowed them to read the map. 'This little drive doesn't go anywhere else but that farm up there,' he said. 'And I doubt very seriously that our Ms. Pierson plans to take her sedan very far off-road.'

'So what's the plan?' Smith asked.

'I suggest we back up a quarter-mile or so,' Peter said. 'I noticed a small copse of trees there which we can use as cover for the cars. Once we've got the rest of our gear on, we can make our way quietly up to that farmhouse on foot.' He showed his teeth again. 'I, for one, should very much like to know who Ms. Pierson has chosen to visit so late at night. And what exactly they are discussing.'

Smith nodded grimly. He was suddenly quite sure that some of the answers he needed were locked away in that dimly lit house on the hill.

CHAPTER TWENTY-NINE

Near Meaux, East of Paris

The ruins of the Château de Montceaux, known as the Château of the Queens, were hemmed in by the forest of Montceaux – a stretch of woods rising above the southern bank of the undulating River Marne, roughly thirty miles east of Paris. First built in the mid-1500s on the orders of the powerful, cunning, and crafty Queen Catherine de Medici, the wife of one king of France and the mother of three more, the elegant country palace and its vast park and hunting preserve had at last been abandoned around 1650. Now, after centuries of neglect, little remained – only the hollow shell of a grand stone entrance pavilion, the oblong moat, and sections of crumbling wall lined with gaping windows.

Strands of mist curled between the surrounding trees, slowly burning away as the morning sun climbed higher. The bells of the Cathedral of St-Etienne in Meaux, five miles away, rang out, summoning the faithful, few though they were these days, to Sunday Mass. Other bells pealed across the peaceful countryside as the smaller parish churches in the nearby villages echoed the summons.

Two vans hauling a pair of trailers sat in a large clearing not far from the ruins. Signs emblazoned on the vehicles identified them as part of an organization called the *Groupe d'Aperçu Météorologique*, the Meteorological Survey Group. Several technicians were busy near the rear of each trailer, erecting two angled launch rails aimed almost due west. Each launch rail included a pneumatic catapult system powered by compressed air. Other men were fussing over a pair of propeller-driven unmanned aerial vehicles, UAVs, each roughly five feet long, with an eight-foot wingspan.

The tall auburn-haired man who called himself Nones stood close by, watching his team complete their work. Periodic reports from the sentries posted in the woods around the clearing crackled through his radio headset. There were no signs of any unwanted observation by the local farmers.

One of the UAV technicians, a stoop-shouldered Asian man with thinning black hair, rose slowly to his feet. He turned to the third of the *Horatii* with a relieved expression on his lined and weary face. 'The payloads are secure. All engine, avionics, UHF, and autonomous control systems have been tested and are online. All global positioning navigation waypoints have been configured and confirmed. Both craft are ready for flight.'

'Good,' Nones replied. 'Then you may prepare for launch.'

He stepped back out of the way as the technicians carefully lifted the UAVs, which weighed roughly one hundred pounds apiece, and carried them over to the twin launch rails. His bright green eyes followed them appreciatively. These two unmanned aircraft were modeled on drones used by the U.S. Army for short-range tactical reconnaissance, communications jamming, and airborne nuclear, biological, and chemical weapons detection. Now he and his men would pioneer an entirely new use for these robotic fliers.

Nones switched frequencies, contacting the newly arrived surveillance team he had stationed in Paris. 'Are you receiving data from the target area, Linden?' he asked.

'We are,' the Dutchman confirmed. 'All remote sensors and cameras are operational.'

'And the weather conditions?'

'Temperature, air pressure, humidity, wind direction,

and wind speed are all well within the preset mission parameters,' Linden reported. 'The Center recommends that you proceed when ready.'

'Acknowledged,' Nones said quietly. He swung round to the waiting UAV technicians. 'Don masks and gloves,' he ordered.

They quickly obeyed, putting on the gas masks, respirators, and thick gloves intended to give them enough time to escape the immediate area if one of their aircraft crashed on launch. The third member of the *Horatii* did the same, donning his own protective gear.

'Catapults pressurized and standing by,' the Asian technician told him. The technician crouched at a control console set between the two angled rails. His fingers hovered over a set of switches.

Nones smiled. 'Continue.'

The technician nodded. He flicked two switches. 'Engine and propeller start.'

The twin-bladed propellers on both UAVs suddenly whirled into motion, spinning with a low-pitched whir that was almost impossible to hear more than a few yards away.

'Engines at full power.'

'Launch!' the tall green-eyed man commanded.

With a soft *whoosh*, the first pneumatic catapult fired – hurling the UAV attached to it up the angled rail and into the air in a high, curving arc. For an instant, at the end of this arc, the unmanned aircraft seemed ready to fall back toward the ground, but then it climbed again – buoyed now by the lift provided by its own wings and propeller. Still ascending, it cleared the trees and headed west on its preprogrammed course.

Ten seconds later, the second unmanned flier followed its counterpart into the air. Both drones, now almost invisible from the ground and too small to register on most radars, climbed steadily toward their cruising altitude of three thousand feet and flew toward Paris at roughly one hundred miles per hour.

Rural Virginia

Staying low, Jon Smith followed Peter Howell west across a wide field choked with tall weeds and thickets of jagged brambles. Their surroundings glowed faintly green through their night-vision goggles. A couple of hundred yards off to their left, the paved county road cut a straight line across the darkened landscape. Ahead, the ground sloped up, rising gently above a stagnant scum-covered pond on their right. The gravel access road Kit Pierson had turned onto snaked back and forth as it climbed the low hill in front of them.

Something sharp snagged Smith's shoulder, stabbing right through the thick cloth deep enough to draw blood. He gritted his teeth and went on. Peter was doing his best to lead them through the worst of the tangled vegetation, but there were places where they just had to bull through, ignoring the thorns and briars tearing at their dark clothing and black leather gloves.

Halfway up the hill, the Englishman dropped to one knee. He scanned the terrain around them carefully and then waved Smith forward to join him. The lights were still on at the farmhouse up on the crest.

Both men were dressed and equipped for a night reconnaissance mission across rough ground. Besides their AN/PVS 7 goggles, each wore a combat vest stuffed with the surveillance gear – cameras and various types of listening devices – left waiting for them at Andrews Air Force Base. Smith had a holster for his SIG-Sauer pistol strapped to his thigh, while Peter had the same kind of rig for the Browning Hi-Power he favored. For extra firepower in a real emergency, each also carried a Heckler & Koch MP5 submachine gun slung across his back.

Peter shook off one of his gloves and then held up a wetted finger to test the direction of the soft, cool night breeze whispering around them. He nodded, pleased by the result. 'Now there's a bit of good fortune. The wind is from the west.'

Smith waited. The other man had spent decades in the field, first for the SAS and then for MI6. Peter Howell had forgotten more about moving through potentially hostile territory than Smith had ever learned.

'This wind won't carry our scent ahead of us,' Peter explained. 'If there are any dogs up there, they won't smell us coming.'

Peter slid his glove back on and led the way again. Both men crouched even lower as they came out onto the top of the shallow rise. They were within yards of an old, ruined barn – a hollowed-out, roofless wreck that was more a pile of broken, rotting boards than a standing structure. Beyond that, they could make out the shapes of two parked cars, the Volkswagen Passat belonging to Kit Pierson, and another, this one an older American make. And there was enough light leaking out through the mostly closed drapes of their target, a small one-story farmhouse, to make it glow brightly in their night-vision gear.

Smith saw that whoever owned the place had gone to the trouble of whacking away the tallest weeds and brambles in a rough circle around the building. He followed Peter down onto his belly and wriggled through the low grass after him, crossing the open space as quickly as possible to gain the cover provided by the parked cars.

'Where to now?' he murmured.

Peter nodded toward a big picture window on this side of the house, not far from the front door. 'Over there, I should think,' he said softly. 'I thought I saw a shadow moving behind those drapes a moment ago. Worth a look anyhow.' He glanced at Smith. 'Cover me, will you, Jon?'

Smith tugged his SIG-Sauer out of the holster. 'Whenever you're ready.'

The other man nodded once. Then he crawled rapidly across the patch of oil-stained concrete and disappeared into a patch of tall brush growing right up against the side of the farmhouse. Only the night-vision goggles he was wearing let Smith keep track of him. To anyone watching with unaided eyes, Peter would have seemed nothing more than a moving shadow, a shadow that simply vanished into blackness.

The Englishman raised himself up onto his knees, carefully examining the window above him. Satisfied, he dropped flat and signaled Jon to come ahead.

Smith crawled over to join him as fast as he could, feeling terribly exposed along every inch of the way. He wriggled the last few feet into the weeds and lay still, breathing heavily.

Peter leaned close to his ear and motioned to the window. 'Pierson is definitely inside.'

Smith smiled tightly. 'Glad to hear it. I'd sure hate to have just wrecked my knees for nothing.' He rolled onto his side and tugged a handheld laser surveillance kit out of one of the Velcro-sealed pouches on his combat vest. He slipped on the attached headset, flipped a switch to activate the low-powered IR laser, and carefully aimed the device at the window above them.

If he could hold it steady enough, the laser beam would bounce back off the glass and pick up the vibrations induced in it by anyone talking inside the room. Then, assuming everything worked right, the electronics package should be able to translate those vibrations back into understandable sounds through his headphones.

Almost to his surprise, the system worked.

'Damn it, Kit,' he heard a man's voice growl angrily. 'You can't back out of this operation now. We're going ahead, whether you like it or not. There are no other options. Either we destroy the Lazarus Movement – or it destroys us!'

CHAPTER THIRTY

Lazarus' Private Office

The man called Lazarus sat calmly behind a solid, age-darkened teak desk in his private office. The room was quiet, cool, and dimly lit. A ventilation system hummed softly in the background, bringing in air rigorously scrubbed clean of any trace of the outside world.

Much of the desk was taken up with a large computer-driven display. With the gentle flick of a finger on his keyboard, Lazarus switched rapidly between views relayed from cameras around the globe. One, apparently mounted aboard an aircraft, showed the winding trace of a river unrolling two or three thousand feet below. Villages, roads, bridges, and tracts of forest came into view and then slid off-camera. Another camera showed a dingy street crowded with stripped and vandalized automobiles. The street was lined with drab concrete-block buildings. Their windows and doors were heavily barricaded with steel bars.

Below the images on his display, three digital readouts showed the local time, the time in Paris, and the time along the eastern seaboard of the United States. A secure satellite phone system sat next to the computer. Two blinking green lights indicated pending connections to two of his special action teams.

Lazarus smiled, reveling in the exquisite sensation of watching a complex, intricately crafted plan unfolding with absolutely perfect timing. With one command, he had set in motion the last of his needed field experiments –

the tests so necessary to refine his chosen instruments of the planet's salvation. With another, he would begin the series of actions intended to throw the CIA, the FBI, and the British Secret Intelligence Service into self-destructive chaos.

Soon, he thought coldly, very soon. As the sun rose higher today, a horrified world would start to see its worst fears about the United States confirmed. Alliances would shatter. Old wounds would reopen. Long-held rivalries would burst again into open conflict. And by the time the full magnitude of what was really happening became clear, it would be impossible for anyone to stop him.

His internal phone chimed once. Lazarus tapped the speaker button. 'Yes?'

'Our drones are within fifty kilometers of the target,' reported the voice of his senior technician. 'Both are operating within the expected norms.'

'Very good. Continue as planned,' Lazarus ordered. He tapped the button, cutting the circuit. Another gentle flick of his finger completed the satellite connection to one of his action teams.

'The Paris operation is under way,' he told the man waiting patiently on the other end. 'Be ready to carry out your instructions on my next signal.'

Rural Virginia

Three big 4×4 trucks were parked just inside a patch of scrub pines growing along the crest of a ridge several hundred yards west of Burke's ramshackle farm. Twelve men wearing black jackets and sweaters and dark-colored jeans waited in the shelter of this clump of stunted trees. Four of them were posted as sentries at different points around the outside edge, keeping watch through British-made Simrad night-vision binoculars. Seven squatted patiently on the sandy soil farther inside the grove. They were busy making last-minute weapons checks on their assortment of assault rifles, submachine guns, and pistols.

The twelfth, the tall green-eyed man named Terce, sat in the cab of one of the 4×4s. 'Understood,' he said into his secure cell phone. 'We are standing by.' He hung up and went back to monitoring a heated conversation relayed through his radio set. An angry voice sounded in his headset. 'Either we destroy the Lazarus Movement – or it destroys us!'

'Melodrama doesn't suit you, Hal,' a woman's voice answered icily. 'I'm not suggesting that we surrender to the Movement. But TOCSIN itself is no longer worth the price we're paying – or the risks we're running. And I meant what I said over the phone earlier: If this lousy operation blows up in my face, I don't plan to be the only one taking a fall.'

Listening to the transmission from a bug he had planted earlier that night, the second member of the *Horatii* nodded to himself. The CIA officer was quite right. FBI Deputy Assistant Director Katherine Pierson was no longer reliable. Not that it mattered very much anymore, he thought with a trace of grim amusement.

Automatically Terce checked the magazine on his Walther, screwed on the silencer, and then slid the pistol back into his coat pocket. He glanced at the luminous dial of his watch. There were only minutes at most remaining before he would need to act.

A soft, insistent *beep* signaled a priority call from one of his sentries. He switched channels. 'Go ahead.'

'This is McRae. There's something moving up near the house,' the lookout warned in a soft lowland Scots burr.

'I'm on my way,' Terce said. The big man slid out of the 4×4, ducking his head to clear the frame, and hurried to the edge of the pine woods. He found McRae crouched behind a fallen tree trunk overgrown with vines and moved low into position beside him.

'Take a look for yourself. In those bushes and tall grass close to the front door,' the short, wiry Scot said, pointing.

'I can't make out anything now, mind you, but I saw movement there just a minute ago.'

The green-eyed man raised his own binoculars, slowly scanning the south side of Burke's house. Two man-shaped blotches leaped immediately into focus, bright white thermal blooms against the cooler gray of the dense vegetation in which they lay hidden.

'You have very good eyes, McRae,' Terce said calmly. The night-vision gear used by his sentries worked by amplifying all available ambient light. They turned night into eerie, green-tinted day, but they could not see 'heat' in the way his special equipment could. Weighing over five pounds and with a price tag of nearly sixty thousand dollars, his French-made 'Sophie' thermal-imaging binoculars were top-of-the-line in every way and far more effective. At night, under these overcast skies, the best passive light intensifier systems had a maximum range of three or four hundred yards, and often much less. In contrast, using thermal imaging he could detect the heat signature made by a human being up to two miles away – even through thick cover.

Terce wondered whether it was mere coincidence that these two spies appeared so soon after Kit Pierson arrived. Or had she brought them with her – either knowingly or unknowingly? The big man shrugged away the thought. He did not believe in coincidences. Nor, for that matter, did his ultimate employer.

Terce considered his options. For a moment he regretted the Center's decision to transfer his specialist sniper to the Paris-based security force. It would have been simpler and far less dangerous to eliminate these two enemies with a pair of well-aimed long-range rifle shots. Then he quickly realized wishing would not alter the circumstances. His team was trained and equipped for close-quarters action – so those were the tactics he would have to employ.

Terce handed the binoculars to McRae. 'Keep an eye

on those two,' he ordered coolly. 'Let me know if they make any sudden moves.' Then he pulled out his cell phone and hit a preset number.

The phone on the other end rang once. 'Burke here.'

'This is Terce,' he said quietly. 'Do not react openly in any way to what I am about to say. Do you understand me?'

There was a short pause. 'Yes, I understand you,' Burke said at last.

'Good. Now then, listen carefully. My security team has detected hostile activity near your house. You are under close observation. Very close observation. Within meters, in fact.'

'That's very . . . interesting,' the CIA officer said tightly. He hesitated briefly. 'Can your people handle this situation on their own?'

'Most definitely,' Terce assured him.

'And do you have a time frame for that?' Burke asked.

The big man's bright green eyes gleamed in the darkness. 'Minutes, Mr. Burke. Only minutes.'

'I see.' Again Burke hesitated. Finally, he asked, 'Should I consider this an interagency matter?'

Terce knew that the other man was asking if Kit Pierson was somehow responsible for the snoopers now almost literally on his doorstep. He smiled. At this point, whether that was true or not was immaterial. 'I think it would be wise to do so.'

'That's too bad,' the CIA officer said edgily. 'Really too bad.'

'Yes, it is,' the big man agreed. 'For now, hold tight where you are. Out.'

Terce flipped the phone shut. Then he retrieved his thermal-imaging binoculars from McRae. 'Go back to the vehicles and bring the others here,' he said. 'But I want them to come quietly.' He grinned wolfishly. 'Tell them they're going hunting.'

*

'Who was that, Hal?' Kit Pierson asked, clearly puzzled.

'The duty officer at Langley,' Burke told her, speaking slowly and distinctly. His voice sounded strained and unnatural. 'The NSA just sent over a courier with a few Movement-related intercepts. . . .'

Jon Smith listened closely. He frowned. Still holding the laser microphone aimed at the window above him, he glanced at Peter Howell. 'Something's wrong,' he whispered. 'Burke just got a phone call and now he's gone all stiff. He's just bullshitting, not really saying anything.'

'Do you think he's tumbled to us?' Peter asked quietly.

'Maybe. But I don't see how.'

'We may have underestimated this fellow,' Peter said. The corners of his mouth turned down. 'A cardinal sin in this line of work, I'm afraid. I suspect Mr. Burke of the CIA has more resources available to him here than we had hoped.'

'Meaning he has backup?'

'Quite possibly.' The Englishman dug the USGS survey map out of one of the pockets on his vest and studied it, tracing the contour lines and terrain features with one gloved finger. He tapped the outline of a wooded ridge not far off to the west. 'If I wanted to keep a good, close eye on this house, that's where I would put my observation post.'

Smith felt the hairs on the back of his neck rise. Peter was right. That ridge offered a clear view of most of the ground around the farmhouse, including their current position. 'What do you suggest?'

'An immediate retreat,' the pale-eyed man said crisply, stuffing the survey map back into his vest pocket. He pulled the Heckler & Koch MP5 submachine gun over his head and yanked back on the cocking handle, chambering a 9mm round. 'We don't know how strong the opposition is, and I don't see any point in loitering about to learn the hard way. We've acquired some useful information, Jon. Let's not push our luck further tonight.'

Smith nodded, already putting the laser microphone

and its associated gear away. 'Good point.' He readied his own submachine gun.

'Then follow me.' Peter rolled to his feet and then, bent almost double, scurried back to the cover offered by the two cars parked close to the house. Smith followed him, moving as fast as he could while also staying low to the ground. At any second he expected to hear a startled shout or feel the sudden impact of a bullet. But he heard and felt only the silence of the night and the pounding of his own accelerating pulse.

From there, they moved past the ruined barn and on down the slope into the bramble-choked field below, trying to keep the bulk of the little hill between them and the higher ridge to the west. Peter led the way, ghosting quietly through the snarled clumps of thorns and waist-high weeds with a grace born out of years of training and experience.

They were close to the edge of the stagnant pond when the Englishman suddenly went prone, hugging the dirt behind a patch of raspberry bushes. Smith dropped flat behind him and then crawled forward, using his elbows and knees while cradling the MP5 against his chest. He tried hard not to breathe in too deeply. They were below the level of the cool breeze whispering across the field, and the air was thick with the pent-up stench of algae and rotting fruit.

'Christ,' Peter muttered. 'That's torn it! Listen.'

Smith heard the faint noise of a powerful engine, growing steadily louder. Cautiously he raised his head to peer over the top of the closest bush. About two hundred yards away a large black 4×4 cruised slowly past on the county road, traveling east. It was driving without lights.

'You think they'll spot our cars?' he asked softly.

Peter nodded grimly. The small stand of trees in which they had parked would not hide their vehicles from a determined search. 'They're sure to,' he said. 'And when they do, all hell will break loose – if it hasn't already.' He glanced back over his shoulder. 'And it has, alas,' he murmured. 'Take a look behind us, Jon. But do it slowly.'

Smith carefully turned his head and saw a skirmish line of five men wearing night-vision goggles and dark clothing slowly descending the gentle slope behind them. Each carried a submachine gun or an assault rifle cradled in both hands.

Jon felt his mouth go dry. The closest of the armed men hunting them was already just a little more than one hundred yards away. He and Peter were trapped.

'Any ideas?' Smith hissed.

'Yes. We drive those five men to ground and then we both run like rabbits,' Peter answered. 'Stay away from the road, though. Not enough cover in that direction. We'll head north.' He spun around and came up on one knee with his submachine gun at the ready, followed a second later by Smith.

For an instant Jon hesitated, pausing with his finger already on the trigger – wondering if he should shoot to kill or simply to frighten. Were these some of the same men who had already tried to kill him? Or allied to them? Or were they regular CIA personnel or private security guards roped in by Burke to guard his property?

Their sudden movement attracted the attention of one of the gunmen moving down the hill. He froze. 'Contact, front!' he yelled in heavily accented English. Then he opened fire with his submachine gun, spraying a hail of 9mm bullets toward the two kneeling men.

Smith's doubts dissolved as the incoming rounds snapped and whined through the air around him. These guys were mercenaries, and they were not trying to take prisoners. He and Peter fired back, squeezing off a series of aimed three-round bursts with their MP5s – walking their fire from opposite ends of the enemy skirmish line toward the middle. One of the five gunmen screamed suddenly and folded over, hit in the stomach. The other four dived for cover.

'Let's go!' Peter said sharply, tapping Smith on the shoulder.

Both men jumped to their feet and sprinted off into the darkness, angling north, well away from the county road. Again, the Englishman led the way, but this time he did not waste any time trying to find easier paths through the tangle of brush and brambles. Instead, he crashed right through even the densest briar patches at full bore. Stealth was out in favor of speed. They needed to cover as much ground as possible before the surviving gunmen recovered from their surprise and started shooting again.

Smith ran fast, his heart pounding as he followed right in Peter's wake. He kept his gloved hands and the submachine gun out in front of him, trying to keep his face from being lacerated by the welter of splintered branches and sharp-edged thorns. Brambles tugged and tore at his arms and legs, jabbing and slashing right through the thick cloth. Sweat trickled down his forearms, stinging like fire when it mingled with his new puncture wounds, cuts, and scrapes.

More gunfire erupted behind them. Rounds zipped through the thick undergrowth on either side – clipping off leaves and twigs and spattering the fragments in all directions.

The two men threw themselves down and wriggled round to face the way they had come, seeking cover in a slight depression worn away by runoff from the hill above them. 'Determined bastards,' Peter commented coolly as rifle bullets and submachine gun rounds ripped past right over their heads. 'I'll give them that.' He listened intently. 'That's only two men firing. We hit one. So where are the other two?'

'Closing in on us,' Smith said grimly. 'While their pals cover them.'

'Quite likely,' Peter agreed. He smiled suddenly. 'Let's teach them that's not such a good idea, shall we?'

Jon nodded.

'Right,' Peter said calmly. 'Here we go.'

Ignoring the bullets still tearing up the brush around them, both men reared up and began firing – again sweeping three-round bursts back and forth across the field in front of them. Smith had a quick impression of startled yells and barely glimpsed shapes diving behind clumps of tall weeds and brambles. More weapons opened up with a stuttering, clattering roar as the gunmen they had driven prone began shooting back.

Smith and Peter dropped back into the shallow drainage ditch and crawled rapidly away along its meandering trace. It fell away to the east, following the slight slope of the long-abandoned field. After moving about fifty yards, they risked poking their heads up for another quick look. One of their pursuers was still firing short bursts in their general direction in an effort to pin them down. The other three gunmen were in motion again, but they were also heading east – rapidly deploying into a dispersed firing line across the width of the forty-acre field.

'Damn it,' Peter said under his breath. 'What the hell are they up to now?'

Smith's eyes narrowed. Their enemies no longer seemed interested in closing with them. Instead, the bad guys were setting up a cordon that would effectively cut them off from the road and from the vehicles they had left hidden in among the trees still several hundred yards away. 'We're being herded!' he realized suddenly.

The Englishman stared at him for a second or two. Then his jaw tightened and he nodded abruptly. 'You're right, Jon. I should have seen it sooner. They're acting as beaters – setting up to flush us out for the rest of the shooting party.' He shook his head in disgust. 'We're being treated like a covey of bloody grouse or quails.'

Almost against his will, Smith grinned back at him, fighting down the urge to laugh out loud. His old friend sounded genuinely insulted at being manipulated so contemptuously by their enemies.

Peter turned his head, speculatively eyeing the rougher, even more overgrown stretch of old farmland to the north. 'They'll have a nasty little ambush set out somewhere up that way,' he said, stripping out the used magazine on his submachine gun and inserting a new thirty-round clip. 'Getting past that will be tricky.'

'Sure,' Smith said. 'But we do have at least one advantage.'

Peter raised an eyebrow in surprise. 'Oh? Care to enlighten me?'

'Yep.' Smith patted his own MP5. 'The last time I checked, grouse and quails don't shoot back.'

This time it was Peter's turn to suppress a snort of rueful laughter. 'True enough,' he agreed quietly. 'Very well, Jon, let's go and see if we can turn the hunters into the hunted.'

They left the drainage ditch and crawled off to the north. Their path through the thick undergrowth was a circuitous one. They were following the rambling narrow trails made by small animals that made their dens and warrens in the overgrown fields. Both men stayed very low, hugging the ground and using their feet, knees, and elbows to wriggle forward as fast as they could without making too much noise or shaking the tangled tufts of brush and grass above them. The knowledge that an enemy force lurked unseen somewhere ahead in the darkness again made stealth nearly as vital as speed.

Smith could feel droplets of sweat rolling down through the dirt streaking his forehead. He shook them away impatiently, not wanting them to drip into his eyes under the mask holding his night-vision goggles. Plant stalks and curling vines loomed up suddenly in his green-tinted vision and then vanished off to the sides as he squirmed past. Deep in the heart of these jumbled thickets, his field of view was down to just a few feet. The air was warm and thick with the smell of dank, mossy earth and fresh animal droppings.

From time to time bullets hissed over their heads or shredded the bushes and thickets off on either flank. All four of the mercenaries deployed in a line behind them were shooting now – firing occasional bursts into the field to force their unseen quarry toward the ambush set to kill them.

Smith's breathing was becoming labored under the strain and physical exertion imposed by crawling so far and so rapidly. He concentrated on following Peter as closely as he could – watching carefully to see where the older man put his elbows and feet to avoid disturbing the vegetation through which they were moving.

Suddenly Peter froze. For long seconds he stayed absolutely motionless, watching and listening. Then, slowly and carefully, he held out one gloved hand and waved Jon forward to his side.

Smith peered cautiously through a screen of tall grass, studying the terrain in front of them. They were very near the northern edge of the field. The weathered and rotting remnants of an old rail fence stretched to the east and west. Just beyond the broken-down fence, the ground fell away gently into a little hollow before rising again in a low embankment that ran off to the northeast. A few patches of scrub brush and small birch trees dotted the forward slopes of this rise, but the countryside was generally more open here – offering less cover and concealment.

Peter jabbed a finger toward this elevation. Then he made the hand signal for 'enemy.'

Smith nodded. That embankment was a likely spot for the ambush they were being herded toward. Anyone stationed just behind its crest would have decent fields of observation and fire along most of this side of the run-down farm. He frowned. The odds against them were stacking up fast.

Peter saw the look on his face and shrugged. 'Can't be helped,' he murmured. He pulled the spent magazine for his MP5 out of the ammo pouch on his combat vest. He waited while Jon followed suit.

'Very well,' Peter said very quietly. 'Here's the plan.' He held up the empty magazine. 'As a distraction, we toss these as far to the right as we can. Then we make a dash over the crest, turn right, and assault along the reverse slope – killing hostiles we meet.'

Smith stared back at him. 'That's it?'

'There's no time for anything fancy, Jon,' the Englishman told him patiently. 'We must hit them hard and fast. Speed and audacity are the only cards we have to play. If either of us goes down, the other must press on without him. Agreed?'

Smith nodded. He did not like any of this, but the other man was right. In this situation, any delay – for any reason, even helping an injured friend – would be fatal. They were so heavily outnumbered that their only chance of escape was to fight their way through anyone in front of them and then keep on moving.

Holding the empty magazine in his left hand and gripping the MP5 in his right, he rose slowly to one knee, getting ready to rush across the tumbledown fence and the open ground beyond it. Beside him, Peter did the same.

Another burst of random gunfire broke out behind them. It faded, leaving only silence.

'Here we go,' Peter hissed. 'Get ready. Set. Now?'

Both men hurled the empty clips as hard as they could, flinging them high into the air and off to the right. The curved metal magazines landed with a rustle and a clatter – suddenly loud in the night.

Instantly Smith jumped up and ran forward. He dived straight over the split-rail fence, hit the ground rolling, and bounced back up on his feet with Peter just a few yards away.

Smith heard startled shouts from behind them and off to the right, but the enemy had spotted them too late. Still running flat out, he and Peter charged up the gentle slope and over the top of the low rise.

Smith spun immediately to the right, submachine gun gripped in both hands, searching for targets in the weird green half-light supplied by his night-vision gear. There! He saw a shape moving beneath the low-hanging branches of a birch tree less than ten yards away. It was a man, who had been lying prone peering over the crest, turning frantically toward them – trying to bring his own weapon, an Uzi, to bear.

Reacting faster, Jon swung his own MP5 on-target and squeezed the trigger, sending three 9mm rounds into the enemy gunman at point-blank range. All three slammed home with tremendous force. The impact hurled the man backward. He slid to the ground and lay splayed against the chalk-white trunk of the birch tree.

They glided on, following the embankment as it angled northeast and separating as they moved so that no single enemy burst could hit them both. The slope on this side was a mix of birch trees, scrub pines, and clumps of brush, all broken up by tiny patches of open ground. Confused by the sudden burst of shooting, the four mercenaries deployed as 'beaters' to drive them into the ambush were firing wildly now – flaying the wrong side of the rise. Bullets ricocheting off trees tumbled high overhead, buzzing angrily like bees.

Smith moved cautiously into a small clearing and caught a sudden flicker of movement out of the corner of his right eye. He spun around and saw the blackened barrel of an M16 assault rifle poking out from behind a vine-covered tree stump. It was traversing in his direction! He threw himself down just as the hidden gunman fired. One 5.56mm round grazed his left shoulder, tearing a bloody gash through cloth and skin. Two more rifle bullets tore long furrows through the earth close by.

Jon rolled away, desperately trying to shake the enemy rifleman's aim. More rounds followed him, again slashing at the ground only inches away from his head. Still rolling, he looked for cover – any kind of cover – within reach.

There was nothing. He was trapped out in the open.

And then Peter appeared behind him and opened fire, methodically hammering the tree stump with controlled bursts. Pieces of bark and shredded vine flew away through the air. The hidden rifleman screamed once, a piercing shriek, and then fell silent.

'Are you all right, Jon?' Peter called softly.

Smith checked himself over. The graze on his shoulder was bleeding and it would hurt like hell soon enough. But miraculously that was the only wound he had taken.

'I'm okay,' he reported, still breathing hard as he recovered from the shock of nearly being gunned down so easily. Moving out into that clearing had been a big mistake, he realized – the kind of screwup raw recruits made in training. He shook his head once, angry with himself for the error.

'Then go make sure that bastard's really down and dead. I'll cover you,' Peter said urgently. 'But do it quickly.'

'On my way.' Smith scrambled back to his feet and moved out of the little space of open ground, circling through the undergrowth to come at the tree stump from behind and out of the Englishman's field of fire. He pushed cautiously through a tangle of tall brush and saw a body on the ground, facedown. The M16 lay several feet away.

Was the gunman really dead or badly wounded or only lying doggo? he wondered. For a moment, Jon thought about firing a quick burst into the body to finish the job. His finger tightened on the trigger. Then he eased off, with a frown. In the heat of battle, he could gun down an enemy without hesitating, but he would not shoot someone who might be lying helpless and in terrible pain. Not and stay true to the oaths he had sworn and, perhaps more important, to his own sense of right and wrong.

Smith stepped closer, sighting along the barrel of the MP5. He could see blood on the ground, trickling out from under the man's body. The fallen rifleman was short and wiry, with a dusting of cropped reddish hair on the back of his small round head. Jon drew nearer still, preparing to bend down and feel for a pulse.

More gunshots rang out from somewhere not far ahead. They were answered immediately by a short burst from Peter's weapon.

Distracted, Smith turned his head to try to see where the fire was coming from. He crouched lower, seeking cover.

That was when the 'dead' man lunged at him, hurling himself forward with lightning speed. He slammed headlong into Jon's stomach and knocked him down. The submachine gun went flying off into the bushes.

Smith writhed away and saw a knife driving toward him. He rolled to the side and came back up, just in time to block another thrust with the outer edge of his left arm. The blade sliced through his sleeve and slashed the skin beneath. It grated off the bone, sending a wave of pain flaming through his mind. He forced the agony aside and struck back with the edge of his right hand, hacking down hard on the red-haired man's wrist.

The knife fell out of the man's suddenly paralyzed fingers.

Smith kept moving, reversing his strike – slamming his right elbow straight back into the shorter rifleman's nose. He felt a sickening crunch as the impact shattered pieces of cartilage, driving them upward and into his enemy's brain. The red-haired man dropped without a sound and lay motionless, dead for real this time.

Jon sat back, breathing deeply. He could feel blood dripping from the deep gash on his left arm. I had better bind that up now, he thought dully. No point in leaving a blood trail for the bad guys to follow. He shook out a field dressing from one of the pockets on his vest and quickly wound the gauze and cotton around the injured arm.

There was a soft whistle from the woods. He looked up as Peter loomed out of the darkness.

'Sorry about that,' Peter said. 'Another one popped his head up and took a shot at me.'

'Did you nail him?'

'Oh, yes,' Peter said with satisfaction. 'Well and truly.' He dropped to one knee and rolled the red-haired man Smith had killed over onto his back. Peter's pale blue eyes widened slightly at the sight of the man's face, and he sucked in his breath.

'You recognize that guy?' Jon asked, watching his reaction.

Peter nodded. He looked up with a grim, worried expression on his weathered face. 'Fellow's name was McRae,' he said softly. 'When I knew him he was a trooper in the SAS. Had a reputation as a troublemaker – very good in any fight, a very nasty bastard out of one. Several years back he crossed the line once too often and got himself booted out of the regiment. Last I heard, he was working as a mercenary in Africa and Asia – with the occasional bit of freelance work for various intelligence services.'

He got up and went over to retrieve Smith's submachine gun.

'Including MI6?' Jon asked quietly, taking the weapon from him and climbing stiffly to his feet.

Peter nodded reluctantly. 'On occasion.'

'Do you think some of your people in London could be involved in this covert war Pierson and Burke are running?' Smith said.

Peter shrugged. 'At the moment, I don't really know what to think, Jon.' He looked up as the rippling chatter of automatic weapons fire crashed out again from the other side of the low embankment. 'But for now, our friends over there are getting restless. And they'll be coming in this direction in force very soon. I think we'd best break contact while we can. We need to find a place where we can safely arrange new transport.'

Smith nodded. That made good sense. By now, their enemies were sure to have found the cars they had brought with them from Andrews Air Force Base. Trying to retrieve the two vehicles would only mean walking back into the trap they had just escaped.

He felt the dressing on his left arm, checking to make sure it had not yet soaked all the way through. It was still dry on the outside. He turned back to the Englishman. 'Okay, lead on, Peter. I'll keep an eye on the rear.'

The two men turned and trotted north, fading deeper into the darkened countryside – keeping to the shelter of the trees and tall brush whenever possible. Behind them, the harsh, echoing rattle of gunfire slowly died away.

CHAPTER THIRTY-ONE

The first burst of automatic weapons fire outside the farmhouse brought Kit Pierson to her feet in a rush. Drawing her service pistol, a 9mm Smith & Wesson, the FBI agent moved rapidly to the window, peering out through the narrow slit between the drapes. She could not see anything, but the sound of gunfire continued, echoing loudly across the low, rolling hills of the Virginia country-side. Heart pounding, she crouched lower. Whatever was going on had all the hallmarks of a pitched battle being fought close by.

'Trouble, Kit?' she heard Hal Burke say with a nasty edge in his voice.

Pierson glanced over her shoulder at him. Her eyes widened. The square-jawed CIA officer had drawn his own weapon, a Beretta. And he held it aimed right at her.

'What kind of game are you playing, Hal?' she de-manded, holding perfectly still – all too aware that, drunk or not, he could not miss at this range. Her mouth felt dry. She could see beads of sweat forming on Burke's forehead. The muscles around his right eye twitched slightly.

'This is no game,' he snapped back. 'As I'm sure you know.' He motioned with the muzzle of the Beretta. 'Now I want you to put your weapon down on the floor – but care-fully . . . very carefully. And then I want you to sit back down in your chair. With your hands where I can see them.'

'Take it easy, Hal,' Pierson said softly, trying hard to conceal her fear and her sudden conviction that Burke had lost his grip on reality. 'I don't know what you think I've done, but I promise you that – '

Her words were drowned by another burst of shooting from outside the house.

'Do what I say, damn it!' the CIA officer growled. His finger tightened dangerously on the trigger. 'Move!'

Feeling ice-cold, Pierson slowly knelt and put her Smith & Wesson down on the floor, butt first.

'Now, kick it toward me – but do it gently!' Burke ordered.

She complied, sliding the pistol toward him across the stained hardwood floor.

'Sit!'

Angry now, both at the other man and with herself for being so afraid of him, Pierson obeyed, slowly lowering herself into the lumpy, frayed armchair. She held her hands up, palms outward, so that he could see that she was not an immediate threat. 'I'd still like to know what I'm supposed to have done, Hal – and what all that shooting is about.'

Burke raised a skeptical eyebrow. 'Why try to pull the innocent act, Kit? It's too late for that. You're not an idiot. And neither am I, for that matter. Did you really think you could sneak an FBI surveillance team onto my property without my knowing?'

She shook her head, desperately now. 'I don't know what you're talking about. Nobody came with me – or followed me. I was clean all the way out from D.C. to here!'

'Lying won't get you anywhere,' he said coldly. His right eye twitched again, fluttering rapidly as the muscles contracted and then relaxed. 'In fact, it just pisses me off.'

The phone on his desk rang once. Without taking his eyes or his pistol off her, Burke reached out and grabbed it before it could ring again. 'Yes?' he said tightly. He listened for a moment and then shook his head. 'No, I have the situation here under control. You can come ahead. The door's unlocked.' He hung up.

'Who was that?' she asked.

The CIA officer smiled thinly, without any humor at all. 'Someone who wants very much to meet you,' he said.

Bitterly regretting her earlier decision to confront Burke in person, Kit Pierson sat tensely in the armchair – rapidly considering various plans to extricate herself from this mess and then equally rapidly discarding them as impractical, suicidal, or both. She heard the front door open and then close.

Her eyes widened as a very tall and very broad-shouldered man stepped quietly into the study, moving with the dangerous grace of a tiger. His curiously green eyes gleamed in the dim light cast by the lamp on Burke's desk. For a moment she thought he was the same man described by Colonel Smith in his report on the aftermath of the Teller Institute disaster – the leader of the 'terrorist' unit that had conducted the attack. Then she shook her head. That was impossible. The leader of that attack had been consumed by the nanophages released by the bombs that had shattered the Institute's labs.

'This is Terce,' Hal Burke said brusquely. 'He commands one of my TOCSIN action teams. His men were on guard outside. They're the ones who spotted your covert surveillance guys prowling around this house.'

'Whoever's out there isn't connected to me,' Pierson said again, straining to put every ounce of conviction she could muster into her voice. Every FBI manual on the psychology of conspiracies stressed the inherent and overwhelming fears of those involved of betrayal from within. As head of the Bureau's Counter-Terrorism Division, she had often made use of those fears – playing on them to break apart suspected cells, turning the would-be terrorists on one another like rats trapped in a pit. She bit down on her lower lip, tasting the salt tang of her own blood. Now the same forces of paranoia and suspicions were at work here, threatening her life.

'No dice, Kit,' Burke told her coldly. 'I don't believe in

coincidences, so you're either a liar – or a screwup. And this operation can't afford either one.'

The big man named Terce said nothing at first. Instead, he reached down and scooped her pistol off the floor. He slid it into one of the pockets of his black windbreaker and then turned to the CIA officer. 'Now, give me your own weapon, Mr. Burke,' he said gently. 'If you please.'

The smaller man blinked in surprise, plainly caught off-guard by the request. 'What?'

'Give me your weapon,' Terce repeated. He stepped closer to Burke, looming over the CIA officer. 'It would be . . . safer . . . for us all.'

'Why?'

The green-eyed man nodded at the half-empty bottle of Jim Beam on the desk. 'Because you have been drinking a bit more than is wise, Mr. Burke, and I do not fully trust either your judgment or your reflexes at this moment. You can rest easy. My men have the situation well in hand.'

More gunfire rattled in the distance, farther away now.

For the space of a heartbeat Burke sat staring up at the taller man. His eyes narrowed angrily. But then he did as he was asked, handing the Beretta to Terce with a sullen frown.

Kit Pierson felt some of the tension leave her shoulders. She breathed out. Whatever else he was, the leader of this TOCSIN action team was no fool. Disarming Burke so quickly was a sound move. It was also one that might help her defuse this ridiculous and incendiary situation. She leaned forward. 'Look, let's see what we can do to sort this mess out rationally,' she said coolly. 'First, if anyone from the FBI did tail me here, they certainly did it without my knowledge or my consent – '

'Be silent, Ms. Pierson!' the green-eyed man said coldly. 'I do not care how or why you were followed. Your motives and your competence, or lack of it, are immaterial.'

Kit Pierson stared back at him, suddenly aware that she

was in as much danger from this man as she had been with Burke – and perhaps a great deal more.

Near Paris

Engines buzzing softly, the two UAVs flew on at three thousand feet. Below, forests, roads, and villages slid past and then vanished in the early morning haze behind them. The sun, rising east above the deep, undulating valleys of the Seine and the Marne, was a large ball of red fire outlined against the thin fading gray mist.

Closer to Paris, the landscape began changing, becoming more congested and crowded. Ancient villages surrounded by woods and farmland gave way to larger, more modern suburbs surrounded by intertwined motorways and rail lines. High-rise apartment buildings appeared ahead, stabbing up at irregular intervals in a great arc around the inner core of the city itself.

Long white contrails formed in the sky high above the two robot aircraft, vast trails of ice crystals floating in the clear, cold air, each marking the passage of a large passenger jet. The UAVs were nearing the flight paths to and from two airports – Le Bourget and Charles de Gaulle. Given their very small size, the odds of radar detection were very low, but those who controlled them saw no point in taking unnecessary risks. Responding to preprogrammed instructions, each drone dropped lower, descending to just five hundred feet and throttling back to maintain a near-constant airspeed of around one hundred miles per hour.

Field Experiment Operations Room,
Inside the Center

The Center's operations room was located deep within the complex, secure behind a number of locked doors accessible only to those with the very highest clearances. Inside the darkened chamber, several scientists and technicians sat in front of large consoles, constantly monitoring the pictures and data streaming in from Paris – both from the ground sensors planted at various points and those on-board the two UAVs. Updates of wind direction, speed, humidity, and barometric pressure were automatically fed into a sophisticated targeting program. Two large screens showed the terrain ahead and below the twin drones. Numbers in the lower right corner of each display – the range to target – counted down, flickering from time to time as the program made carefully calculated adjustments to each robot aircraft's aim point. The control room personnel sat up straighter, watching with growing tension and excitement as those range numbers steadied up and began sliding ever more rapidly toward zero.

0.4 km, 0.3 km, 0.15 km . . . the command 'Initiate' flashed in red on both screens. Instantly the targeting program transmitted an encrypted radio signal, relaying it through a communications satellite high above the Earth and then back down to the drones aloft just north of Paris.

La Courneuve

More and more people ventured out on the dingy, run-down streets around the slum housing complexes of La Courneuve. A few were heading for the nearest Metro station on their way to whatever menial jobs they had been able to find. More were women carrying baskets and bags – mothers, wives, and grandmothers sent out to shop for the day's food. Some were families strolling toward the wooded spaces and parkland north of the suburb. Sunday morning was a rare opportunity for parents to give their children a taste of the open air away from the crime-ridden, graffiti-smeared streets and alleys, and the trash-heaped hallways of the *Cité des Quatre Mille*. The thieves, thugs, pushers, and drug addicts who preyed on them were mostly asleep, barricaded in the bare concrete apartments provided by the French welfare state.

*

Flying on parallel courses now, the two UAVs climbed again, rising to just over one thousand feet. Still moving at one hundred miles an hour, they crossed over a wide avenue and entered the airspace above La Courneuve. Aboard first one and then the other drone, control relays cycled, triggering the twin canisters slung below their wings. With a sinister hiss, each canister began spewing its contents in an invisible stream.

Hundreds of billions of Stage III nanophages fell across a huge swathe of La Courneuve, slowly raining down out of the sky in an undetected cloud of death and imminent slaughter. Vast numbers drifted among the thousands of unsuspecting people caught outside and were inhaled unnoticed – pulled into their lungs with every breath. Tens of billions more of the microscopic phages were drawn into the huge air ducts atop the slum high-rises and spread through ventilation shafts to apartments on every floor. Once the phages were inside, air currents wafted them through every room, settling unseen on those sleeping, drowsing in a drugged stupor, or mindlessly watching television.

Most of the phages stayed inert, conserving their limited power, silently spreading through the blood and tissues of those they had infected while waiting the go signal that would unleash them. Like the Stage II nanodevices used at the Teller Institute, however, roughly one out of every hundred thousand was a control phage – a larger silicon sphere packed with a wide array of sophisticated biochemical sensors. Their power packs went active immediately. They scoured through their host bodies, seeking any trace of one of dozens of precoded conditions, illnesses, allergies, and syndromes. The first positive reading by any single sensor triggered an immediate burst of the messenger molecules that would send the smaller killer phages into a frenzy of destruction.

Several miles south and west of La Courneuve, the six-man surveillance team occupied the upper floor and attic of an old gray stone building in the heart of the Marais District of Paris. Microwave and radio antennae dotted the steep, sloping tiled roof above them – gathering every scrap of data beamed their way by the sensors and cameras set up around the nanophage target area. From there the data flowed down into banks of networked computers. There it would be stored and evaluated to eventually be relayed by coded signal and satellite to the distant Center. To conserve bandwidth and preserve operational security, only the most crucial information was passed on in real time.

The white-haired man named Linden stared over the shoulder of one of his men, watching the data pour into his machines. Linden was careful to avoid looking too closely at a TV monitor showing images captured from the streets surrounding the *Cité des Quatre Mille*. Let the scientists observe their own handiwork, he thought grimly. He had his own tasks to perform. Instead, he glanced at another screen, this one showing pictures relayed from the two UAVs. They had completed their orbits over La Courneuve and they were now flying east, roughly paralleling the course of the Canal de l'Ourcq.

He keyed the radio mike attached to his headset, reporting to Nones at the launch site near Meaux. 'Field Experiment Three is proceeding. Data collection is nominal. Your drones are on their programmed course and speed. ETA is roughly twenty minutes.'

'Is there any sign of detection?' the third of the *Horatii* asked calmly.

Linden glanced at Vitor Abrantes. The young Portuguese was charged with monitoring all police, fire, ambulance, and air traffic control frequencies. Computers set to scan for certain key words aided him in this task. 'Anything?' Linden asked.

The young man shook his head. 'Nothing yet. The Parisian emergency operators have received several calls from the target area, but nothing they have so far been able to understand.'

Linden nodded. He and his team had received a cursory briefing on the effects of the Stage III nanophages – enough to know that the soft tissues of the mouth and tongue were among the first to dissolve. He clicked his mike again. 'You are clear so far,' he told Nones. 'The authorities are still asleep.'

Brown-eyed, brown-haired, still slender, and pretty, Nouria Besseghir gripped the hand of her five-year-old daughter, Tasa, tightly, urging the little girl across the street at a rapid pace. Her daughter, she knew, was both curious and easily distracted. Left to her own devices, Tasa was perfectly capable of standing still right in the middle of the road – caught up in the study of an interesting pattern in the cracked and potholed cement or of some intriguing bit of graffiti on a nearby building. True, there were not many cars on the streets of La Courneuve at this hour, but few drivers here paid much attention to traffic laws or to pedestrian safety. In this lawless neighborhood, part of what the French called the Zone, hit-and-runs were a fairly common occurrence, certainly far more common than any police investigation of such 'accidents.'

Almost as important to Nouria was her desire to keep moving – to avoid drawing unwanted attention from any of the predatory men who loitered along these dingy streets or squatted in the shadowed alleys. Six months ago, her husband had returned to his native Algeria on what he had told her was 'family business.' And now he was dead, killed in a clash between the Algerian security forces and the Islamic rebels who periodically challenged that nation's authoritarian government. Word of his death had taken weeks to reach her, and she still did not know which of the two warring factions had murdered him.

That made Nouria Besseghir a widow – a widow whose French birth entitled her to a modest welfare allowance from the French government. In the eyes of the thieves, pimps, and rogues who essentially ran the affairs of the

Cité des Quatre Mille, that small weekly stipend also made her a valuable commodity. Any one of them would be only too glad to offer her his dubious 'protection' – at least in return for the chance to plunder her body and her money.

Her lip curled in disgust at the thought. Allah only knew that her dead husband, Hakkim, had been no great prize himself, but even so she would rather die than be fondled and then robbed by the human parasites she saw lurking all around her. And so Nouria walked quickly whenever and wherever she went outside her tiny apartment, and she always kept her gaze fixed firmly on the ground before her. Both she and her daughter also wore the *hijab* – the loose-fitting clothing, including head scarf, that marked them as Muslim females of decency and propriety.

'Mama, look!' Tasa exclaimed suddenly, pointing up into the blue sky above them. The little girl's voice was excited and shrill and piercing. 'A big bird! Look at that big bird flying up there! It's enormous. Is it a condor? Or perhaps a roc? Like one from the stories? Oh, how Papa would have loved to have seen it!'

Annoyed, Nouria shushed her daughter sternly. The very last thing they needed to be right now was conspicuous. Still walking fast, she pulled on Tasa's wrist, tugging her along the littered pavement. It was too late.

A drunk with a matted beard and acne-pitted skin reeled out from a nearby alley, blocking their path. Nouria gagged as a choking stench of sour liquor and unwashed flesh rolled over her. After her first appalled look at this shambling wreck, she lowered her gaze and tried to walk around the man.

He staggered closer, forcing her to step back. The drunk, with his eyes bulging, coughed and spat and then moaned – uttering a low, guttural groan that was more dog-like than human.

Disgusted, Nouria grimaced and stepped back farther, pulling Tasa with her. Part of her ached that her beautiful little girl was being exposed to so much filth and degradation and depravity. Why, this *cochon* was so intoxicated that he could not even speak! She averted her eyes from the sight, wondering what she should do to get away from this stinking brute. Should she scoop Tasa up in her arms and make a dash back across the street? Or would that only draw even more unwanted attention?

'Mama!' her daughter murmured. 'Something awful is happening to him. See? He's bleeding all over!'

Nouria looked up and saw with horror that Tasa was right. The drunk had collapsed in front of her, falling onto his hands and knees. Blood trickled onto the pavement, dripping from his mouth and from the terrible wounds spreading along the length of his arms and legs. Strips of flesh peeled away from his face and dropped to the ground, already turning into a reddish, translucent slime. He moaned again, quivering wildly as spasms of agony wracked his disintegrating body.

Stifling her own terrified screams, Nouria backed away from the dying man, putting her hand over her daughter's eyes to shield her from the gruesome sight. Hearing more anguished howls behind her, she whirled round. Many of the other men, women, and children who had also been out along the street were on their knees or curled up in agony – screaming, groaning, and clawing at themselves in a mindless, twitching frenzy. Dozens were already affected. And even as she watched, more and more fell prey to the invisible horror stalking their neighborhood.

For several seemingly endless seconds Nouria only stared at the hellish scene around her in mounting dread, scarcely able to comprehend the magnitude of the slaughter happening right before her panicked eyes. Then she gathered Tasa in her arms and ran, scrambling toward the nearest doorway in a frantic effort to find shelter.

But it was already far too late.

Nouria Besseghir felt the first burning waves of pain rippling outward from her heaving lungs, spreading with every breath through the rest of her body. Shrieking aloud in fear, she stumbled and fell – trying vainly to cushion her daughter against the impact with arms that were already disintegrating, shredding apart as skin and muscle tissue dissolved, pulling away from her bones.

More knives of fire stabbed at her eyes. Her vision blurred, dimmed, and then vanished. With the last traces of nerves remaining in what was left of her once-pretty face she felt something wet and soft sliding out of her eye sockets. She sank to the pavement, praying for oblivion, praying for a death that would stop the pain wracking every part of her flailing, shuddering body. She also prayed desperately for her daughter, hoping against hope that her little girl would be spared this same suffering.

But in the end, before the final darkness claimed her, she knew that even this last prayer had been denied.

'Mama,' she heard Tasa whimper. 'Mama, it hurts . . . it hurts so much. . . .'

CHAPTER THIRTY-TWO

Rural Virginia

Terce leaned back against one dark-paneled wall of Burke's small study. His posture was relaxed, almost casual, but his gaze was alert and focused. He still held the Beretta he had taken from the CIA officer. The 9mm pistol looked small in his large gloved right hand. He smiled coldly, sensing the growing unease of the two Americans sitting motionless under his watchful eye. Neither Hal Burke nor Kit Pierson was used to being wholly subject to the will of another. It amused Terce to keep these two senior intelligence officials so completely under his thumb.

He checked the small antique clock on Burke's desk. The last burst of gunfire outside had died away several minutes ago. By now, the spies his men were hunting should be dead. No matter how good their training was, no pair of FBI agents could possibly be a match for his own force of ex-commandos.

A voice crackled through his radio headset. 'This is Uchida. I have a situation report.'

Terce straightened up, hiding his surprise. Uchida, a former Japanese airborne trooper, was one of the five men he had assigned to drive the two intruders into the ambush carefully laid along the north edge of Burke's farm. Any reports should have come from the ambush party itself. 'Go ahead,' he replied.

He listened to the other man's tale of utter disaster in silence, keeping a tight rein on his rising anger. Four of his men were dead, including McRae, his best tracker and scout. The ambush he had planned had been rolled up from the flank and wiped out. That was bad enough. Worst of all was the news that the shocked survivors of his security team had completely lost contact with the retreating Americans. Hearing that his forces had found and disabled two automobiles belonging to the intruders was small consolation. By now they were undoubtedly in touch with their headquarters, reporting whatever they had heard and requesting urgent reinforcements.

'Should we pursue?' Uchida ended by asking.

'No,' Terce snapped. 'Fall back on your vehicles and await my instructions.' He had been overconfident, and his team had paid a high price as a result. In the dark, the odds of regaining contact with the Americans before they received help were too low. And even in this open, unpopulated country the sound of so much gunfire was bound to draw unwelcome attention. It was time to leave this place before the FBI or other law-enforcement agencies could begin throwing a cordon around it.

'Trouble?' Kit Pierson asked icily. The dark-haired woman had detected the anger and uncertainty in his voice. She sat up straighter in the armchair.

'A minor setback,' Terce lied smoothly, working hard to conceal and control his growing irritation and impatience. All of his training and psychological conditioning had taught him the uselessness of the weaker emotions. He waved her back down using a small, almost imperceptible, gesture with the Beretta. 'Calm yourself, Ms. Pierson. All will be made clear in due time.'

The second of the *Horatii* checked the desk clock again, mentally adjusting for the six-hour time difference between Virginia and Paris. The call would come soon, he thought. But would it come soon enough? Should he act without receiving specific orders? He pushed the thought away. His instructions were clear.

His secure cell phone buzzed abruptly. He answered it. 'Yes?'

A voice on the other end, distorted faintly by encryption software and by multiple satellite relays, spoke calmly, issuing the command he had been waiting to hear. 'Field Experiment Three has begun. You may proceed as planned.'

'Understood,' Terce said. 'Out.'

Smiling slightly now, he looked across the room at the dark-haired FBI agent. 'I hope you will accept my apology in advance, Ms. Pierson.'

She frowned, clearly puzzled. 'Your apology? For what?'

Terce shrugged. 'For this.' In one smooth motion, he lifted the pistol he had confiscated from Burke and squeezed the trigger twice. The first shot hit her in the middle of the forehead. The second tore straight through her heart. With a soft sigh, she slumped back against the blood-spattered back of the armchair. Her dead slate-gray eyes stared back at him, eternally fixed in an expression of utter astonishment.

'Good God!' Hal Burke gripped the arms of his chair. The blood drained from his face, leaving it a sickly hue. He pulled his horrified gaze away from the murdered woman, turning to the big man towering over him. 'What . . . what the hell are you doing?' he stammered.

'Following my orders,' Terce told him simply.

'I never asked you to kill her!' the CIA officer shouted. He swallowed convulsively, plainly fighting down the urge to be sick.

'No, you did not,' the green-eyed man agreed. He placed the Beretta gently on the floor at his feet and pulled Kit Pierson's Smith & Wesson out of his pocket. He smiled again. 'But then, you do not truly understand the situation, Mr. Burke. Your so-called TOCSIN was only a blind for a much larger operation, never a reality. And you are not the master here – only a servant. An expendable servant, alas.'

Burke's eyes opened wide in sudden horrified understanding. He scrambled backward, trying desperately to stand up, to do something, anything, to fight back. He failed.

Terce fired three 9mm rounds into the CIA officer's stomach at point-blank range. Each bullet tore a huge hole through his back, spraying blood, bone fragments, and bits of internal organs across the swivel chair, desk, and computer screen behind him.

Burke fell back into his seat. His fingers scrabbled vainly at the terrible wounds in his abdomen. His mouth opened and closed like a netted fish gasping frantically for breath.

With contemptuous ease, Terce reached out with his foot and shoved the swivel chair over, spilling the dying CIA officer onto the hardwood floor. Then he strode over and dropped the Smith & Wesson in Kit Pierson's blood-soaked lap.

When he turned around, he saw Burke lying motionless, curled inward on himself in his final death agony. The tall green-eyed man reached into his coat pocket and brought out a small plastic-wrapped package with a digital timer attached to the top. Moving swiftly, with practiced ease, he set the timer for twenty seconds, triggered it, and set the package on the desk – just below the racks of Burke's computer and communications equipment. The digital readout began counting down.

Terce stepped carefully around the CIA officer's body and out into the narrow hallway. Behind him, the timer hit zero. With a soft whoosh and a sudden white incandescent flash, the incendiary device he had planted detonated. Satisfied, he walked outside and pulled the front door closed behind him.

Then he turned. Flames were already visible through the nearly closed drapes of the study window, dancing and growing as they spread rapidly across the furniture, books, equipment, and bodies inside. He punched in a preset number on his cell phone and waited patiently for the reply.

'Make your report,' ordered the same calm voice he had heard earlier.

'Your instructions have been carried out,' Terce told him. 'The Americans will find only smoke and ashes – and evidence of their own complicity. As ordered, my team and I are returning to the Center at once.'

Several thousand miles away, sitting in a cool, darkened room, the man called Lazarus smiled. 'Very good,' he said gently. Then he swung back to watch the data streaming in from Paris.

PART FOUR

PART FOUR

CHAPTER THIRTY-THREE

Paris

The leader of the Center's surveillance team, Willem Linden, flipped quickly from image to image on the large monitor set up in front of him, swiftly checking the TV pictures transmitted by the sensor packages mounted on lampposts around La Courneuve. The images were nearly identical. Each revealed long stretches of pavement and avenues strewn with small, sad heaps of slime-stained clothing and whitened bone. Shots from several cameras, those deployed around the perimeter of the target area, showed wrecked police cars, fire trucks, and ambulances – most with their engines running and their roof lights still flashing. The first emergency crews, rushing to answer frantic calls for help, had driven straight into the invisible nanophage cloud and died with those they had come to aid.

Linden spoke into his mike, reporting to the distant Center. 'There appear to be no survivors among those outside.'

'That is excellent news,' the faintly distorted voice of the man named Lazarus said. 'And the nanophages themselves?'

'One moment,' Linden said. He entered a series of codes on the keyboard set up before him. The TV pictures disappeared from his screen, replaced by a series of graphs – one for each deployed sensor package. Every gray box included an air scoop and collection kit designed to gather a representative sample of the nanophages falling through the air around them. As the white-haired man watched, lines on each graph suddenly spiked upward. 'Their self-destruct sequences have just activated,' he reported.

The spherical semiconductor shell of each Stage III nanophage contained a timed self-destruct mechanism to scramble its working core – the chemical loads that smashed peptide bonds. As these microscopic bomblets detonated, they released a small burst of intense heat. IR detectors inside the collection kits were picking up those bursts of heat.

Linden saw the lines on each graph drop back to zero. 'Nanophage self-destruct complete,' he said.

'Good,' Lazarus replied. 'Proceed to the final phase of Field Experiment Three.'

'Understood,' Linden said. He entered another series of command sequences on his keyboard. Flashing red letters appeared on his screen. 'Charges activated.'

Several miles to the north and east, the demolition charges rigged at the base of each gray sensor box exploded. Fountains of blinding white flame soared high into the air as the white phosphorus filler in each charge ignited. In milliseconds, temperatures at the heart of each towering column of fire reached five thousand degrees Fahrenheit – consuming every separate element of the sensor boxes, inextricably mingling their metals and plastics with the now-molten steel and iron of the lampposts. When the smoke and flames faded away, there were no usable traces left of the instruments, cameras, and communications devices set out to study the slaughter in La Courneuve.

The White House

The persistent chirping of his phone roused President Sam Castilla from an uneasy, dream-filled sleep. He fumbled for his glasses, put them on, and saw from the clock on his nightstand that it was nearly four-thirty in the morning. The sky outside the White House family quarters was still pitch-black, untouched by any hint of the approaching dawn. He grabbed the phone. 'Castilla here.'

'I'm sorry to wake you, Mr. President,' Emily Powell-Hill said. His national security adviser sounded both weary and depressed. 'But there's a situation developing outside Paris that you need to know about. The first news is just hitting the airwaves – CNN, Fox, the BBC, all of them have the same rough details.'

Castilla sat up in bed, automatically glancing apologetically to his left for the early morning interruption before remembering that his wife, Cassie, was away on yet another international goodwill tour, this one through Asia. He felt a sharp pang of loneliness and then fought off the wave of sadness that came with it. The demands of the presidency were inexorable, he thought. You could not dodge them. You could not ignore them. You could only soldier on and try to honor the trust the people had placed in you. Among other things, that meant accepting periodic separations from the woman you loved.

He punched the TV remote, bringing up one of the several competing twenty-four-hour cable news channels. The screen showed the deserted streets of a suburb just outside Paris, filmed from a helicopter orbiting high overhead. Suddenly the picture zoomed in, revealing hundreds of grotesque clumps of melted flesh and bone that had once been living human beings.

'. . . many thousands of people are feared dead, though the French government steadfastly refuses to speculate on either the cause or the magnitude of this apparent disaster. Outside observers, however, have commented on the striking similarities between the horrible deaths reported here and those blamed on nanophages released from the Teller Institute for Advanced Technology in Santa Fe, New Mexico, only days ago. But so far, it is impossible to confirm their suspicions. Only a few civil defense units equipped with full chemical protective suits have been allowed to enter La Courneuve in a frantic quest for survivors and answers. . . .'

Shaken to his core, Castilla snapped off the television. 'My God,' he murmured. 'It's happening again.'

'Yes, sir,' Powell-Hill replied grimly. 'I'm afraid so.'

Still holding the phone, Castilla levered himself out of bed and threw a bathrobe over his pajamas. 'Get everybody in here, Emily,' he said, forcing himself to sound calmer and more in control than he felt. 'I want a full NSC meeting in the Situation Room as soon as possible.'

He disconnected and punched in a new number. The phone on the other end rang only once before it was picked up.

'Klein here, Mr. President.'

'Don't you ever sleep, Fred?' Castilla heard himself ask.

'When I can, Sam,' the head of Covert-One replied. 'Which is far less often than I would like. One of the hazards of the trade, I fear – just like your job.'

'You've seen the news?'

'Yes, I have,' Klein confirmed. He hesitated. 'As a matter of fact, I was just about to call you.'

'Concerning this new horror in Paris?' the president asked.

'Not exactly,' the other man said quietly. 'Though I'm afraid that there may well be a connection. One I do not yet fully understand.' He cleared his throat. 'I've just received a very troubling report from Colonel Smith. Do you remember what Hideo Nomura said about his father's belief that the CIA was waging a covert war on the Lazarus Movement?'

'Yes, I do,' Castilla said. 'As I recall, Hideo first thought it was an indication of Jinjiro's increasingly shaky mental state. And we both agreed with him.'

'So we did. Well, I'm sorry to have to tell you that it seems Jinjiro Nomura was right,' Klein said somberly. 'And we were both wrong. Dead wrong, Sam. I'm afraid that senior officials in the CIA and the FBI, and possibly other services, *have* been conducting an illegal campaign of sabotage, murder, and terrorism designed to discredit and destroy the Movement.'

'That's an ugly accusation, Fred,' Castilla said tightly. 'A real ugly accusation. You'd better tell me exactly what you've got to back it up.'

The nation's chief executive listened in stunned silence while Klein recounted the damning evidence gathered by Jon Smith and Peter Howell – both in New Mexico and outside Hal Burke's country house. 'Where are Smith and Howell now?' Castilla asked when the head of Covert-One finished bringing him up to speed.

'In a car on their way back to Washington,' the other man said. 'They were able to break contact with the mercenaries who ambushed them roughly an hour ago. I dispatched support and transportation as soon as Jon was able to safely make contact with me.'

'Good,' Castilla said. 'Now, what about Burke, Pierson, and their hired guns? We need to arrest them and start getting to the bottom of this mess.'

'I have more bad news there,' Klein said slowly. 'My staff has been listening in on the police and fire department frequencies for that part of Virginia. Burke's farmhouse is on fire. Right now, the blaze is still out of control. And the local sheriff's department hasn't been able to find anyone responsible for all the shooting his neighbors reported. Nor have they found any bodies in the fields outside the house.'

'They're running,' Castilla realized.

'Someone is running,' the head of Covert-One agreed. 'But who and how far remain to be seen.'

'So exactly how high up does the rot go?' Castilla demanded. 'All the way up to David Hanson? Is my Director of Central Intelligence conducting a clandestine war right under my nose?'

'I wish I could answer that, Sam,' Klein said slowly. 'But I can't. Nothing Smith found proves his involvement.' He hesitated. 'I will say that I don't think Burke and Katherine Pierson could have organized an operation like this TOC-SIN all on their own. For one thing, it's too expensive. Just taking into account what little we know, the tab has to run into the millions of dollars. And neither of them had the authority to draw covert funds of that magnitude.'

'This fellow Burke was one of Hanson's top men, wasn't he?' the president said grimly. 'Back when he ran the CIA's Operations Directorate?'

'Yes,' Klein admitted. 'But I'm wary of jumping to conclusions. The CIA's financial controls are rock-solid. I don't see how anyone inside the Agency could hope to divert the kind of federal money necessary – not without leaving a trail a mile wide. Tampering with the Agency's computerized personnel system is one thing. Ducking its auditors is quite another.'

'Well, maybe the money came from somewhere else,' Castilla suggested. He frowned. 'You heard what else Jinjiro Nomura believed – that corporations and other intelligence services besides the CIA were going after the Lazarus Movement. He might have been right about that, too.'

'Possibly,' Klein agreed. 'And there is another piece of the puzzle to consider. I ran a quick check on Burke's most recent assignments. One of them sticks out like a sore thumb. Before taking over the Agency's Lazarus Movement task force, Hal Burke led one of the CIA teams searching for Jinjiro Nomura.'

'Oh, hell,' Castilla muttered. 'We put the goddamned fox in charge of the chicken coop without even knowing it. . . .'

'I'm afraid so,' Klein said quietly. 'But what I don't understand in any of this is the connection between the nanophage release in Santa Fe – and now possibly in Paris – and this TOCSIN operation. If Burke and Pierson and others are trying to destroy the Lazarus Movement, why orchestrate massacres that will only strengthen it? And where would they get access to this kind of ultra-sophisticated nanotechnology weapon?'

'No kidding,' agreed the president. He ran a hand through his rumpled hair, trying to smooth it down. 'This is one hell of a mess. And now I learn that I can't even rely on the CIA or the FBI to help uncover the truth. Damn it, I'm going to have to put Hanson, his top aides, and every senior Bureau official through the wringer before the word of this illegal war against the Movement leaks out. Because it will leak out.' He sighed. 'And when it does, the congressional and media firestorm is going to make Iran-Contra look like a tempest in a teapot.'

'You still have Covert-One,' Klein reminded him.

'I know that,' Castilla said heavily. 'And I'm counting on you and your people, Fred. You have to get out there and find the answers I need.'

'We'll do our best, Sam,' the other man assured him. 'Our very best.'

The Chiltern Hills, England

Early Sunday morning traffic was light on the multi-lane M40 Motorway connecting London and Oxford. Oliver Latham's silver Jaguar sped southeast at high speed, racing through a landscape of green rolling chalk hills, tiny villages with gray stone Norman churches, stretches of unspoiled woodland, and mist-draped valleys. But the wiry, hollow-cheeked Englishman paid no attention to the natural beauty around him. Instead, the head of MI6's Lazarus surveillance section was wholly focused on the news pouring out of his car radio.

'Initial reports from the French government do appear to connect the deaths in La Courneuve with those outside the American research institute in the state of New Mexico,' read the BBC announcer in the calm, cultured tones reserved for serious international developments. 'And tens of thousands of residents of the surrounding suburbs of Paris are said to be fleeing in panic, clogging the avenues and motor routes leaving the city. Army units and security forces are being deployed to control the evacuation and maintain the rule of law – '

Latham reached out and snapped the radio off, annoyed to find his hands trembling slightly. He had been fast asleep in his weekend country home outside Oxford when the first frantic call from MI6 headquarters reached him. Since then, he had experienced a succession of shocks. First came his inability to contact Hal Burke to find out what the devil was really happening in Paris. Just as TOCSIN seemed to be flying apart at the seams, the American had dropped completely out of sight. Next came the horrifying discovery that his superior, Sir Gareth Southgate, had put his own agent, Peter Howell, into the Lazarus Movement without Latham's knowledge. That was bad enough. But now the head of MI6 was asking pointed questions about Ian McRae and the other freelancers Latham sometimes hired for various missions.

The Englishman grimaced, considering his options. How much did Howell know? How much had he reported to Southgate? If TOCSIN was well and truly blown, what kind of cover story could he produce to conceal his involvement with Burke?

Deep in thought, Latham shoved down hard on the Jaguar's accelerator, swerving left to overtake and pass a heavy, lumbering lorry in the blink of an eye. He cut back into the same lane with just a meter to spare. The lorry driver flashed his lights at him in irritation and then leaned on his horn – sending a piercing note blaring across the motorway. The horn blast echoed back from the surrounding slopes.

Latham ignored the angry gestures, concentrating instead on getting to London as quickly as possible. With luck, he could extricate himself unscathed from this mess. If not, he might be able to make some sort of deal – trading information about TOCSIN for the promise that he would not be prosecuted.

Suddenly the Jaguar rattled and banged, shaken by a succession of small explosions. Its right front tire shredded and flew apart. Bits of rubber and metal bounced and rolled away, scattering across the road surface. Sparks flew high in the air, spraying over the bonnet and windscreen. The car swerved sharply to the right.

Swearing loudly, Latham gripped the steering wheel in both hands and spun it right, trying to regain control over the skid. There was no response. The same series of tiny charges that had blown out the Jaguar's front tire had destroyed its steering system. He screamed shrilly, still desperately spinning the now-useless wheel.

Completely out of control now, the car careened across the motorway at high speed and then flipped over – sliding upside down for several hundred meters along the paved surface. The Jaguar came to rest at last in a tangle of torn metal, broken glass, and crumpled plastic. Less than a second later, another tiny explosive charge ignited the fuel seeping from its mangled gas tank, turning the wreckage into a blazing funeral pyre.

The lorry drove past the burning wreck without stopping. It continued on, heading southeast along the M40 toward the crowded streets of London. Inside the cab, the driver, a middle-aged man with high Slavic cheekbones, slid the remote control back into the duffel bag at his feet. He leaned back, satisfied with the results of his morning's work. Lazarus would be pleased.

CHAPTER THIRTY-FOUR

Washington, D.C.
Lieutenant Colonel Jonathan Smith looked down at K Street from the window of his eighth-floor room in the Capital Hilton. It was just after dawn and the first rays of sunlight were beginning to chase the shadows from Washington's streets. Newspaper vans and delivery trucks rumbled along the empty avenues, breaking the silence of an early Sunday morning.

There was a knock on his door. He turned away from the window and crossed the room in several long strides. A cautious glance through the peephole showed him Fred Klein's familiar pale, long-nosed face.

'It's good to see you, Colonel,' the head of Covert-One said, once he was inside and the door was safely closed and bolted behind him. He glanced around the room, noting the unused bed and the muted television tuned to an all-news channel. It showed footage shot live from the military and police cordon set up around La Courneuve. Vast throngs of Parisians were gathering just beyond the barricades, screaming and chanting in soundless unison. Placards and protest signs blamed *'Les Américaines'* and their *'armes diaboliques,'* their 'devil weapons,' for the disaster that had claimed at least twenty thousand lives by the most recent estimates.

Klein raised a single eyebrow. 'Still too wound up to sleep?'

Smith smiled thinly. 'I can sleep on the plane, Fred.'

'Oh?' Klein said calmly. 'Are you planning some travel?'

Smith shrugged his shoulders. 'Aren't I?'

The other man relented. He tossed his briefcase onto the bed and perched himself on a corner. 'As a matter of fact, you're quite right, Jon,' he admitted. 'I do want you to fly out to Paris.'

'When?'

'As soon as I can get you out to Dulles,' Klein told him. 'There's a Lufthansa flight leaving for Charles de Gaulle around ten. Your tickets and travel documents are in my case.' He pointed to the bandage wrapped around Smith's left arm. 'Will that knife wound give you any trouble?'

'It could use some stitches,' Jon said carefully. 'And I should take some antibiotics as a precaution.'

'I'll arrange it,' Klein promised. He checked his watch. 'I'll have another medical doctor meet you at the airport before your flight. He's discreet, and he's done some good work for us in the past.'

'What about Peter Howell?' Smith asked. 'I could use his help in whatever mission you've got planned for me in Paris.'

Klein frowned. 'Howell would have to make his own way there,' he said firmly. 'I won't risk compromising Covert-One by making travel arrangements for a known British intelligence agent. Plus, you'll have to maintain the fiction that you're working for the Pentagon.'

'Fair enough,' Smith said. 'And my cover for this jaunt?'

'No cover,' Klein said. 'You'll be traveling as yourself, as Dr. Jonathan Smith of USAMRIID. I've arranged your temporary accreditation to the U.S. Embassy in Paris. With all this political hysteria building,' he nodded at the TV screen, where protesters were now burning several American flags, 'the French government can't afford to be seen working with any U.S. intelligence service or with the American military. But they are willing to allow medical and scientific experts in to 'observe.' At least so long as they do so with 'maximum discretion.' Of course, if you land in any trouble, the authorities there will deny you were ever extended an official invitation.'

Smith snorted. 'Naturally.' He paced back to the window, staring down, still restless. Then he turned back. 'Do you have anything specific for me to look into once I get there? Or am I just supposed to sniff around to see what turns up?'

'Something specific,' Klein said quietly. He reached over and pulled a manila folder out of his briefcase. 'Take a look at those.'

Smith flipped open the folder. It contained two single sheets – each a copy of a TOP SECRET cable from the CIA's Paris Station to its Langley headquarters. Both had been sent within the past ten hours. The first reported a series of astonishing observations made by a surveillance team trailing a terrorist suspect inside La Courneuve. Smith felt his hackles rise as he read the description of the 'sensor boxes' rigged on street lamps around the district. The second cable reported the progress being made in tracing the license plate numbers of the vehicles driven by those involved. He looked up at Klein in amazement. 'Jesus! This stuff is red-hot. What are the boys at Langley doing about it?'

'Nothing.'

Smith was bewildered. 'Nothing?'

'The CIA,' Klein patiently explained, 'is too busy right now investigating itself for gross malfeasance, murder, money laundering, sabotage, and terrorism. So, for that matter, is the FBI.'

'Because of Burke and Pierson,' Smith realized.

'And possibly others,' Klein agreed. 'There are indications that at least one senior official in MI6 may also have been involved in TOCSIN. The head of their Lazarus surveillance section was killed in a single-car accident a couple of hours ago . . . an accident the local police are already labeling suspicious.' He looked down at his finger-tips. 'I should also tell you that the sheriff's department has found both Hal Burke and Kit Pierson.'

'And they're dead, too, I suppose,' Smith said grimly.

Klein nodded. 'Their bodies were discovered inside the charred remains of Burke's farmhouse. The preliminary forensics work seems to indicate that they shot each other before the fire took hold.' He sniffed. 'Frankly, I find that far too convenient. Someone out there is playing a series of dirty games with us.'

'Swell.'

'It's a bad situation, Jon,' the head of Covert-One agreed somberly. 'The collapse of this illegal operation is paralyzing three of the best intelligence services in the world – right at the moment when their skills and efforts are most needed.' He fumbled in his jacket pocket for his pipe and tobacco pouch, saw the no-smoking sign prominently displayed on the door, and then stuffed them back with a distracted frown. 'Curious, isn't it?'

Smith whistled softly. 'You think that was intended all along, don't you? By whoever's really responsible for these mass nanophage attacks?'

Klein shrugged. 'Maybe. If not, it's all one hell of a nasty coincidence.'

'I don't put much faith in coincidences myself,' Smith said flatly.

'Nor do I.' The long, lean head of Covert-One stood up. 'Which means we're up against a very dangerous opponent here, Jon. One with enormous resources, and with the ruthlessness to make full use of every scrap of power it possesses. Worse yet,' he said softly, 'this is an enemy whose identity is still completely unknown to us. Which means we have no way to discern its purposes – or to defend ourselves against them.'

Smith nodded, feeling chilled to the bone by Klein's warning. He paced back to the window, again staring down at the quiet streets of the nation's capital. What was the real aim behind the two separate nanophage releases in Santa Fe and Paris? Sure, both attacks had killed thousands of innocent civilians, but there were easier – and cheaper – ways to commit mass murder on that scale. The nanodevices used in those two places represented an incredibly sophisticated level of bioengineering and production technology. Developing them had to have cost tens of millions of dollars – maybe even hundreds of millions.

He shook his head. None of what was happening made much sense, at least on the surface. Terrorist groups with that kind of money would find it far safer and more convenient to buy nukes or poison gas or existing biological weapons on the world black market. Nor would ordinary terrorists find it easy to gain access to the kind of high-tech lab equipment and space needed to produce these killer nanophages.

Smith straightened up, suddenly sure that this unseen enemy had a far deeper and darker goal in mind, a goal it was moving toward with speed and precision. The slaughters in New Mexico and France were only the beginning, he thought coldly, the mere foretaste of acts even more diabolical and destructive.

CHAPTER THIRTY-FIVE

Nanophage Production Facility, Inside the Center

An endless succession of numbers and graphs passed on by satellite link from Paris scrolled slowly across a large computer screen. In the darkened room, the flowing numbers and graphs were eerily reflected in the thick safety glasses worn by two molecular scientists. These men, the chief architects of the nanophage development program, were studying each piece of new data as it arrived.

'It's clear that releasing the nanophages from altitude was extremely effective,' the senior member of the pair remarked. 'The enhanced sensor arrays in our control phages also achieved optimal results. For that matter, so did our new self-destruct system.'

His subordinate nodded. By every practical measure, the remaining engineering problems of their early-design nanophages had been solved. Their Stage III devices no longer needed specific sets of narrowly defined biological signatures to home in on their targets. In one short step, their kill ratio had risen from only around a third of those contaminated to nearly everyone caught inside the nanophage cloud. Plus, the improved chemical loads contained inside each shell had proved their effectiveness by almost entirely consuming all those attacked. The pale, polished bone fragments left on the pavements of La Courneuve were a far cry from the bloated half-eaten corpses littering Kusasa or the unpleasant blood-tinged slime strewn across the grounds outside the Teller Institute.

'I recommend that we declare the weapons fully operational and move immediately to a full production run,' the younger man said confidently. 'Any further design modifications suggested by new data can be carried out later.'

'I agree,' the chief scientist said. 'Lazarus will be pleased.'

Outside the Center

Flanked by two plainclothes bodyguards, Jinjiro Nomura stepped out into the open air for the first time in almost a year. For a moment the small, elderly Japanese man stood rooted to the earth, blinking, briefly dazzled by the sight of the sun high overhead. A cool sea breeze ruffled through the thin wisps of white hair on his head.

'If you please, sir,' one of the guards murmured politely, offering him a pair of sunglasses, 'they are ready for us now. The first of the *Thanatos* prototypes is on final approach.'

Jinjiro Nomura nodded calmly. He took the glasses and put them on.

Behind him, the massive door slid shut, again sealing the main corridor that led to the Center's living quarters, control center, administrative offices, and, ultimately, nanophage production facility hidden deep within the huge building. From the outside and from the air the whole complex appeared to be nothing more than a metal-roofed concrete warehouse – one essentially identical to the thousands of other low-cost industrial storage facilities scattered around the globe. Its intricate systems of chemical storage and piping, air locks, concentric layers of ever more rigidly maintained 'clean' rooms, and elaborate banks of networked supercomputers were completely camouflaged by that plain, rusting, weather-beaten exterior.

Paced by his guards, Nomura marched down a gravel path and onto the edge of a tarmac, part of an immensely long concrete runway that stretched north and south for thousands of feet. Large aircraft hangars and aviation fuel tanks were visible at either end, along with several parked cargo and passenger jets. A tall metal fence, topped by coils of razor wire, surrounded the airfield and its associated buildings. The western horizon was an unbroken vista of rolling waves, crashing and foaming all along the coast. Off to the east, flat green fields dotted by grazing sheep and cattle ran for miles, rising toward a distant peak covered with trees.

He stopped near a small knot of white-coated engineers and scientists, all of whom were eagerly scanning the northern horizon.

'Soon,' one of them told the others, consulting his watch. He turned his head, checking the position of the sun through eyes narrowed against the glare. 'The craft's solar power system is functioning perfectly. And the on-board fuel cells have finished cycling into standby mode.'

'There it is!' another said excitedly, pointing north. A thin dark line, at first barely visible against the clear blue sky, suddenly appeared there – growing steadily as it slowly descended toward the runway.

Jinjiro Nomura watched intently as the strange aerial vehicle, code-named *Thanatos* by its designers, drew nearer. It was an enormous flying-wing aircraft, without a fuselage or a tail but with a wingspan larger than that of a Boeing 747. Fourteen small twin-bladed propellers mounted along the length of the huge wing whirred almost noiselessly, pulling it through the air at less than thirty miles an hour. As the aircraft banked slightly, lining up with the runway, the sixty thousand solar cells installed on its gossamer-thin upper surface shimmered brightly in the sun.

Footsteps crunched softly across the tarmac behind him. Nomura stayed motionless, watching the enormous craft drift lower still as it came in for a landing. For the first time, the engineering specifications and drawings he had studied took shape in his mind.

Modeled on prototypes first flown by NASA, *Thanatos* was an ultra-light all-wing aircraft constructed of radar-absorbent composite materials – carbon fiber, graphite epoxy, Kevlar and Nomex wraps, and advanced plastics. Even with a full payload, it weighed less than two thousand pounds. But it could reach altitudes of nearly one hundred thousand feet and stay aloft under its own power for weeks and months at a time, spanning whole continents and oceans. Five underwing aerodynamic pods carried its flight control computers, data instrumentation, backup fuel-cell systems for night flying, and attachment points for the multiple cylinders that would contain its sinister payload.

NASA had designated its test aircraft *Helios*, after the ancient Greek god of the sun. It was an apt name for a vehicle meant to soar through the upper reaches on solar power. Jinjiro frowned. In the same way, *Thanatos*, the Greek personification of Death, was the perfect appellation for the intended use of this flying wing.

'Beautiful, is it not?' an all-too-familiar voice said quietly in his ear. 'So large. And yet, so delicate . . . so graceful . . . so featherlight. Surely you can see that *Thanatos* is more a wisp of cloud blown by the breath of the gods than it is a creation of brutish man.'

Jinjiro nodded gravely. 'That is so. In itself, this device *is* beautiful.' Grimly he turned to face the man standing close behind him. 'But your evil purposes pervert it, as they do all things you touch . . . Lazarus.'

'You honor me with that name . . . Father,' Hideo Nomura replied, smiling tightly. 'All that I have done, I have done to achieve our common goals, our shared dreams.'

The older man shook his head forcefully. 'Our goals are not the same. My fellows and I wanted to restore and redeem the Earth – to save this ravaged world from the perils posed by uncontrolled science. Under our leadership, the Movement was dedicated to life, not to death.'

'But you and your comrades made one fundamental error, Father,' Hideo told him quietly. 'You misunderstood the nature of the crisis facing our world. Science and technology do not threaten the survival of the Earth. They are only tools, the means to a necessary end. Tools for those like me with the courage and the clarity of vision to make full use of them.'

'As weapons of mass slaughter!' Jinjiro snapped. 'For all your noble words, you are nothing more than a murderer!'

Hideo replied coldly. 'I will do what must be done, Father. In its present state, the human race itself is the enemy – the true threat to the world we both love.' He shrugged. 'In your heart, you know that I am right. Imagine seven billion greedy, grasping, violent animals roaming this one small, fragile planet. They are as dangerous to the Earth as any unchecked cancer would be to the body. The world cannot sustain so heavy a burden. That is why, like any mutating cancer, the worst of mankind must be eliminated – no matter how painful and unpleasant the task will be.'

'Using your devil's weapon, these nanophages,' his father said harshly.

The younger Nomura nodded. 'Imagine *Thanatos* and dozens like it. Imagine them gliding high above the surface – silent and almost entirely invisible to radar. From them will fall a gentle rain, drops so small that they, too, will go unnoticed . . . at least until it is far too late.'

'Where?' Jinjiro asked, ashen-faced.

Hideo showed his teeth. 'First? *Thanatos* and its kin will fly to America, a country that is soulless, powerful, and corrupt. It must be destroyed to make room for the new world order to come. Europe, another source of material-ist contagion, will follow. Then my nanophages will cleanse Africa and the Middle East, those cesspools of ter-ror, disease, starvation, cruelty, and religious fanaticism. China, too, bloated and too mindful of its ancient power, must be humbled.'

'And how many people will die before you are fin-ished?' his father whispered.

Hideo shrugged. 'Five billion? Six billion?' he suggested.

'Who can say exactly? But those who are left alive will soon understand the value of the gift they have been given: A world whose balance has been restored. A world whose resources and infrastructure are left intact, undamaged by the madness of war or all-consuming greed.'

For a long moment the older man could only stare at his son, the man who was now Lazarus, in horror. 'You shame me,' he said at last. 'And you shame our ancestors.' He turned to his guards. 'Take me back to my prison cell,' he said softly. 'The very presence of this monster in human form sickens me.'

Hideo Nomura nodded tightly to the two poker-faced men. 'Do as the old fool asks,' he said icily. Then stepped back and stood in silence, watching his father march away to renewed captivity.

His eyes were hooded. As so often before, Jinjiro had disappointed him – had even betrayed him – with the shallowness of his thoughts and with his lack of courage. Even now his father was too blind to admire the achievements of his only son. Or perhaps, Hideo thought, savoring an old and bitter resentment from his vanished childhood, his father was simply too jealous or coldhearted to offer the praise that was his due.

And praise *was* due; of that he was sure.

For years the younger head of Nomura PharmaTech had worked almost day-and-night to make his vision of a cleaner, less crowded, and more peaceful world a reality. First, careful planning had made it possible to build, staff, and fund this hidden nanotechnology lab without drawing unwelcome attention from his shareholders or from anyone else. None of his many competitors had ever suspected that Nomura, apparently lagging behind in the nanotech applications race, was, in truth, months or years ahead of them.

Next had come the intricate task of subverting the Lazarus Movement, of bending the loose organization slowly and inexorably to his unseen will. Movement leaders who opposed him had been pushed aside or killed, usually by one of the *Horatii*, the trio of assassins whose creation and training he had financed. Best of all, every unexplained death had acted as a spur toward further radicalism by those who were left alive.

Arranging the mysterious disappearance of his own father, the last of the original Lazarus Nine, had been comparative child's play. Once that was accomplished, Hideo had been free to secretly gather all of the frightened Movement's reins into his own hands. Best of all, though, the CIA-led search for Jinjiro had brought him into contact with Hal Burke. And with that, the last piece of Hideo's plan had fallen suddenly into place.

Hideo laughed coldly and quietly, remembering the ease with which he had gulled the CIA agent and, through him, others in the American and British intelligence services – playing on their paranoid fears of terrorism. By feeding them ever more damaging information about the Movement, he had manipulated Burke and his associates into launching their foolish and illegal war. From that day forward, all events had been managed according to his will, and his will alone.

The results spoke for themselves: The world's population was increasingly terrified and hunting for scapegoats. His competitors like Harcourt Biosciences were helpless, buried by an avalanche of new government restrictions on their research. The Lazarus Movement was growing stronger and more violent. And now the American and British spy services were rendered helpless by scandal and corrosive suspicion. By the time the first murderous rain of nanophages fell on Washington, D.C., New York, Chicago, and Los Angeles, it would be impossible for anyone to uncover the terrible truth.

Hideo Nomura smiled to himself. After all, he thought savagely, how better to win a game than to play both sides at once?

CHAPTER THIRTY-SIX

Lazarus Address

The new digital video of Lazarus released by the Movement repeated the pattern of his first world broadcast in the wake of the Teller Institute Massacre. Pieces of untraceable footage arrived simultaneously in TV studios around the globe, each one with a different digitally constructed image of Lazarus designed to appeal to a particular audience.

'It is no longer possible to hide from the truth,' Lazarus said sadly. 'The horrors we have witnessed testify that a new weapon is being unleashed on humanity – a weapon forged by a cruel and unnatural science. Humankind stands at a crossroads. Down one road, the road charted by our Movement, lies a world of peace and tranquillity. Down the other, a path laid down by greedy men obsessed by power and profit, lies a world wracked by war and genocide – a world of carnage and catastrophe.'

The Lazarus figure stared straight into the camera. 'We must choose which of these two futures we will embrace,' he said. 'The ruinous advances of nanotechnology, genetic meddling, and cloning must be abandoned or suppressed before they destroy us all. Accordingly, the Movement calls on all governments – especially those in the so-called civilized nations of the West and the United States in particular – to immediately ban the study, development, and use of these sinister, life-destroying technologies.'

The face of Lazarus grew stern. 'Should any government fail to heed this demand, we will take matters into our own hands. We must act. We must save ourselves, our families, our races, and the Earth we all love. This is a struggle for the future of humankind and there is no time for further delay, no more room for neutrality. In this conflict, anyone who will not join us stands against us. Let those who are wise heed this warning!'

Berlin
Thousands of demonstrators poured onto Berlin's grand central boulevard, Unter den Linden, their numbers swelling fast with every passing minute. Scores of scarlet and green Lazarus Movement banners fluttered near the front of the chanting crowd as it moved east from the chariot-topped Brandenburger Tor. Behind them came a growing array of other flags, placards, and posters. The Greens and Germany's other major environmental and antiglobalization groups were joining the Movement in a major show of force.

Their chants echoed harshly off the stone facades of the enormous public buildings lining the wide avenue. 'NO TO NANOTECH! STOP THE MADNESS! BREAK THE AMERICAN WAR MACHINE! LET LAZARUS LEAD!'

The CNN crew covering the protest moved back up the steep steps of the Staatsoper, the state opera house, a still-elegant nineteenth-century building fronted by massive columns, seeking both a better vantage point and shelter from the angry crowd. The reporter, a slender, pretty brunette in her early thirties, had to shout into her microphone to be heard over the tumult spreading through the streets of the German capital. 'This demonstration seems to have taken the authorities here almost completely by surprise, John! What began two hours ago as just a small band of protesters inspired by the most recent Lazarus video has now become one of the largest political gatherings seen since the Wall came down! And now we understand that similar mass rallies against nanotechnology and U.S. policy are developing in cities around the world – in Rome, Madrid, Tokyo, Cairo, Rio de Janeiro, San Francisco, and many others.'

She looked out over the sea of flags and signs flowing past the opera house. 'So far the crowd here in Berlin has stayed relatively peaceful, but officials fear that anarchists may peel off at any moment to begin smashing stores and office buildings owned by various American corporations – corporations the Lazarus Movement calls "part of the death machine culture." As the situation develops, we'll be standing by to bring it to you live!'

Near Cape Town, South Africa
Twenty-five kilometers south of Cape Town, thick columns of black smoke billowed high above the Capricorn Business and Technology Park, staining the red-hued evening sky. Nearly a dozen once-gleaming buildings were on fire inside the high-tech industrial and research facility. Thousands of rioters swarmed along the ring road circling a central lake, smashing windows, overturning cars, and setting new blazes wherever they could. At first, the rampaging mob had aimed its efforts at American-owned biotech labs, but now, gripped by hysteria and rage, they were lashing out at every science-based business and firm in sight – destroying property and equipment worth tens of millions of dollars with total abandon.

The police, heavily outnumbered and unwilling to confront the screaming crowd with deadly force, had withdrawn from Capricorn and now manned a perimeter well outside the complex – hoping only to keep the destruction from spilling over into the surrounding suburbs. More pillars of smoke began rising from the ruined technology park as the strengthening wind whipped new fires through the looted buildings.

CBS News – Breaking Story: 'America's Secret War'
America's daytime TV viewers, tuning in to watch their favorite game shows or soap operas, instead found themselves watching nonstop news bulletins as the major networks and cable channels raced to keep up with events around the world.

As the violence spread through countries on five continents, not even the veteran CBS anchor could contain his growing excitement. 'Hold on to your hats, folks,' he said, in a Southern drawl that deepened with every passing minute. 'Because this wild ride is getting even wilder. French television has just dropped a bombshell – charging that the CIA and the FBI, with help from the British, have been conducting a secret campaign of murder and sabotage against the Lazarus Movement. Reporters in Paris say they can prove that former U.S. and British commandos and spies are responsible for the deaths of Lazarus leaders and activists around the world, including here in the United States. They also claim these attacks could only have been authorized at "the very highest levels of the American and British governments." '

The anchor looked up, speaking right into the camera with a grave expression on his face. 'Now when our reporters asked officials in Washington and London to comment, they were given the royal brush-off. Everyone from the president and prime minister on down is refusing to say anything of substance to the press. No one knows whether that's just the usual reluctance to comment on intelligence operations and on criminal investigations or if it's because there's fire under all this smoke. But one thing is certain. The angry people across the globe burning all those American flags and smashing up American-owned businesses aren't going to wait to find out.'

White House Situation Room
'Listen very closely, Mr. Hanson. I don't want to hear any more waffling or evasion or bureaucratic mumbo jumbo. I

want the truth, and I want it now!' President Sam Castilla growled. He glared down the long table at his uncharacteristically silent CIA director.

Ordinarily trim and dapper under even the most trying circumstances, David Hanson looked a wreck. There were deep shadows under his eyes and his rumpled suit looked as though he had slept in it. He held a pen clutched tightly in the fingers of his right hand in a futile effort to hide the fact that his hands were trembling slightly. 'I've told you what little I know, Mr. President,' he said warily. 'We're digging as deeply as we can into our files, but so far we haven't found anything even remotely connected to this so-called TOCSIN operation. If Hal Burke was involved in anything illegal, I'm certain that he was running it on his own hook – without authorization or help from anyone else in the CIA.'

Emily Powell-Hill leaned forward in her seat. 'Just how stupid do you think people are, David?' the national security adviser asked bitterly. 'Do you think anyone's going to believe that Burke and Pierson were paying for a multimillion-dollar covert operation out of their own pockets – all with their personal savings and government salaries?'

'I understand the difficulties!' Hanson snapped in frustration. 'But my people and I are working on this as hard and as fast as we can. Right now I've got my security personnel combing through the records and logs of every operation Burke was ever involved in, looking for anything remotely suspicious. Plus, we're setting up polygraph tests for every officer and analyst in Burke's Lazarus Movement section. If anyone else inside the CIA was involved, we'll nail them, but it's going to take time.'

He frowned. 'I've also sent orders to every CIA station around the world immediately terminating any operation that involves the Movement. By now there shouldn't be an Agency surveillance team within shouting distance of any Lazarus building or operative.'

'That's not good enough,' Powell-Hill told him. 'We're

getting killed over this – both domestically and overseas.'

Heads nodded grimly around the Situation Room conference table. Coming as it did right on the heels of the nanophage butchery in La Courneuve, the press reports of an illegal clandestine operation against the Lazarus Movement had been perfectly timed to inflict the maximum amount of damage on American credibility around the world. It had landed on the world stage like a match tossed into a room full of leaking gasoline drums. And the Movement was perfectly positioned to profit from the resulting explosion of anger and outrage. What had been a relatively minor nuisance for most governments and businesses was rapidly growing into a major force in global politics. More and more countries were aligning themselves with the Movement's demands for an immediate ban on all nanotech research.

'And now every lunatic who claims that we're testing some sort of nanotech-based genocide weapon is being treated respectfully by the international media – by the BBC, the other European networks, al-Jazeera, and the rest,' the national security adviser continued. 'The French have already recalled their ambassador for so-called consultations. A lot of other nations are going to do the same thing in a tearing hurry. The longer this drags on, the more damage we're going to suffer to our alliances and our ability to influence events.'

Castilla nodded tightly. The phone call he had received from the French president had been full of ugly accusations and barely concealed contempt.

'We're in almost as much trouble on the Hill,' Charles Ouray added. The White House chief of staff sighed. 'Practically every congressman and senator who was screaming at us to go after the Lazarus Movement has already pulled a full 180-degree turn. Now they're falling all over themselves to put together a Watergate-style investigative committee. The wilder talking heads are already discussing a possible impeachment, and even our usual friends are lying low while they wait to see which way the political winds are blowing.'

Castilla grimaced. Too many of the men and women serving in Congress were political opportunists by habit, inclination, and experience. When a president was popular, they crowded in close, hoping to share in the limelight. But at the first sign of trouble or weakness they were only too eager to join the pack baying for his blood.

The White House

Estelle Pike, the president's longtime executive secretary, opened the door to the Oval Office. 'Mr. Klein is here, sir,' she said waspishly. 'He doesn't have an appointment, but he claims that you'll see him anyway.'

Castilla turned away from the windows. His face was lined and weary. He seemed to have aged ten years in the past twenty-four hours. 'He's here because I asked him to be here, Estelle. Show him in, please.'

She sniffed, plainly disapproving, but then obeyed.

Klein stepped past her with a murmured 'thank you' that went unacknowledged. He stood waiting until the door closed behind him. Then he shrugged. 'I don't think your Ms. Pike likes me very much, Sam.'

The president forced a dutiful smile. 'Estelle isn't exactly a warm and cuddly people person, Fred. Anyone who bucks her daily calendar gets the same treatment. It's nothing personal.'

'I'm relieved,' Klein said drily. He looked narrowly at his old friend. 'I assume from your pained expression that the NSC meeting did not go well?'

Castilla snorted. 'That's almost on par with asking Mrs. Lincoln how she liked the play.'

'That bad?'

The president nodded glumly. 'That bad.' He motioned Klein toward one of the two chairs set in front of the big table that served him as a desk. 'The senior people inside the CIA, FBI, NSA, and other agencies are too god-damned busy trying to dodge the blame for this TOCSIN fiasco. Nobody knows how far up the ladder the conspiracy reached, so nobody knows how far anybody else can be trusted. Everybody's circling one another warily, waiting to see who gets it in the neck.'

Klein nodded quietly, not greatly surprised. Even at the best of times, debilitating turf wars were a fact of life within the American intelligence community. Their long-standing feuds and internecine conflicts were largely why Castilla had asked him to organize Covert-One in the first place. Now, with a major scandal embroiling the two biggest over-seas and domestic intelligence agencies, tensions would be rising fast. In the circumstances, no one with a career to protect was going to risk sticking his or her neck out.

'Is Colonel Smith on his way to Paris?' Castilla asked at last, breaking the silence.

'He is,' Klein said. 'I expect him there by late tonight, our time.'

'And you honestly believe Smith has a chance to find out what we're really facing here?'

'A chance?' Klein repeated. He hesitated. 'I think so.' He frowned. 'At least, I hope so.'

'But he *is* your best?' Castilla asked sharply.

This time Klein did not hesitate. 'For this mission? Yes, absolutely. Jon Smith is the right man for the job.'

The president shook his head in exasperation. 'It's ridiculous, isn't it?'

'Ridiculous?'

'Here I sit,' Castilla explained, 'the commander in chief of the most powerful armed forces in the history of mankind. The people of the United States expect me to use that power to keep them safe. But I can't. Not this time. Not yet at least.' His broad shoulders slumped. 'All the bombers, missiles, tanks, and riflemen in the world don't matter worth a damn unless I can give them a target. And that's the one thing I cannot give them.'

Klein stared back at his friend. He had truly never envied the president any of the various perks and privileges of his position. Now he felt only pity for the tired, sad-eyed man in front of him. 'Covert-One will do its duty,' he promised. 'We'll find you that target.'

'I hope to God you're right,' Castilla said quietly. 'Because we're running out of time and options fast.'

CHAPTER THIRTY-SEVEN

Monday, October 18
Paris

Jon Smith looked out the windows of the taxi, a black Mercedes, speeding south from Charles de Gaulle International Airport toward the sleeping city. Dawn was still several hours away, and only the hazy glow of lights on both sides of the multi-lane A1 Motorway marked the suburban sprawl around the French capital. The highway itself was almost deserted – allowing the cabdriver, a short, sour-faced Parisian with bloodshot eyes, to push the Mercedes up to the legal limit and then well beyond.

Moving at more than 120 kilometers per hour, they flashed past several darkened neighborhoods where flames danced skyward, licking red and orange against the black night. Dilapidated apartment blocks were on fire there, casting a flickering glow across the neighboring buildings. Near those areas, rolls of barbed wire and hurriedly deployed concrete barriers blocked all entrance and exit ramps off the motorway. Each checkpoint was manned by heavy concentrations of police and soldiers in full combat gear. Armored cars fitted with tear-gas grenade launchers and machine guns, tracked personnel carriers, and even fifty-ton Leclerc main battle tanks were parked at strategic points along the route.

'Les Arabes!' The taxi driver sniffed contemptuously, stubbing his cigarette out in an overflowing ashtray. He shrugged his narrow shoulders. 'They are rioting against

what happened in La Courneuve. Burning down their own homes and shops – as usual. Bah!'

He paused to light another unfiltered cigarette with both hands, using his knees to steer the heavy German-made sedan. 'They are idiots. Nobody much cares what happens inside those rats' nests. But let them put one foot outside and *ppffft*.' He drew a line across his throat. 'Then the machine guns will begin talking, eh?'

Smith nodded silently. It was no real secret that the overcrowded and crime-ridden housing projects outside Paris had been carefully designed so that they could be swiftly and easily sealed off in the event of serious unrest.

The Mercedes turned off the A1 and onto the boulevard Périphérique, swinging south and east around the crowded city's maze of alleys, streets, avenues, and boulevards. Still grumbling about the stupidity of a government that taxed *him* to pay welfare to thugs, thieves, and *'les Arabes,'* the taxi driver abandoned this ring road at the Porte de Vincennes. The cab plunged west, circled the Place de la Nation, roared along the rue du Faubourg-St. Antoine, screeched around the Place de la Bastille, and then threaded its way deeper into the narrow one-way streets of the Marais District, in the city's Third Arrondissement.

Once a swamp, this part of Paris was one of the few untouched by the grandiose nineteenth-century demolition and reconstruction projects carried out by Baron Hausmann at the orders of the emperor Napoléon III. Many of its buildings dated back to the Middle Ages. Seedy and run-down in the mid-twentieth century, the Marais had experienced a rebirth. It was now one of the city's most popular residential, tourist, and shopping areas. Elegant stone mansions, museums, and libraries sat beside trendy bars, antique shops, and fashion-conscious clothing salons.

With a final flourish of his tobacco-stained hands, the driver pulled up outside the front door of the Hôtel des Chevaliers – a small boutique hotel scarcely a block from the ancient tree-lined elegance of the Place des Vosges. 'We arrive, *m'sieur*! And in record time!' he announced. He grinned sourly. 'Perhaps we should thank the rioters, eh? Because I think the *flics*,' he used the French slang word for policemen, 'are too busy cracking their heads to hand out traffic tickets to honest men like me!'

'Maybe so,' Smith agreed, secretly relieved to arrive in one piece. He shoved a handful of euros at the cabdriver, grabbed his small carry-on bag and the travel kit he had picked up before boarding his flight at Dulles, and scrambled out onto the pavement. The Mercedes roared away into the night almost the second he closed the passenger door.

Smith stood quietly for a moment, savoring the restored silence and stillness of the damp street. It had rained here not long ago, and the cool night air carried a clean, crisp scent that was refreshing. He stretched limbs that had grown stiff in a cramped airline seat, then breathed deeply a few times to clear the lingering second-hand traces of the cabdriver's harsh tobacco out of his lungs. Feeling better and more awake, he slung his luggage over his shoulder and turned to the hotel. There was a light on over the door, and the night clerk – alerted by an earlier phone call from the airport to expect him – buzzed him in without trouble.

'Welcome to Paris, Dr. Smith,' the clerk said smoothly, in clear, fluent English. 'You will be staying with us long?'

'A few days, perhaps,' Jon said carefully. 'Can you accommodate me that long?'

The night clerk, a neatly attired middle-aged man alert despite the early hour, sighed. 'In good times, no.' He shrugged his shoulders expressively. 'But, alas, this unpleasantness at La Courneuve has caused many cancellations and early departures. So it will be no problem.'

Smith signed the register, automatically checking the names above his for anything suspicious. He saw nothing there to worry him. There were only a few other guests, almost all of them from other European countries or from France itself. Most, like him, seemed to be traveling alone. They were either here on urgent business or else scholars delving into the various nearby historical archives and museums, he judged. Couples bent on romance would have been among the first to abandon Paris in the wake of the nanophage attack and the ensuing riots.

The clerk brought out a small square cardboard box and laid it on top of the desk. 'Also, this package came by courier for you an hour ago.' He glanced down at the note on top. 'It is from the MacLean Medical Group in Toronto, Canada. You were expecting it, I think?'

Smith nodded, smiling inwardly. Trust Fred Klein to be on the ball, he thought gratefully. MacLean was one of the many shell companies Covert-One used for clandestine shipments to its agents around the world.

Upstairs in the privacy of his small but elegantly furnished room, he broke open the seals on the box and ripped through the packing tape. Inside he found a hard plastic case containing a brand-new 9mm SIG-Sauer pistol, a box of ammunition, and three spare magazines. A leather shoulder holster came wrapped separately.

Smith sat down on the comfortable double bed, stripped the pistol down to its constituent parts, carefully cleaned each component, and then put them back together. Satisfied, he snapped in a loaded magazine and slid the SIG-Sauer into the shoulder holster. He went to the window, which looked out onto the tiny courtyard behind the hotel. Above the dark slate rooftops of the ancient buildings on the other side, the eastern sky was touched by the first faint hint of gray. Lights were beginning to flick on behind some of the other windows facing the little cobblestone enclosure. The city was waking up.

He punched in Klein's number on his cell phone and reported his safe arrival in Paris. 'Any new developments?' he asked.

'Nothing here,' the head of Covert-One told him. 'But

it appears that the CIA team in Paris has traced one of the vehicles it spotted in La Courneuve to an address not far from where you are now.'

Smith heard the uncertainty in Klein's voice. 'It appears?' he said, surprised.

'They're being very coy,' the other man explained. 'The team's most recent signal to Langley claimed preliminary success but omitted any specific location.'

Smith frowned. 'That's odd.'

'Yes,' Klein said flatly. 'It is very odd. And I don't have a satisfactory explanation for the omission.'

'Isn't Langley pressing the Paris Station for specifics?'

Klein snorted. 'The head of the CIA and his top people are far too busy running emergency audits of the whole Operations Directorate to pay much attention to their officers in the field.'

'So what makes you think this surveillance team is zeroing in on a building in or around the Marais?' Jon asked.

'Because they've set their primary RV in the Place des Vosges,' Klein said.

Smith nodded to himself, understanding the other man's reasoning. The RV – or rendezvous point – for a covert surveillance team operating inside a city was almost always set up within easy walking distance of its intended target. It was usually a fairly public place, one busy enough to camouflage discreet meetings between agents as they exchanged information or relayed new orders. The Place des Vosges, built in 1605, was the oldest square in Paris and was perfect for this purpose. The bustling restaurants, cafés, and shops lining its four sides would provide ideal cover.

'Makes sense,' he agreed. 'But knowing that doesn't do me much good, does it? They could be snooping around any one of several hundred buildings in this neighborhood.'

'It's a problem,' Klein agreed. 'Which is why you're going to have to make direct contact with the CIA team.'

Smith raised an eyebrow in amazement. 'Oh? And just how do you suggest I go about doing that?' he asked. 'Parade up and down the Place des Vosges waving a big sign asking for a meeting?'

'Something rather like that, actually,' Klein said drily.

With growing surprise and amusement, Smith listened to the other man explain what he meant. When they were through, Smith disconnected and entered another number.

'Delights of Paris, LLC,' a rich, resonant English voice answered. 'No service too small. No bed left unmade. No reasonable request refused.'

'You thinking of a career move, Peter?' Smith asked, grinning.

Peter Howell chuckled. 'Not at all. Merely a possible sideline to supplement my meager retirement pay.' He turned serious. 'I assume you have news?'

'I do,' Smith confirmed. 'Where are you?'

'A charming little *pension* on the Left Bank,' Peter replied. 'Not far from the boulevard Saint-Germain. I arrived here all of five minutes ago, so your timing is impeccable.'

'How are you fixed for equipment?'

'No problems,' the Englishman assured him. 'I paid a little call on an old chum on my way in from the airport.'

Smith nodded to himself. Peter Howell seemed to have reliable contacts across most of Europe – old friends and comrades-in-arms who would provide him with weapons, other gear, and assistance without asking awkward questions.

'So, where and when do we meet?' Peter asked quietly. 'And with what purpose precisely?'

Smith filled him in – passing along the information relayed by Klein, though he described it as coming to him only from a 'friend' with good contacts inside the CIA. By the time he was finished, he could hear the undisguised astonishment in the other man's voice.

'It's a funny old world, Jon, isn't it?' Peter said at last. 'And a damned small one, too.'

'It sure is,' Smith agreed, smiling. Then his smile faded as he thought of the terrors that might lie in store for this small, interconnected world if he and the Englishman were only chasing yet another dead end. Somewhere out there, those who had designed the nanophages were surely busy brewing up an even deadlier batch of their new weapons. Unless they could be found and stopped – and soon – a great many more innocent people were going to die, eaten alive by new waves of murderous machines too small to be seen.

CHAPTER THIRTY-EIGHT

Paris

An autumn breeze ruffled through the leaves of the chestnut trees planted around the neatly landscaped edges of the Place des Vosges. As the wind freshened, small gusts whipped through the spray of one of the burbling fountains. A fine mist of water droplets swirled sideways – staining the broad pavements and glistening like early morning dew on the lush green grass.

Impishly the breeze danced and curled around the weathered gray and pale rose stone facades of the covered galleries, the arcades, lining the square. In the northwest corner of the Place, cloth napkins pinned down by water goblets fluttered on the highly polished wicker tables of the Brasserie Ma Bourgogne.

Jon Smith sat alone at a table on the edge of the arcade, lounging comfortably in one of the restaurant's red leather-backed chairs. He looked out over the fenced-in square, paying careful attention to the many people strolling casually along its sidewalks or occupying park benches, idly tossing bread crumbs to the murmuring pigeons.

'*Un café noir, m'sieur,*' a glum voice said nearby.

Smith looked up.

One of the waiters, a serious, unsmiling, older man wearing the bow tie and black apron that was a hallmark of Ma Bourgogne, slid a single cup of black coffee onto the table.

Smith nodded politely. '*Merci.*' He slid a few euros across the table.

Grumbling under his breath, the waiter pocketed the money, turned away, and stalked toward another table, this one occupied by two local businessmen making a deal over what looked like an early lunch. Smith could smell the fragrant odor of the plates piled high with *saucisson de Beaujolais* and *pommes frites*. His mouth watered. It had been a long time since breakfast at the Hôtel des Chevaliers, and the two cups of strong coffee he had already consumed while waiting here were eating away at his stomach lining.

For a moment he debated calling the waiter back, but then he decided against it. According to Klein, this was the CIA surveillance team's primary rendezvous point. With a bit of luck, he might not have to sit here idle much longer.

Smith went back to watching the people moving through the square and among the surrounding buildings. Even at mid-morning, the Place des Vosges was reasonably crowded, full of students and teachers on break from the nearby schools, young mothers pushing infants in strollers, and squealing tots happily digging in the sandbox set in the shadow of an equestrian statue of Louis XIII. Old men arguing about everything from politics, to sports, to the odds of winning the next national lottery stood around in small groups, slicing the air with wide, vigorous gestures as they made their points.

Before the French Revolution, when it was still called the Place Royal, this beautiful little patch of open ground had been the site of innumerable duels. On every square inch where ordinary Parisians now enjoyed the autumn sun and let their pampered dogs run free, cavaliers and young aristocrats had fought and died – hacking at each other with swords or exchanging pistol shots at close range, all to prove their courage or to defend their honor. Though it was fashionable now to deride these duels as the hallmarks of a savage and bloodthirsty age, Smith wondered whether or not that was especially fair. After all, how might future historians characterize this so-called modern era – a time when some men were determined to slaughter innocents whenever and wherever they could?

A plain, plump, dark-haired young woman in a knee-length black coat and blue jeans passed close by his table. She noticed him watching her and flushed red. She walked hurriedly on with her head down. Jon followed her with his eyes, debating with himself. Was she the contact he had been waiting for?

'This seat? It is taken, *m'sieur*?' rasped a gravelly voice made hoarse by decades of smoking three or four packs of cigarettes a day.

Smith turned his head and saw the slender, ramrod-straight figure of an aged Parisian dowager glaring down at him. He had the overriding impression of a mass of immaculately coiffed gray hair, a deeply lined face, a prominent hawk-like nose, and a fierce, predatory gaze. She raised one finely sculpted eyebrow in apparent disgust at his slowness and stupidity. 'You do not speak English, *m'sieur*? *Pardon. Sprechen Sie Deutsch*?'

Before he could recover, she turned away to address her dog, a small, equally elderly poodle who seemed intent on gnawing one of the empty chairs to death. She yanked on his leash. 'Heel, Pascal! Let the damned furniture fall to pieces on its own!' she snapped in idiomatic French.

Apparently satisfied that Smith was either deaf, dumb, or an imbecile, the old woman seated herself across the table from him – groaning slightly as she slowly lowered her creaking bones into the chair. He looked away, embarrassed.

'Just what the hell are you doing trespassing on my patch, Jon?' he heard a very familiar and very irritated voice ask quietly. 'And please don't try to sell me some cock-and-bull story that you're here to see the glories of Paris!'

Smith turned back toward the old woman in amazement. Somewhere behind that mass of gray hair, wrinkles, and lines were the smooth, blond good looks of CIA officer Randi Russell. He felt himself flush. Randi, the sister of his dead fiancée, was a very good friend, someone with whom he shared dinner or drinks whenever they found themselves in Washington at the same time. Despite that, and though he had known that his presence right at her team's rendezvous point would eventually draw her attention, she had still managed to slip past his guard.

To buy himself some time to recover from his surprise, he took a cautious sip of his coffee. Then he grinned back at her. 'Nice disguise, Randi. Now I know what you'll look like in forty or fifty years. The little dog's a nifty touch, too. Is he yours? Or standard CIA-issue?'

'Pascal belongs to a friend, a colleague at the embassy,' Randi replied briefly. Her mouth tightened. 'And the poodle is almost as much of a pain in the ass as you are, Jon. Almost, but not quite. Now quit stalling and answer my question.'

He shrugged. 'Okay. It's pretty simple, really. I'm here following up on the reports you and your team have been sending to the States for the past twenty-four hours.'

'*That's* what you call simple?' Randi said in disbelief. 'Our reports are strictly internal CIA product.'

'Not anymore they're not,' Smith told her. 'Langley's in a hell of a mess right now over this clandestine war against the Lazarus Movement. So is the FBI. Maybe you've heard.'

The CIA officer nodded bitterly. 'Yeah, I've heard. Bad news spreads fast.' She frowned down at the table. 'That stupid son of a bitch Burke is going to wind up giving the Agency the biggest black eye we've ever had.' Her gaze sharpened. 'But that still doesn't explain who you're working for this time.' She paused significantly. 'Or at least who you're going to *claim* you're working for.'

Inwardly Smith cursed the continuing need to keep Covert-One's existence a tightly held secret. Like Peter

Howell's, her affiliation with another intelligence outfit meant Smith had to tread carefully around her, concealing whole aspects of his work – even from those who were his closest friends, people to whom he would entrust his life. He and Randi had managed to work together before, in Iraq and Russia, here in Paris, and most recently in China, but it was always awkward dodging her pointed questions.

'It's no great secret, Randi,' he lied. He felt guilty for lying to her but did his best to hide it. 'You know I've done some work for Army Intelligence in the past. Well, the Pentagon brass pulled me in again for this mission. Someone is developing a nanotech weapon, and the Joint Chiefs of Staff don't like the sound of that at all.'

'But why you, exactly?' she demanded.

Smith looked her straight in the eye. 'Because I was working at the Teller Institute,' he said quietly. 'So I know what this weapon can do to people. I saw it myself.'

Randi's face softened. 'That must have been terrible, Jon.'

He nodded, mentally pushing away the sickening memories that still haunted his sleep. 'It was.' He looked across the table. 'But I guess it was even worse here – at La Courneuve.'

'There were many more deaths, and no apparent survivors,' Randi agreed. 'From the press accounts, what happened to those poor people was absolutely horrible.'

'Then you should understand why I want a closer look at the men you spotted installing some kind of quote-unquote sensor equipment there the night before the attack,' Smith told her.

'You think the two events are related?'

He raised an eyebrow. 'Don't you?'

Randi nodded reluctantly. 'Yes, I do.' She sighed. 'And we've managed to trace most of the vehicles those guys were using.' She saw the next question in his eyes and answered it before he could speak. 'Right, you guessed it:

They're all tied to a single address right here in Paris.'

'An address you've carefully avoided naming in any of your cables home,' Smith pointed out.

'For some damned good reasons,' Randi snapped back. She grimaced. 'I'm sorry to sound so pissed off, Jon. But I can't fit much of what we've learned into any kind of rational, coherent pattern, and frankly, it's getting on my nerves.'

'Well, maybe I can help sort out some of the anomalies,' he offered.

For the first time, Randi responded with a faint smile. 'Possibly. For an amateur spook you do have an uncanny knack for stumbling into answers,' she agreed slowly. 'Usually by accident, of course.'

Smith chuckled. 'Of course.'

The CIA officer leaned back against the chair, absently studying the people strolling past them on the pavement. Suddenly she stiffened, plainly incredulous. 'Jesus,' she muttered in dismay. 'What is this . . . old home week?'

Smith followed her gaze and saw what appeared to be an old, untidy Frenchman in a beret and an often-patched sweater ambling toward them, whistling, with both hands stuck into the pockets of his faded workingman's trousers. He looked more closely and hid a grin. It was Peter Howell.

The sun-browned Englishman sauntered across the street separating the restaurant from the square, came right up to their table, and politely doffed his beret to Randi. 'A pleasure to see you looking so well, *madame*,' he murmured. His pale blue eyes gleamed with amusement. 'And this is your young son, no doubt. A fine, stout-looking lad.'

'Hello, Peter,' Randi said resignedly. 'So you've joined the Army, too?'

'The American army?' Peter said in mock horror. 'Heavens, no, dear girl! Merely a spot of informal collaborating between old friends and allies, you see. Washing the hand that feeds me and all that. No, Jon and

I simply popped by to see if you were interested in joining our little pact.'

'Grand. I'm so glad.' She shook her head. 'Okay, I surrender. I'll share my information, but that has to work both ways. I want all of your cards on the table, too. Get it?'

The Englishman smiled gently. 'Clear as crystal. Fear not. All will be revealed in due course. You can trust your Uncle Peter.'

'Sure I can.' Randi snorted. 'Anyway, it's not as if I have much real choice, not under the circumstances.' She pushed herself up slowly, carefully maintaining the illusion that she was an elderly woman somewhere in her mid-seventies. She tugged at the small poodle, dragging him firmly out from under the table where he had been futilely gumming one of Smith's shoes for the past few minutes. She switched back to her raspy, nasal French. 'Come, Pascal. We must not intrude further on these gentlemen's company.'

Then she lowered her voice, making sure that only they could hear her instructions. 'Now here's how we're going to play this. When I'm gone, wait five minutes and then head over to Number Six – the Victor Hugo house. Pretend you're tourists or literary critics or something. A white Audi with a dent on the right rear door will pull up there. Climb in without making a big fuss about it. Understand?'

Jon and Peter nodded obediently.

Still frowning, Randi moved away without looking back at them. She strolled briskly toward the nearest corner of the Place des Vosges – looking for all the world as though she truly were the epitome of a Paris *grande dame* out for her morning constitutional with her much-pampered poodle.

Ten minutes later, the two men stood outside the Maison de Victor Hugo, staring curiously up at the second floor, where the great writer, the author of *Les Miserables* and *The Hunchback of Notre-Dame*, had spent sixteen years of his long life. 'A curious fellow,' Peter Howell remarked meditatively. 'Prone to fits of madness in later life, you know. Someone once found him trying to carve furniture with his teeth.'

'Much like Pascal,' Smith suggested.

Peter looked surprised. 'The famous philospher and mathematician?'

'No,' Smith said, grinning. 'Randi's dog.'

'Dear me,' Peter replied wryly. 'The things one learns in Paris.' He glanced casually over his shoulder. 'Ah, our chariot awaits.'

Smith turned around and saw the white Audi, complete with its dented rear door, stopping alongside the curb. He and Peter slid into the backseat. The car pulled away immediately, drove around the Place des Vosges, and swung left back onto the rue de Turenne. From there, the sedan began making a series of seemingly random turns, moving ever deeper into the heart of the maze of one-way streets that made up the Marais District.

Jon watched the sallow-faced driver, a heavyset man wearing a cloth cap, for a few moments. 'Hello, Max,' he said at last.

'Morning, Colonel,' the other man said, grinning in the rearview mirror. 'Nice to see you again.'

Smith nodded. He and Max had once spent a great many hours in each other's company – trailing a group of Arab terrorists all the way from Paris to the Spanish coast. The CIA operative might not be the brightest star in the Agency's firmament, but he was a very competent field agent.

'Are we being followed?' Smith asked, seeing the way the other man's eyes were always in motion, checking every aspect of the environment around the Audi as he drove through the traffic-choked Paris streets.

Max shook his head confidently. 'Nope. This is just a

precaution. We're being extra careful, is all. Randi's sort of on-edge right now.'

'Care to tell me why?'

The CIA agent snorted. 'You'll find out soon enough, Colonel.' He turned the Audi off into a narrow passageway. Tall stone buildings soared on either side, blotting out any real sight of the sun or sky. He parked right behind a gray Renault van blocking most of the alley. 'Last stop,' he said.

Smith and Peter got out.

The back doors of the van popped open, revealing a crowded interior crammed full of TV, audio, and computer equipment. Randi Russell, still wearing her disguise as an old woman, was there – along with another man, one Jon did not recognize. Pascal the poodle was nowhere to be seen.

Jon scrambled up into the Renault, followed closely by the Englishman. They pulled the doors shut behind them and then stood awkwardly hunched over in the cramped space.

'Glad you could make it,' Randi said. She flashed a quick smile at them and waved a hand at the equipment mounted in racks on both sides of the van interior. 'Welcome to our humble abode, the nerve center of our surveillance operation. Besides human watchers, we've been able to rig a number of hidden cameras at key points around the target.'

She nodded to the other man, who was sitting on a stool in front of a computer screen and keyboard. 'Let's show them what we've got, Hank. Bring up Camera Two first. I know our guests are dying to find out what we're doing here.'

Her subordinate obediently entered a series of commands on his keyboard. The monitor in front of him flashed on immediately, showing a clear TV picture of a steep gray-blue slate roof. Antennae of every size, shape, and description sprouted from the roof.

Smith whistled softly.

'Yeah.' Randi nodded flatly. 'These guys are set to send and receive just about every kind of signal you can think of. Radio, microwave, laser pulse, satellite . . . you name it.'

'So what's the problem?' Jon asked her, still puzzled. 'Why run so scared about feeding Langley the whole scoop?'

Randi smiled sardonically. She leaned forward and tapped her equipment operator on the shoulder. 'Bring up Camera One, Hank.' She glanced back at Smith and Peter. 'Here's the street entrance of the same building. Take a good close look.'

The picture on the screen showed a building five stories high. Centuries of pollution and weather had pitted and darkened its plain stone facade. High, narrow windows looked down on the street from every level, rising all the way up to a series of dormer windows that must open into attic chambers just below the roof.

'Now zoom in,' Randi told her assistant.

The image expanded rapidly, centering at last on a small brass plaque beside the front door. In deeply incised lettering it read:

18 RUE DE VIGNY
PARTI LAZARE

'Oh, bloody hell,' Peter murmured.

Randi nodded grimly. 'Exactly. That building just happens to be the Paris headquarters for the Lazarus Movement.'

CHAPTER THIRTY-NINE

An hour later, Jon Smith stood outside the door to his room at the Hôtel des Chevaliers. He knelt down, checking the telltale – a thick black hair stretched between the door and the jamb, about a foot off the hall carpet. It was still there, completely undisturbed.

Satisfied that the room was secure, he ushered Randi and Peter inside. The CIA team's Renault van was too cramped for a prolonged meeting, and the nearby cafés and restaurants were far too crowded and public. They needed somewhere more private to try to find a solution to the predicament they suddenly faced. And at the moment, the Hôtel des Chevaliers was the closest thing they had to a safe house.

Now back in her own likeness with short neat blond hair and wearing a black jumpsuit, Randi moved restlessly around the room. With her long legs and slender five-foot-nine-inch frame, she had often been mistaken for a dancer. No one seeing her now would make that mistake. She drifted back and forth like a caged and dangerous animal seeking a way out. She was deeply frustrated by the self-inflicted paralysis she sensed engulfing the CIA – paralysis that was robbing her of any serious backup or advice just when she needed it most. Her uncertainty over what to do with the stunning discovery her team had made left her feeling uneasy, even with her old friends and allies.

Randi cast a skeptical eye over the room's elegant furnishings and decor and glanced over her shoulder at

Smith. 'Not bad for someone on a U.S. Army expense account, Jon.'

'Just your tax dollars at work,' he replied with a quick grin.

'Typical Yank soldier,' Peter said, with a quiet chuckle. 'Overpaid, overindulged, and overequipped.'

'Flattery will get you nowhere,' Smith told him drily. He dropped into the closest chair and looked across the room at his two friends. 'Look, we should stop fencing with each other and start talking seriously about what we're going to do next.'

The other two turned to face him.

'Well, I do admit that the position is a bit difficult,' Peter said slowly, settling himself into an overstuffed armchair.

Randi stared at the Englishman's leathery face in disbelief. 'A *bit* difficult?' she repeated. 'For crying out loud, why don't you ditch the stiff upper lip routine, Peter? The *position* is pretty well impossible, and you know it.'

' "Impossible" is an awfully big word, Randi,' Smith said, forcing a slight smile.

'Not from where I'm standing,' she snapped back. She shook her head in dismay, still pacing back and forth between the two men. 'Okay, first you two heroes go and prove that some of our own people have been fighting a very nasty and very illegal secret war against the Lazarus Movement. Which puts everybody, including the president and prime minister, into panic mode, right? So they start piling onto the intelligence agencies – hitting us with immediate cease and desist orders for *any* covert actions involving Lazarus. Not to mention gearing up for congressional and parliamentary investigations that could easily run for months, maybe even years.'

The two men nodded.

Randi frowned deeply. 'Mind you, I've got no real problem with that. Anybody dumb enough to fall in with Hal Burke, Kit Pierson, and the others deserves to be crucified. Using blunt nails.' She took a deep breath. 'But now, *now*, with all of this flak raining down around our ears, you both want to turn right around . . . and do what? Why, break into a Lazarus Movement building, of course! And not just any old building, naturally, but the headquarters for its whole Paris-based operation!'

'Certainly,' Peter told her calmly. 'How else do you propose that we learn what they're up to in there?'

'Jesus,' Randi muttered. She swung toward Smith. 'And you see it the same way?'

He nodded somberly. 'I'm pretty sure that somebody outside the intelligence services was manipulating Burke and the others. Using their undeclared war as a cover for something even worse, something like what happened at the Teller Institute or here in Paris . . . only magnified a hundred times over,' he said quietly. 'I'd like to find out who – and why. Before we learn the hard way.'

Randi bit down on her lip, mulling that over. She crossed the room to stare out the window at the little courtyard behind the hotel.

'Lazarus Movement or not, at least some of the people working inside 18 rue de Vigny knew the nanophage attack that hit La Courneuve was coming,' Smith continued. He leaned forward in his chair. 'That's why they were setting up those sensors you saw. That's why they were willing to kill anyone who got in their way.'

'But the movement is anti-technology to its core – especially nanotechnology!' she burst out in frustration. 'Why would Lazarus supporters help anyone commit mass murder, especially using a means they oppose so vehemently? It doesn't make sense!'

'That may well mean that Jon's mysterious somebody – perhaps we should call him Mr. X, for short – is using the Movement as a cover for his real plans,' Peter pointed out. 'In much the same way that we believe he used a few fools inside the CIA and the FBI. And MI6, alas.'

'You're giving this Mr. X a hell of a lot of credit,' Randi remarked acidly. She swung away from the window to face them both with her chin held stubbornly high. 'Maybe too much.'

'I don't think so,' Smith said, with a grim look settling on his face. 'We already know that X, whether it's a person or a group, has enormous resources. You can't design and produce hundreds of billions of nanophages without access to serious money. At least a hundred million dollars and probably a whole lot more. If you spent even a fraction of that on bribes, I'll bet you could buy the loyalty of quite a few people inside the Lazarus Movement.'

He stood up suddenly, unable to bear just sitting still any longer. Then he walked over to Randi. He put his hand gently on her arm. 'Can you think of any other way to make the pieces we've got come together?' he demanded quietly.

The CIA officer was silent for a long, painful moment. Then, slowly, she shook her head and sighed. All her pent-up energy and irritation seemed to drain away.

'Well, neither can I,' Smith said softly. 'That's why we have to get inside that building. We have to discover what those sensor arrays were gathering at La Courneuve. Maybe even more important, we have to find out what happened to the information they collected.' He frowned. 'Your technical people haven't been able to pick up anything being said inside, have they?'

Reluctantly she shook her head again, admitting defeat. 'No. The place seems to be remarkably bug-proof. Even the windows are set to vibrate slightly to defeat laser surveillance.'

'Every window?' Peter asked curiously.

She shrugged. 'No. Just those on the top floor and in the attic spaces.'

'Nice of them to hang out a sign for us,' the Englishman murmured, looking across the room at Jon.

Smith nodded. 'Very convenient.'

Randi frowned at the two men. 'Maybe too convenient,' she suggested. 'What if it's a setup?'

'Chance we have to take,' Peter said lazily. 'Ours is not to reason why, and so forth.' Before she could snap back at him, he donned a more suitably serious expression. 'But I doubt it. That would mean these Lazarus chaps deliberately allowed you and your people to spot them setting up those little gray boxes of theirs. Why go to all that trouble and expense and risk just to nab a couple of broken-down old soldiers?'

'Plus one top-notch CIA field officer,' she said, after a brief hesitation. She looked down modestly. 'That would be me, of course.'

Smith raised an eyebrow. 'You're planning on coming along?'

Randi sighed. 'Somebody responsible has to keep an eye on you two overaged kids.'

'You know what'll happen to your career if we get caught?' Smith asked quietly.

She shot him a lopsided grin. 'Oh, come on, Jon,' she said, forcing herself to sound cheerful. 'If we get caught inside that building, you know that saving my career will be the least of our worries!'

Now that she had made her decision, Randi busied herself by spreading a set of still photos of the Lazarus Movement's Paris headquarters out on the floor in front of them. The pictures showed the old stone building at 18 rue de Vigny from almost every angle, taken at different hours of the day and night. She also unfolded a detailed map depicting the Movement headquarters in relation to its nearest neighbors and the surrounding streets and alleys.

The three of them knelt down, closely scrutinizing the photos and the map – each looking for a way in that would not lead to immediate discovery and certain disaster. After a few moments, Peter sat back on his haunches. He regarded Randi and Jon with a slight smile. 'There's only one realistic option, I'm afraid,' he said, shrugging. 'It may not be particularly elegant or original, but it should serve.'

'Please tell me you're not planning a head-on charge

through the front door and straight up four or five flights of stairs,' Randi begged.

'Oh, no. Not my style at all.' He tapped the map gently with one finger. It came to rest on one of the apartment blocks adjoining 18 rue de Vigny. 'To mangle *Hamlet*, there are more ways into a building, dear girl, than are dreamt of in your philosophy.'

Smith looked at the map more closely and saw what the other man intended. He pursed his lips. 'We'll need some specialized gear. Know anyone who can provide them for us, Peter?'

'I might just have a few bits and pieces of equipment stashed around Paris,' Peter admitted calmly. 'The remnants of my old and wicked life in the service of Her Majesty. And I'm sure Ms. Russell's friends at the CIA station here can provide us with anything else we need. If she asks nicely, that is.'

Frowning, Randi studied the map and the pictures again. Her eyebrows rose. 'Oh, great, let me guess,' she said, sighing under her breath. 'You're planning one of those "defying the laws of gravity" deals again, aren't you?'

Peter looked at her in pretended shock. 'Defying the laws of gravity?' he repeated, shaking his head. 'Not at all. In point of fact, we shall be obeying gravity's imperious demands,' he said with a sly grin. 'After all, what goes up must come down.'

CHAPTER FORTY

Tuesday, October 19

It was after midnight, but there were still quite a few revelers and pleasantly sated late-night diners strolling home through the well-lit streets of Paris. Set apart from most of the bustling cafés, brasseries, and clubs of the Marais District, the rue de Vigny was quieter than most, but it, too, had its share of pedestrians.

One, a wrinkled old woman well bundled up against the chill of the autumn night, hobbled painfully up the street. Her high heels echoed on the worn cobblestones. She kept her large cloth handbag clutched tightly under one arm, clearly determined to defend her property against any lurking thieves. Footsore and weary, she paused briefly outside Number 18, resting for a moment to catch her breath. Lights glowed in the upper-floor windows beneath the old stone building's steeply angled slate roof. Those facing the street on the lower floors were dark.

Muttering under her breath, the old lady limped on to the adjoining four-story block of flats at Number 16. She stood in the recessed entryway outside the front door for a long, painful moment – first fumbling inside her enormous handbag and then apparently having trouble fitting her key into the lock. At last, she seemed to manage it. The lock clicked. With an effort, she pulled the heavy door open and tottered slowly inside.

The street was quiet again.

Minutes later, two men, one dark-haired, the other gray-headed, walked up the rue de Vigny. Both men wore dark-colored overcoats and carried heavy duffel bags slung over their shoulders. They walked side by side, chatting amiably in colloquial French about the weather and the absurdities of airport security these days – looking for all the world like two travelers returning home after a long weekend away.

They turned off the street at Number 16. The younger, dark-haired man pulled the door open and held it for his older companion. 'After you, Peter,' he said quietly with a wave.

'Age before beauty, eh?' the other man quipped. He moved into the small, dark foyer beyond, murmuring a polite greeting to the elderly woman who stood there waiting.

Jon Smith ducked into the apartment building himself, but not before casually removing a strip of duct tape the 'old woman' had stuck there to prevent the door lock from engaging. He balled it up, shoved it into his coat pocket, and allowed the door to close gently behind him.

'That was a nice piece of lock picking,' Smith complimented the bundled-up old lady standing beside Peter Howell.

Randi Russell grinned back at him. Beneath the disguise of wrinkles and lines that added forty years to her apparent age, her eyes were bright with nervous energy and excitement. 'Well, I did graduate at the head of my class at the Farm,' she said, referring to Camp Perry, the CIA training facility near Williamsburg, Virginia. 'It's nice to know my time there wasn't a total waste.'

'Where to now?' Smith asked.

She nodded toward a hallway leading out of the foyer. 'Through there,' she said. 'A central staircase runs all the way to the top. There are landings at each floor with doors leading to the separate flats.'

'Any restless natives?' Peter wondered.

Randi shook her head. 'Nope. There are lights showing under a few doors, but otherwise it's pretty quiet. And let's try to keep it that way, shall we, guys? I'd rather not spend the next twenty-four hours answering awkward questions down at the nearest Prefecture of Police.'

With Randi in the lead, the trio made their way carefully up the stairs – moving quietly past landings cluttered with bicycles, baby strollers, and small two-wheeled shopping carts. Another locked door, this one at the very top, yielded quickly to her lock picks. They stepped through the door and out into a rooftop garden of the kind so beloved by Parisians – a miniature urban glade created by a maze of large clay pots filled with dwarf trees, shrubs, and flowering plants. They were at the rear of the apartment building, separated from the rue de Vigny by a row of tall soot-stained chimneys and a forest of radio and TV antennae.

This high up, the chill autumn breeze carried the muted sounds of the city to them – car horns honking on the boulevard Beaumarchais, the shrill whine of motor scooters racing through narrow streets, and laughter and music drifting out through the open door of a nightclub somewhere close by. The floodlit white domes of the Byzantine-inspired Sacré Coeur basilica gleamed to the north, set high on the crowded slopes of Montmartre.

Smith moved carefully to the edge and looked down over an ornate wrought-iron railing. In the darkness far below he could just make out a row of trash bins crowding a narrow alley. The wall of another old building, also converted into a block of flats, rose vertically on the other side of that tiny lane. Patches of warm yellow lamplight showed through the cracks in closed shutters and drapes. He stepped back a few paces, rejoining Peter and Randi in the modest cover provided by the roof garden's trees and shrubs.

On their right loomed the shadowy mass of the Lazarus Movement's Paris headquarters. The two buildings were adjacent, but 18 rue de Vigny was one story higher. A twenty-foot-high blank wall of stone separated them from the steeply sloping roof of their goal.

'Right,' Peter whispered, already kneeling down to

open the first of their two duffel bags. He began handing out articles of clothing and gear. 'Let's get started.'

Moving quickly in the cold night air, the three began transforming themselves from ordinary-appearing civilians to fully equipped special operators. First, Randi started by tugging off the gray wig confining her own blond hair. Then she peeled away the specially crafted wrinkles and lines that had added decades to her appearance.

All of them shed their heavy coats, revealing high-necked black sweaters and black jeans. Dark-colored watch caps covered their hair. They blackened their faces and foreheads with camouflage sticks. Their street shoes came off and were replaced by climbing boots. Heavy leather gloves protected their hands. All three donned Kevlar body armor and followed that by shrugging into SAS-style assault vests and belting on holsters for their personal weapons – Smith's SIG-Sauer pistol, a Browning Hi-Power for Peter, and a 9mm Beretta for Randi. Next, they struggled into rappelling harnesses and slung bags containing coils of climbing rope over their shoulders.

Peter handed around an assortment of special equipment. Last of all, he gave each of them two cylindrical canisters, about the size of a can of shaving cream. 'Flash/bang grenades,' he said coolly. 'Very handy for throwing the enemy into confusion. Quite popular as a gag at all the best parties, too, or so I'm told.'

'We're supposed to do this covertly,' Randi reminded him tartly. 'Not plunge in shooting and start World War Three.'

'To be sure,' Peter replied. 'But better safe than sorry, I think. After all, those fellows,' he nodded toward the high, dark shape of the Lazarus Movement headquarters, 'may react badly if they spot us peeping in at them.' He moved around Jon and Randi, inspecting and tugging at their harnesses and various items of equipment to make sure everything was secure. Then he submitted patiently while Smith performed the same last-minute check on him.

'Now for that little bit of wall,' Peter announced. He reached into his duffel bag and pulled out a small air pistol already rigged with a titanium-barbed dart attached to a spool of nylon-coated wire. With a slight bow, he handed the assembly to Randi. 'Would you care to do the honors?'

Randi stepped back a few feet. She peered up at the shadow-cloaked stretch of wall in front of them, scanning for what looked like a good anchor point. A narrow crack caught her eye. She sighted along the barrel of the air pistol, aiming carefully. She squeezed the trigger. The pistol coughed quietly and the tiny titanium dart shot out, trailing the wire behind it. With a soft *clang*, the barbs of the small grappling hook bit deep into the stonework and held fast.

Smith reached up and tugged firmly on the dangling nylon-coated wire. It stayed put. He turned to the others. 'All set?'

They nodded.

One by one, they swarmed up the wall and hauled themselves cautiously onto the peak of the steep slate roof of the building at 18 rue de Vigny.

The Lazarus Center, the Azores

Seated behind the plain teak desk in his private office, Hideo Nomura observed the compressed-time computer simulation of the first *Thanatos* sorties with growing pleasure. A large screen showed him a digitized map of the Western Hemisphere. Icons indicated the constantly updated position of each *Thanatos* aircraft dispatched from his base here in the Azores – roughly twenty-five hundred miles off the American coast.

As each blinking dot crossed the Atlantic and soared above the continental United States, whole swathes of territory on the digital map began changing color – indicating areas struck by the windblown clouds of Stage IV nanophages his stealthly high-altitude aircraft would release. Different hues showed the predicted casualty rates for each pass. Bright red indicated near-total annihilation for anyone caught inside the indicated zone.

While Nomura watched, the metropolitan areas of New York, Washington, D.C., Philadelphia, and Boston glowed scarlet, signaling the calculated deaths of more than 35 million American men, women, and children. He nodded, smiling to himself. In and of themselves, those deaths would be meaningless, merely the first taste of the necessary carnage he planned to inflict. But this first onslaught would serve a much larger purpose. The rapid destruction of so many of its most populous centers of governmental and economic power was sure to plunge the United States into crisis – rendering its surviving leaders completely unable to detect the origin of the devastating attacks being carried out against their helpless nation.

His internal phone chimed once, demanding his attention.

Reluctantly Nomura drew his eyes away from the computer-generated glory unfolding before him. He tapped the speaker button. 'Yes? What is it?'

'We have received all the necessary data from the Paris relay point, Lazarus,' the dry, academic tones of his chief molecular scientist informed him. 'Based on the results of Field Experiment Three, we see no need for further design modifications at this time.'

'That is excellent news,' Nomura said. He glanced back at the simulation. The dead zones it showed were spreading inland fast, reaching deep into the American heartland. 'And when will the first Stage Four production run be complete?'

'In approximately twelve hours,' the scientist promised cautiously.

'Very good. Keep me informed.' Nomura switched off the attack simulation and called up another – this one constantly updating the work being carried out inside the huge aircraft hangars at both ends of his airfield. It showed him that the crews assembling the components of his fleet of *Thanatos* drones were on schedule. By the time the first cylinders of the new nanophages rolled out of his hidden production facility, he would have three aircraft ready to receive them.

Nomura picked up his secure satellite phone and punched in a preset code.

Nones, the third of the *Horatii* he had created, answered immediately. 'What are your orders, Lazarus?'

'Your work in Paris is finished,' Nomura told him. 'Return here to the Center as soon as possible. Tickets and the necessary documents for you and your security unit will be waiting at the Air France desk at Orly Sud.'

'What about Linden and his surveillance team?' Nones asked quietly. 'What arrangements do you wish made for them?'

Nomura shrugged. 'Linden and the others have completed their appointed tasks efficiently. But I see no need for their services in the future. None whatsoever. Do you understand my meaning?' he asked coldly.

'I understand,' the other man confirmed. 'And the equipment at 18 rue de Vigny?'

'Destroy it all,' Nomura ordered. He smiled cruelly. 'Let us prove to a horrified world that American and British spies are still waging their illegal war against the noble Lazarus Movement!'

CHAPTER FORTY-ONE

Paris

Smith crawled out along the high, sharp peak of the roof at 18 rue de Vigny. He used his hands and arms to pull himself along, preferring not to risk the noise his rubber-soled boots would make scraping and scrabbling across the roof's cracked slate tiles. He moved slowly, seeking whatever handholds he could find along the slick, slippery surface.

The Lazarus Movement headquarters was among the highest buildings in this part of the Marais, so there was nothing to block the cold east wind rushing across Paris. The frigid breeze keened through the array of antennae and satellite dishes clustered on the roof. A stronger gust swirled suddenly along the sheer slopes, tugging hard at his clothing and equipment.

Buffeted by this gust, Jon felt himself starting to slide off the ridge of the roof. He gritted his teeth and desperately tightened his grip. A hundred-foot drop beckoned, with nothing below to break his fall but iron-spiked railings, parked cars, and cobblestones. He could feel his pulse hammering in his ears, drowning out the faint sounds drifting up from the city streets far below. Sweating despite the cold, he pressed closer to the roof, waiting until the force of the wind eased just a bit. Then, still shaking slightly, he pushed himself back up and crawled on.

A minute later, Smith reached the modest shelter afforded by a large brick chimney. Randi and Peter were there ahead of him. They had already rigged an anchor line around the base of the chimney. He clipped on to it with a quiet, grateful sigh and then sat up, breathing heavily – uneasily perched like the others on the sharp ridge of the roof.

Peter chuckled, looking along the row at his two companions. 'So here we sit,' he said quietly. 'Looking for all the world like a rather sad and bedraggled band of crows.'

'Make that two ugly crows and one graceful swan,' Randi corrected him with a slight smile of her own. She clicked the transmit button on her tactical radio. 'Anything stirring, Max?' she asked.

From his concealed post some distance down the rue de Vigny, her subordinate radioed back. 'Negative, boss. It's all real quiet. One light came on a few minutes ago, up on the third floor, but otherwise there's no sign of anyone coming or going.'

Satisfied, she nodded to the others. 'We're clear.'

'Right,' Smith said flatly. 'Let's get this done.'

One by one, they edged closer to the chimney and prepared their rappelling gear – taking special care to ensure that their ropes, harnesses, and snap and descending links were correctly rigged.

'Who wants to go first?' Randi asked.

'I will,' Smith volunteered, looking down at the roof stretching away in front of him. 'Tackling this was my bright idea, remember?'

She nodded. 'Sure. Though "bright" isn't exactly the adjective I would have used.' But then she laid a gloved hand gently on his shoulder. 'Just watch yourself, Jon,' she said softly. Her eyes were troubled.

He flashed her a quick, reassuring grin. 'I'll do my best,' he promised.

Smith took a couple of deep breaths, steadying his jangled nerves. Then he swung around and slid slowly backward down the slope, carefully controlling his descent with one hand on the rope as it uncoiled. Tiny pieces of broken slate pitter-pattered ahead of him and then fell away into the darkness below.

Inside Number 18 rue de Vigny, the tall auburn-haired giant called Nones strode out of the third-floor office he had commandeered immediately upon arriving in Paris. Ordinarily reserved for the head of the Movement's African aid and education programs, it was the largest and the most beautifully furnished in the whole building. But the local activists had known better than to protest his curt decisions or to ask inconvenient questions. After all, Nones carried authorizations from Lazarus himself. For the time being, his word was law. He smiled coldly. Very soon, the Movement's followers would have cause to regret their unhesitating obedience, but by then it would be far too late.

Five men from his security detail waited patiently for him on the landing outside the office. Their packs and personal weapons were ready at their feet. They stood up silently at his approach.

'We have our orders,' he told them. 'From Lazarus himself.'

'The orders you expected?' the short Asian man called Shiro asked calmly.

The third member of the *Horatii* nodded. 'Down to the last detail.' He drew his pistol, checked it over, and then slid it back into his shoulder holster. His men did the same with their own weapons and then bent down to pick up their packs.

They split up. Two headed down the main staircase toward the small garage at the rear of the building's ground floor. The rest followed Nones up the stairs, moving determinedly toward the fifth-floor rooms occupied by the field experiment surveillance team.

Smith stopped his descent and balanced himself precariously right on the very edge of the roof. Holding the rope tight, he forced himself to lean far back into thin air, taking a good long look at the dormer windows raised above the slope on either side. These windows opened into small attic rooms just below the roof and just as the pictures they had studied earlier had shown – they were securely shuttered.

Smith nodded to himself. They weren't going to be able to break through those heavy wooden shutters, at least not without making a hell of a lot of noise. They were going to have to find another way into this building.

He leaned out farther, now peering down the side of the building below him. Lights glowed in the windows on the fifth floor, and their shutters were open. Moving in short, cautious bounds, he rappelled down the wall. There was very little noise – just the quiet creak of the rope as it slid through the metal descending link on his harness and the soft thud of his boots as he hit the wall and then pushed off again. Twenty feet down, he tightened his grip on the rope, braking himself to a stop right next to one of those lighted windows.

He glanced up.

Randi and Peter were there at the edge of the roof, two dark shapes outlined against the black, star-filled sky. They were looking down over their shoulders at him – waiting for his signal that it was safe to come ahead.

Smith motioned for them to hold where they were. Then he craned his neck, trying to take a good look through the closest window. He had the fleeting impression of a long, narrow room – one that ran at least half the length of this side of the building. Several of the other windows on this floor opened into this large chamber.

Inside, an assortment of computers, video monitors, radio receivers, and satellite relay systems were stacked on a row of tables pushed up against the opposite wall. Other tables and more equipment were set at right angles, breaking the room up into a series of improvised computer workstations or bays, and power and data transfer cables snaked across a bare hardwood floor. The walls themselves were dingy, stained by centuries of use and roughly daubed with cracked and peeling paint.

Off in one dark corner Smith could make out a row of six cots. Four of them were occupied. He could see stocking feet protruding out from under coarse woolen blankets.

But at least two men were awake and hard at work. One, an older man with white hair and a scruffy beard, sat at a computer console, entering keyboard commands with lightning-fast fingers. Images flashed on and off the monitor in front of him at a dizzying pace. The second man wore a headset and sat in a chair next to one of the satellite communications systems. He leaned forward, listening closely to the signals coming through his earphones and occasionally making small adjustments to its controls. He was younger and clean-shaven, and his dark brown eyes and olive-toned skin somehow suggested the sun-drenched lands of southern Europe. Was he a Spaniard? An Italian?

Jon shrugged. Spaniard, Italian, or someone from the South Bronx. What did it really matter? The Lazarus Movement recruited its activists from around the world. At the moment, only one thing was important. They were not going to be able to enter 18 rue de Vigny unobserved – at least not on this floor. He glanced down, examining the rows of darkened windows below.

Suddenly, on the very edge of his vision, he caught a flicker of movement inside the room. Smith saw the bearded white-haired man swivel away from his keyboard and stand up. He seemed surprised but not unduly alarmed as four more men filed into the room through a narrow arched doorway.

Smith watched carefully. These newcomers were hard-faced men dressed in dark clothing, with bulging satchels slung over their shoulders. Two carried drawn pistols. A third held a shotgun cradled in his arms. The fourth man, much taller than the others and evidently the leader, snapped an order to his men. They split up immediately – each moving purposefully toward a different part of the room. The big auburn-haired giant glanced briefly toward the row of windows and then turned away. With a sinister fluid grace he drew a pistol out of his shoulder holster.

Jon felt his eyes widen in stunned disbelief. A shiver of superstitious dread ran down his spine. He had seen that same face and those same startling green eyes before – just six days ago. They belonged to the terrorist leader who had nearly killed him in personal combat outside the Teller Institute. This was impossible, he thought desperately. Absolutely impossible. How could a man wholly consumed by nanophages rise from the grave?

CHAPTER FORTY-TWO

Nones turned away from the windows toward Willem Linden. Slowly, he brought his pistol on-target. He flipped the safety off with one huge thumb.

The white-haired Dutchman stared at the weapon aimed straight at his forehead. He turned pale. 'What are you doing?' he stammered.

'This is your severance package. Your services are no longer required,' Nones told him drily. 'But Lazarus thanks you for your efforts on his behalf. Farewell, Herr Linden.'

The third of the *Horatii* waited just long enough to watch the horrified understanding enter the other man's eyes. Then Nones pulled the trigger twice – firing two rounds into Linden's head at point-blank range. Blood, shards of bone, and bits of brain flew out the back of the Dutchman's shattered skull and spattered against the wall. The dead man fell away and crumpled to the floor in a heap.

In that same moment, a shotgun blast echoed from the darkened corner of the room – followed immediately by a second and then a third blast. Nones glanced in that direction. One of his three men had just finished slaughtering the four surveillance team members who had been sleeping. Trapped in their cots, they were easy prey. Fired at a range of less than ten feet, three twelve-gauge rounds filled with buckshot tore them into pitiful shreds of torn flesh and broken bone.

The big man heard a sudden choked-off cry of fear off

349

to his left. He swiveled that way fast, seeing the youngest member of Linden's team, the Portuguese signals expert named Vitor Abrantes, staggering to his feet. Abrantes yanked frantically at his headset, but he was still tethered to the satellite transmitter by a twisted length of audio cable.

Nones fired twice more while moving. The first 9mm round hit the young man high up in the chest. The second tore into his left shoulder and spun him around in a complete circle. White-faced with shock, Abrantes toppled backward against the transmitter. Moaning, he slid to the floor and sat clutching his smashed shoulder.

Frowning at his own sloppiness, Nones took a step closer to the wounded man, raising his pistol again. This time he would aim with more care and precision. He sighted along the barrel. His finger tightened on the trigger, starting to squeeze it . . .

But then the window beside him exploded inward – flying apart in a tinkling cloud of sharp-edged glass shards.

Still hanging in his rappelling harness just outside the room, Jon Smith saw the wave of cold-blooded butchery begin inside. These bastards were killing their own people, he realized abruptly – clearing away loose ends, evidence, and potential witnesses. Witnesses and evidence he urgently needed. Gripped by a wave of white-hot fury, he reacted instantly, tugging his SIG-Sauer pistol out of the holster on his hip. He aimed at the glass.

Three rapid shots fired from top to bottom blew open the window, spraying broken glass and bullets through an arc inside the room. Before the last shards stopped falling, he shoved the pistol back into its holster and yanked one of his two flash/bang grenades out of a leg pouch strapped to his left thigh. His gloved right thumb pulled the ring. The grenade's safety spoon flipped up.

Smith lobbed the black cylinder in through the shattered window and shoved off hard from the wall with his boots, moving directly away from the opening. He reached the end of his pendulum arc, pushed away again even harder, and began swinging back toward the window, flying even faster now.

And then the grenade went off – detonating in a rapid-fire burst of blinding flashes and earsplitting explosions intended to stun and disorient anyone caught within its burst radius. A dense cloud of smoke rolled outward, swirling madly in air roiled by the continuing staccato series of bangs.

Jon came soaring through the window feetfirst. He landed heavily on the floor, folded up, and then rolled prone. Small pieces of glass crunched beneath him. He pulled his SIG-Sauer out again, already searching for targets through the haze and smoke.

Smith looked first for the big green-eyed man. There were smeared streaks of blood on the hardwood floor where he had been standing when the window exploded in on him, but nothing else. The auburn-haired giant must have dived for cover when the flash/bang grenade went off. The blood trail he had left behind disappeared out through the arched doorway.

Stumbling footsteps sounded nearby, on the other side of a heavy table.

Smith reared up and saw one of the other gunmen come reeling out of the rapidly thinning smoke cloud. Though dazed by the grenade's nerve-shattering burst of noise and dazzling light, the gunman still held his pistol in a two-handed shooting grip. Blinking rapidly to clear his eyes, he caught sight of Jon's head poking above the table and swung around, trying to draw a bead on him.

Smith shot him twice, hitting him once in the heart and once in the neck.

The gunman folded over and fell forward, plainly dead before he hit the floor.

Jon dropped back behind the table and rolled frantically the other way, rapidly hitting the release on his rappelling harness to detach the climbing rope still trailing in through the window. While he was still hooked to it, the rope would hamper his movements. It would also act as a giant arrow pointing straight at him wherever he went. At last, he managed to tug the length of rope clear and crawled away across the scarred floor, staying low.

One down. Counting the big man, that left three to go, he thought grimly. Where exactly had the other enemy gunmen been when his grenade came sailing through the window? More important, where were they now?

He wriggled around the corner of a table and saw the white-haired man sprawled in front of him. Smith grimaced at the sight of the ugly mess seeping out from under the dead man's shattered skull. That bullet-riddled brain had held information they needed.

He crawled past the corpse, heading toward the darker corner of the room he had seen being used as makeshift sleeping quarters.

From somewhere behind him, a pistol barked three times in rapid succession. One round ripped low over his head. Another tore jagged splinters off the solid oak table leg next to his face. The third 9mm round slammed into his back and then tumbled away, deflected by his Kevlar body armor. It was like being kicked by a mule between the shoulder blades.

Gasping through a searing wave of white-hot pain, trying to suck air into lungs that felt as though they had been hammered flat, Smith threw himself onto his side. Two more shots tore into the floor, right where he had been lying a second before – gouging out huge chunks of wood before they ricocheted away. He curled around, frantically seeking a glimpse of the gunman firing at him.

There!

A shape wavered in his pain-filled vision. One of the gunmen knelt behind a table just about twenty feet away, coolly taking aim. Jon shot back wildly with the SIG-Sauer, squeezing the trigger as rapidly as he could. The pistol bucked upward in his hands. Rounds crashed through the table and hammered into the computer equipment piled on top of it. A hail of wood splinters, sparks, and broken pieces of plastic and metal went flying away through the air. Startled, the gunman ducked out of sight.

Smith rolled away across the floor, trying to find better cover. He stopped about midway down one of the U-shaped bays formed by three joined tables and risked a cautious glance back the way he had come. Nothing.

Then he looked up at the TV monitor on the table in front of him. He froze suddenly, seeing his own death reflected in its darkened screen.

The third enemy gunman rose up from the next bay over – already aiming a combat shotgun right at the back of his head.

Poised on the edge of the roof, Peter and Randi heard the sudden burst of gunfire, saw the blinding flash of a grenade, and then watched Jon abruptly hurl himself into the building below them. They exchanged appalled glances.

'Dear me. So much for subtlety and discretion,' Peter murmured. He pulled his Browning Hi-Power clear of his holster and held it ready.

More gunshots rang out in a rising crescendo, echoing back from the brickwork and stone of the surrounding buildings.

'Come on!' Randi snarled, already rappelling down the wall in short, fast bounds. Peter came flying down after her, moving with equal speed and longer jumps.

Knowing it was far too late, knowing that the gunman's finger was already starting to squeeze the shotgun's trigger, Smith twisted around desperately, trying to bring his own weapon on-target. The adrenaline pulsing through his system seemed to slow time itself – stretching out the nightmare moment before a hail of twelve-gauge buckshot blasted his head into bloody ruin . . .

And then another window exploded inward – torn apart by multiple 9mm rounds fired through it at close range. Hit several times in the chest and neck and head, the enemy gunman staggered to the side and then sagged across one of the tables. The shotgun fell from his lifeless fingers and clattered to the floor.

First Randi and then Peter swung in through the shattered window and dropped to the floor. Quickly they detached their ropes and took up positions on either side of Jon, scanning the long, narrow room around them for signs of movement.

Smith smiled weakly, still shaken by his narrow escape. 'Glad you could make it,' he whispered. 'Thought I'd have to handle this all on my own.'

'Idiot,' Randi murmured back, but her eyes were warm.

'Never miss a party,' Peter said softly. 'How many have you left us?'

'One for sure,' Smith replied. He nodded toward the far side of the room. 'He's in cover somewhere off that way. Another guy, their leader, I think, already hightailed it out through the door.'

Peter looked at Randi. 'Shall we show our medical friend here how professionals flush game?' Peter turned to Smith. 'You cover the door, Jon.' Then he took a flash/bang grenade out of the pouch on his thigh, pulled the ring, and held the safety spoon closed. 'On five. Four. Three. Two . . .'

Peter popped up briefly and lobbed the grenade over the table. It sailed through a long, low arc, dropped out of sight, and exploded. A new cloud of smoke boiled across the room, lit from within by blinding, strobe-like flashes.

Randi was already in motion, running fast and bent low. She caught a glimpse of a darker shape moving in the smoke and dived for the floor. The surviving gunman staggered toward her. She fired her Beretta twice and watched him go down. He shuddered once and then lay still, staring back at her with lifeless eyes.

For a moment longer Randi stayed prone, waiting for the smoke and haze to dissipate. 'All clear on this end!' she called out when she could see well enough to be sure.

'Check around to see if you can find anyone else still alive,' Smith suggested, rising painfully to his feet. He glanced at Peter. 'Meanwhile, I think we should go after that other big bastard I saw.'

'The one you say scarpered out the door?'

Smith nodded grimly. 'That's right.' He explained the uncanny resemblance between the tall green-eyed man he had seen here and the terrorist leader he had watched die in New Mexico.

Peter whistled softly. 'Now, there's a nasty coincidence.'

'That's just it,' Smith said slowly. 'I don't think it is a co-incidence at all.'

'Probably not,' Peter agreed. He looked troubled. 'But we'll have to be quick, Jon. The French may have most of their police deployed outside Paris at the moment, but all this racket is bound to attract their attention.'

Weapons drawn and ready, the two men moved cautiously toward the narrow arched doorway. Smith pointed silently at the smeared bloodstains on the floor. The large red drops led straight toward the open door. Peter nodded his understanding. They were tracking a wounded man.

Smith stopped just inside the room. He stared out through the doorway, seeing part of a black-and-white-tiled landing enclosed by a waist-high wrought-iron railing.

The spatters of blood continued on, heading right for the wide marble staircase that led down to the building's lower floors. The big man they were hunting might be getting away! Determined not to lose him, Jon impulsively darted forward through the arch, ignoring Peter's startled warning.

Too late Jon realized that the blood trail ended abruptly just two steps down. His eyes opened wide. Unless he had somehow learned to fly, the green-eyed man must have doubled back. . . .

Smith felt himself hurled violently to the side. Knocked completely off his feet, he slid across the landing and slammed shoulder-first into the iron railing. His SIG-Sauer skittered away across the tile floor. For a moment he stared through the bottom of the railing out into a dizzying void.

Sickened and dazed by the impact, he heard a sudden muffled cry and then saw Peter thrown past him. The Englishman tumbled head over heels over the wide lip of the staircase. He disappeared out of sight in a diminishing clatter and rattle of loose equipment.

Smiling cruelly, the auburn-haired giant swung back toward Smith. His face, flayed by razor-sharp shards of glass, was a mask of bright red blood. One ravaged socket was empty, but a single green eye gleamed fiercely out of the other.

Jon scrambled to his feet, coldly aware of the enormous drop right at his back. Quickly he drew the combat knife sheathed at his waist. He crouched lower, holding the blade at his side.

Undeterred by the sight of the knife, the big man stalked toward him. His huge hands moved in small, deceptively lazy circles as he came forward, ready to strike out, to maim, and then to kill. His smile grew wider.

Through narrowed eyes, Smith watched him come closer. Just a bit nearer, you son of a bitch, he thought. He swallowed hard – fighting down a growing sense of fear at the other man's implacable approach. He did not have any real illusions about the likely outcome of sustained close-quarters combat against this man. Even half-blinded, this foe was much taller, stronger, and undoubtedly far more skilled in hand-to-hand fighting than he was.

The big auburn-haired man saw the fear on his face. He laughed and shook more blood away before it dripped in his one good eye. 'What? No stomach for battle without a gun in your hand?' he asked softly in a cynical, mocking tone.

Refusing to be goaded into premature action, Jon stayed still, ready to react fast to any opening. He kept his own gaze fixed on the other man's single eye – knowing that it would telegraph any real move.

The bright green eye flickered suddenly. There it was! Smith came on-guard.

Moving with terrifying speed, the big man spun through a tight arc, aiming a dazzlingly fast elbow strike at Jon's face. He yanked his head to the side just in time. The killing blow missed by a fraction of an inch.

Smith blocked another powerful strike with his own left forearm. The world blurred red around him and he felt the stitches there rip loose. The massive impact knocked him backward against the railing. Panting, he crouched lower still.

Grinning hugely now, the green-eyed man closed in again. One of his hands stayed ready to block any knife thrust. The other powerful fist drew back, preparing yet another hammer blow – one that would either drive Smith back over the railing to his death or crush his skull.

Instead, Jon threw himself forward, diving right under the taller man's legs. He whirled around and scrambled upright just in time to meet another series of attacks – rapid-fire blows that he narrowly parried with his own left hand and both forearms. The force in them slammed him back against the wall, driving the air out of his lungs. Desperately he slashed out with the knife, forcing the other man back – not far, just a few short steps, just far enough to put his back against the iron railing.

It was now or never, Smith told himself.

With a wild yell, he yanked the last flash/bang grenade out of his leg pouch and hurled it with all his remaining strength straight into his foe's face. Reacting instinctively, the big man batted the harmless grenade aside with both hands, laying himself wide open for the first time.

In that single frozen moment of time, Jon lunged – striking with the point of his combat knife. Only the very tip of the blade plunged into the middle of the big man's remaining green eye. But that was enough. Blood and fluid poured out of the new and terrible wound.

Blinded, the auburn-haired giant roared in mingled fury and agony. He lashed out violently, knocking the knife from Smith's hand. He stumbled forward with his arms spread wide in one last bid to trap his unseen opponent and crush him.

Moving fast, Jon ducked under those massive outstretched arms and punched the bigger man hard in the throat – crushing his larynx. Immediately Jon jumped back again, determined to stay safely out of reach.

Gasping, panting, straining frantically for the oxygen he desperately needed but could no longer draw in, the giant slid slowly to his knees. Beneath the dripping blood, his skin was turning blue. Despairingly he reached out one last time – still trying to seize the man who had killed him. Then his arm dropped. He slumped to the floor and rolled over onto his back, lying there with his empty eye sockets staring blindly up at the ceiling.

Exhausted, Smith fell to his own knees.

From somewhere down below a new fusillade of gunfire thundered suddenly, echoing noisily up the central staircase. Smith staggered upright, scooped up his pistol from the floor where it had fallen, and ran toward the head of the stairs.

He saw Peter trudging slowly up the staircase, limping painfully. 'Took a damned long, hard spill, Jon,' the other man explained, seeing his concerned face. 'Managed to hang on to my Browning, though.' He smiled thinly. 'That was just as well. You see, I tumbled right into two more of those fellows coming up the other way.'

'I guess they won't be bothering us any longer?' Smith suggested.

'Not in this life, at least,' Peter agreed drily.

'Jon! Peter! Come here! Quick!'

Both men turned at the sound of Randi's voice, urgently summoning them. They ran back into the room.

The CIA officer was kneeling beside one of the bodies. She looked up at them in amazement. 'This guy is still alive!'

CHAPTER FORTY-THREE

With Peter right on his heels, Smith hurried to Randi's side and knelt down to examine the lone survivor. It was the younger man he had seen through the window, the one who had been listening to signals sent over a satellite communications relay. He had been shot twice, once in the shoulder and once in the chest.

'See what you can do for the poor fellow,' Peter suggested. 'Find out what he knows. Meanwhile I'll take a quick prowl around to see what else I can uncover in this shambles.'

Peter moved off to begin a systematic search of the bodies and any equipment and electronics that might be left undamaged in the bullet-riddled room. Meanwhile, Smith stripped off one of his gloves and felt for a pulse in the wounded man's neck. The pulse was still there, but it was very weak, fast, and fading. The young man's skin was also pale and cold and wet to the touch. His eyes were closed, and he was breathing in shallow, labored gasps.

Smith glanced at Randi. 'Elevate his feet a few inches,' he said quietly. 'He's pretty deep in shock.'

She nodded and lifted the injured man's feet slightly. To hold them in place, she grabbed a thick computer manual from the nearest table and slid it carefully under his calves.

Working swiftly, with gentle fingers, Smith carefully probed the young man's wounds, pulling away clothing to get a good look at the various bullet entry and exit points. He frowned. The shattered left shoulder was bad enough. Most surgeons would urge the immediate amputation of that arm. The other injury was far worse. His face darkened as he traced the extent of the massive exit wound high up on the young man's back. Moving at the speed of sound, the 9mm round had inflicted enormous damage as it tore through his chest – shattering bone, shredding blood vessels, and pulverizing vital tissue across an ever-wider area.

Jon did what little he could. First, he shook out a field dressing kit from one of the pouches on his assault vest. Among other things, it contained two rolled-up sheets of plastic in a sealed bag. He tore the bag open with his teeth, unrolled the pieces of plastic, and then firmly pressed them into place over the two holes in the wounded man's chest – making the injury airtight. With that done, he taped sterile gauze dressings over the plastic in an effort to control the bleeding.

He looked up to find Randi watching him. She raised an eyebrow in an unspoken question.

Smith shook his head slightly. The wounded man was dying. His efforts would only slow the process, not prevent it. There was simply too much damage, too much internal hemorrhaging. Even if they could get him to an emergency room in the next few minutes, the effort would be wasted.

Randi sighed. She stood up. 'Then I'll go take another look around myself,' she said. She tapped her watch. 'Don't wait too long, Jon. By now someone in the neighborhood will have called the cops about all the noise. Max will give us a heads-up if he hears anything definite on the scanner, but we need to be long gone before they get here.'

He nodded. Coming right on the heels of Burke and Pierson's secret war against the Lazarus Movement, the arrest of a serving U.S. Army officer and a CIA agent inside the Movement's shot-up Paris headquarters building would only confirm every paranoid conspiracy theorist's worst fears and suspicions.

Randi tossed him a bloodstained wallet. 'I found this in one of his pockets,' she said. 'The ID could be a fake, I suppose. But if so, it's a top-notch job.'

Smith flipped it open. It contained an international driver's license made out in the name of Vitor Abrantes, with a permanent address shown in Lisbon. Abrantes. He spoke the name out loud.

The dying man's eyes fluttered open. His skin was ashen.

'You're Portuguese?' Smith said.

'*Sim*. Yes. *Eu sou Portuguese*.' Abrantes nodded faintly.

'Do you know who shot you?' Smith asked quietly.

The young Portuguese shivered. 'Nones,' he whispered. 'One of the *Horatii*.'

The *Horatii*? Smith puzzled over that. The word, which sounded Latin, rang a bell somewhere in the back of his mind. He thought it was something he had seen or heard here in Paris in the past, but he couldn't pin it down – at least right away.

'Jon!' Randi called in excitement. 'Take a look at this!'

He glanced up. She was standing at the computer where he had seen the older white-haired man working. She swung the monitor toward him. Caught in some kind of programming loop, the computer was playing the same piece of digital imagery over and over again – footage of pedestrian-filled streets, apparently captured and transmitted by an aircraft flying low overhead. Three words blinked in red in the lower right-hand corner of the imagery: NANOPHAGE RELEASE INITIATED

'My God!' Smith realized suddenly. 'They hit La Courneuve from the air.'

'Looks that way,' Randi agreed grimly. 'I suppose that's easier and more effective than setting these horrible weapons loose on the ground.'

'A lot more effective,' Smith said, thinking it through fast. 'Deploying the nanophages at altitude avoids relying solely on the wind or internal pressurization to spread the cloud. You get more control that way, and you can blanket a much larger area with the same number of devices.'

He turned back to Abrantes. The wounded man was drifting on the edge of death, barely aware of his surroundings. With luck, he might now answer questions that he would certainly have refused earlier. 'Why don't you tell me about the nanophages, Vitor?' he suggested carefully. 'What is their real purpose?'

'Once our tests are complete, they will cleanse the world,' the dying man said, coughing. Bubbles of blood flecked the side of his mouth. But his eyes held a fanatical gleam. With an effort, he spoke again. 'They will make all things new again. They will rid the Earth of a contagion. They will save it from the plague of untamed humanity.'

Smith felt a shiver of horror run through him as the full impact of just what Abrantes was talking about hit home. The massacres at Teller and La Courneuve had only been trial runs. And that, in turn, meant the deaths of tens of thousands had been planned right from the start as field experiments – as tests to evaluate and further refine the effectiveness of these murderous nanophages outside the sterile confines of a laboratory.

He stared blindly at the images repeating over and over on the screen. The nanophages were more than just another weapon of war or terrorism. They had been designed as instruments of genocide – genocide planned on a scale unmatched in history.

Jon felt enormous anger welling up inside him. The thought of anyone rejoicing in the kind of cruel, inhuman butchery he had seen outside the Teller Institute triggered a feeling of fury beyond anything he had felt in years. But to extract the information they needed it was vital that this young Portuguese hear the voice of a friend – of someone who shared his warped beliefs. With that in mind, Jon fought to regain control over his rampaging emotions.

'Who will control this cleansing, Vitor?' he heard himself ask gently. 'Who will remake the world?'

'Lazarus,' Abrantes said simply. 'Lazarus will bring life out of death.'

Smith sat back. A terrible and frightening image was taking shape in his mind. It was an image of a faceless puppeteer coolly staging a drama of his own maniacal creation. In one moment, Lazarus denounced nanotechnology as a danger to mankind. In the next, he perverted that same technology for his own vicious purposes – using it to slaughter even his own most devoted followers as though they were laboratory mice. With one hand, he manipulated officials of the CIA, FBI, and MI6 into conducting a covert war against the Movement he controlled. With the other, he turned that same illegal war against them, rendering his enemies blind, deaf, and dumb at the critical moment.

'And where is this man you call Lazarus?' he asked.

Abrantes said nothing. He drew in a single short breath and then began coughing uncontrollably, retching, unable to clear his lungs. He was literally drowning in his own blood, Smith knew.

Quickly he turned the young man's head to the side, momentarily clearing a passage for the air he needed. Scarlet rivulets of blood spattered from Abrantes' twitching mouth. The coughing fit eased.

'Vitor! Where is Lazarus?' Smith repeated urgently. Randi left the computer she had been examining and came back to his side. She stood listening closely.

'*Os Açores,*' Abrantes whispered. He coughed once more and spat more blood onto the floor. He drew in another short, shallow breath. '*O console do sol. Santa María.*' This time the effort was too great. He jerked and spasmed suddenly, convulsed by another long, wracking paroxysm. When it passed, he was dead.

'Was that a prayer?' Randi asked.

Smith frowned. 'If it was, I doubt he'll get any credit for it.' He looked down at the twisted body on the floor and then shook his head. 'But I think he was trying to answer the question I asked him.'

Forty feet away, Peter stooped beside the corpse of the gunman Randi had shot. He rifled through the dead man's pockets, collecting a wallet and a passport. Quickly he flipped through the passport, mentally noting the most recent entry stamps – Zimbabwe, the United States, and France, in that order, and all within the last four weeks. His pale blue eyes narrowed in calculation. Most revealing, he thought coldly.

He pocketed the documents and moved on to inspect a bulky pack he had noticed earlier. The plain green cloth satchel stood off on its own in the nearest corner. And now that he thought back, it was identical in appearance to two other packs he had seen dumped in other parts of the room.

Peter drew aside the flap and peered inside.

He sucked in his breath, staring down at two foot-long blocks of plastic explosive wrapped together. They were wired to a detonator and a digital watch. Czech-made Semtex or American-manufactured C4, he decided, with an improvised timer. Either way, he knew that was enough plastic explosive to make one devil of a bang when it went off. And now he saw that the numbers on the watch were blinking rhythmically, steadily falling toward zero.

CHAPTER FORTY-FOUR

The White House

'Ambassador Nichols is on the phone, sir,' the White House waiter said deferentially. 'The secure line.'

'Thank you, John,' said President Sam Castilla, pushing away his plate of untouched food. With his wife away and the Lazarus crisis growing worse with every passing hour, he was taking his meals alone, usually, like tonight, on a tray in the Oval Office. He picked up the phone. 'What's up, Owen?'

Owen Nichols, the U.S. ambassador to the UN, was one of Castilla's closest political allies. They had been friends since college. Neither man felt any need to stand on ceremony with the other. And neither believed in sugar-coating bad news. 'The Security Council is moving toward a final vote on the nanotech resolution, Sam,' he said. 'I expect it within the hour.'

'That fast?' Castilla asked in surprise. The UN almost never acted quickly. The organization preferred consensus and lengthy, almost interminable discussion. He had thought it would take the Council another day or two to bring the nanotech resolution up for a vote.

'That fast,' Nichols confirmed. 'The debate's been strictly *pro forma*. Everybody knows the votes are there to pass this damned thing unanimously – unless we veto it.'

'What about the UK?' Castilla asked, shocked.

'Their ambassador, Martin Rees, says they can't afford to buck the international consensus on this issue, not after the revelations that MI6 was tied into this secret war against Lazarus. They have to go against us on this one. He says the PM's job is hanging by a thread as it is.'

'Damn,' Castilla muttered.

'I only wish that were the worst news I had,' Nichols said quietly.

The president tightened his grip on the phone. 'Go on.'

'Rees wanted me to pass on something else he picked up from the British Foreign Office. France and Germany and some of the other European countries have been working on another nasty surprise for us, behind the scenes. After we veto the Security Council resolution, they plan to demand our immediate suspension from all NATO military and political roles – on the grounds that we might otherwise use NATO resources as part of our illegal war on Lazarus.'

Castilla breathed out, trying to control the anger he felt boiling up inside. 'The vultures are circling, I guess.'

'Yes, they are, Sam,' Nichols said tiredly. 'Between the massacres in Zimbabwe, Santa Fe, and Paris and now these stories about CIA-sponsored murders, our good name overseas is completely shot. So this is the perfect time for our so-called friends to cut us down to size.'

After he finished speaking with Nichols and hung up, Castilla sat for a moment longer, his head bowed under the weight of events that were moving beyond his ability to control. He glanced tiredly at the elegant grandfather clock along one curved wall. Fred Klein had said he thought Colonel Smith was on the trail of something significant in Paris. The corners of his mouth turned down. Whatever Smith was chasing had better pan out – and quickly.

Paris

For a fraction of a second longer, Peter stared down at the activated demolition charge, unwillingly admiring the sheer thoroughness of the opposition. When it came to covering their tracks, he thought, these fellows never stopped at half-measures. After all, why be satisfied with killing a few potential witnesses when you could blow apart the whole building as well? The timer flickered through another second, still inexorably counting down toward its predetermined end.

He jumped to his feet and ran toward Jon and Randi, dodging around the worktables and bullet-smashed electronics gear. 'Out!' he yelled, pointing to the windows. 'Get out now!'

They stared at him, plainly mystified by the sudden urgency in his voice.

Peter skidded to a stop beside the two perplexed Americans. 'There's at least one ruddy great bomb set to go off in this building – and probably more!' he explained fast, the words tumbling out of his mouth. Then he grabbed each of them by a shoulder and shoved them toward the two windows they had smashed open to get inside. 'Go on! If we're lucky, we might have thirty seconds!'

Horrified understanding at last dawned on Jon's and Randi's faces.

They each grabbed one of the three ropes still dangling in through the windows. 'No time to waste trying to clip into a harness,' Peter told them. 'Just use the bloody rope!'

Smith nodded. He jumped up onto the stone window ledge, whipped a length of the rappel rope around behind his hip, brought it diagonally up and over the opposite shoulder, back across to the same hip, and then along his arm down to the hand he would use as a brake. He saw Peter and Randi doing the same thing with their own ropes.

'Ready?' Peter asked.

'Set!' Jon confirmed. Randi nodded.

'Then go! Go! Go!'

Smith leaned out, turned sideways toward the ground, and simply let gravity do most of the work, plunging down the side of the building in huge bounds. The ground rushed up at him at a dizzying pace. He could smell the nylon rope scorching through his leather gloves and feel it burning across his shoulder and hip.

He was aware of Peter and Randi keeping pace with him. All three of them came hurtling down the wall at high speed.

When he judged he was just twenty feet or so above the little cobblestone alley running behind the Movement headquarters, Smith tightened the grip of his braking hand and pulled that same arm sharply across his chest in a hard, fast movement. He did not want to risk hitting the ground at that speed, and going that fast there was no way he could brake gently or slowly. He slammed to a stop, dangling only ten or twelve feet above the ground.

In that instant, a series of enormous explosions tore through the upper floors of the building soaring above him – rippling from one end of Number 18 rue de Vigny to the other in a growing fury of flame and glowing super-heated air. Hellish tongues of fire burst through every window, scorching the night and turning the darkness as bright as day in one blinding, awful moment. Broken pieces of stone and slate and other debris tumbled high into the air, lit from beneath by the inferno consuming the Lazarus Movement headquarters.

Smith felt his rope give way – ripped apart by the blast. He dropped, hit the ground hard, and rolled. Randi and Peter thudded down beside him. They scrabbled to their feet and ran for it, streaking down the darkened alley as fast as they could go, slipping and skidding on the dank, smooth cobblestones. Huge chunks of rubble were falling all around them – smashing onto nearby roofs or crashing down into the tight confines of the alley with killing force.

The trio burst out of the mouth of the alley and turned onto a wider cross street. Still running at full speed, they ducked into the recessed door of a small tobacco shop, seeking cover. A new wave of white-hot debris cascaded down across the surrounding streets and buildings, punching craters in roofs and pavements and setting new fires in its wake. The shrill anti-theft alarms going off in parked cars pummeled by the falling wreckage only added to the unholy din rising on all sides.

'Anyone have any brilliant ideas?' Randi said quickly. They could all hear sirens in the distance, drawing nearer with every passing second.

'We need to get clear of this area and drop out of sight,' Smith said grimly. 'And fast.' He looked at her. 'Can you call for help on that radio of yours?'

She shook her head. 'My radio's kaput.' She yanked off the headset with a disgusted look. 'I must have landed right on the damned thing when those bombs cut my rope. It sure feels like I did, anyway!'

A blue Volvo sedan came screeching around the corner from the rue de Vigny. It swung sharply in their direction and came roaring ahead. They were caught in its glaring twin headlights, silhouetted against the locked and barred door of the little tobacco shop. They were trapped, with nowhere to run and nowhere to hide.

Wearily Smith turned, fumbling for his SIG-Sauer, but Randi caught his arm and shook her head. 'Believe it or not, Jon,' she said in amazement, 'that's actually one of ours.'

The sedan braked hard, skidding to a stop just a few feet away. A window rolled down. They saw Max's astonished face peering up at them from behind the wheel. He grinned weakly. 'Man! When that building blew up, I never thought I'd see you folks again – not in one piece anyway.'

'I guess it's just your lucky day, Max,' Randi told him. She scrambled into the front seat while Jon and Peter piled into the back.

'Where to?' the CIA agent asked her.

'Anywhere for now,' Randi said tersely. 'Just put some distance between us . . . and that!' She jerked a thumb over her shoulder at the blazing pillar of fire roaring high into the night sky.

'Sure thing, boss,' Max replied quietly. He spun the steering wheel through a half-circle and pulled back onto the street. Then, keeping a wary eye on his rearview mirror, he drove away at a sedate but steady pace.

By the time the first fire trucks and police cars pulled up outside the blazing, bomb-gutted ruins of Number 18 rue de Vigny, they were already more than a mile away and heading for the outskirts of Paris.

The Forest of Rambouillet lay roughly thirty-five miles southwest of the city. It was a lovely expanse of woods, lakes, and ancient stone abbeys tucked away amid the tall trees. The elegant mansion and beautiful grounds of the château of Rambouillet stood in the heart of this rolling woodland. The château itself, more than six centuries old, had once been a weekend country retreat for several French kings. Now it served the same purpose for presidents of the French Republic.

The northern fringes of the woods, however, were miles removed from the glories of the château and mostly deserted – a haven for herds of skittish deer and a few wild boars. Narrow roads wandered here and there under the trees, providing access for hikers and for the occasional government forester.

In a small clearing just off one of those rough woodland tracks, Lieutenant Colonel Jon Smith sat on a tree stump, bandaging the reopened knife wound on his left forearm. Finished, he put aside the tape and unused gauze. Then he tested his new field dressing, rotating his arm back and forth to make sure it would stand the strain of sudden movement.

Smith realized that at some point, the wound would need new stitches, but at least this bandage should stop the worst of the bleeding. With that accomplished, he pulled on a fresh shirt, wincing slightly as the cotton knit slid over fresh cuts, bruises, and knotted muscles.

He stood up, stretching and twisting as he did so in an

effort to clear away some of the fatigue crowding in on his exhausted mind. A half-moon hung low in the west, barely visible above the canopy of the surrounding forest. But a small hint of pale gray light on the eastern horizon signaled the slow approach of dawn. The sun would be up in a couple of hours.

He glanced across at his companions. Peter was sleeping on the front seat of the Volvo, snatching whatever rest he could with the practiced ease of a veteran soldier. Randi stood next to a small black Peugeot parked at the far end of the clearing, quietly conferring with Max and another CIA agent – a junior officer named Lewis who had just driven out from Paris to deliver the new civilian clothes they needed. She was undoubtedly arranging for the immediate disappearance of their assault gear, weapons, and old clothing – of anything that might tie them to the carnage inside 18 rue de Vigny.

No one was in earshot.

Smith took out his encrypted cell phone, took a deep breath, and punched in the code for Covert-One headquarters.

Fred Klein listened to Smith's report of the night's events in silence. When he finished, Klein sighed heavily. 'You're riding an awfully narrow rail between disaster and utter catastrophe, Colonel, but I suppose I can't argue much with success.'

'I sure hope not,' Smith said drily. 'That would smack of rank ingratitude.'

'You're satisfied that this Abrantes was telling you the truth?' Klein asked. 'About the relationship between Lazarus and the nanophages, I mean? What if he was only trying to lay another false trail – trying to send us rushing off in the wrong direction?'

'He wasn't,' Jon said. 'The guy was dying, Fred. For all he knew, I was his sainted grandmother come down from heaven to escort him to the Pearly Gates. No, Vitor Abrantes was telling me the truth. Whoever Lazarus really is, he's the son of a bitch who's been behind these attacks from the beginning. Plus, he's been throwing sand in everyone's eyes by stage-managing both ends of this war between the Movement and the CIA and FBI.'

There was a long silence on the other end of the phone. 'To what end, Jon?' Klein asked finally.

'Lazarus has been buying time,' Smith told him. 'Time to run these perverted "field tests" of his. Time to analyze the results and to reengineer the nanophages – making them more and more powerful and deadly. Time to develop and evaluate new methods of delivering them to his chosen targets.' He grimaced. 'While we've all been running around in circles, Lazarus has been out there designing, developing, and testing a weapon that could wipe out most of the human race.'

'At Kusasa in Zimbabwe, the Teller Institute, and now La Courneuve,' Klein realized. 'All the places showing up in those passports and other travel documents Peter Howell retrieved.'

'Exactly.'

'And you think this weapon is ready for use?' Klein asked quietly.

'I do,' Smith said. 'There's no other reason for Lazarus to destroy the people and equipment he was using to monitor those experiments. He's clearing the decks – getting ready to strike.'

'What's your recommendation?'

'We pinpoint Lazarus and whatever lab or factory he's using to produce this stuff. Then we kill him and capture his nanophage stocks before they're dispersed for any large-scale attack.'

'Short and sweet, Colonel,' Klein said. 'But not very subtle.'

'Do you have any better ideas?' Smith demanded.

The head of Covert-One sighed again. 'No, I don't. The trick will be finding Lazarus before it's too late. And that's something no Western intelligence agency has managed in more than a year of trying.'

'I think Abrantes told me most of what we need,' Smith argued. 'The trouble is: My Spanish is fair to middling, but my Portuguese is nonexistent. I need a clear translation of what he said when I asked him where Lazarus was now.'

'I can find someone to handle that,' Klein promised. He faded from the phone a moment. There was a small *click* in the background, and then he came back on the line. 'Okay, we're set to record, Colonel. Go ahead.'

'Here goes,' Smith said. From memory, and trying to make sure he used the same pronunciation he had heard the dying man use, he repeated Vitor Abrantes' last words. '*Os Açores. O console do sol. Santa María.*'

'Got it. Anything else?'

'Yeah.' Smith frowned. 'Abrantes told me he was shot by a man he described as "one of the *Horatii*." If I'm right, I've already run into two of them – first outside Teller and now here in Paris. I'd like a better read on what those big identical bastards were . . . and how many more of them might be out there!'

Klein said, 'I'll see what I can dig up, Jon. But this might take a while. Can you stay where you are for a bit?'

Smith nodded, looking around at the tall trees dappled in shadow and in fading moonlight. 'Yeah. But make it as quick as you can, Fred. I have a bad feeling that the clock is running fast on this situation.'

'Understood, Colonel. Hold tight.'

The line went dead.

Smith paced back and forth across the clearing. He could feel the tension inside mounting. His nerves were stretched almost to the breaking point. More than an hour had gone by since Klein had promised to get back to him. The gray light in the east was much stronger now.

The sudden sound of a car engine startled him. He swung around in surprise and saw the little black Peugeot drive away, bouncing and rolling awkwardly along the heavily rutted forest track.

'I sent Max and Lewis back to Paris,' Randi explained. She had been sitting calmly on his tree stump, watching him pace. 'We don't need them here right now, and I'd like to find out more about anything the French police have dug up inside what's left of the Movement headquarters.'

Smith nodded. That made sense. 'I think – '

His cell phone vibrated. He flipped it open. 'Yes?'

'Are you alone?' Klein asked abruptly. His voice sounded strained, almost unnatural.

Jon checked his surroundings. Randi was perched just a few feet away. And, operating on some sixth sense honed by years in the field, Peter had woken up from his catnap. 'No, I'm not,' he admitted.

'That's extremely unfortunate,' Klein said. He hesitated. 'Then you'll have to be very careful of what you say on your end. Clear?'

'Yes,' Smith said quietly. 'What have you got for me?'

'Let's start with the *Horatii*,' Klein said slowly. 'The name comes from an old Roman legend – a set of identical triplets sent into single combat against warriors from a rival city. They were renowned for their courage, strength, agility, and loyalty.'

'That sure fits,' Smith said, thinking back over his deadly encounters with the two tall green-eyed men. Both times, he had been very lucky to emerge alive. He winced. The thought of a third man with the same strength and skills still lurking out there was disconcerting.

'There's a famous painting done by the French neo-classical artist Jacques-Louis David,' Klein went on. 'Called *The Oath of the Horatii*.'

'And it's hanging in the Louvre,' Smith said, suddenly realizing why the name had conjured up old memories.

'That's right,' Klein confirmed.

Smith shook his head grimly. 'Swell. So our friend Lazarus has a love for the classics and a nasty sense of humor. But I guess that doesn't bring us any closer to finding him.' He took a deep breath. 'Were you able to secure a translation of Abrantes' last words?'

'Yes,' Klein said quietly.

'Well?' Smith asked impatiently. 'What was he trying to tell me?'

'He said, "The Azores. The island of the sun. Santa María," ' the head of Covert-One reported.

'The Azores?' Smith shook his head, surprised. The Azores were a group of small Portuguese-settled islands far out in the Atlantic Ocean, close to the line of latitude linking Lisbon and New York. Centuries ago, the archipelago had been a strategic outpost of the now-vanished Portuguese empire, but today it survived largely on beef and dairy exports and on tourism.

'Santa María is one of the nine islands of the Azores,' Klein explained. He sighed. 'Apparently, the locals sometimes refer to it as "the island of the sun." '

'So what the hell is on Santa Maria?' Smith asked, barely controlling the irritation in his voice. Fred Klein was not usually so slow to get to the point.

'Not much on the eastern half of the island. Just a few tiny villages, really.'

'And in the west?'

'Well, that's where things get tricky,' Klein admitted. 'It seems that the western end of Santa María is leased by Nomura PharmaTech for its global medical charity work – complete with a very long hard-surfaced runway, enormous hangar facilities, and a huge medical supply storage complex.'

'Nomura,' Jon said softly, at last understanding why his superior sounded so strained. 'Hideo Nomura is Lazarus. He's got the money, the scientific know-how, the facilities, and the political connections to pull something like that off.'

'So it appears,' Klein agreed. 'But I'm afraid it's not enough. No one's going to be persuaded by the purported last words of an unknown dying man. Without hard evidence, the kind of evidence we can show to wavering friends and allies, I don't see how the president can possibly approve an open attack on Nomura's Azores facility.'

The head of Covert-One continued. 'The situation here is worse than you can imagine, Jon. Our military and political alliances are shredding like wet tissue paper. NATO is up in arms. The UN General Assembly is planning to designate us as a terrorist nation. And a sizable bloc in Congress is arguing seriously for the impeachment of the president. In these circumstances, an apparently unprovoked air or cruise missile attack on a world-renowned medical charity would be the last straw.'

Smith knew that Klein was right. But knowing that didn't make the situation they faced any more acceptable. 'We may be damned if we do. But we'll die if we don't,' he argued.

'I know that, Jon,' Klein said emphatically. 'But we need evidence to back our claims before we can send in the bombers and missiles.'

'There's only one way to get that kind of proof,' Smith pointed out grimly. 'Someone has to go in on the ground in the Azores and get right up close.'

'Yes,' Klein agreed slowly. 'When can you head to the airport?'

Smith looked up from the phone at Randi and Peter. They looked equally grim, equally determined. They had heard enough of his side of the conversation to know what was going on. 'Now,' he said simply. 'We're going *now*.'

CHAPTER FORTY-FIVE

The Lazarus Center, Santa María Island, the Azores
Outside the windowless confines of the Lazarus Movement nerve center, the sun was just rising, climbing higher above the embrace of the Atlantic. Its first dazzling rays touched the sheer cliffs of São Laurenço Bay with fire and lit the steep stone-terraced vineyards of Maia. From there, the growing daylight rolled westward across verdant forests and pastures, gleamed off the white sand beach at Praia Formosa, and at last chased the night's lingering shadows away from the treeless limestone plain surrounding the Nomura PharmaTech airfield.

Inside the Center, secure in neon-lit silence, Hideo Nomura read through the most recent messages from his surviving agents in Paris. Based on details supplied by paid informants on the police force, it was clear that Nones and his men were dead – killed along with all the others inside the bomb-ravaged building at 18 rue de Vigny.

He furrowed his brow, both puzzled and worried by this news. Nones and his team should have been well away before their demolition charges exploded. Something had gone badly wrong, but what?

Several witnesses reported seeing 'men in black' running away from the building right after the first explosions occurred. The French police, though dubious at first, were now treating these reports seriously – blaming the mysterious forces opposing the Lazarus Movement for what looked like a major terrorist attack on its Paris headquarters.

Nomura shook his head. That was impossible, of course. The only terrorists targeting the Movement were men under his command. But then he stopped, considering the matter more carefully.

What if someone else *had* been snooping around inside 18 rue de Vigny? True, his intricately laid plans had succeeded in throwing the CIA, FBI, and MI6 into confusion. But there were other intelligence organizations in the world, and any number of them might be trying to pry into the activities of the Lazarus Movement. Could they have found anything there that might tie the La Courneuve surveillance operation to him? He bit his lower lip, wondering if he had been overconfident, entirely too sure that his many elaborate ruses would escape detection.

Nomura pondered that possibility for a while. Though it was likely that his cover was intact, it might be best to take certain precautions. His original plan envisioned a simultaneous strike on the continental United States by at least a dozen *Thanatos* aircraft – but assembling the required number of the giant flying-wing drones would take his work crews another three days. More important, he lacked the hangar space here to conceal so many planes from any unexpected aerial or space surveillance.

No, he thought coldly, he should act *now*, while he was certain that he still could, instead of waiting for a perfect moment that might never arrive. Once the first millions were dead, the Americans and their allies would be leaderless and too horror-stricken to hunt effectively for their hidden foes. When fighting for control over the fate of the world, he reminded himself, flexibility was a virtue, not a vice. He tapped a button on his internal phone. 'Send Terce to me. At once.'

The last of the *Horatii* arrived moments later. His massive shoulders filled the doorway and his head seemed almost to brush against the ceiling. He bowed obediently and then stood motionless in front of Nomura's teak desk, patiently waiting for orders from the man who had made him so powerful and efficient a killer.

'You know that both of your companions have failed me?' Nomura said.

The tall green-eyed man nodded. 'So I understand,' he said coolly. 'But *I* have never failed in my duty.'

'That is true,' Nomura agreed. 'And in consequence, the rewards promised to them now fall to you. When the time comes, you will stand at my right hand – exercising dominion in my name, in the name of Lazarus.'

Terce's eyes gleamed. Nomura planned to reorder the world to create a paradise for those few he believed worthy of continued life. Most nations and peoples would die, consumed over months and years by waves of unseen nanophages. Those allowed to live would be forced to obey his commands – reshaping their lives, cultures, and beliefs to fit his idyllic vision. Nomura and those who served him would wield almost unimaginable power over the frightened remnants of humanity.

'What are your orders?' the surviving member of the *Horatii* asked.

'We are going to attack earlier than first planned,' Nomura told him. 'Three *Thanatos* aircraft should be ready for launch in six to eight hours. Inform the nanophage production team that I want enough full canisters to load those planes as soon as their preflight checks are finished. The first targets will be Washington, D.C., New York, and Boston.'

Lajes Field, Terceira Island, the Azores

Three people, two men and a woman, stood out among the small crowd of passengers deplaning from Air Portugal's Lisbon flight. Unencumbered by luggage, they moved swiftly through the slower currents of locals and bargain-hunting tourists and made their way from the tarmac into the airport terminal.

Once inside, Randi Russell stopped dead in her tracks.

She stared up at a large clock showing the local time as noon and then back to the board showing flight arrivals and departures. 'Damn!' she muttered in frustration. 'There's only one connecting flight to Santa María a day – and we've already missed it.'

Walking on, Jon shook his head. 'We're not taking a commercial flight.' He led them toward the outer doors. A short line of taxis and private cars stood at the curb, waiting to pick up arriving passengers.

She raised an eyebrow. 'Santa María must be close to two hundred miles away. You planning to swim?'

Smith grinned back over his shoulder. 'Not unless Peter really fouls up.'

Randi glanced at the pale-eyed Englishman walking beside her. 'Do you know what he's talking about?'

'Haven't a clue,' Peter told her breezily. 'But I noticed our friend there making a few *sotto voce* phone calls in Paris while we were waiting for the Lisbon flight. So I rather suspect he has something up his sleeve.'

Still smiling slightly, Smith pushed through the doors out into the open air. He raised his hand, signaling a green, brown, and tan camouflaged Humvee idling just down the road. It pulled forward to meet them.

'Colonel Smith and company?' the U.S. Air Force staff sergeant behind the wheel asked.

'That's us,' Smith said, already tugging open the rear doors and motioning Randi and Peter inside. He hopped in after them.

The Humvee pulled away from the curb and drove on down the road. A quarter mile farther on, it swung toward a gate in the perimeter fence. There a pair of stern-faced guards carrying loaded M16s checked their identity cards, carefully comparing faces and pictures. Satisfied, the soldiers waved them through onto the U.S. Air Force base at Lajes.

The vehicle turned left and raced down the flight line. Gray-camouflaged C-17 transports and giant KC-10 tanker planes lined the long runway. On one side of the tarmac, the ground fell away, eventually plunging almost straight down toward the Atlantic. On the other, bright green slopes rose high above the airfield, broken up into innumerable small fields by low walls of dark volcanic rock. The sweet scents of wildflowers and the fresh salt smell of the ocean mixed oddly with the sharp, acrid tang of half-burnt jet fuel.

'Your bird arrived from the States an hour ago,' the Air Force sergeant told them. 'It's being prepped now.'

Randi turned toward Smith. 'Our *bird?*' she asked pointedly.

Jon shrugged. 'A U.S. Army UH-60L Black Hawk helicopter,' he said. 'Dispatched here by C-17 about the same time we flew from Paris to Lisbon. I thought it might come in handy.'

'Good thinking,' Randi said with barely contained sarcasm. 'Let me get this straight: You just snapped your fingers and had the Army and the Air Force ship you a multimillion-dollar helicopter for our personal use? Is that about right, Jon?'

'Actually, I asked a couple of friends in the Pentagon to pull a string or two,' Smith said modestly. 'Everybody's so worried about this nanophage threat that they were willing to bend some of the rules for us.'

Randi rounded on the leathery-faced Englishman. 'And I suppose you think you can fly a Black Hawk?'

'Well, if I can't, we'll soon find out the hard way,' Peter told her cheerfully.

CHAPTER FORTY-SIX

PharmaTech Airfield, Santa María Island

Hideo Nomura paced slowly along the edge of the long concrete runway. The wind, blowing from the east, whispered through his short black hair. The light breeze carried the rich, sun-warmed smell of tall grass growing on the plateau beyond the fence. He looked up. The sun was still high overhead, just beginning its long slide toward the western horizon. Far to the north, a few clouds drifted slowly past, solitary puffs of white in a clear blue sky.

Nomura smiled. The weather was perfect in every respect. He turned, seeing his father standing behind him between two of Terce's hard-faced guards. The older man's hands were handcuffed behind his back.

He smiled at his father. 'It's wonderfully ironic, isn't it?'

Jinjiro eyed him with a stony, cold reserve. 'There are many ironies here, Lazarus,' he said coldly, refusing even to call his treacherous son by his own name. 'To which do you refer?'

Ignoring the gibe, the younger man nodded toward the runway in front of them. 'This airfield,' he explained. 'The Americans built it in 1944, during their war against Germany and our beloved homeland. Their bombers used this island as a refueling point during their long transatlantic flights to England. But today, I will turn their own work against them. This airfield is about to become the staging area for America's annihilation!'

Jinjiro said nothing.

Hideo shrugged and turned away. It was clear now that

he had kept his father alive out of a misguided sense of filial piety. Once the first *Thanatos* drones were airborne, there would be time to arrange a fitting end for the old fool. Some of his scientists were already working on different variations of the Stage IV nanophages. They might find it useful to test their new designs on a live human subject.

He strode toward a small knot of flight engineers and ground controllers waiting beside the runway. They wore headsets and short-range radios for communications between the aircraft hangars and the tower. 'Is everything ready?' he asked sharply.

The senior ground controller nodded. 'The main hangar crew reports they are ready for rollout. All canisters are onboard.'

'Good.' Nomura looked at his ranking flight engineer. 'And the three aircraft?'

'All of their systems are functioning within the expected norms,' the man told him confidently. 'Their solar power cells, fuel-cell auxiliaries, flight controls, and attack programs have all been checked and rechecked.'

'Excellent,' Nomura said. He glanced again at the ground controller. 'Are there any unidentified air contacts we need to worry about?'

'Negative,' the controller said. 'Radar reports nothing airborne within one hundred kilometers. We're in the clear.'

Hideo took a deep breath. This was the moment he had spent years planning, scheming, and killing to make a reality. This was why he had tricked, trapped, and betrayed his own father – all for this single glorious instant of sure and certain triumph. He breathed out slowly, savoring the delightful sensation. Then he spoke. 'Commence *Thanatos* operations.'

The ground controller repeated his order over the radio.

'Open hangar doors.'

In response, at the southern end of the airfield huge metal doors on the nearest hangar began groaning apart, revealing a vast interior crowded with men and machines. Sunshine streamed inside through the rapidly expanding opening. It fell on the solar cells of the first *Thanatos* flying wing. They gleamed like golden fire.

'The first aircraft is taxiing,' the senior flight engineer reported.

Slowly, the enormous drone, with a wingspan wider than that of a 747, lumbered forward, clearing the doors with only feet to spare. Fourteen twin-bladed propellers whirred silently, pulling it out onto the runway. Clusters of thin-walled plastic cylinders were visible on each of the aircraft's five underwing pods.

'Don masks and gloves,' Nomura ordered. The controllers and engineers hurriedly obeyed, shrugging into the heavy gear that would give them limited protection if anything went wrong during takeoff.

Terce moved to his side, offering him a gas mask, respirator, and thick gloves. Hideo took them with a curt nod.

'And the prisoner?' the tall green-eyed man asked, in a voice muffled by his respirator. 'What about him?'

'My father?' Hideo glanced back at Jinjiro, who was still standing bareheaded in the sun, rigid and unbending between his two gas-masked guards. He smiled coldly and shook his head. 'No mask for him. Let the old man take his chances.'

'The second aircraft is taxiing,' the flight engineer reported, speaking loudly enough to be heard through his mask and breathing apparatus.

Nomura looked back at the runway. The first *Thanatos* drone was already two hundred meters away, slowly accelerating as it rolled north on its takeoff run. The second flying wing was emerging from inside the mammoth hangar – with a third just visible behind it. He pushed his father's impending death to the back of his mind and focused instead on watching his cruel dreams take flight.

Terce moved away, unslinging a German-made Heckler & Koch G36 assault rifle from his shoulder as he went. His head swiveled from side to side, checking the armed guards he had posted at intervals along the runway. All of them appeared alert.

A slight frown crossed the big man's face. Counting the two men watching Jinjiro, there were ten sentries stationed at the airfield. There should have been twice as many – but the unexpectedly heavy losses he had sustained in New Mexico and then again in Virginia could not be made up in time. The deaths of Nones and his Paris-based security detail only made the manpower shortage worse.

Terce shrugged, looking westward out to sea. In the end, it would not matter. Nomura was right. Stealth outweighed firepower. No matter how many soldiers, missiles, and bombs they possessed, the Americans could not attack a target they could not find.

He froze. Something was moving out there above the Atlantic, right near the edge of his vision. He stared harder. Whatever it was, the object was drawing closer at high speed. But it was difficult to make out through the thick, distorting lenses of his gas mask.

With a snarl, Terce tore off the mask and attached respirator and tossed them aside. At least now he could see clearly! A small dark green dot, racing low just above the ocean waves. It curved toward him, tilting slightly – growing larger fast. Sunlight flashed off spinning rotor blades.

Aboard the UH-60L Black Hawk, Smith leaned forward in the co-pilot's seat, peering at the airfield ahead of them through a pair of high-powered binoculars. 'Okay,' he said loudly, shouting to be heard above the howl of the troop carrier's two powerful engines and its large, clattering rotors. 'I count two An-124 Condor cargo planes near the north end of the runway, parked next to a big hangar. Also what looks like a much smaller executive jet, maybe a Gulfstream.'

'What's that moving down near the south end of the runway?' Randi yelled in his ear. She crouched behind the forward cabin's two seats, holding on tight with whitened knuckles. The Black Hawk was shuddering and bouncing wildly as Peter fought to hold the helicopter just fifty feet above the rolling crests of the ocean waves – all the while flying at more than one hundred knots. He had brought them in at very low altitude to avoid being picked up by the airfield's radar.

Smith swung his binoculars to the right. For the first time, he saw the three huge flying wings lined up one after another on the long concrete strip. The lead aircraft was already moving faster and faster, rolling smoothly toward takeoff. At first, his exhausted mind refused to accept that anything so big and, at the same time, so fragile-looking could possibly be airworthy.

Then, in a flood of understanding, the facts and images fell into place, pulled from memory. Several years ago he had read up on NASA's scientific experiments with high-altitude solar-powered long-endurance robot planes. Nomura must have stolen the same technology for his own vicious ends. 'Good lord!' he said, rocked by the sudden realization. 'Those are Nomura's attack aircraft!'

Quickly he briefed the others on what he remembered of their flight profile and capabilities.

'Can't our fighter planes shoot them down?' Randi asked somberly.

'If they're flying at close to a hundred thousand feet?' Smith shook his head. 'That's beyond the maximum ceiling for any fighter in our inventory. There's not an F-16 or F-15 or anything else we own that can fly and fight that high up!'

'What about your Patriot missiles?' Peter suggested.

'One hundred thousand feet is above their effective ceiling, too,' Smith replied grimly. 'Plus, I'll bet those damned drones out there are built to avoid most radar.' He gritted his teeth. 'If they're at high altitude, they'll be invulnerable and probably undetectable. So once those planes are operational, Nomura will be able to hit us at will – unleashing nanophage clouds over any city he chooses!'

Horrified by the danger he saw looming before the United States, Jon focused his binoculars on a small group of men standing together just off the runway. He drew in a short, sharp breath. They were wearing gas masks.

The world around him seemed to blur, slowing while his mind raced. Why were they wearing masks? And then, suddenly, the answer – the only possible answer – leaped out at him.

'Take us in, Peter!' Smith snapped. He jabbed a finger at the airfield. 'Straight in!'

The Englishman glanced at him in surprise. 'This isn't an attack mission, Jon. We're supposed to be scouting – not riding in with sabers drawn like the bloody cavalry.'

'The mission just changed,' Smith told him tightly. 'Those planes are armed. That son of a bitch Nomura is launching his attack now!'

CHAPTER FORTY-SEVEN

Frowning, Peter banked the Black Hawk tightly, turning in toward the airfield. Santa María's coastline loomed larger, rapidly taking on shape and definition as they flew toward it at one hundred knots. The Englishman turned his head for just a moment, looking at Randi. 'You'd better break out the weapons.'

She nodded. The three of them were already wearing Kevlar body armor, and the helicopter had come equipped with three M4 carbines, cut-down versions of the U.S. military's M16 assault rifle. She moved back into the troop compartment, careful to keep a tight grip with at least one hand on anything bolted down.

Abruptly Peter banked the Black Hawk through another tight turn – this time swinging the helicopter north to fly parallel to the runway. 'Half a tick,' he said. 'Why do this the hard way? Why not just hover above these damned drones and shoot them down over the sea?'

Smith thought the suggestion through. It made perfect sense. He reddened. 'I should have thought of that,' he admitted reluctantly.

Peter grinned. 'Studying medicine when you should have been studying tactics, eh?' He pulled back on the controls. The UH-60 rose steadily, climbing several hundred feet above the sea in a matter of seconds. 'Keep an eye on that first drone, Jon. Let me know when it's aloft.'

Smith nodded. He leaned back in his seat to stare out the cabin's right-side window, over Peter's shoulder. A sudden bright white flash and a puff of dust near the airfield caught his eye. A small dart sped toward them, riding fast on a pillar of fire. For a fraction of a second he stared in disbelief. Then his survival instincts kicked in. 'SAM! SAM!' he roared. 'At three o'clock!'

'Hell's teeth!' Peter exclaimed. He yanked hard on the controls, adroitly handling the foot pedals, collective, and cyclic stick to throw the Black Hawk into a tight descending turn toward the oncoming missile. At the same time, he stabbed a switch on the control panel, activating the helicopter's IR flare dispenser.

Incandescent flares spewed through a wide arc behind the diving UH-60. Looking up, Smith saw the incoming surface-to-air missile streak right overhead and then curve away sharply, following one of the decoy flares as it tumbled slowly toward the ocean. He breathed out. 'Must have been a heat seeker,' he commented, irked to hear a tremor in his voice.

Peter nodded. His lips were pressed tight together. 'Man-portable SAMs usually are.' He sighed. 'Back to square one, I'm afraid. We daren't mess about at altitude – not with a missile threat like that sitting right behind us.'

'So in we go?' Smith suggested.

'Too right,' Peter said, baring his teeth in a fierce fighting grin. He brought the Black Hawk down so low that its main landing gear seemed to be skimming right over the curling waves. The airfield, now dead ahead, grew rapidly through the forward canopy. 'We go in hard and fast, Jon. You clear the left. I'll clear the right. And Randi, God bless her, will do whatever else needs doing!'

'Sounds like a plan!' Randi agreed from behind them. She handed Smith one of the M4 carbines and three thirty-round magazines. With a shortened barrel and a telescoping stock, the M4 was a somewhat lighter and handier weapon than its parent, the M16. He snapped one magazine into the rifle and tucked the spare clips away in his pockets. The third carbine went to Peter, who wedged it beside him on the pilot's seat.

'Thanks! Now, buckle in,' Peter yelled back at her. 'The landing will be just a tad bumpy!'

There were more flashes rippling along the runway ahead of them. Several men were standing out in the open, steadily firing at the oncoming helicopter with assault rifles. Five-point-fifty-six mm rounds smacked into the Black Hawk – pinging off the main rotor, ricocheting off its armored canopy and cockpit, and punching through the thin alloy sides of the fuselage.

Smith saw Nomura's first flying wing lift off the ground and begin climbing. He slammed his fist onto the side of his seat in frustration. 'Damn!'

'There are still two more on the ground! We'll deal with that one later,' Peter assured him. 'Assuming there is a later, that is,' he added under his breath.

The Black Hawk clattered low over the tarmac and spun rapidly through a half-circle, flaring out to thump heavily into the long grass growing beside the runway. More rifle bullets spanged off the canopy and went whirring away in showers of sparks. Smith hammered the seat belt buckle hard, opening it, grabbed his M4 carbine, and forced his way back into the troop compartment. Peter followed closely, pausing only to set a couple of switches on the control panel. Overhead, the rotor blades slowed dramatically – but they kept turning.

Randi already had the left-side door open. She crouched in the opening, sighting down the barrel of her carbine. She glanced over her shoulder. 'All set?'

Jon nodded. 'Let's go!'

With Randi right behind him, he leaped out of the helicopter and dashed south along the fringe of the runway. Rifle rounds cracked low overhead, coming from a pair of guards running toward them across the concrete. Smith threw himself down in the tall grass and opened fire – squeezing off three-round bursts in an arc from left to right.

One of the guards screamed shrilly and flopped forward,

cut almost in half by two high-velocity bullets. The other dropped flat on the concrete and kept shooting.

From her position on Smith's right, Randi coolly took aim. She waited until the sights settled on the goggles of the guard's gas mask and then gently pulled the trigger. His head exploded.

Jon swallowed hard, looking away. He checked their surroundings. They were about a third of the way along the runway – just a few hundred meters from the massive hangar at the southern end. An enormous tin-roofed warehouse stretched east not far behind them. There appeared to be only one entrance on this side, a solid-looking steel door with a keypad lock. His eyes narrowed as suspicion hardened into certainty. No one put that kind of fortress-like door on a run-of-the-mill storage facility. Nomura's secret nanophage lab must be somewhere inside. You could hide a dozen biochemical factories inside that vast, cavernous space and still have plenty of room left over.

The second of the huge flying-wing planes was rolling down the runway in their direction, slowly gathering speed as its propellers spun faster and faster. Jon could see the deadly canisters clustered beneath its single enormous wing. The third drone aircraft was stopped just outside the hangar, waiting for its turn in the takeoff pattern.

Gunfire erupted to the north, on the other side of the Black Hawk. Another guard screamed and fell back – riddled with bullets fired by Peter. As he toppled, the dying man triggered the Russian-made SA-16 SAM he had been trying to aim. The missile ignited. Trailing a dense cloud of gray and white smoke, it soared straight up, turned east, and then plummeted harmlessly to explode in the empty pastures beyond the perimeter fence.

Smith spotted more movement to the south, not far from the second aircraft. Three more gunmen, led by a much taller man, were advancing along the western edge of the runway – generally keeping pace with the oncoming drone plane. They were bounding in pairs, taking turns covering each other as they came forward.

He winced. Great, he thought. These guys were professionals. *And* they were being led by the third of the superhuman *Horatii*.

'Watch your front, Jon!' Randi called. She gestured toward the open ground on the other side of the runway. A little knot of men in gas masks and respirators was falling back there, retreating from the battle raging around the tarmac. Most appeared to be unarmed. But two carried submachine guns slung over their shoulders, and they were dragging an older white-haired man between them. A man who was not wearing a gas mask. A man in handcuffs.

'I'll deal with the planes,' Smith said. He pointed toward the retreating men. 'You take care of them!'

Randi nodded, seeing Jon already moving along the edge of the runway – heading toward the giant flying wing lumbering north. Smoke from the errant SAM launch wafted across the tarmac, cutting off her view of him.

Left alone, she jumped to her feet and sprinted across the wide bare stretch of oil- and jet fuel-stained concrete. One of the fleeing men saw her coming. He yelled a frantic warning to his companions. They threw themselves prone in the grass. The two guards tossed the old man down beside them and turned toward her. Their submachine guns came up.

Randi fired from the hip, squeezing off three-round bursts on the run. One of the guards spun away and fell heavily, bleeding from several wounds. The other shot back, firing off a full twenty-round clip from his Uzi.

The air around Randi was suddenly full of bullets and fragments of shattered concrete. She dived to the side. Something smashed into her left arm – hurling her backward. A ricochet tumbling off the concrete had hit hard enough to break her arm just above the elbow. Whitehot agony sleeted up from the injury. She rolled away, desperately trying to get clear before the gunman could zero in and nail her.

Stunned to see her still alive, the guard yanked out his empty clip and fumbled for another.

Gritting her teeth against the pain, Randi brought her carbine up again. She fired another burst. Two copper-jacketed rounds slammed home, hurling the gunman onto his back in bloodred ruin.

She forced herself back to her feet and ran on across the runway. The unarmed men jumped up and scattered in front of her, running wildly in all directions. They all looked alike in their hooded gas masks. Suddenly the old man in handcuffs kicked out, tripping one of the fleeing men. Snarling, the old man rolled over onto the man he had knocked down – pressing him facedown into the tall, tangled grass.

Randi moved closer, aiming the carbine with her good hand. 'Who the hell are you?' she snapped.

The old man smiled beatifically up at her. 'I am Jinjiro Nomura,' he said quietly. 'And this,' he nodded toward the figure squirming beneath him, 'is Lazarus – the traitor who was once my son, Hideo.'

Scarcely able to believe her luck, Randi grinned back at the old man. 'Delighted to meet you, Mr. Nomura.' She kept the M4 aimed at the man writhing on the ground while Jinjiro climbed awkwardly to his feet.

'Now stand up and take off that gas mask,' she ordered. 'But do it slowly. Otherwise I might just twitch and blow your head off.'

The younger man obeyed. Slowly, with exaggerated caution, he tugged off the mask and respirator – revealing the gray, shocked features of Hideo Nomura.

'What will you do with him?' Jinjiro asked curiously.

Randi shrugged her good shoulder. 'Take him back to the United States for trial, I guess.' She heard a new burst of firing, this time from the north.

'Speaking of which, I suggest the three of us head back

to the helicopter right this minute. This neighborhood seems to be getting distinctly unhealthy.'

Peter ghosted through the drifting haze of smoke, with his carbine cradled against his shoulder. He heard a metallic *click* close by and dropped quietly to one knee, searching ahead of him for the source of the sound.

A guard loomed up out of the slowly clearing pall. His hand was still on the firing selector for his German-made assault rifle, switching it from single-shot to fire three-round bursts. His mouth dropped open when he saw the Englishman aiming at him.

'Very careless,' Peter told him softly. He squeezed the trigger.

Hit by all three shots fired at close range, the guard crumpled into the blood-soaked grass.

Peter waited a few moments longer, allowing the smoke to clear. It rolled west toward the ocean, slowly shredding in the light wind. He scanned the open ground stretching before him. Nothing moved.

Satisfied, he turned and trotted back toward the helicopter.

White-faced with pain from her broken arm, Randi prodded her prisoner toward the waiting Black Hawk. She stumbled once and Hideo Nomura glanced swiftly back at her, with hatred written all over his face. She shook her head and lifted the M4, aiming right at his chest. 'I wouldn't try that. Not unless you really believe you can rise from the dead. Even one-handed, I'm a very good shot. Now hop in!'

Walking behind her, Jinjiro chuckled – plainly enjoying his treacherous son's discomfiture.

The man who had called himself Lazarus turned and scrambled inside the helicopter. Standing by the door, Randi motioned him into one of the forward-facing rear seats. Scowling, he obeyed.

Peter loomed up beside her. He peered into the troop compartment at her prisoner. His eyebrows rose. 'Nicely done, Randi. Very nicely done indeed.'

Then he looked around in growing unease. 'But where on earth is Jon?'

CHAPTER FORTY-EIGHT

Smith sprinted toward the four gunmen advancing alongside the rolling drone aircraft. They were still moving in pairs. At any given moment, two of them were prone – ready to provide covering fire for their comrades. Most of their attention was focused on the battle raging around the grounded Black Hawk, but they were sure to spot him soon enough.

The back of his mind yammered that this headlong charge was a particularly stupid form of suicide, but he furiously shoved those doubts away. He did not have any other options. He had to hit this enemy team quickly, before they spotted him, pinned him down with suppressive fire, and then came in for the kill.

His only real chance against these men was to seize the initiative and hold it. Their tactics showed that they were professionals, probably more of the veteran mercenary soldiers recruited to do the dirty work for Nomura's Lazarus operation. In a set-piece skirmish Smith might be able to take out one of them, possibly even two – but trying to fight all four of them at once would only be a good way to die quickly. Still, he knew that it was the presence among them of the third of the *Horatii* that tipped the scales toward this seeming recklessness.

Twice before Smith had gone up against one of those powerful and deadly killers. In both fights he had been lucky to limp away alive and he was not going to be able to rely on stumbling into good fortune again. This time he needed to make his own luck – and that meant taking chances.

He ran on, with his feet flying through the tall grass lining the eastern edge of the runway. The range to the oncoming drone and the four enemy gunmen was closing fast – falling rapidly as they moved toward each other with increasing speed.

Two hundred and fifty meters. Two hundred. One hundred and fifty meters. Jon felt his lungs laboring under the strain. He brought the M4 up to his shoulder and sprinted on.

One hundred meters.

The flying wing came whirring along the runway toward him. All fourteen of its propellers were spinning now, carving bright flashing circles in the air.

Now!

Smith squeezed the trigger on the M4, firing short bursts on the move – walking his rounds across the tarmac toward the startled enemy gunmen. Pieces of concrete and then tufts of grass flew skyward.

They dropped prone and began shooting back.

Jon swerved left, zigzagging away from the tarmac. Bullets tore through the grass behind him and cracked past his head. He dived forward, hit the ground, shoulder-rolled back onto his feet, and kept running. He fired again, then swerved right.

More rifle rounds screamed past, reaching out to tear him apart. One tore through the air close to his face. The superheated gases trailing in its wake slapped his head back. Another clipped his side, glanced off his body armor, and knocked him down into the grass. Frantic now, Smith rolled away – hearing bullets rending the earth right behind him.

In the midst of all the shooting, he heard a deep, bull-like voice shouting angry orders somewhere on the other side of the runway. The last of the *Horatii* was issuing new commands to his troops.

And then, suddenly, astonishingly, the firing stopped.

In the silence, Jon cautiously raised his head. He

grinned weakly in relief. As he had intended, the second drone flying wing, still serenely taxiing toward its programmed takeoff, had come rolling between him and the men who were trying to kill him. For a brief moment they could not shoot at him, at least without the risk of hitting one of their own precious aircraft.

But he knew their self-imposed cease-fire would not last long.

Smith pushed himself up, and crouching low, he moved backward – trying to keep pace with the huge slowly accelerating solar-powered plane. He peered beneath the enormous wing, looking for any sign of movement on the concrete runway.

He caught a quick glimpse of running combat boots through the narrow gaps between the flying wing's five sets of landing gear and its aerodynamically shaped avionics and payload pods. Two of the gunmen were sprinting across the wide tarmac, cutting behind the drone in an effort to gain a clear field of fire.

Jon kept backing up, waiting with the M4 tucked against his shoulder and his finger ready on the trigger. He breathed out, feeling his pulse pounding in his ears. Come on, he urged the running men silently. Make a mistake.

They did.

Impatient or overconfident or spurred on by the wrath of the auburn-haired giant who commanded them, both gunmen crossed into the open in the same instant.

Smith opened fire – pouring rounds downrange into the suddenly appalled pair. The carbine hammered back against his shoulder. Spent cartridges flew away from the weapon, tinkling onto the concrete. Fifty meters away, the two gunmen screamed and fell away into the grass. Multiple 5.56mm hits ripped them apart.

And then Smith felt a series of hammer blows punching across his own chest and right flank – a cascade of agonizing impacts on his Kevlar body armor that spun him around in a half circle and threw him to his knees.

Somehow he held on to the M4.

Through vision blurred by pain, he looked up.

There, only forty meters away across the tarmac, a tall green-eyed man stared back at him, smiling coldly down the barrel of an assault rifle. In that instant, Jon understood the mistake he had made. The last of the *Horatii* had expended two of his own men – throwing them forward to draw fire in the same way a chess player sacrifices pawns to gain an advantage in position. While Jon killed them, the big man had slipped quickly around the front of the taxiing drone aircraft to strike at him from the flank.

And now there was nothing Smith could do to save himself.

Still smiling, the green-eyed man raised his rifle slightly, this time aiming at Smith's unprotected head. Beside him, just at the edge of Jon's wavering, unfocused vision, the leading edge of the huge flying wing came into view, liberally studded with the plastic cylinders containing its murderous payload.

The fear-ridden primitive part of Jon's brain screamed in silent terror, raging futilely against its approaching death. He did his best to ignore that part of himself, straining instead to hear what it was that the colder, more clinical, more rational side of his mind was trying to tell him.

The wind, it said.

The wind is from the east.

Without thinking further, Smith threw himself sideways. He fired the carbine in that same moment, pulling the trigger as fast as he could. The M4 barked repeatedly, kicking higher with every shot as he emptied what was left of his thirty-round magazine. Bullets lashed the huge flying wing – punching holes in carbon fiber and plastic surfaces, slicing flight control cables, smashing onboard computers, and shattering propellers.

The drone plane rocked under the force of the high-velocity impacts. It began slewing west, slowly turning off the runway.

*

400

Terce watched the dark-haired American's last desperate move without pity or concern. One side of his mouth curved up in a wry, predatory grin. This was like seeing a wounded animal thrashing in a trap. That was something to savor. He stood motionless, choosing only to follow his target with the rifle barrel – waiting for his sights to settle on the other man's head. He ignored the bullets shrieking off to his right. At this range, the American could not possibly hope to hit him with unaimed fire.

But then he heard the smooth hum made by the drone aircraft's fourteen electric motors change pitch – roughening in fits and starts as they shorted out or lost power. Bits and pieces of shattered plastic and carbon fiber spun away across the tarmac.

Terce saw the huge plane swinging toward him, veering wildly off-course. He scowled. The American's last gamble would not save his life, but the damage to one of his three irreplaceable attack aircraft would infuriate Nomura.

Suddenly Terce stared in disbelief at the thin-walled plastic cylinders slung under the huge wing, noticing for the first time the rough-edged star-shaped punctures torn through so many of them.

It was only then that he felt the murdering east wind gently kiss his face. His green eyes widened in horror.

Terror-stricken, Terce stumbled backward. The assault rifle fell from his shaking hands and clattered onto the concrete.

The auburn-haired man groaned aloud. Already he could feel the Stage IV nanophages at work inside his body. Billions of the horrid devices were clawing their way outward from deep inside his heaving lungs – spreading their poisons wider with every fatal breath. The flesh inside his thick transparent gloves turned red, sloughing off his muscles and tendons and bones as they disintegrated.

His two surviving men, temporarily secure in their gas masks, looked up at him from their firing positions. Eyes wide in fear, they scrambled to their feet and began backing away.

Desperately he raised his haggard melting face in mute appeal. 'Kill me,' he whispered, choking out the words past a tongue that was falling to pieces. 'Kill me! Please!'

Instead, panicked by the horror they saw before them, they threw their rifles aside and fled toward the ocean.

Screaming again and again, the last of the *Horatii* doubled over, wracked by incomprehensible and unending pain as the teeming nanophages ate him alive from within.

Smith ran north along the runway, moving fast despite his fatigue and the terrible punishment he had taken. His jaw was set, held tight against the pain from several cracked ribs grinding under his body armor. He stumbled once, swore under his breath, and pushed himself onward.

Keep going, Jon, he told himself savagely. Keep going or die.

He did not look back. He knew the horror he would see there. He knew the horror he had deliberately set in motion. By now the nanophage cloud was spreading west across the whole southern end of the airfield – drifting on the wind toward the Atlantic.

Smith came pounding up to the grounded Black Hawk. The rotors were still spinning slowly. Torn blades of grass and lingering traces of missile exhaust swirled lazily in the air around the waiting helicopter. Peter and Randi saw him coming. Their worried looks vanished and they moved toward him, smiling and laughing with relief.

'Get aboard!' Jon roared, waving them back to the Black Hawk. 'Get that thing spooled up!'

Peter nodded tightly, seeing the shot-up drone careening off the runway out of control. He knew what that meant. 'Give me thirty seconds, Jon!' he called.

The Englishman swung himself back aboard the helicopter and scrambled into the pilot's seat. His hands danced across the control panel, flicking switches and watching indicators lighting up. Satisfied, he rotated the throttle, pushing the engines toward full power. The rotors began spinning faster.

Smith skidded to a stop beside the troop carrier's open door. He noticed Randi's left arm dangling at her side. Her face was still pale, drawn with pain. 'How bad is it?' he asked.

She smiled wryly. 'It hurts like hell, but I'll live. You can play doctor some other time.'

Before he could react, she glared at him. 'And you will not make any smart-ass comments. You hear me?'

'I hear you,' Smith told her quietly. Hiding the pain from his own injuries, he helped her climb up into the Black Hawk. Then he swung himself aboard. His eyes took note of the two other passengers – recognizing both Hideo and Jinjiro Nomura from their pictures in the files Fred Klein had made him study so long ago in Santa Fe. So long ago, he thought coldly. Six days ago. A lifetime ago.

Randi dropped into a rear-facing seat across from Hideo. Wincing, she cradled the M4 carbine in her lap, making sure its deadly black muzzle was pointing straight at his heart. Jon settled in beside her.

'Hold tight!' Peter called from the control cabin. 'Here we go!'

Engines howling, the Black Hawk slid forward across the runway and then lifted off – already turning as it climbed away from the airfield.

CHAPTER FORTY-NINE

At three hundred feet, Peter leveled out. They were high enough now to be safe from the nanophage cloud blowing across the Nomura PharmaTech airfield and complex. Or so he hoped. He frowned, reminding himself that hope ran a very poor second to absolute certainty. With a twitch of the controls, he took them up another hundred feet.

Happier now, Peter pulled the Black Hawk into a gentle turn, beginning a slow orbit over the corpse-strewn runway. Then he glanced back over his shoulder into the troop compartment. 'Where to now, Jon?' he asked. 'After our friend Lazarus' first drone? The one that got away?'

Smith shook his head. 'Not quite yet.' He stripped the empty magazine out of his carbine and inserted a fresh clip. 'We still have a couple of things to finish up here first.'

He slid out of his seat and lay prone on the floor of the helicopter, sighting along the M4 out through the open door. 'Give me a shot at that third drone, Peter,' he called. 'It's still trying to take off on autopilot.'

In response, the Black Hawk tilted, swinging back to the south. Smith leaned a bit farther out, watching the huge flying wing grow even larger in his sights. He squeezed the trigger – firing a series of aimed bursts down into the drone rolling determinedly down the runway. The carbine hammered back against his shoulder.

The UH-60 roared past the aircraft and pulled up sharply, already curving back through a full circle.

The carbine's bolt locked open at the rear. Jon pulled

out the empty clip and slapped in another – his last. He hit the catch. The M4 was loaded and ready to fire again.

The helicopter finished its turn and flew north, heading back for another pass.

Smith stared down. Battered by thirty rounds of 5.56mm ammunition, the third drone now sat motionless on the tarmac. Whole sections of the single long wing sagged, shattered by multiple hits. Fragments of engine pods and nanophage cylinders littered the concrete paving behind the wrecked aircraft. 'Scratch one drone,' he announced in a matter-of-fact voice. 'That's two down and one to go.'

Hideo Nomura stiffened in his seat.

'Not a move,' Randi warned him. She hefted the weapon on her lap.

'You will not shoot me inside this machine,' the younger Nomura snarled. Every trace of the amiable cosmopolitan facade he had cultivated for so many long years of deception had vanished. Now his face was a rigid, hate-filled mask that revealed the raw malice and egomania that truly drove him. 'You would all die, too. You Americans are too soft. You do not have the true warrior spirit.'

Randi smiled mockingly back at him. 'Maybe not. But the fuel tanks behind you are self-sealing. And I'm willing to bet that you're not. Shall we find out which one of us is right?'

Hideo fell silent, glaring at her.

Jinjiro Nomura looked out through the door, smiling calmly as he watched the rapid destruction of his son's twisted dreams. All that Jinjiro had suffered in twelve months of cruel confinement was now being dealt out in full to Hideo.

Guided by Jon, Peter flew the Black Hawk to the north end of the runway and passed low over the two large cargo planes and the much smaller executive jet parked there.

Again leaning out through the open door, Smith fired another series of bursts right into their cockpits – smashing windows and flight controls. 'I don't want any survivors leaving this island until we can get Special Forces units and decontamination teams here,' he explained. Randi handed him her spare ammunition.

Now Peter took the helicopter higher, climbing steadily in a tight, spiraling circle while they searched for signs of Nomura's first drone. For long minutes they anxiously hunted through the skies around them. Randi saw it first – catching a tiny glint of gold-flecked light high above. 'There it is!' she cried, pointing out through the side door. 'At our three o'clock now. And it's heading due west!'

'Toward the States,' Smith realized.

Hideo smiled thinly. 'For Washington, D.C., and its surrounding suburbs, to be precise.'

The helicopter clattered through another turn as Peter swung onto a parallel course. He stared up through the forward windshield with a worried expression on his face. 'That damned thing is already devilishly high,' he called. 'It's probably flying at ten or twelve thousand feet and climbing fast.'

'What's the service ceiling on this bird?' Smith asked, buckling back into his seat.

'It tops out somewhere around nineteen thousand feet,' Peter replied, frowning. 'But the air will be very thin at that altitude. Perhaps too thin.'

'You're too late,' Hideo told them gleefully. His eyes gleamed in triumph. 'You cannot stop my *Thanatos* aircraft now! And there are enough nanophages aboard that plane to kill millions. You may hold me captive, but I have already struck a blow against your greedy, materialistic country that will live down through the centuries!'

The others ignored his ranting, entirely intent on catching the *Thanatos* flying wing before it escaped above their reach.

Peter pulled the Black Hawk's nose up as steeply as he could, chasing that distant fleeing speck. The helicopter soared higher, climbing fifteen hundred feet higher with every passing minute. Everyone inside could feel the air growing steadily colder and thinner.

By the time the UH-60 reached twelve thousand feet, their teeth were chattering and it was becoming markedly more difficult to catch their breath. The density of the air around them was now only a little over half the norm at sea level. People could live and work and even ski at this altitude, but usually with a much longer time to acclimate. Hypoxia, altitude sickness, was now a serious danger.

The *Thanatos* drone was much closer now, but it was still above them and climbing steadily. Its single enormous wing tilted occasionally as the onboard flight controls adjusted for small changes in wind speed, direction, and barometric pressure. Otherwise the aircraft held its course, flying doggedly on toward its preordained target – the capital city of the United States.

Peter pushed the Black Hawk higher. His head and lungs ached, and he was finding it increasingly difficult to concentrate on what he was doing. His vision blurred slightly around the edges. He blinked hard, trying to get a clearer view.

The altimeter crawled slowly through fourteen thousand feet. This far above the Earth's surface, the helicopter's rotors provided far less lift. Their rate of climb and airspeed were both rapidly diminishing. Fifteen thousand feet. And still the giant aircraft hung above them, tantalizingly close, but well out of reach.

Another minute passed, a minute of increasing cold and exhaustion.

Again Peter glanced up through the forward windshield. Nothing. The *Thanatos* drone was gone. 'Come on, you devil,' he growled. 'Stop playing silly buggers with me! Where have you got to now?'

And suddenly sunlight blazed on a huge wing surface below him, reflected back by tens of thousands of mirror-bright solar cells.

'We've done it! We're above the beast!' Peter crowed. He coughed, trying to draw more air into his straining lungs without hyperventilating. 'But you'll have to be quick, Jon. Very quick. I can't hold us up here much longer!'

Nodding, Smith unbuckled his seat belt and again dropped onto his stomach by the open door. Every piece of metal he touched was chilled so far below the freezing point that it burned like fire. The outside air temperature was now well below zero.

Frantically Jon blew on his hands, knowing that they were all in real danger of losing fingers and other exposed patches of skin to frostbite. Then, cradling the M4, he leaned out into the slipstream, feeling the wind tearing at his hair and clothes.

He could make out the drone now. It was roughly two hundred feet below them. The Black Hawk slowed, matching its speed to that of its prey.

Smith's eyes teared up in the frigid wind. He squeezed them shut and roughly brushed away the tears before they froze. He peered through his sights. The upper surface of the flying wing wavered slightly and then steadied up.

He squeezed the trigger.

Rounds slammed into the *Thanatos* drone, shattering hundreds of solar cells. Fragments of glass and plastic swirled away and vanished astern. For a moment the wing flexed alarmingly. It slid lower.

Jon held his breath. But then the giant machine's on-board flight computers corrected for the sudden loss of power, revving its propellers higher. The drone steadied up and began climbing again.

Smith swore quietly, already fumbling for a new magazine.

Amid the noise and cold and thin, scarcely breathable air, Randi fought to remain conscious. The sharp, stabbing pain from her broken arm was merging now with a terrible throbbing ache behind her temples. She gritted her teeth, feeling nauseated. The pain in her head was now so intense that it seemed to send little pulses of red light flashing into her eyes with every beat of her heart.

Her head fell forward.

And in that brief moment, Hideo Nomura attacked.

One hand batted aside her carbine. The other chopped down hard on Randi's collarbone. It snapped like a dry twig.

With a muffled groan, she fell back against the seat and then flopped forward again. Only the safety belt buckled at her waist kept her from sliding onto the floor of the troop compartment.

Nomura snatched the M4 and held it to her head.

Smith glanced over his shoulder in surprise. He rolled over and sat up – and then froze, taking in the changed situation in one appalled glance.

'Throw your weapon out the door,' Nomura ordered. His eyes glittered, as hard as ice and just as cold. 'Or I will blow this woman's brains across this compartment.'

Jon swallowed hard, staring at Randi. He could not see her face. 'She's dead already,' he said, desperately trying to buy time.

Nomura laughed. 'Not yet,' he said. 'Observe.' He wrapped one hand in Randi's short blond hair and yanked her head back. She moaned softly. Her eyes fluttered open briefly and then closed. The man who was Lazarus released his grip contemptuously, allowing her head to flop forward again. 'You see?' he said. 'Now do as I say!'

Defeated, Smith let the carbine fall out of his hands. The weapon whirled away and disappeared.

'Very good,' Nomura told him cheerfully. 'You learn obedience quickly.' He moved back, keeping Randi's weapon carefully aimed at Jon's chest. His face grew harder. 'Now order your pilot to fly away from my *Thanatos* drone.'

Smith raised his voice. 'Did you hear what the man wants you to do, Peter?'

The Englishman looked back over his shoulder. His pale blue eyes were expressionless. 'I heard him,' he replied coolly. 'It seems we have no choice, Jon. At least not with the situation as it stands.'

'No,' Smith agreed. 'Not as it *stands*,' he said, putting the emphasis on the last word. He tilted his head slightly.

An almost imperceptible wink fluttered in Peter's left eye. He turned back to the Black Hawk's controls.

Nomura laughed again. 'You see, Father,' he said to Jinjiro. 'These Westerners are soft. They value their own lives above all else.'

The old man said nothing. He sat stone-faced, cast again into despair by the sudden reversal of fortune.

Smith sat near the helicopter's open door, waiting tensely for Peter to make his move.

Abruptly the Englishman banked the helicopter hard right – almost tipping the Black Hawk over on its side. Nomura toppled backward, thrown completely off his feet. He crashed into the back wall of the troop compartment and then slid to the floor. His finger, curled around the trigger of Randi's M4, tightened involuntarily. Three rounds tore through the roof and ricocheted off the spinning rotors.

As soon as the helicopter tilted, Smith threw himself forward, away from the open door. He dived across the floor and slammed headlong into Nomura. He tore the carbine out of Nomura's hands and tossed it away across the cabin. It clattered somewhere among the seats, well out of reach.

The Black Hawk leveled out and began climbing again.

Snarling, Nomura kicked out at Jon, shoving him back. Both men scrambled to their feet. Hideo attacked first – striking out with his hands and feet in a maddened frenzy.

Jon parried two blows with his forearms, shrugged a kick off his hip, ducked under a third strike, and then closed in. He grabbed Nomura by one arm, punched him hard in the face, and then hurled him across the row of seats.

The other man landed in a heap – right next to the open door. Though dazed, with blood streaming from a broken nose, he struggled to get back up.

Smith grabbed hold of a seat and roared, 'Peter! Now! Reverse! Reverse!'

The Englishman complied, again throwing the Black Hawk into a steep bank, but this time sharply left. The helicopter tilted on its side, for a moment seeming to hang in space, high above the Atlantic Ocean, as it spun through a tight turn. The *Thanatos* drone came into view not more than fifty feet below them, still heading west on its pro-grammed mission of mass murder.

Hideo Nomura made a desperate lunge and grabbed a seat strut. His legs dangled in mid-air, flailing, trying to find a foothold that did not exist.

Arms straining, he began to pull himself back inside the helicopter. With his teeth bared in a rictus grin, he looked up and saw his father staring down at him.

Jinjiro Nomura looked deep into the maddened eyes of the man who had once been his beloved son. 'You mis-judged these Americans,' he said softly. He sighed in sor-row. 'Just as you have misjudged me.'

And with that, the old man leaned forward and kicked Hideo's hands away from the seat strut.

Face fixed in horror, the younger Nomura slid out the door, his fingernails clawing wildly, seeking a hold any-where on the smooth metal. Then, with a despairing wail, he fell away into thin air, tumbling toward the *Thanatos* drone as it flew past under the turning Black Hawk.

Still kicking and flailing with his arms and legs, the man who was Lazarus crashed onto the fragile surface of the enormous flying wing. The drone shuddered, rocked by the sudden impact. And then, overloaded and already damaged, the *Thanatos* aircraft simply snapped in half –

folding up like the closing pages of a book. Propeller blades, avionics pods, and clusters of nanophage cylinders ripped loose in a growing cloud of debris.

Slowly at first, and then faster, the tangled wreckage spun around and around, plunging all the way down to the hungry and waiting waters of the vast and merciless sea.

EPILOGUE

Early November
The White House
Although it was still early in the afternoon, President Samuel Adams Castilla had abandoned the excited hustle and bustle around the Oval Office – preferring instead the quiet comfort and privacy of his den upstairs in the East Wing. This room was all his own, exempt from the whims of the fashionable designers who had redecorated the rest of the White House under orders from his wife. There were shelves full of well-read books, a large Navajo rug covering the polished hardwood floor, a big black leather sofa, a couple of recliners, and a big-screen television. Hung on the walls were prints of works by Fredric Remington and Georgia O'Keeffe together with photographs of the rugged mountains around Santa Fe.

Castilla glanced over his shoulder with a smile. His hand was poised over a bottle and a pair of glasses on the sideboard. 'Care for a Scotch, Fred?'

Fred Klein grinned back at him from his place on the long sofa. 'I certainly would, Mr. President.'

Castilla poured the drinks and carried them over. 'This is the Caol Ila, Jinjiro's favorite.'

'Very appropriate, Sam,' Klein said quietly. The head of Covert-One nodded toward the television. 'He should be on any second now.'

'Yep. And I wouldn't miss this for the world,' Castilla said. He set down his Scotch and tapped a key on the TV remote. The screen lit up, showing the vast chamber of the UN General Assembly in New York. Jinjiro Nomura stood alone on the dais, looking out over the sea of delegates and cameras with perfect poise – although he knew his words and his image were being beamed around the world to more than a billion people watching this live broadcast. His face was solemn, still bearing the deep marks of sorrow left by betrayal, a year's imprisonment, and the death of his son.

'I stand before you today on behalf of the Lazarus Movement,' Jinjiro began. 'A movement whose noble ideals and dedicated followers were betrayed by the malice of one man. This man, my own son Hideo, murdered my friends and colleagues and imprisoned me – destroying those of us who founded the Movement so that he could seize power in secret. Then, masquerading as Lazarus, he used our organization to conceal his own cruel and genocidal aims, aims utterly at odds with everything for which our Movement truly stands . . .'

Castilla and Klein listened in satisfied silence while the older Nomura carefully and precisely recounted the details of Hideo's treachery, revealing both his secret creation of the nanophages and his plans to use them to destroy most of humanity so that he could make himself absolute master over the frightened survivors. Briefed earlier by Jinjiro, America's allies had already begun returning to the fold – all expressing profound relief that their earlier suspicions had proved unfounded and anxious to repair their damaged relations with the U.S. before the truth became widely known. This UN speech was only the first part of a determined campaign to unveil the subversion of the Lazarus Movement and salvage America's reputation.

Both men knew it would take time and a great deal of effort, but they were also sure the wounds left by Hideo Nomura's vicious deceptions would heal. A few isolated fanatics might cling to their belief in America's guilt, but most would accept the truth – swayed by the calm conviction and powerful presence of the last surviving founder of the Lazarus Movement and by the release of documents captured inside Nomura's secret Azores labs. The Movement itself was already crumbling, rocked by the first revelations of its leader's lies and murderous plans. Whatever survived would only do so by returning to Jinjiro's original vision of a force for peaceful change and environmental reform.

Castilla felt himself beginning to relax for the first time in weeks. America and the whole world had had an incredibly narrow escape. He sighed and saw Fred Klein looking at him.

'It's over, Sam,' the other man told him quietly.

Castilla nodded. 'I know.' He raised his glass. 'To Colonel Smith and the others.'

'To them all,' Klein echoed, raising his own glass. '*Slainte.*'

The Mall, Washington, D.C.

A crisp, rain-washed autumn breeze rustled through the leaves still clinging to the trees lining the Mall. Sunlight slanted through branches, dappling the grass with moving patterns of red- and gold-tinged shadows.

Jon Smith walked through the shadows toward a woman standing pensively near a bench. Her short golden hair gleamed in the afternoon light. Despite the thick cast encasing her left arm and shoulder, she still appeared slender and graceful.

'Waiting for me?' he called softly.

Randi Russell turned toward him. A slight smile creased her lips. 'If you're the guy who left a message on my answering machine suggesting dinner, I guess so,' she said tartly. 'Otherwise, I'll be eating alone.'

Smith grinned. Some things would never change. 'How's the arm?' he asked.

'Not bad,' she told him. 'The doctors tell me this hunk of plaster can come off in a few more weeks. Once that's done, and the collarbone heals, a little more rehab should clear me for field duty. Frankly, I can't wait. I'm not cut out for sitting behind a desk.'

He nodded. 'Are things at Langley still in a mess?'

Randi shrugged carefully. 'The situation seems to be calming down. The files our people snagged in the Azores have pretty well nailed everyone involved in TOCSIN. You heard that Hanson is resigning?'

Smith nodded again. The director of the CIA had not been directly involved in Burke and Pierson's illegal operation. But no one could doubt that his failures of judgment and his willingness to turn a blind eye were partly responsible. David Hanson's resignation 'for personal reasons' was purely a face-saving alternative to being fired.

'Have you heard anything from Peter?' Randi asked in turn.

'I had a call from him last week,' Smith told her. 'He's back in retirement at his place in the Sierras. For good this time, he claims.'

She raised a skeptical eyebrow. 'Do you believe him?'

He laughed. 'Not really. I can't imagine Peter Howell sitting idle on his front porch for very long.'

She looked across at Jon through slightly narrowed eyes. 'What about you? Still playing spook for the Joint Chiefs? Or was it Army Intelligence this time?'

'I'm back at Fort Detrick, in my old post at USAM-RIID,' Smith told her.

'Back to the infectious diseases grind?' Randi asked.

He shook his head. 'Not exactly. We're developing a program to monitor potentially hazardous nanotech R&D around the world.'

She stared at him.

'We stopped Nomura,' Smith told her quietly. 'But now the genie's out of the bottle. Someone else out there may try something similar – or equally destructive – someday.'

Randi shivered. 'I'd hate to imagine that.'

He nodded somberly. 'At least this time we know what to look for. Manufacturing biologically active nanodevices requires biochemical substances in large quantities – and those are substances we can track.'

She sighed. 'Maybe we should just do what the Lazarus Movement wanted in the first place. Ban nanotech completely.'

Smith shook his head. 'And lose out on all the potential benefits? Like curing cancer? Or wiping out pollution?' He shrugged. 'It's like any other advanced technology, Randi. Nothing more. How we use it – for good or ill – is up to us.'

'Now there's the scientist in you talking,' she said drily.

'It's what I am,' Smith said quietly. 'Most of the time, anyway.'

'Right,' Randi replied with a wry grin. She relented. 'Okay, Dr. Smith, you promised me dinner. Are you going to honor your promise?'

He sketched a bow and offered her his arm. 'Never let it be said that I'm not a man of my word, Ms. Russell. Dinner is on me.'

Together, Jon and Randi turned and walked back toward his waiting car. Above them, the last clouds were drifting away, leaving behind a clear blue sky.

All Orion/Phoenix titles are available at your local bookshop or from the following address:

Mail Order Department
Littlehampton Book Services
FREEPOST BR535
Worthing, West Sussex, BN13 3BR
telephone 01903 828503, *facsimile* 01903 828802
e-mail MailOrders@lbsltd.co.uk
(Please ensure that you include full postal address details)

Payment can be made either by credit/debit card (Visa, Mastercard, Access and Switch accepted) or by sending a £ Sterling cheque or postal order made payable to *Littlehampton Book Services*.
DO NOT SEND CASH OR CURRENCY

Please add the following to cover postage and packing

UK and BFPO:
£1.50 for the first book, and 50p for each additional book to a maximum of £3.50

Overseas and Eire:
£2.50 for the first book plus £1.00 for the second book and 50p for each additional book ordered

---

BLOCK CAPITALS PLEASE

name of cardholder ....

delivery address
(if different from cardholder)

address of cardholder ....

....

....

postcode ....

postcode ....

☐ I enclose my remittance for £.............................

☐ please debit my Mastercard/Visa/Access/Switch (delete as appropriate)

card number ☐☐☐☐ ☐☐☐☐ ☐☐☐☐ ☐☐☐☐

expiry date ☐☐☐☐   Switch issue no. ☐☐

signature ....

prices and availability are subject to change without notice